Class of 1964

A Novel

Also by James Y Hung:

Finding Fat Lady's Shoe: A Memoir of Growing up in Hong Kong and Malaysia (2013)

FOB in Paradise: A Memoir (2014)

Silk Road on My Mind (2015)

Practical Ophthalmology: A Concise Manual for the Non-Ophthalmologist (2016)

The Chinese Language Demystified (2018)

Introduction to Tang Poetry (2019)

Sightless: A Novel (2019)

I Left My Heart in Malaya (2020)

Available through Amazon in paperback and Kindle e-book. E-book also available through Barnes & Noble.

Finding Fat Lady's Shoe

An intensely reflective tale of a family uprooted by war, cast adrift onto a sea of uncertainty.—Kirkus Review

Dr. James Hung's life story echoes others that will probably never be written, and offers a fascinating perspective on Hong Kong's recent past that deserves to be widely read. [4 stars out of 5]—South China Morning Post

FOB in Paradise

Hung has written an absorbing and witty book. Dramatic, nuanced vignettes and vivid descriptions of people and places create a rich tapestry that shows the medical profession at its best and worst.—Kirkus Review

Silk Road on My Mind

Hung is an endearing mix of benevolence, wryness, and curiosity....there is an appealing Marco Polo-ishness to his project: a boundless wonder for a society unlike his own, not for its differences but for the infinitely recognizable humanity at its center.—Kirkus Review

Practical Ophthalmology

More specialists should create guides of this caliber for nonspecialists. An indispensable ophthalmological volume for any general practitioner's office.—Kirkus Review (featured article 11/15)

The Chinese Language Demystified

An engrossing introduction to the riches of Chinese that should delight casual language mavens and more experienced speakers alike.—Kirkus Review (featured article 6/15)

Introduction to Tang Poetry

...will be accessible to novices and a rich resource for experts.... A compelling, detail-rich resource about Tang verse.—Kirkus Review (featured article 3/1)

Sightless: A Novel

An engaging tale about a singular friendship that gives voice to the struggles of the sightless.—Kirkus Review (featured article 2/15)

I Left My Heart in Malaya

With great tenderness, he recounts the beautiful simplicity of that stretch of his youth...—Kirkus Review

Class of 1964

A Novel

James Y Hung MD

Class of 1964: A Novel

Contents

Author's Note

MOST STUDENTS IN LA SALLE COLLEGE'S CLASS OF 1964 were born in 1946 or 1947. We were spared the horrors of WWII, but most of us had to endure the consequences of the Chinese Civil War, which ended in the communist rule of China. Many of our families had to flee our homes, our lives uprooted. My family, like many of my classmates' families, was among those who fled communist China.

We grew up in a unique city, one that has been the crossroads of many worlds and many pasts; and La Salle was a microcosm of Hong Kong itself, with its students representing many worlds.

Some described Hong Kong as a city that existed on borrowed land and borrowed time, a city without a future. Throughout our lives, we all knew that Hong Kong would eventually be returned to China. That knowledge influenced many of our plans for the future.

As far back as I could remember, perhaps as young as seven or eight, and probably from my parents' conversations, I always knew that Hong Kong was not to be my permanent home. It would be a stepping stone to someplace far away from the Chinese communists.

Many of us vowed that we would never live under communist rule, and we studied very hard to accomplish just that, so that we could study and remain in America, Canada or Australia.

Hong Kong has never been an easy place to live, except for the really rich. For most residents, life has always been a struggle. It is one of the world's most expensive places to live, ranking above New York, London and Tokyo. In Hong Kong people learn to survive, not live. Even the climate can make life difficult, with the furnace of summertime Hong Kong heat and the typhoons.

In our days, we often had to worry about what temper tantrums the Chinese communists might throw and what punishments they would inflict on the people of Hong Kong, such as limiting the water flowing into the city.

We all remember how the communist government in 1962 let tens of thousands of impoverished and hungry Chinese cross the border into Hong Kong. We were all worried that the already crowded city would be overwhelmed by these poor migrants seeking a better life. Things were already difficult enough for us as it was.

It was under these circumstances that we grew up. They say that Hong Kong people are tough. The song *New York, New York* says if you can make it in New York, you can make it anywhere. I believe that's even more true of Hong Kong. If you can make it in Hong Kong, you can definitely make it anywhere.

The class of 1964 is a product of the East and West. For the longest time, most people in Hong Kong had come from somewhere else. During the first 50 years of the 20th century, the mainland was wracked by civil war, invasions and revolution, leading to successive waves of refugees seeking the relative security of the colony.

Growing up in Hong Kong, life was full of uncertainties. The school that you had been going to for the last ten years might decide to get rid of you simply because they didn't think you would do well enough in the HKSC Exam to maintain its excellent passing rate. Everything in Hong Kong was about "face"—respect, honor and social standing, and this was even true for schools.

This book is an intimate look of some of the people of Hong Kong, the real people, my classmates. Most of the characters existed. A few are fictional, while others are a composite of different characters. Almost all the names have been changed to protect their privacy.

As we get into our mid-seventies, the class of 1964 will be fading into oblivion. The class of 2020, after many years of hard work, has just begun to seek their place in the world, just as we did almost sixty years ago.

Perhaps someone in the class of 2020 would feel sorry that we are now old men. I would say to him, "I was what you are and you will be what I am."

I am grateful that my life has mostly been wonderful. So far, I have lived an exciting, rewarding and meaningful life.

I hope you enjoy reading this book as much as I have writing it.

Thank you,

James Y Hung, MD FACS
Honolulu, Hawaii
June 2021

Hong Kong and its surroundings.

CHAPTER 1:

La Salle College

MY HEART WAS RACING as I sat in the waiting room.

It was about ten in the morning, the first Monday in February of 1962, and I was waiting nervously at the office of the principal of La Salle College (High School) in Kowloon, Hong Kong.

How I found myself at that place at that time is an amazing story.

In 1949, when I was three, our family fled communist China to Hong Kong. With over a million and a half refugees flooding Hong Kong in a matter of a few months, the colony was overwhelmed. Jobs were scarce and my parents were unemployed for five years. We managed to survive through the largess of friends and relatives, although with great hardship. I was extremely fortunately that I never missed any school.

In 1957, my parents were recruited to teach in a Chinese medium high school in Malaya. During the five years we were there, I attended St. Andrew's School, a school run by the same Christian Brothers as La Salle College. In January 1962, our family returned to Hong Kong. At the suggestion of Brother Robert, the principal of St. Andrew's, I sought transfer to La Salle. Brother Robert happened to be roommates with Brother Felix, the principal of La Salle College, when they were in the seminary in Ireland almost three decades ago.

Our family left Malaya because the country had become independent from the British and they no longer needed teachers like my parents. We arrived in Hong Kong on a Friday in early February, four days after boarding an Italian passenger ship, the *Michelangelo*. In order to save money, we stayed in an inexpensive hotel off Nathan Road.

Two days later, on a Monday, I asked a hotel employee for directions to La Salle College. I took bus number 1A and got off at the intersection of La Salle Road and Boundary Street, which, as the named implied, at one time separated Kowloon from the New Territories. The cross street was the namesake of the school. The building, a very European-looking structure, sat on the top of a hill in Kowloon Tong, an exclusive residential area in Kowloon.

The magnificent, sprawling Romanesque structure was much larger than I had imagined, and could easily have belonged in Rome or Paris. It had a dome, under which was the chapel. The beautiful and impressive school astounded me.

After some enquiries, I found my way to the administrative offices. A man who looked Caucasian but spoke perfect Cantonese guarded the front office. It turned out that he was half English and half Chinese and went by the name of Ah Hung. He had a habit of closing his eyes with every other word—whether it was a nervous twitch or a mild form of Tourette's syndrome, I don't know. He was busy making copies at a small printing machine and asked me what my visit was for. I handed him the letter from Brother Robert and said, "My family has just moved back from Malaya, and I'm hoping to attend La Salle."

He took the letter and told me to wait while he checked with Brother Felix, who was in his office.

Brother Felix was the opposite of Brother Robert both physically and temperamentally. He was tall and lean. He had a full head of wavy, salt-and-pepper colored hair and a slender face, and he struck me as kind and somewhat reserved. He invited me into his office to sit down, telling me that he was sorry my family couldn't stay in Malaya and had to leave the country on such short notice.

It was now February, and the new school year had begun in late August—Malaya and Hong Kong had different academic years. I had to either repeat the second half of Form 2 (eighth grade) or skip half a year and join Form 3 (the ninth grade) midyear. Giving me an assessing look, Brother Felix spoke in a reassuring voice.

"James, you look like an intelligent and determined young man. I will place you in Form 3A. Brother Lawrence is an excellent teacher."

Hong Kong followed the same system as the British. The first six years were Primary one to six. Form 1 was the seventh grade; Form 2, the eighth grade, and so on. Form 5 was the last year of high school, at the end of which all students sat for the all-important Hong Kong School Certificate (HKSC) Exam and the O-level of the London University Overseas Exam. Forms 6 and 7 were the pre-university years, with university being only three years.

Brother Felix's decision to place me in the A class showed that he had faith in me. One grade at La Salle had up to six sections, i.e. from A to F. The students were usually ranked from the previous grade. As a rule—with the exception of the students taking French, who had to stay together as a group for logistical reasons—the top 40 or so would be placed in the A class. From 41 to 80 would be the B class and so on. With this system, which was widespread in Hong Kong, the students' academic standings could be determined by which class they belonged to, identifying the "underachievers" immediately.

Brother Felix asked me about my family. He listened kindly as I told him that my parents were Chinese schoolteachers and were currently looking for work in Hong Kong.

He advised me that the school fee was 40 Hong Kong dollars (about five US dollars) a month, and asked me if that would be a problem. I was surprised that such an important man would take so much interest in a new student.

"Brother Robert has always been gruff," he mused. "He was in the IRA—the Irish Republican Army—during the fight for Ireland's independence. He was shot in the neck, but the bullet missed the important structures and he wasn't even hospitalized."

I remembered the scar on Brother Robert's neck and that my good friend at St. Andrew's, Chua Huck Cheng, had said something about the war.

Brother Felix smiled and seemed to be reminiscing about his seminary days with Brother Robert. "I have heard that he is very strict with the boys in Malaya," he commented.

I smiled weakly and nodded but said nothing, remembering the canings I had from him in my first two years at the school when I misbehaved.

Brother Felix expressed his concern about my parents and said that he wished he could help them. Then, in a surprise move, he told me that he would waive the 40 dollar monthly fees for the rest of the school year and that I should see him if I needed continuing assistance the following year.

Brother Robert must have written me an excellent letter of recommendation and Brother Felix had taken his good words seriously. He was the principal of one of the most prestigious and largest high schools in Hong Kong, and he was spending his valuable time on one new student who he knew very little about. I vowed to myself that I wouldn't disappoint them.

"Now James," he said, "are you ready to run?"

For a second I didn't know what he meant. The confusion must have shown on my face, because Brother Felix explained, "Brother Robert mentioned in his letter that you are a good sprinter. I would like you to work with the coach to be on the relay team."

I readily agreed, and shortly after that the coach, Mr. Chong, arrived at the office.

I thanked Brother Felix profusely as I exited his office. I was truly moved by his kindness.

***

Mr. Chong, a swarthy and sinewy man, must have been in his mid or late 50s. What little hair he had remaining had been cut close to his scalp. As he spoke, which he did rapidly, foam appeared in both corners of his mouth, and he constantly wiped it off with his hand. In the depth of winter, he was wearing a pair of white shorts and a sweater. Around his neck he wore a shiny silver whistle.

I later learned that in the 1930s he was the top sprinter in all of China, and was captain of the Chinese team at the Berlin Olympics. Like so many educated people, Mr. Chong along with his family fled to Hong Kong when Mao was taking over China. With his excellent credentials, he was hired as the coach at La Salle.

Communication with Mr. Chong wasn't easy. Nobody knew how much English he had studied in college or who interviewed him and gave him the job at La Salle, but few people understood him or were even certain that he was speaking English. Coming from Fujian Province, he never learned Cantonese, which happened to have different tones compared to the Fujian dialect. Nobody understood his "English" or his "Cantonese," and the students began calling him "Ku Lay Lou" (i.e., *the coolie man*) because he sounded so uneducated. Some students would call him that to his face, and when they did, Mr. Chong would chase down the offender and pull on his ears. It became a game of cat and mouse. Surprisingly, at his age, he could outrun most of the city slicker students.

That first day, he took me to the Olympic-sized track field behind the main building, telling me that La Salle College had consistently been number one in sports amongst all the schools in Hong Kong. The school had dominated sprinting and soccer for years. He showed me some techniques on the starting block, somewhat different from Mr. Goddard's, our coach in Malaya. With a clock in his hand, he asked me to run the 100 meter dash as fast as I could.

Still in my street shoes, pants and jacket, I told him that I was still adjusting to the new land, having arrived only three days ago.

He asked me for my best time, which was 12.0 seconds. He remarked that Tony Hu, the best sprinter at La Salle, and second in all of Hong Kong, had a best time of 11.5 seconds; I would be second or third, depending on Ed King who was an inconsistent runner, on a few occasions running it around 12.0 seconds. The difference of 0.5 seconds between Tony's and my best times was night and day in the sprinting world. Tony Hu belonged to another league! I was pleased to know that I would be within the top three.

"By the way," said the coach, "there will be an invitation meet at Wah Yan College, the Jesuit High School on Hong Kong Island, this Saturday and I want you to be on the 4 x 100m relay team."

He again asked if he could time my 100m. Since he had asked me to run for La Salle in a few days, I thought it would only be fair to show him that at least I could run. It was a particularly cold day. Taking off my jacket, tightening my belt and shoelaces, shivering in the wind, I did some warm ups and stretching. Then

I told the coach I was ready and took off running as fast as I could.

When I finished, Mr. Chong beamed with approval and showed me his stopwatch—12.3 seconds. Considering the circumstances, he thought it wasn't bad and felt that I certainly belonged on the relay team.

I could see the steam from my breath, and I quickly put on my jacket. The coach shook my hand and patted me on the shoulder as a sign of welcome. It was a wonderful feeling. For a few moments, I forgot my uncertainties and felt ready for the challenges of my new life. By now, I had heard all the wonderful things about La Salle and how difficult it was to get into. I had also heard that they rarely accepted transfer students.

I took the same number 1A bus back to the hotel and told my parents what had transpired. I was gone for most of the day and they were beginning to worry. They were ecstatic that I was accepted to La Salle and that I didn't have to pay any fees.

***

La Salle College, Kowloon, Hong Kong, 1962

Later I learned how fortunate I was to be admitted to La Salle and also learned about the school's long history.

In early 1900, Kowloon was expanding rapidly and there was demand for a school. On April 23, 1928, Brother Aimar Sauron (1873-1945), the Director of St. Joseph's on Hong Kong Island, acquired a 10-acre hilly plot near Prince Edward Road as a site for the new La Salle College, for a sum of $120,000 HK. The site was immediately north of the city boundary, and thus was technically in New Kowloon. That section of Boundary Street was not yet a formal road when the school site was bought.

On November 5, 1930, Sir William Peel, the Governor of Hong Kong, laid the foundation stone of the new building. By December 3, 1931, work on the building and the playgrounds was sufficiently advanced to allow the opening of eight classes for 303 pupils, under the management of five Brothers from St. Joseph's College and a few lay teachers.

The formal inauguration of the college took place on January 6, 1932. Seven Brothers, headed by Reverend Brother Aimar as Director, took over. A few days later 40 boarders occupied the quarters to the west of the building. There were 540 students in 14 classes. About one-third of the students had a European (mostly Portuguese) connection. La Salle would always welcome students from different countries.

Brother Aimar was the principal of the school for its first seven years. The statue of St. John Baptist de La Salle that now stands in front of the College was erected during that time. The number of students increased to 805 in 1935 and 1,060 in 1939.

In 1939, La Salle College was affected when World War II commenced in Europe. On September 3, 1939, Britain declared war on Germany, and the British War Department in Hong Kong designated the La Salle College campus as an internment camp for German nationals arrested in Hong Kong. All buildings were occupied, including the College Annex across the road, which would become La Salle Primary School in 1957.

On December 8, 1941, the Japanese attacked Hong Kong, and the school building was again taken over by the British Military, this time as a relief hospital. After the surrender of Hong Kong on Christmas Day 1941, the Japanese took over the building. In February 1942, the Brothers were expelled from the college, and the school's operation was suspended until September 1946. During the Japanese occupation, the college was believed to have been used as a Number One Japanese military hospital (out of four in Kowloon) until August 1945.

School recommenced in September 1946. By the end of 1949, the Chinese Civil War ended, and China was now controlled by the communist government of Mao Zedong. The Chinese People's Liberation Army was rapidly advancing southwards toward the Hong Kong border. Owing to that threat, the British Army reinforced their garrisons in Hong Kong. In need of a hospital, they expropriated the use of the college grounds, originally agreed upon for a duration of 12 to 18 months. Meanwhile, the Hong Kong government erected a number of wooden huts on a plot at Perth Street in Ho Man Tin. The temporary occupation unfortunately dragged on for ten years. It took the concerted efforts of the local government, some members of the British Parliament, and even the Vatican to finally dislodge the Army in August 1959.

Brother Felix was appointed Director of the school in 1956 and re-acquired the college buildings from the military authorities on August 1, 1959. Student numbers grew steadily, which led to a separation of primary and secondary divisions.

La Salle Primary School was founded in 1957 and Brother Henry Pang was appointed its founder and first headmaster.

From February 1962 to June 1965, this majestic building was a big part of my life. Even though I attended the school for only three and a half years, I made many friendships that would last for a lifetime.

In 1977 a decision was made to replace the aging building. While classes were continuing, a portion of the school grounds was used to erect a new building. The project was funded via the sale of approximately one-third of the school grounds to Cheung Kong Holdings, owned by the richest man in Hong Kong, Li Ka Shing.

The Governor of Hong Kong, Sir Murray MacLehose officially opened the new school building on February 19, 1982, in its Golden Jubilee year.

By tradition, alumni of La Salle College are called the La Salle old boys, and the alumni association is called the La Salle College Old Boys' Association.

The Old Boys' Association has always been active. Our class celebrated its 25th, 50th and 55th anniversaries with good attendance each occasion. I maintained contact with many of my classmates through the 55 years since we left school.

CHAPTER 2:
Form 3

I WAS FILLED WITH EXCITEMENT and apprehension that I had been accepted to Form 3 at La Salle. I was excited for new adventures; I was apprehensive because I was in a big, strange city at an extremely competitive school.

I began classes the day after my interview with Brother Felix. Brother Lawrence, another Irish monk, was my homeroom teacher. He looked to me like a tall version of the British actor Peter O'Toole. He was a handsome man in his early thirties with sandy hair, and he seemed much taller than six feet. When I entered the room, he pointed to the extra desk and chair that had been moved there for me. As he pointed, I noticed that his finger was twice as long as mine and his hand was so massive that he could have easily grabbed a basketball. In contrast to his impressive size, he was a soft-spoken man and seemed to be a serious teacher.

For two weeks, we stayed at the fleabag hotel while I was attending La Salle. I was too embarrassed to tell my classmates where I was staying. It was strange to be living in a hotel without a desk or other things I needed for school.

The night before I started classes, my mother had taken me to a nearby clothing store in Mongkok and bought me a blue blazer—all schools in Hong Kong had blazers varying from blue to brown to green—for my winter uniform. I also got a pair of gray pants. Many of the students in class had fine cashmere or camel hair blazers and well-pressed gray wool pants. Their white shirts with firm collars were impeccable, without a wrinkle, and their school ties sat neatly in place. They looked wealthy. The clothes I had bought were obviously of poor quality. The pants felt coarse and already the fibers were shedding and getting thinner by the day. I felt as if I was wearing a pair of disposable pants. Even though the material was thick, I didn't feel warm and I thought it might have been woven out of remnants and discarded wool. How ironic that the uniform intended to make us equal exposed the disparity between the richer and poorer students with one quick glance. I was embarrassed, and I was ashamed that I was embarrassed because I knew it was my vanity making me feel that way.

The first day was overwhelming. I was skipping half a year and only four months remained in the school year. My brother Chung found a second-hand textbook store on Nathan Road and I was able to get almost all my books used at two-thirds the price of new ones. In those days, textbooks were really expensive as they were usually printed in England.

On Friday, Mr. Chong reminded me about the invitational track meet at Wah Yan College on Saturday. The top sprinter, Tony Hu, happened to be in my class and said he would take me there. I was fortunate to have brought my track shoes when we left Malaya.

We got there early the next morning to warm up and practice passing the baton. It was an unusually cold winter day and I was shivering.

Our third runner was Ed King, a stocky fellow who looked more like a discus thrower than a sprinter. He had thick eyelids and high cheekbones on his square, reddish face. Judging from his fair complexion and slightly accented Cantonese, I suspected he was from northern China.

The fourth runner was Frankie Sing, who was from Fiji and was half Chinese and half Indian. He was the captain of the sports team and champion of the 400m, but his time for the 100m was also good enough for him to be on the relay team. The fifth runner, the reserve, was Wing Man Ko, who was in Form 5.

After warming up and practicing our baton passing, we only had the one event to run. We came in first. On the way back to the hotel, Tony asked me where I was staying. I was too embarrassed to tell him the truth, so I said I was staying at the better-known Nathan Hotel, which was half a block away from our hotel. In Muar, I felt that our family was one of the wealthier ones, but at La Salle I felt like a pauper.

I hadn't studied Chinese for five years, and now I was expected to resume the language at a high school level. The Chinese language teacher, a short, kind, bespectacled man in his fifties asked about my background with the language.

Mr. Wong had had a mild stroke some years ago and was left with a mild paralysis of the left facial nerve. As a result, his mouth drifted to the left and looked like a kind of fish—probably flounder—common in the Hong Kong fish market. The students had given him the nickname "Jor Hau Yeu" (*left mouth fish*).

The assignment for the class was an essay on Chinese New Year, which was a week away. I tried and tried but was only able to write three simple sentences. After I handed in my assignment, Mr. Wong took me aside and remarked that it was not an essay as I had only written three short sentences.

That year, Form 3A just happened to contain all the students taking French, in addition to the top students. Scattering the French language students across all six sections would have been disruptive, so almost half of Form 3A consisted of students taking French. There were a number of Portuguese, Eurasians and a few Indians in the class, and even one with a Russian connection, one with a Jewish background, as well an assortment of overseas Chinese who for one reason or another ended up in Hong Kong.

The class also included two ethnic Chinese from Indonesia who had encountered persecution and sought refuge in Hong Kong.

Those who didn't want to take Chinese as a second language were offered French, and the class was the first session each morning. When Mr. Wong pulled me aside, he asked if I would rather take French, because he felt my Chinese wasn't at the Form 3 grade level. I told him that I had never taken any French and wouldn't be able to join at the third year level.

French was offered in Form 1, i.e. the seventh grade, and would go on for five years. By the end of eleventh grade, the students would take French as a second language in the HKSC Exam instead of Chinese. In my case, it was assumed that I'd studied Chinese since the kindergarten. In addition to Chinese language, there was also Chinese history and literature.

Fortunately I could use the Malay language, which I had studied for five years, if I failed Chinese for the second language requirement.

***

Housing in Hong Kong had gone up astronomically since we left. A small two bedroom, one bath apartment near La Salle was well over $600 HK (about $75 US) a month. Father looked at several apartments near Kowloon City, but the area was very noisy and not much cheaper.

Father had his mail forwarded to an old friend's dry goods store prior to our arriving in Hong Kong. Mr. Lo suggested my father consider Shatin, saying that he had a friend who was constructing a three-story building. He had one of his sons accompany my father to see the house. In the sixties, Shatin was very much in the New Territories. Getting there was a pain and involved taking a train.

Father decided on a unit on the second floor, which had been completed. Three Hakka women, day after day, added one block of granite after another to continue the rest of the building.

The truck came on Sunday morning to move us to Shatin. After two weeks, I was glad to be leaving the fleabag hotel at last. It hadn't been a pleasant experience, but it was only $40 HK a night. Had we stayed at the nicer Nathan Hotel, it would have been two or three times as expensive. Our parents were pleased that we'd saved a few hundred dollars.

The new place was a strange looking house, built on the cheap, without a permit. There was no steel rib bar for support. The owner had acquired doors and windows from buildings that had been torn down. None of the doors were the same and the windows came in varying shapes and sizes. I often feared that the entire building would tumble down. Even the interior walls were whitewashed instead of painted. If by accident our clothes touched the wall, they would turn white. My dark blue winter blazer uniform was the most problematic as it was difficult to get rid of the whitewash. My hair would catch particles from it and always felt gritty.

There was one more problem with the house—its distance. It was built in the middle of a rice paddy and was accessible only by a path three feet wide above fields and fields of rice paddies. It was a good half hour walk to the train station. From the train station, the ride was another half hour to the city. Once in the city, it was yet another half hour walk or a twenty-minute bus ride to La Salle. The commute to school was over an hour and a half each way.

The bus ride from the hotel to La Salle had been about fifteen or twenty minutes. In the new place, I had to plan carefully to allow enough time to get to school. My sister Cathy's Maryknoll Convent School was also on Boundary Street and two bus stops before La Salle, so we traveled to school together.

Classes began at eight. We had to get up around five, leave the house before six and catch the 6:30 train, which would arrive in the city after seven. We could then either get off one stop before the terminal and walk half an hour or continue to the terminal in Tsim Sha Tsui and take the number 1A bus for the 25 to 30 minute ride to Boundary Street. Getting to school was a real ordeal.

The monthly rent in Shatin was three hundred dollars, and an equivalent apartment near the school would have been two or three times that. We had no idea how soon our parents would find work or how long the several thousand dollars in savings would last the family.

Each morning, by the time I arrived at school, I was exhausted. With so many adjustments and so much to catch up on, I was staying up until one or two in the morning. When five o'clock rolled around, I would finally be sound asleep, only to be jolted awake by the alarm clock. Dragging myself out of the warm bed, I would walk to the cold bathroom and splash cold water on my face to wake up. Cathy and I would then walk in the dark, facing the biting wind, to the train station. I often thought how wonderful it would be to have an apartment near the school. I could roll out of bed at seven and simply walk to school leisurely. But sometimes in life we aren't given a choice. I was resentful that in addition to the adjustments of a new school system and a new place, we were burdened with the stress of living in the middle of nowhere.

***

In class, a fellow by the name of Michael Sze was especially friendly and helpful, filling me in on the happenings at school. After the move to Shatin, I saw two familiar faces at the train station the first morning. One was Michael, and the other was a

Eurasian-looking fellow I'd seen in class but hadn't had the chance to be acquainted with.

Michael introduced me to Juan Trujillo. He was a handsome fellow with olive-toned skin, luxuriant wavy black hair, thick eyebrows and long dark eyelashes. His large hazel eyes were friendly and expressive.

Michael explained that Juan was part Chinese and part Mexican.

I had always been curious about people's heritage. "Is your father Mexican?" I asked.

With a slight smile, he replied, "My father is part Chinese and part Mexican. I have a Spanish surname because of the naming custom in Mexico. You see, when a child is born, he or she is usually given three names. The first is the given name, the middle is the father's surname, and last is the mother's surname. For example, as my father's name is Pedro Chu Trujillo and my mother's name is Elena Wong Martinez, I should have been named Juan Chu Wong. But since I was born in Hong Kong, my name followed the British custom of using my father's last name and hence Juan Chu Trujillo. It's a long story. My father is part Chinese and part Mexican and so is my mother."

Over a number of days, I listened with interest as Juan told me more about his family history.

His paternal grandfather went to Mexico as an indentured worker on an island (Isla San Martin) off the coast of Baja California to collect guano to be used as fertilizer, a job no locals would do. It was hell on earth—the place was hot and filthy, and no vegetation grew on the island. The hot salty air laden with bird droppings burned many of the workers' throats and lungs, and fresh water was scarce. To add to the misery, the dusty air carried all sorts of germs. Many Chinese workers suffered all kinds of skin and respiratory ailments and many died. They lived in huts and had to sleep underground because it was so hot.

After five years, his grandfather had paid off his debt and left the job, moving to Mexicali where there was a growing Chinese population. There, he opened a small grocery store with his brother. After a decade of hard work, they bought some desert land and brought in irrigation to grow cotton on land that had never been utilized before. In 1900, entrepreneurs of the California Development Company under an American named Chandler managed to divert the water from the Colorado River to the Mexicali area, making it possible to have a stable year-round water supply for agriculture. Juan's grandfather owned hundreds of acres of cotton fields as well as his own processing plant.

As almost no Chinese women were allowed to go to Mexico, many Chinese men married Mexican women. At age forty, Juan's grandfather married an eighteen-year-old Mexican girl, and Juan's father was born.

His maternal grandfather also went to Mexico around 1910, to work on the railroad. After his five-year contract was up, he worked as a foreman in a cotton gin owned by a Chinese man, and he too married a Mexican woman.

Later, his maternal grandfather, with a few relatives and friends, opened a casino in the La Chinesca section of Mexicali— at the time the town was almost all Chinese. He made a fortune during the Prohibition years in the 1920s, as many Americans crossed the border to drink and gamble, and some to smoke opium.

In the 1930s, during the Depression, there were few jobs. The Chinese in Mexicali were doing relatively better than most of the natives because they saw opportunities few had seen before, such as bringing irrigation to the desert land. Thousands of acres were planted with cotton and other crops. Most of the Chinese were able to get by while many Mexicans went hungry.

The Mexicans became very resentful of the Chinese and blamed them for their misery, even though they were a miniscule fraction of the total population.

The anti-Chinese movement emerged during the Mexican Revolution and peaked during the Depression. The treatment of the Chinese in Mexico was similar to what they experienced in California in the second half of the 19th century. They were initially welcomed into unpopulated areas, which needed large amounts of cheap manpower. The frontier situation in both areas also allowed the Chinese to carve out economic niches for themselves. The Chinese as a whole turned out to be hardworking, frugal, mutually supportive within their communities, and often succeeded as entrepreneurs in agriculture and small commercial enterprises. In both cases, when their numbers reached a certain percentage of the local population and they attained a certain amount of monetary success, backlashes occurred on both sides of the border. Many of their properties were looted and burnt and hundreds of innocent Chinese were killed by mobs.

The Mexican Government eventually passed a law that the Chinese must leave Mexico, including their Mexican wives and children. In early 1930, Juan's grandfather and his father, who was fourteen at the time, went back to their ancestral village in Guangdong. His father had gone to school in Mexicali and Spanish was spoken at home.

During the 1930s and 1940s, China was in turmoil. Juan's father was unable to attend school much of the time because he knew little Chinese.

His mother's family was also expelled from Mexico and returned to their ancestral village in Guangdong.

In 1941, the Japanese occupied China and Hong Kong, so the families fled to Macau, which was neutral during WWII. With names like Trujillo and Martinez, they could blend in with the

Macanese. Juan's parents met in Macau, and when the war ended in 1946, they moved to Hong Kong. Juan was born in 1947.

In 1952, the family moved to Shatin where they had some relatives. His father opened a dry goods store. His mother, a devout Catholic, would take Juan and his sister to church.

After primary school in Shatin, when Juan was twelve, the priest suggested that he apply to La Salle for Form 1. In 1961, he enrolled at La Salle, and his sister Julia, who was a year and a half younger, enrolled at Maryknoll Convent School in Form 1 a year later.

At La Salle, Juan decided to take French as a second language instead of Chinese because he found Chinese too difficult. Since his parents spoke Spanish with each other, he thought studying French might be easier.

I first met Julia on the train one morning. Juan's sister was as beautiful as Juan was handsome. Her luxuriant wavy black hair fell to her shoulders, partially hiding her slender neck. She had dark brown eyebrows and long eyelashes, and her large, sparkling hazel eyes were most striking. They reminded me of one of my favorite Spanish songs, *Aquellos Ojos Verdes*. I was instantly attracted to her. On the train, sometimes, I would throw glances at her, and I thought she too threw glances at me.

She was in Form 2 and my sister Cathy was in Form 1, also at Maryknoll, which was two blocks from La Salle. The two girls became good friends and began traveling to and from school each day.

Later, Julia and I exchanged letters with Cathy as the carrier.

***

Michael and Juan's houses were just a few minutes' walk from the train station. They felt bad that I lived so far away from it.

Michael was God-sent, an angel. Not knowing a soul in a big school, in a big city, I was overjoyed to meet someone who was so warm and helpful. When he suggested that I borrow his old bicycle that wasn't being used, it was a gift from heaven! Instead of a torturing, time-wasting and boring half-hour walk to the train station, we could ride the bike there in less than ten minutes. My sister Cathy sat on the bar, and when we arrived we would lock the bike up near the station. Such a simple machine took so much pressure off of our busy lives.

The train was always crowded with students heading for school, and often there were no seats so we had to stand between the cars. When it passed through the tunnel, it would be pitch black. Sometimes soot from the coal-burning engine would settle on our white shirts.

Most mornings as we rode the train, Michael would help me with Chinese language and Chinese history and literature. Fortunately, even though I didn't have any lessons in Chinese in Malaya, I was reading or trying to read the Chinese newspaper each day. Those characters came back to me with some practice.

When Michael wasn't helping me, the three of us would catch up on the gossip in school. Over several months of daily commutes, I learned a lot about both of them.

Michael's family was from Hong Kong. He had lived in Shatin his entire life. His ancestral village was Dongguan in the nearby Guangdong province. Even though he was Cantonese, he had learned to speak Hakka, as most of the original people in the Shatin area were Hakka. His father was the manager of a textile company in Shatin.

Michael and Juan introduced me to their friends, explained the culture at La Salle, and told me who was who. Without their help, my transition to La Salle would have been so much more difficult.

***

24

One Friday morning, the three of us decided to get off at the Yau Ma Tei train station and take the half hour walk to La Salle while Cathy and Julia continued on to Star Ferry to take the bus.

Halfway through our walk, a tall fellow, over six feet, with a very fair complexion approached us. He looked Caucasian, so I was surprised when he spoke to Michael in perfect Cantonese.

"Good morning Michael. How are you parents?" he asked.

"Good," Michael answered. "My father was just talking about getting together with your family the other day."

"I'll tell my mother," said the tall fellow. "We haven't seen each other for over a year." After saying goodbye to us, he walked on ahead with another friend.

I was curious, so when we were out of earshot I commented to Michael that I thought the fellow was a "Gweilo," literally *devil man*, a term the Cantonese in Hong Kong used for the white man.

With a smile on his face, Michael explained, "He's the son of General Claire Chennault. You know, the American who came to China's aid when the Japanese had a blockade on China. The only way China was able to get weapons and ammunitions from America was the Flying Tigers that flew over the Himalaya Mountains to Kunming, Yunnan in western China to supply Chiang Kai-shek and his Kuomintang soldiers. His father was the founder of the Flying Tigers.

"His mother is my father's cousin on his mother's side," Michael continued. "She met General Chennault in Kunming during WWII when she was eighteen and they had Henry a year later. They never got married because he was already married, but General Chennault took very good care of them and even got Henry into La Salle. He's in Form 5. From what Henry told me, he'll be going to San Francisco next year when he turns eighteen. Because of his father, he was born an American citizen. The general died in 1958, but before he did, he hired a lawyer and had all the papers drawn up to make sure that Henry and his mother would be well taken care of. His father was a nice man."

I was fascinated by the story. My father had told me stories about the Flying Tigers, and now I had actually met the founder's son.

Michael explained that Henry's full name was Henry Fei Fu Chennault, and in Chinese he went by Chen Fei Fu, using the first syllable of Chennault for Chen, a common surname. Fei Fu in Chinese means *flying tiger*. I was impressed that he had such a strong Chinese name and how perfectly it translated into Chinese.

La Salle never ceased to amaze me with such a diverse student body. I thought that in itself was educational.

Another kind fellow in my class, Mark Moy, noticed that I was in need of help with my Chinese language. Mark spoke American English, and I soon found out that he was actually an American, born in New York City to Toi Shan parents. His father was a physician in New York City's Chinatown who had sent his wife and two sons to Hong Kong so that the boys would be exposed to Chinese culture.

Mark admitted that he had the lowest marks in the Chinese language in class, but nevertheless, he knew more Chinese than I did. He had an air of self-confidence and spoke clearly, carefully enunciating each word in both English and Chinese. He impressed me as an extremely intelligent fellow.

***

My parents had sent out many job applications. During the five years we were away, Hong Kong had changed a great deal. The British colonial government had risen to the occasion and was doing a great job of housing hundreds of thousands of refugees. Many new schools were built. Hospitals were added. Many of my parents' friends from Sun Yat-sen University had found employment and were doing well.

In late June, Father received his contract to teach chemistry at the Tang King Po Technical School in Hung Hum. In July, Mother got her contract to teach in a Catholic primary school in Kwun Tong. My father's salary would be $1000/month and Mother's was $800/month. They had been making that much in Malayan dollars, which converted to twice as much, but we were very happy that they would be employed.

Four months later, the school term ended. When the results were posted, I ranked 32nd for the entire Form 3 (9th grade) and I was promoted to Form 4A (10th grade).

Now that my parents would be working, we moved out of Shatin at the end of summer to a two bedroom, one bath apartment on Prince Edward Road, a fifteen- to twenty-minute walk to La Salle, or a less than ten-minute bus ride if I was late.

My ninth grade had ended well and I was eager to begin the tenth grade.

CHAPTER 3:
Form 4

U NLIKE THE PREVIOUS YEAR, I knew I could survive Form 4 (10th grade) at La Salle. Chinese was no longer a big problem. However, I had never been gifted in math, and although I found physics manageable, I was struggling with trigonometry.

La Salle was well known for its students' superior command of English in Hong Kong. This was in part due to the fact that there were sizeable numbers of overseas Chinese (Chinese born outside of China and Hong Kong), and also Hong Kong-born Portuguese, Eurasian and Indian students who preferred to speak English even though most of them also spoke Cantonese.

It was a common practice for families who could afford it to have private tutors for their children to help them gain an edge at school. Such practice is still widespread all over Asia where education is highly valued. Some La Salle students would make pocket money by working as tutors. When the mother of five who lived in our apartment building approached me about tutoring her two sons, both La Salle Primary School students aged nine and twelve, I jumped at the chance. I was happy to have the extra money.

***

Laissez-faire Society
The "leave it alone" or non-interference attitude of the colonial government had worked for Hong Kong. With so many talented

people wanting to succeed, business thrived. It was survival of the fittest in the truest sense.

Competition could be found in all aspects of life in Hong Kong. Parents would do anything to get their children into the top schools. For a school like La Salle, a young boy had to have an interview to get into kindergarten. My acceptance into La Salle was a source of great pride for my parents.

It was a brutal system; in order to have a high percentage of passing students in the HKSC examination, many top schools utilized a pyramid system. To gain admission into the La Salle high school, a student had to have done well in the also all-important exam that every sixth grader had to take. As with the HKSC Exam, the results of this exam were posted openly in school and printed out in almost all the newspapers. Only those who had done well would be privileged enough to continue at La Salle.

Even after getting into La Salle, there was no guarantee that a student could remain there. From one grade to the next, the students at the bottom would be asked to leave. These poor students then had to continue their education in a lower-tiered school. If the family was rich, they would often continue their high school education overseas in boarding schools. By the time a student got to the eleventh grade at La Salle, they had been screened and tested so many times that they were almost guaranteed to pass the exam.

This survival-of-the-fittest atmosphere spawned an industry of after-school "review sessions" in some of the teachers' homes. Some of the wealthy underachieving students paid up to twenty Hong Kong dollars an hour to have the teacher help them do their homework. More importantly, the teacher dispensed tips and hints to help these students in the forthcoming exams; they often walked into an exam already knowing two-thirds of the contents. But these teachers were smart enough to give only enough tips to allow a student to score a passing grade instead of an A. Otherwise it would have been too obvious. What an example of conflict of interest! Some of the students who managed to get promoted year after year would then leave Hong Kong to continue in boarding schools overseas before entering Form 5 (11th grade) because they knew that the HKSC Exam was the great equalizer; no teacher could help them there.

In Hong Kong, students could be identified by their school uniforms—the badge on the blazer and the school tie. Those in the lower-tiered schools were a source of embarrassment and shame for their parents, as they were already considered failures in life.

***

We knew that things were not well in China, but there was a media blackout and officially no one knew what was happening. There were power struggles between Mao and some other founding members of the new China, such as Deng Xio-ping and Lin Piao. For reasons unknown, waves of hungry Chinese were allowed to rush the border. Many broke through and many more thousands entered Hong Kong by boats under the cover of darkness. In the papers there suddenly appeared pictures of men, women and children with hollow cheeks, sunken eyes, and dry, dull, lifeless hair, all signs of extreme malnourishment.

When I was commuting from Shatin, the saddest thing to witness were the refugees from China who had escaped to the New Territories trying to enter the city—once in the city, they would be relatively safe. I learned that the Hong Kong government had enacted the so-called "Touch Base" policy by which a refugee caught in the New Territories would be questioned to discover their motives, and most of them would be handed over to the Chinese authorities. If they were lucky enough to reach the urban side of the Kowloon hills, however, they were deemed to have reached "home base" and would be allowed to stay in the colony. But it wasn't easy for them to blend in with people like us on the train. They stood out so much with their nervous looks and obvious physical signs of malnutrition. There were police officers walking around the stations keeping an eye out for these people. I always felt very bad to see them get caught. I imagined being one of them, having escaped to the New Territories only to be caught on my way to the city.

A second fence was erected to prevent more refugees from entering the colony. The people of Hong Kong were very worried. Hong Kong was a tiny colony, and it simply couldn't accommodate any more people. It would overwhelm the infrastructure and there were fears that anarchy would ensue.

I was very worried. Where could we go? Just as life was starting to have some semblance of order, Mao had ruined it. It was frightening because there was really nothing we could do. Those who had the means were making plans to go to England, America, Australia or Canada.

Hong Kong, with its swelling population, had been dependent on China for years for its water supply, which was transported from Guangdong via a large pipeline. The Chinese government decided to cut down on the flow of water to Hong Kong—another way of harassing the colonial government. Water rationing was instituted and water was only available for a few hours each day and sometimes only two or three days a week. To store the water when it was available, we bought a huge tank, which occupied almost half our bathroom. We also had to make sure someone was home during the hours when water was available. It was another hassle in our hectic lives, but we managed.

One date most people in Hong Kong dreaded was the year 1997. In 1997 the lease of Kowloon and the New Territories would run out, at which point they would be reverted back to China. It was also common knowledge that if China really wanted the land back earlier, they could simply open the gate and let Hong Kong be overrun. The British wouldn't be able to defend the colony.

***

Hong Kong has always tried to take care of its refugees. With the upheaval in Indonesia, many Chinese were massacred, and many fled to China even though most of them had been born in Indonesia. China had its own turmoil, and the great hardships caused by the Great Leap Forward made life for the Indonesian Chinese impossible. They decided they had enough of China and secured exit visas; about 30,000 were able to find new countries in which to resettle. Those who couldn't find new homes were refused reentry to Indonesia and ended up, like my family, staying in Hong Kong. Like the Shanghainese before them, the Indonesian Chinese began to form a neighborhood with its own distinct identity. In the fifties, the Shanghainese had created a Little Shanghai in Causeway Bay. North Point, the district along the eastern corridor of Hong Kong waterfront, became known as Little Indonesia.

***

When our family left Hong Kong for Malaya at the end of 1956, the standard of living was much higher in Malaya because of its rich natural resources. Changes had occurred in Hong Kong while we were away. After the communist takeover, Shanghai, the Paris of the East, was undergoing a difficult time and all capitalistic activities ceased in 1953. The people who made Shanghai the hugely successful financial center that it was came to Hong Kong. Among the Chinese, many of whom were Shanghainese, was an exotic mix: Russians escaping from the Bolsheviks, Ashkenazi Jews escaping persecution and discrimination in Russia, Sephardic Jews who made the long trek from Baghdad to China via India. These people made up a great part of the financial establishment. With their capital and know-how, they were transforming Hong Kong.

In class I noticed two fellows who looked fully Caucasian, yet I didn't think they were British because they didn't have the typical English accent. After getting acquainted with them, I learned that both of them had very unusual backgrounds.

Felix Sapanov

Felix had slightly wavy, fine blond hair and intense light gray eyes. I had never really met a Russian before, so I had no idea that he was one. I wasn't even aware that there were any Russians in Hong Kong. He was articulate and self-assured and often asked pertinent questions in class.

During recess one day in the canteen, I was standing beside him in line to grab a bun and a bottle of soymilk, and we struck up a conversation. After paying for our food, we walked outside to sit on a bench. The conversation led to our families, and I told him a bit about my family history.

"My family background is somewhat similar to yours," Felix commented, "in that we're both refugees fleeing the communists. My maternal grandmother was a countess in Russia before the Bolshevik Revolution. During the Revolution of 1917, my grandmother's family escaped to Siberia. But the communists continued to pursue the White Russians, so they fled south to Harbin in China when she was about twenty years old. With the money her family brought, they got into the fur trade business and did well. They led a very comfortable life in Harbin, where there were many other White Russians as well as Russians Jews.

"While in Harbin, she married another White Russian, and soon my mother was born.

The beautiful Saint Sophia Russian Orthodox Cathedral where my grandparents got married still stands in the city.

"My mother grew up in Harbin and went to Russian schools there. She could speak fluent Mandarin. She was hoping to go to university but couldn't because of the political situations in both China and Russia.

"My paternal grandfather, who was a White Russian originally from Moscow, had gone to Harbin in the 1920s to work for the Railway Company. He was one of the senior managers. My father was also born in Harbin like my mother. They attended the same Russian high school there. My father too was hoping to attend university, but like my mother wasn't able to because of the political climate. Both my parents' families were better off than most other Russians in Harbin because they were able to bring a substantial amount of gold and jewelry with them.

"In 1940, the Japanese occupied Harbin and made life difficult for the inhabitants by harassing them with new laws, arresting some, and taking over some properties. The two families decided to leave, but news from Russia wasn't good. The communist regime had executed a number of nobility and put others in prisons in Siberia, which had deplorable conditions. Since both families were part of the nobility being persecuted in Russia, they chose to travel south to Shanghai and join the large number of exiled White Russians who were already there.

"Initially, both families could afford to live in the French Concession in Shanghai and actually led comfortable lives. But after a year, with nobody finding any work, their wealth dwindled and they had to live more frugally, moving into much smaller apartments."

I chewed on my bun and sipped my soymilk, nodding occasionally but otherwise listening intently to Felix's story.

"Life was difficult in Shanghai," he continued. "There were so many refugees and work was scarce. With no income, they continued to further deplete their savings. Grandmother's fur business was long gone, as few people had money to buy furs anymore. Before long, most of the White Russians in Shanghai were poor. Unlike many of the Russian Jews, most White Russians never had to work and now found themselves without skills. A lot of the Russian Jews were trades and crafts people and they had always worked very hard.

"My parents got married in Shanghai on Saturday December 6, 1941, the day before the Japanese bombed Pearl Harbor. After that, life became even more difficult.

"The strange thing is that even though both the White Russians and Russian Jews were refugees, the White Russians didn't have much to do with the Russian Jews because they looked down on them, which I thought was sad. They had so much in common, but the White Russians thought they were better than the Russian Jews. In the end, the Russian Jews survived better because they were willing to work hard.

"Ironically," he continued, "the White Russians in Shanghai became so poor and desperate that the British looked down on them. They felt the lifestyles and poverty of White Russians were undermining the 'white privilege' that the British and other white people were enjoying. Other Europeans even tried to avoid associating with the White Russians.

"You know James," Felix said as he munched on his beef curry bun and took sips of his soymilk, "even before WWII, many Russians were hired by the Royal Hong Kong Police Force because there was just no other work to be found. They had to abandon their lives of leisure in Shanghai and move to Hong Kong. They were paid much less than the other Europeans. At one point, Russians comprised almost 15% of all Europeans in the Hong Kong police.

"After the Japanese surrendered in September, 1945, my parents realized that Shanghai was no place for them. They knew there would be no peace and that the civil war between

Mao and Chiang would resume. They really wanted to immigrate to America, Canada or Australia, but there were so many other refugees with the same idea, and visas were difficult to get because preference was given to the refugees who had relatives in those countries.

"In September of 1946, about a year after the Japanese surrendered, my parents moved to Hong Kong where my father was hired as a police inspector. Fortunately, while in Shanghai, he had studied English seriously because he knew that in order to survive he would need it.

"I was born a year later. So, as you can see, I am a true Hong Kong native. I guess I am more of a Hong Kong native than you!" Felix chuckled.

He had a smile on his face as he finished off his bun. The autumn morning sun felt good and there was a gentle breeze in the air.

I was fascinated by his family stories, which I thought were somewhat similar to mine. "If you had remained in Russia, would you have inherited the title of Count from your grandmother?" I asked.

Felix looked perplexed and answered, "That's a good question. I'm not sure. I've never thought about it. Perhaps I'll ask my parents.

"My mother studied English in Shanghai as well," he continued, "but didn't work as hard as my father. She found the English language very difficult and very different from Russian and Chinese. She really struggled with the pronunciations, and still has problems with the language here. She speaks Mandarin, but as you know, it's useless here in Hong Kong, and she has tremendous difficulty with Cantonese because it's so different from Mandarin. In spite of that, she has able to earn some income by giving piano lessons to wealthy Chinese children. Both of my parents have worked hard here and managed to build a decent life. They bought a house in Kowloon Tong, not far from La Salle College.

"Even though life is good here, we know that we don't belong in Hong Kong," Felix remarked. "It's a Chinese city and we just don't fit in. My parents are still planning to immigrate to Canada or Australia. They would rather go to America, but they know that America is very difficult for us Russians to immigrate to. I'm not sure what the reason is.

"I love Hong Kong," he continued. "This is the only place I know and I feel I'm a true native. But my parents worry about my future if I decide to stay. If they do get their visas to Australia or Canada, of course I'll go with them. But I'll keep my Hong Kong papers so I can always come back."

"I think your parents are right," I said. "Hong Kong will eventually return to China, and life will be difficult. I won't stay here if I can help it. I'm hoping to study in America and stay there. All my life I've heard from my parents that the communists will rule Hong Kong one day and that I should study hard and go to America."

"I guess our parents have their reasons," he mused. "They're a lot wiser than we are."

The school bell rang, so we got up from the bench and returned to class for the physics period.

Max Mandel

I had no idea that Max Mandel was Jewish. In 1963, I only had some vague ideas about the history of the Jewish people. Max had wavy light brown hair and grayish-blue eyes, which was not the picture I had in my mind of a typical Jewish person.

At lunch break on a beautiful fall Tuesday, I spotted Max sitting alone on the grass of our sports field behind the main building eating a sandwich and drinking a bottle of Coke. I had also brought my own sandwich, and I went to join him.

As we ate our lunch and chatted, I learned that he was born

in Shanghai shortly after WWII.

"How did your family end up Shanghai?" I asked.

"It's a long story," replied Max with a smile. "In 1933 Hitler came to power and made the situation more and more hostile to the Jews in Germany. My father, Otto, had just graduated from the medical school at the University of Vienna, Austria. He was interested in psychiatry, so he continued his studies at the Sigmund Freud Clinic in Vienna. Later, he worked there for a year, until 1938, when Freud left Austria to escape Nazi persecution. At that point, my father couldn't find any work, because by then Jews were banned from many professions, including medicine.

"My grandfather Baruch was a banker in Vienna and the family led a very comfortable life there, living in a mansion with several servants.

"After the *Kristallnacht* in 1938, the situation rapidly worsened for the almost 200,000 Austrian Jews. Germany had annexed Austria. Most of their businesses were closed. Jews were beaten in the streets for no obvious reasons other than being Jewish."

At this point I interrupted and asked, "Sorry Max, I don't know about *Kristallnacht.* What happened?"

Max nodded and replied, "Of course. *Kristallnacht* or the Night of Broken Glass, also called the November Pogrom, was a pogrom against Jews carried out by Hitler's paramilitary forces and civilians throughout Nazi Germany including Austria, on November 9 and 10 of 1938. The police did nothing and let the mob do whatever they wanted."

I interrupted again to ask, "What does pogrom mean?"

"It's a word used to mean a sort of organized violence, harassment or even massacre," he explained, "especially against the Jews in Russia. I don't know how it originated.

"The name *Kristallnacht*, which is Crystal Night in German, comes from the shards of broken glass that littered the streets after the windows of Jewish-owned stores, buildings and synagogues were smashed. The pretext for the attacks was the assassination of a senior German diplomat in Paris by a 17-year-old German-born Jew.

"Jewish homes, hospitals and schools were ransacked and demolished with sledgehammers. Rioters destroyed many synagogues throughout Germany and Austria. Jewish businesses were damaged or destroyed, and over 30,000 Jewish men were arrested and incarcerated in concentration camps.

"According to Grandpa, hundreds of Jews were murdered during the riot. He also told me that over six hundred Jews who were arrested and suffered torture or terrible treatment later committed suicide. Grandpa said *Kristallnacht* was a prelude to the *Final Solution* and the murder of over six million Jews during the Holocaust."

Max shook his head, looking somber.

"Can you imagine how wonderful my father's life was in Vienna before the Nazis took over and how drastically it changed when the Jews were literally treated like animals without any sort of rights, let alone dignity.

"You know James, I feel my heart ache a little whenever I see pictures of Jewish men, women, boys and girls and even babies wearing their yellow Star of David to indicate that they were Jews. Can you imagine the humiliation?

"My father and Grandpa thought the German and Austrian people had gone mad. Most of them were church-going and supposed to be kind, God-fearing people. Without the help of most of these people, Hitler couldn't have carried out such atrocities," lamented Max.

Max paused and took a few bites of his sandwich followed by a few sips of Coke before resuming his story.

"My grandpa Baruch decided that the family had to leave Austria, as rumors were rampant that all Jews would be rounded up and sent to concentration camps. By 1938, the Jews were no longer protected by law, so the Nazis could do anything to them and they had no recourse.

"The only way for Jews to escape Nazism was to leave Europe. In order to leave, they had to provide proof of emigration, usually a visa from a foreign nation. This was difficult, because at the 1938 Evian Conference in Evian, France, 31 out of 32 countries—including America, Canada, Australia and New Zealand—refused to accept Jewish immigrants.

"The only country willing to accept them was the Dominican Republic, which offered to accept up to 100,000 refugees. But my grandpa had no idea what was in the Dominican Republic and didn't even know how to get there. He knew another Jewish banker from Vienna who had left six months earlier with his family and was now living in the French Concession in Shanghai. This banker friend wrote that they felt safe in Shanghai, and said there was a Jewish community there. He also wrote that if someone had money, life could actually be quite comfortable and that he and his family had adjusted well to life there. He said there were a few very prominent, wealthy Jewish families who had been in Shanghai for many years and were leaders in the city, and they were helping the Jewish refugees settle.

"Grandpa told me that he agonized over what to do, but he realized that there weren't many options and decided to try taking the family to Shanghai.

"In 1938, time was running out for the Jews. By then, the Nazis had confiscated Grandpa's properties, but he managed to hide some gold and diamonds as well as some US dollars. His physician and friend, Dr. Weiss, told him that the Chinese Consul-General in Vienna was issuing visas for Jews to go China, so Grandpa and Father waited in front of the Chinese Consulate the following day and begged to be given visas. There was a long line of Jews there for the same reason.

"James, you know, one Chinese man saved my family. Without him, I'm quite certain that I wouldn't be here talking to you. This man was Ho Feng-shan. He was the Chinese Consul-General in Vienna at the time.

"Grandpa and Father met with Mr. Ho for only a few minutes but they were issued visas that included my grandmother and my father's younger sister Rachel, whose passports they had brought along. Someone at the consulate also gave Grandpa a contact to get train tickets to Moscow, where they would take the Trans-Siberian Railway onward to Harbin and then on to Shanghai."

Max stopped talking and reached into the pocket of his pants for a white handkerchief, using it to dab at the corners of his eyes. He apologized, saying that he got tears in his eyes every time the story came up.

"I think these are tears of gratitude rather than tears of sadness," Max explained as he continued. "My family managed to get to Moscow. They stayed there with some relatives for a few days while they waited for the train. While in Moscow, they learned that the conditions in Russia for Jews were horrible as well, and they too had nowhere to go. Some had fled to China, but conditions there were also bad because there were few jobs. Some Jews in Moscow with money who had gone to Shanghai earlier fared much better, and some of them even managed to resume a life of luxury.

"From Moscow they boarded a train on the Trans-Siberian Railway. After over a week of bone-jarring travel, they arrived in Vladivostok and then took another train to Harbin. In Harbin they stayed for a few days with the Jewish relatives of a friend from Vienna. Grandpa was surprised to learn that not many years earlier, there were actually as many as 30,000 Russian Jews in the city and at least four synagogues. Most of them fled Russia to escape the pogroms that the Russian Tsars waged against them from time to time.

"From Harbin they took a train to Tianjin, the port city east of Beijing. There, Grandpa was again surprised to learn that not many years ago, there were many Jewish families there as well; again most of them had fled Russia for the same reasons as the Jews in Harbin. From there they managed to get to Shanghai on a cargo ship."

I had been listening with interest, only nodding or briefly commenting occasionally. As Max took a few more bites of his sandwich and a few sips of Coke, I said, "I remember hearing that there were over 30,000 Jewish refugees in Shanghai at the time. How did they manage? If the Nazis took all their money, how did they survive?"

"Things were very difficult for most of the Jews," Max remarked. "Some who arrived earlier were able to bring their money and jewelries as well as gold and silver with them before things got really bad. They didn't suffer as much. But those who arrived later had to work or depend on charity, because the Nazis had robbed them of all their wealth. Can you imagine that the Nazis could simply take anything away from these people and there was nothing they could do?" We both shook our heads.

"In Shanghai things were so bad that sometimes ten families shared a house with only one bathroom," Max continued. "My grandma really had a hard time adjusting to the conditions. She was petrified of the rats and cockroaches. She was constantly worried about infectious diseases like diphtheria, typhoid and typhus fevers because people were living so close together."

The warm autumn sun felt wonderful and there was a soft breeze blowing. Summer had been sweltering and longer than usual, and the humidity had only dropped a few weeks earlier. It seemed incongruous with the topic of our conversation, but reminded me that I had many things to be thankful for.

After another bite of his sandwich, Max resumed his story. "After the Japanese bombed Pearl Harbor on December 7, 1941, the Jews were in an even more precarious situation, as Shanghai was now under Japanese occupation. As you know, the Japanese and Germans were allies. Rumors were rampant that Hitler had been urging the Japanese to intern the Jews in China. Finally, the Japanese decided to order the Jews who had arrived in Shanghai after 1937—those the Japanese regarded as stateless—to live in only one section of Shanghai, the Hungkou area, sort of making that their area of confinement.

"This was later known as the Shanghai ghetto for the Jews. Conditions were horrible. There were armed guards surrounding the neighborhood to enforce the 6 pm curfew each night, and anyone in violation would be severely punished. But the Jews were responsible for their own livelihoods and most of them had to work to eat. They had to ask for special permission to return home after 6 pm if their workplaces were outside the ghetto.

"Many of the refugees were resourceful and tried to make their lives as normal as they could. For instance, there was a section of Shanghai called Little Vienna where there were Viennese bakeries and other things that reminded them of home. Those who could afford it could even drink coffee in cafes. Grandpa told me that each day, every refugee with a trade would ply it, standing or pacing in the streets of Little Vienna with cards around their necks to indicate their trades, such as carpenters, electricians, plumbers and barbers. Jobs were scarce and many depended on the soup kitchen funded by the wealthy Jews who had been in Shanghai for a long time, as well as donations from American Jews.

"News from Europe was frightening and depressing. Reports were coming out that the Nazis were systematically killing Jews. After hearing that, my grandma's attitude improved, because she realized that she was one of the lucky ones. Many of her relatives were never heard from again and presumed dead at the hands of the Nazis.

"Sometimes the topic of conversation among the Viennese Jews turned to the subject of Ho Feng-shan, and many of them would say that without his help, they wouldn't be alive."

"Do you know what happened to him?" I asked curiously.

"My grandpa learned that Ho continued to issue visas until he was ordered to return to China in May 1940. I don't think the exact number of visas he issued to Jewish refugees is known, but he issued at least 2,000 in 1938 alone. Some estimate that he probably issued over 5,000.

"This visa requirement thing was just another gigantic obstacle that the Nazis created for the Jews who wanted to leave Austria at the time. Nobody actually needed a visa to go to China at the time, because the central government was breaking down and nobody bothered checking them.

"Not everyone who got a visa from Ho to go to China went to China. Some of Grandpa's friends actually went to Argentina. Some went to Hong Kong. Some managed to end up in Australia, if they were scientists or had a profession that Australia thought they could use. "

"What an incredible story," I exclaimed. "What a good man Ho Feng-shan was! Do you know what happened to him after he was recalled to China?"

"I don't know what he did or where he was during the war. But in 1949 when the Kuomintang lost power to Mao, the Nationalist government fled to Taiwan. Ho and his family followed the Nationalists and settled in Taiwan. I think from there, he continued his job as a diplomat for the Taiwanese government," answered Max.

"You may not know this James," he continued, "but in those days almost all Jewish doctors in Europe played a musical instrument. When the money that Grandpa had brought was depleted, my father helped support the family by playing the violin in one of the many clubs in Shanghai's French Concession. There were too many Jewish doctors there already, so he couldn't find work as a doctor. Besides, most of the refugees were too poor and couldn't afford to pay.

"My grandma almost had a nervous breakdown when she heard the news that her brother Hans and other relatives were being sent to a concentration camp, a place in southern Poland called Auschwitz. She was convinced that it was just a matter of time before the Japanese did the same to them. Grandpa told her that the Japanese wouldn't harm the Jews—he had learned from another former Viennese banker that the Japanese would spare the Jews' lives in China was because a German-born Jewish American investment banker named Jacob Schiff had done the Japanese government a huge favor in 1905 during the Russo-Japanese War. The Japanese were running out of money and approached Mr. Schiff for a loan. I don't know the exact amount Mr. Schiff raised in bonds for the Japanese, but that money helped them beat the Russians. I think because of that, the Japanese were forever grateful to the Jews.

"Grandpa also learned from a Russian Jew that this was probably why the Tsars hated the Jews so much, because they blamed them for the loss of the war to the Japanese."

"How about your mother's family?" I asked.

Max paused for a few moments and took a swallow of Coke before saying, "My mother's family's story was even more incredible. My mother had just finished her training as an architect in Warsaw, Poland. My maternal grandpa Alon was also an architect.

"When the Nazis invaded Poland in 1939, they seized Grandpa Alon's properties. He lost most of his wealth and the family moved to a much smaller house. By then, it was almost impossible to leave Nazi-occupied Europe, but Grandpa Alon knew he needed to get his family out. He had received letters from a Polish Jew who had fled to Shanghai a year earlier saying that it was safe, so he decided to try taking the family there.

"In early autumn of 1940, with the help of a few resistance

fighters, Grandpa Alon and his family were guided through the forests of northeastern Poland and crossed the border into Lithuania, where they stayed with some relatives.

"In June 1940, the Soviet Union occupied Lithuania. At the time, the Soviets didn't have any policies against the Jews, and even though life was difficult, they were left alone.

"Many Jewish   refugees from Poland as   well   as Lithuanian Jews tried to acquire exit visas. Without the visas, it was dangerous to travel; yet it was impossible to find countries willing to issue them. Word got out that the Japanese Consulate was issuing visas, and hundreds of refugees went to the Japanese consulate in Kaunas to apply for visas to Japan. But they all knew their final destination was actually Shanghai. By now, there were perhaps already 20,000 Jewish refugees from all over Europe in Shanghai.

"At the Japanese Consulate was a man named Sugihara Chiune, who was an assistant to the consul general. It was rumored that Sugihara had heard what Ho Feng-shan was doing in Vienna to help the Jews. Mr. Sugihara felt certain that the Germans would invade Lithuania soon, and realized that if these Jews didn't leave Lithuania, they would meet the same fate as many of the Polish Jews. He decided to help them.

"He began issuing ten-day visas to Jews for transit through Japan. Grandpa Alon was able to get visas for the whole family.

"At that time Japan and the Soviets weren't yet at war with each other. Sugihara was able to convince Soviet officials to let the Jews travel through Russia via the Trans-Siberian Railway, although the Soviets demanded a fare five times higher than the standard ticket price. So Grandpa Alon and his family, which included my grandma and my mother's younger brother, along with two Polish Jew families and a Lithuanian Jewish family, took a train from Vilnius to Minsk in Belarus, and continued on to Moscow where they took the Trans-Siberian Railway to Vladivostok.

"From Vladivostok they were supposed to take a ship to Kobe, Japan, but there was a wait for at least two weeks so they decided instead to take a ship to Sapporo in Hokkaido, northern Japan. From Sapporo they took another ship to Kobe.

"While in Kobe, a Polish diplomat there helped them to get to Shanghai on a cargo ship."

At this point I interrupted Max and asked, "Why didn't they go from Vladivostok to China instead, like your father's family?"

Max cocked his head and blinked his eyes a few times. "That's a good question, James. I'm not sure. It may have something to do with the transit visa that was issued to them. Maybe the Russians wouldn't allow them to leave Russia for China directly, since their visas were for transit through Japan. It's a very good question. I'll have to ask my mother.

"In June and July 1941," he resumed, "following the German invasion of the Soviet Union, the Germans occupied Lithuania. By then, it was no longer possible for the Jews to leave. We later learned that most of the Jews in Lithuania were sent to Auschwitz.

"My mother's family arrived in Shanghai with almost no money, and the four of them stayed in a single room at one of the boarding houses provided by the Kadoorie family. Luckily, Grandpa Alon and my mother both found work with the Kadoories, who owned many buildings in Shanghai and needed architects. They were eventually able to rent a small apartment in the French Concession.

"It was in Shanghai that my parents met when they joined the Young Jewish Orchestra of Shanghai. My father played the violin and my mother played the piano. It was a good thing they both could speak Yiddish, although slightly different versions of it," Max chuckled. It turned out that his father was educated in German and his mother, Polish, so Yiddish was the only way they could communicate.

"The Japanese took over Shanghai on December 8, 1941,

including the International Settlement run by the Americans and Brits, as well as the French Concession. Americans, Brits and Australians were rounded up and put into camps.

"Life in Shanghai was unbearable under Japanese occupation. My mother's family had to give up their small apartment in the French Concession and move to the Hungkou district, where they shared a house with five other families. Food and fuel were scarce. The Japanese could do anything they wanted to anybody. What they said was the law.

"In order to survive, some of the young Jewish women became the mistresses of Japanese officials so they would get better rations. It was a terrible situation. Everyone did whatever they could to survive.

"Fortunately Grandpa Alon and my mother were able to continue their work, as long as they were careful to return to Hungkou before the 6 pm curfew.

"The Jews in Hungkou suffered greatly for three years. Some of them were humiliated and beaten by the two Japanese officials who administered the Hungkou ghetto. Both of them seemed to enjoy terrorizing people. All of the residents in Hungkou lived in constant fear of what they would do next.

"Grandpa Alon told me that one of the officials was a little Japanese man, no taller than five feet, and some even said he was about four feet tall. He looked like a cartoon character. He wore a little mustache and reportedly had bucked teeth, although others said he didn't. My grandfather was lucky enough to never see him. Everyone was convinced that he was a sadist or schizophrenic or both. He was unpredictable and terrifying in his treatment of others.

"This little man, Kanoh Ghoya, had tremendous power over the residents, as he was responsible for giving monthly passes to Jewish refugees living in Hungkou to work outside the ghetto. He saw himself as the 'King of the Jews', and he would often slap and kick them for no obvious reason other than to make them beg for their work passes. The story went that he was so short, he had to stand on his desk to slap people. He would scream at them and throw their application papers in their faces, all while standing on his desk.

"I know some of these stories could have been exaggerated," said Max, shaking his head, "but there were really bad people who behaved very badly during the war.

"Grandpa also told me that there were informers among the refugees who would betray other refugees so they would be treated better. He knew for sure of two Polish Jews who were informers, and everyone would keep quiet when they were around. They reported anyone who dared to complain about anything to the Japanese."

Max paused and then smiled. "You know, James, the good guys should always win, but they don't," he remarked. "But this time they did. On August 6, 1945, a big American B-29 bomber dropped the world's first deployed atomic bomb over the Japanese city of Hiroshima. Then another bomb on Nagasaki, and soon after, the Japanese surrendered.

"Grandpa said the refugees in Hungkou were too scared to say anything, even after they heard the news of the bombings in Japan. They were petrified that the Japanese could still do bad things to them. Only when it was clear that the Japanese had been defeated and the officials and soldiers had left did the refugees cheer.

"Of course it's not as if things went well for the Jews from then on, because they were still in Shanghai, away from home with no idea what would happen to them. They didn't know where to go from there. Some were leaving for Palestine, as they longed for a country of their own, and Israel had become independent in 1948. Most were hoping to go to America, Canada or Australia. Others had gotten visas to go to Argentina and Brazil or other countries in Latin America like Venezuela, Dominican Republic and Uruguay.

"My father had great hopes as he watched Chiang Kai-shek and General Chennault of the Flying Tigers fame march into Shanghai after the Japanese had surrendered. But the peace in China didn't last and soon the civil war between Chiang and Mao resumed with a vengeance.

"When the truth of what the Nazis did to 6 million Jews came to light, the world was horrified. Countries like America, Canada and Australia began issuing immigrant visas to Jews. My parents were hoping to go to New York to join some relatives, but there was a long queue.

"I was born in early 1947, by which time over half of the residents in Hungkou had left. Both of my parent's families were waiting to see if they could get visas to America. Staying in Shanghai was out of the question. When the communists started taking over much of China, the extended family decided to all go to Hong Kong in 1949."

I smiled and interjected, "That was about the same time my family arrived in Hong Kong."

Max nodded and continued. "My father couldn't practice medicine in Hong Kong, but he found work as a dishwasher at the Peninsula Hotel, the hotel owned by the Kadoorie family. My father also tried to make ends meet by giving violin lessons while my mother gave piano lessons to children from local wealthy families. Later, he became the manager of Jimmy's Kitchen, a very famous restaurant that serves Western food founded by the Landau family, Jews that had been in Hong Kong for decades.

"My parents' hope to immigrate to America never materialized. There were just too many applicants. So we stayed in Hong Kong.

"Now, our lives are really quite good. We were so lucky that Ho Feng-shan made it possible for my father's family to go to Shanghai. We are also grateful for Sugihara Chiune for saving my mother's family. Then, later, Hong Kong saved our family," declared Max with a smile.

I chimed in, "I know, Hong Kong has saved a lot of people, including my family. If it wasn't for Hong Kong, I don't know where we would have ended up. My father would certainly have been killed by the Chinese communists right away, because he worked for the previous government that Mao defeated!"

I thought Max might be tired of talking, but I was curious about Sugihara so I asked, "Do you know what happened to Mr. Sugihara?"

"Grandpa Alon heard that Mr. Sugihara was arrested by the Soviets somewhere in Europe after the defeat of the Japanese and was imprisoned for a few years," answered Max. "He was later released and returned to Japan. I don't know what happened to him after that."

Max looked thoughtful for a moment and then commented, "You know, James, life is certainly a mystery. Why my family was saved from the Nazis while millions of others perished for no other reason than being Jewish, I don't know. Grandpa Baruch often reminds me to be grateful because our family could have easily suffered the same fate.

"I'm glad to know that not all Japanese were bad during the war. I've heard so many horror stories about the atrocities committed by the Japanese. Why so many of them behaved so badly during the war is a mystery, because they're usually known as such polite and considerate people. I guess, just like the many Germans who helped Hitler with his atrocities, most of them went to church every Sunday. What made ordinary people do such horrific things is puzzling."

I was impressed with how knowledgeable Max was about Jewish history. When the bell rang for us to return to class, I felt like I'd already had a full history lesson. His family's stories were both fascinating and educational.

After the last period, Max and I walked down the 100 steps at the front of La Salle to Boundary Street, and I mentioned how much I enjoyed hearing about his family history. He said if I was interested in Jewish history, especially the Jews in Hong Kong, he could show me around.

"Of course," I declared. "I'd like to learn more about the history of your people." We made plans to meet up again soon, and then Max got on the number 1A bus while I took the fifteen-minute walk back home.

***

Hong Kong was never intended to be my permanent home. It was unnerving to be living right next to the communists, knowing that they could take over the colony at any time. There was never any doubt in my mind that I would immigrate to somewhere, most likely America.

***

Our family was an example of how so many middle class families lived in those days, struggling under internal and external pressures. Internally, we put pressure on ourselves because we wanted to succeed, feared failure, and worked hard to maintain "face." Externally, there were the pressures of living in a crowded city with limited space, crowded buses, and people fighting for the limited resources. Dealing with the water rations and fears of a communist takeover in Hong Kong were constantly lurking in the backs of our minds.

It was at this time in my life that I began to think seriously about going into medicine. I reasoned that it would be a stable life and I probably would never have to worry about unemployment. There was only one medical school in Hong Kong, which took in about 100 students a year. As with the British system, students entered medical school directly from high school, after the 13th grade, and studied there for five years.

My dream was to be a physician because it was the surest way to have a secure life, and I could help people in the most direct way. But I had to be honest with myself about my chances. Medicine was the most competitive faculty to get into. Only the very top students from the very best schools had any real chance of getting in. At La Salle I consistently ranked around thirty to thirty-five. I was nowhere close to the top, and I knew my chances of getting into the medical school at Hong Kong University were slim.

I thought my second best option would be dentistry, although that wasn't easy either and would be expensive to study.

La Salle had a tradition of sending a number of its graduates to the Hong Kong Academy of Police Inspectors. For those who passed the HKSC Exam but didn't do well enough to go on to Form 6 (12th grade) for pre-university, becoming a police inspector was a good option. As many of the higher-ranking police inspectors were British, they liked La Salle graduates to join their ranks because most of them were able to speak at least fairly decent English. Graduates from other English schools might have done equally well on the HKSC Exam, but their spoken English might not be as acceptable. There would be job security and a certain amount of prestige; and I would have been a good candidate: an ex-Boy Scout, an athlete, fluent in English and many Chinese dialects as well as Malay, and five feet seven inches (the minimum height requirement). But being a police inspector was at the bottom of my list because I didn't want to stay in Hong Kong. Also, if the communists took over the colony, it would be equivalent to working for the Kuomintang.

***

Social Life

Now that I lived near the school, I had more time to get to know my classmates. Many of them had known each other since primary school. As a transfer student from Malaya, I was regarded somewhat differently; but rather than working against me, it actually enhanced my acceptability into different social groups.

In Form 4, it was again decided to put all the students taking French in the A section, rather than dividing them based on academics. The majority of people in the French classes were Portuguese or Macanese (Portuguese and Chinese mixture), hence there were many de Silvas and Souzas at La Salle. Most of their parents worked for the major banks, the HSBC and Standard Chartered, and were provided good housing and generally well taken care of. Generally the Portuguese and Macanese socialized amongst themselves outside of school.

There were also a few students with British and Chinese mixed heritage, and then there were the overseas Chinese from many parts of the world. La Salle was truly diverse.

Among the Macanese was Anthony Rosario, the most impeccable dresser at the whole school, with the most neatly combed hair and cleanest face. He always wore the sharpest and bluest cashmere blazer, without a wrinkle in his white, perfectly starched shirt, buttoned around the collar and finished with the straightest and smoothest school tie. His suave gray woolen pants had the crispest crease and were of the finest quality. Anthony stood at only slightly over five feet tall and looked more Chinese than Portuguese. To my amazement, I found out that he was nineteen years old, having repeated a couple of grades since the seventh, and he was now in the tenth. Usually no one was allowed to repeat grades at La Salle. I learned that his father was a senior manager at the HSBC, but in spite of that Anthony was asked to leave at the end of the year. By all indications, he wasn't stupid; he simply didn't believe in doing his homework or studying.

As a runner, I also came into contact with the athletes; most of them were also serious students. One of the coolest guys was Frankie Sing, a fellow runner on the relay team and the 400-meter champion, as well as the team captain. Frankie spoke impeccable English, having grown up in Fiji of a Chinese father and an Indian mother. He had acquired the good features from both parents, and he looked like a swarthy James Dean.

I had also rejoined the Boy Scouts, and found the members very diverse. Then there were the various clubs, some of which I joined. The Legion of Mary and the Novena Club were religious clubs, with praying as the main activities. I was always envious of the members of the model airplane club. On Saturdays they would fly their remote control airplanes on the school field, sometimes flying them out of range and losing them. It was a club that needed good family financial backing!

Then there was the orchestra, the fencing club, the debate club, the history club and the 60-member strong harmonica band—yes, a band of only harmonicas.

Phillip Chan was the lead singer of the rock and roll band, The Astronauts, whose signature song was *Runaway* by Del Shannon, which I thought was as good as the original. Some at La Salle mocked them for being a one-song band, but they had won top prizes in local contests.

In spite of all the diversity, the majority of students at La Salle were very middle class and very Chinese; few of our parents spoke much English. In the sixties, there were very few wealthy Chinese in Hong Kong. With both parents working as teachers, I was perhaps the median, or slightly below. There were a few poor students whose families lived in the government housing estates, although many of them were too embarrassed to let it be known.

CHAPTER 4:

More of Form 4

M R. LIOU, OUR FORM 4A HOMEROOM TEACHER, was leaving us because his visa for immigration to Canada had just been approved. He shared with us that he had learned to be a baker and planned to open a Chinese bakery when he got Alberta, specializing in moon-cakes.

His replacement was a new teacher who had just arrived from South Africa.

One Friday, Clement Tam and I came out of class after writing our trigonometry midterm at the same time. It was my weakest subject, but I was relieved that I'd been able to answer most of the questions. Clement seemed relieved too.

Clement Wing Hung Tam had been in Form 3A with me the year before as well, but since the first few months at La Salle were so hectic, I hadn't gotten to know him. He had the darkest complexion in class, a high forehead, and large ears—the Chinese believe that large ears bring good luck and longevity. He had a kind, round face.

As Juan came out of class and headed toward us, Clement told me that some of the boys had decided to celebrate finishing the exam and invited me along. Juan and Clement had known each other since Form 1 at La Salle, and they had become quite close. We compared notes on how we thought the midterm went, and then Juan and Clement started trying to decide where to go.

Clement suggested that we have lunch in Kowloon City, which was about a fifteen- minute walk from La Salle, to have *hai tu si* in a restaurant near where he lived. It happened to be my favorite food too. *Hai tu si* literally meant *shrimp toast*. It was a large shrimp placed on a piece of toast, then soaked in batter and deep-fried. It was crispy and very savory.

Michael, Tommy and Xavier joined us. It was a beautiful autumn day as we set out, and I was feeling very happy with how things were going. I decided to walk next to Clement as I didn't know him very well and was really curious about his background. It turned out that it was just as exotic as Juan's. I also found out why he spoke Cantonese with an accent, a Shun Tak accent that he had learned from his father in Madagascar.

He had such a dark complexion because he was part Chinese and part Malagasy. His great-grandfather left China to work in Madagascar as a coolie.

I told him I was very interested in different cultures, and it turned out he was a bit of a historian like Max. He seemed pleased to indulge my curiosity. "I don't know how much Chinese history you know," he began, "but around 1910, China was in chaos. It was the last days of the Qing Dynasty. Jobs were scarce and famines were frequent. Sun Yat-sun's revolution had been successful, and in 1911 the Republic of China was formed. But instead of the situation in China getting better, it only got worse, because now the different regions were ruled by warlords. More and more people were leaving China.

"Recruiters were traveling across southern China to get Chinese men to work as indentured laborers all over the world."

"Like Juan's grandfather," I commented. "I've just learned about it from him."

"Yes," said Clement. "So at age nineteen, my great-grandfather signed up with one of these recruiters to go to Madagascar. He had no idea where it even was."

I knew it was a very big island east of Africa, but I didn't know much else about it.

"France had colonized Madagascar," Clement continued. "This general by the name of Gallieni was looking for workers to build the roadway. He found the natives unmotivated and unable to follow orders, so he was hiring contract workers from China, intending for them to return home after their stint on the island. Sadly, many of them became ill while working on the construction of the railway; and many of those who survived and managed to board ships back to China died en route.

"The workers who stayed in Madagascar continued to die from dreadful tropical diseases like malaria and dengue fever, poisonous snakes and insects, and all sorts of parasites. However, among those who survived, many decided to stay, since China was still in turmoil and few of them had made much of a living there before they left. There really was nothing much for them to return to."

I listened with intense interest as Clement went on. "After my great-grandfather fulfilled his contract, he opened a small bakery in the east coast port of Tamatave. He married a Malagasy woman, and they had my grandfather. When my grandfather was fifteen, his father decided to send him to China for a Chinese education.

"After spending six years in China, my grandfather returned to Madagascar with a Chinese wife, and became a teacher at the local Chinese school in addition to running the bakery. He, along with others, helped found the Shun Tak Association, which consisted of a temple and a cemetery for the unfortunate workers who had died.

"My father, who was a quarter Malagasy, was home-schooled in Chinese by his father. When he turned twenty, he married a Malagasy woman—so I'm a quarter Chinese and three quarters Malagasy. But culturally," he mused, "I think I'm much more Chinese than Malagasy.

"My father sent me to a Catholic boarding school in the capital, Antananarivo. The bakery became very popular with the locals, especially the Chinese moon-cakes and all sorts of buns that were popular in southern China. On the weekends, my father would teach me Chinese.

"You know, my father learned enough Chinese from his own father that he was able to help illiterate Chinese workers write home and send money.

"My father expanded the bakery business and hired locals to collect sea cucumbers in the local waters. He processed them and exported them to Hong Kong to be sold at my uncle's store in Kowloon City. He also exported coffee, cloves and vanilla beans. Before long, my father became one of the richest men in town. My family became Catholic and we had a pew in the first row of the new church, because we'd donated the most for its construction.

"When I was eleven, my mother died. My father remarried, also a Malagasy woman. He decided to send me to Hong Kong for my education and to live with my uncle in Kowloon City. This uncle is my father's cousin who owns the dried seafood store. In the 1950s, my father saw that there wasn't much future for the Chinese on the island, as the economy got worse year after year. He was also worried about the increasing lawlessness after the bakery was robbed several times. He shifted some of his assets to Hong Kong with the idea that he would move the whole family here.

"Since I'd gone to a French school and was home-schooled in Chinese by my father, I knew very little English. I had to enroll in a primary school to learn it, which was embarrassing because I was older and I was so dark—I really stood out!" he laughed.
"My uncle also hired a tutor to help with my English. At age 14, I was accepted into Form 1 at La Salle."

We had arrived at the restaurant, and the subject changed to the trigonometry exam as we all joined up and headed inside.

The shrimp toasts were scrumptious and I had two orders, which went down perfectly with a bottle of ice cold Coca Cola.

By the time lunch was over, I had thought of several questions I wanted to ask Clement. With my encouragement, he continued telling me about his background on the walk back to school. He vividly recalled how, at age eleven and under the care of one of his father's friends who was also going to Hong Kong, he left home.

"The miserably long voyage took several months," he lamented. "From Madagascar, I took a ship east to Port Louis in Mauritius, where I was met by some relatives who I stayed with for a week. From there, I boarded another ship and traveled northeast to Colombo in Ceylon and then continued through the Strait of Malacca. After a week-long stop in Singapore, we finally reached Hong Kong. I was so seasick and even more homesick. I cried almost every day."

I found his story mesmerizing. As we walked, our friend Carlos caught sight of us and joined us. "Is James plying you for information about your family history, Clement?" he asked with a laugh.

"Of course he is!" called Juan over his shoulder as he walked ahead of us with the other boys. "He's a bit of a history buff."

"Definitely," agreed Carlos. "He got me talking last week!"

"I'm just curious about people," I defended, although I knew the teasing was good-natured.

"It's a good thing," chimed in Michael. "We learn a lot about each other thanks to James. And it's important to remember our history."

"Speaking of history," said Xavier, "has anyone done the reading yet for Chinese history class?" The subject changed, we strolled back to school chatting about our grades and plans for the future. As we entered the main gate, the school bell sounded and we were just in time.

Carlos Medina Leon Lee had wavy, dark brown hair and light brown eyes. Initially I thought he must be Portuguese or Macanese. I got to know him well early in Form 4.

I learned that his great-grandfather had gone to Cuba as a laborer around 1890. After fulfilling his five-year contract, he worked as a cook for a Spanish nobleman who governed the island. When the Spanish-American War broke out in 1898, he fought bravely for the Spanish, instead of on the side fighting for independence as many Chinese workers did. In one of the skirmishes, his great-grandfather saved the nobleman's life by shooting dead a rebel who was about to shoot him.

When the Spanish lost, he and a few other Chinese men who were loyal to Spain left Cuba and went to Spain, where they tried to settle in Bilbao, the port in Basque country.

Life was difficult for the Chinese men in Bilbao, as they were looked upon as oddities. But the nobleman was kind to them and took good care of them, even encouraging Spanish women to marry them.

Carlos's great-grandfather married a Spanish woman with light brown hair and hazel eyes. Not long after, he decided to leave Bilbao, feeling that there was no future for him there. He and his wife first went to Panama, where he changed his name and got new identity papers. The couple then went on to Cuba.

With the gold and silver coins given to him by the nobleman, he established a grocery store in Havana. The business prospered over the years, and Carlos's grandfather was able to attend Havana University and later also married a Spanish woman. Life was good and the family was doing very well financially.

Carlos was born in Havana in 1947 and attended a Catholic School. By then, his father's store was one of the largest in Havana. In the early 1950s, Cuba had a Chinese population of around 200,000, and Havana had four Chinese theaters and numerous Chinese restaurants.

When Fidel Castro began recruiting workers, including many Chinese ones, for his revolution, Carlos's father was concerned that it would turn communist just as China had in 1949. He decided to leave Cuba for Panama with his extended family just before Castro finally took over all of Cuba on December 31, 1958.

In 1959, Carlos was sent to Hong Kong so that he could get a Chinese and English education. He stayed with relatives and attended the St. Francis of Assisi School in Shum Shui Po. When he did well on the 6th grade public examination, he was accepted to Form 1 at La Salle.

Carlos had many fond memories of Havana. His childhood sounded a lot like mine, with a great deal of freedom. He talked about enjoying all the different fruits and foods cooked with coconut milk just like I did in Malaya.

One of his favorite things to do was to go to the Chinese opera with his mother, who was half Chinese and half Spanish. He saw some of the most famous Cantonese movie stars and opera singers, such as Sun Ma Chai and Pak Shuet Sin from Hong Kong when they toured Cuba. He vividly remembered a beautiful Spanish-looking Cuban girl with hazel eyes and dark brown hair who became the most famous Cantonese opera singer at the time. Caridad Amaran, who went by her Chinese stage name of Ho Chau Lan (*Autumn Orchid*), lost her Spanish father just after she was born and was adopted by a Chinese theater owner. She was taught the Chinese language and to sing the very difficult Cantonese opera, and became the biggest sensation in Havana in the early 1950s. Carlos had photos of her in his bedroom.

Cantonese opera diva Caridad Amaran (aka Ho Chau Lan),
in Cuba circa 1955

Shortly after Carlos's family left Cuba, the properties of the Chinese were confiscated by the new communist government. Over a period of only a few years, almost all of the 200,000 Chinese in the country left the island. Only a few hundred remained. The wealthy ones went to the US and Canada, while those with less money went to nearby countries such as Dominican Republic, Venezuela, Colombia, Costa Rica and Panama. Carlos's father chose Panama because he had some cousins there.

I was fascinated by his life and the history of the Chinese in Cuba, and I asked him a lot of questions. He said when it became more difficult to bring slaves from Africa to work on the sugar plantations, the Spanish sought Chinese coolies, who by then were working in different parts of the world as indentured workers—more or less as slaves.

The Chinese immigration to Cuba started in 1847 when 120,000 Cantonese men arrived under contract for 8 years. When slavery was abolished on October 7, 1886, more Chinese workers were recruited.

Carlos said most Chinese men married black women, because the Chinese workers were considered the bottom of society just as the blacks were. His great-grandfather and grandfather married Spanish women because by then they had achieved some success and financial security. Before slavery was abolished, many Chinese men bought slave women and then freed them expressly for marriage. Their children would then be allowed to own land and properties.

Carlos lamented that life was so much freer and less stressful in Cuba, and that at times he really missed it. On the other hand, he was glad that his family left because he heard that life in Cuba had become exceedingly difficult in every aspect, and there was rationing on everything. Carlos believed that life under communism was miserable, and it would be tragic to live a life like that.

It was certainly educational being at La Salle and learning from so many classmates whose life stories were truly captivating.

***

During lunch break I often ate with Michael. We liked to walk uphill to the sports field behind the main building and get some fresh air and view the planes getting ready to land at the old Kai Tak Airport. They flew so low that I sometimes thought I could see the faces of the passengers!

One Tuesday, Michael was nowhere in sight, so I decided to get some peace and quiet on the marble steps leading to the deck above the chapel, and review the physics notes I had taken. To my surprise there were already two fellows there.

One was Hans Liu Sung Chang, a tall boy with a square face and high cheekbones who always wore a pair of tortoiseshell glasses. He had dense, jet-black hair that stopped just above his eyebrows. He had recently broken his right ankle and had a cast that ran from his foot to just below his knee.

The other fellow was Austin Yung Lok Sing, a well-mannered, soft-spoken young man with a fair complexion. He was tall and loose-jointed.

Hans always had a smile and a good sense of humor. When he saw me, he waved for me join them. I sat down on a marble step as Hans said, "James, we're just talking about what we're going to do in the future. What do you think you'd like to be?"

"I'd really like to go into medicine," I answered, "but I know it's very competitive, so I think I may have to settle for dentistry."

"I see you have strong arms," Hans commented with a laugh. "I'm sure you'll have enough strength to pull teeth."

Austin and I laughed, but inwardly I hoped that if I became a dentist, I would be doing more than just pulling out people's teeth!

Austin said he'd like to go into medicine as well, and Hans chuckled. "I could never go into medicine," he said, making a face. "The sight of blood makes me sick."

We laughed again, and Hans said he thought he would go into chemical engineering like his father. "He was a beer brewer for a German company in Qingdao, Shandong in northeast China," he explained. "When he was young, he went to Germany to study chemical engineering. That's how I got a German name."

"Ahh," I exclaimed. "I wondered. You don't look very German!"

It turned out that Hans and his family left Qingdao in the early summer of 1949, about the same time as my family was leaving Canton for Hong Kong. I joked that we could have run into each other at the Hong Kong Kowloon Railway Station.

In the early part of 1949, Hans's father's German boss advised him to leave China because Mao seemed to be invincible and China would soon turn communist, after which all properties would be confiscated.

His parents and grandparents on both sides sold everything they owned and all came down to Hong Kong, just as our family did before the exodus later that year. Both of his grandparents were quite well off and brought enough gold and silver to live a comfortable life in Hong Kong, buying up some properties before the majority of the refugees came.

Austin's journey from China to Hong Kong was much more complicated. His father, like mine, had worked for the Kuomintang government. "I remember my father driving a car or jeep," Austin said, "and he always carried a gun." He recounted how his father decided to take the family out of China sometime in 1952, after the border had already closed.

Even though he was only five years old, he remembered the arduous journey. He, his parents and his younger sister were led by a guide as they walked long distances day and night, over hills and across rivers. Sometimes they had to hide in the bushes, and once they hid in a fishing boat. His sister, who was two at the time, was too young to understand the need to be quiet, and they were petrified that her cries would give them away. Fortunately, they arrived in Hong Kong safely in a fishing boat.

Tragically, Austin's father died a few years later from a massive stroke and his mother became despondent, falling into depression. With her jewelry and some gold and silver coins they had brought to Hong Kong, his mother frugally budgeted their family expenses each month, calculating that they would have enough to last until Austin finished Form 5, at which time he could find work.

His mother was in a deep depression for many years, often staying in bed for days. With the help of neighbors and church members, Austin's paternal grandmother managed to keep the family together.

As usual, I was curious and wanted to ask more questions, but as we finished our lunches and I drank the last of my soymilk, the school bell sounded and we headed back to the classroom.

I had always understood that many refugees like my family had compelling stories to tell, and it was interesting to hear how different Hans and Austin's were. Some were definitely less fortunate than others.

***

Darius Mody was a handsome, soft-spoken fellow with wavy black hair, light brown eyes, a smooth nose and a square jaw.

We hit it off very well after I told him that I lived in Malaya for five years and had lots of Indian friends. When I asked him which part of India his ancestors came from, I was surprised when he told me that he was a Parsee. I had to confess that I had no idea what a Parsee was.

"My family came from Bombay to Hong Kong over a hundred years ago," Darius explained. "My ancestors worked with the British in the East India Company. You see, I am not really a true Indian.

"The Parsees left Persia and arrived in India as refugees after the Arab Conquistadors invaded the country in 638 AD. They left in order to avoid religious persecution by the Muslims, because they were Zoroastrians and they refused to convert to Islam."

"What's a Zoroastrian?" I asked.

"Zoroastrianism is the world's oldest monotheistic religion, founded almost 4,000 years ago," Darius replied. "It centers on the words of the prophet Zarathushtra, called Zoroaster by the ancient Greeks. The main teaching is about good and evil.

"We believe that humans are intimately involved in this struggle, holding off chaos and destruction through active goodness.

"Many Zoroastrians pray several times a day, always facing a source of fire or light. That's why people think we worship fire, but we really don't. Fire is just a symbol. Zoroastrian temples keep a fire burning at all times to represent the Lord of Wisdom's eternal power. Fire is also recognized as a powerful purifier and is respected for that reason," he explained.

"So what language do you speak at home?" I asked.

"We all speak Cantonese," Darius answered, "but English is truly our mother tongue. It's been spoken in our house for generations. I'm taking French instead of Chinese as a second language, because not being a native speaker makes it impossible for me to keep up with the Chinese students."

I nodded, remembering how worried I was about catching up in the Chinese language class after being away for five years. "Are you related to the Mody that Mody Road was named after in Tsim Sha Tsui in Kowloon?" I asked.

"Yes," he replied with a smile. "In fact, all the Modys in Hong Kong are related in some way."

He explained further, "The Parsees have done well in Hong Kong because they spoke English when few Chinese in Hong Kong did, and it was the Parsees who assisted the British in the trade. There have been quite a few famous Parsees in Hong Kong. Kotewall Road was named after another Parsee, and I know that one of the principal founders and financial supporters of the University of Hong Kong was a Parsee."

I felt my knowledge of cultures and history expand with every new person I got to know at La Salle, and I was constantly amazed at what a diverse group of people we were.

***

Bashir Ajmal

Bashir was a slim fellow, swarthy, with wavy black hair and dark eyes. Like most South Asians who were born in Hong Kong, he couldn't write Chinese, but he spoke perfect Cantonese. At La Salle, he took French as a second language.

He wasn't entirely clear how his ancestors came to Hong Kong, but he believed that his grandfather was a sailor from Karachi in what is now Pakistan who came to Hong Kong on a ship and stayed to work as a watchman in a warehouse. He later went back to Karachi and found a wife, then returned with her to Hong Kong.

With the help of the money Bashir's grandfather saved, his father opened a store selling spices from India and Ceylon as well as Indonesia. The store did well. When Bashir was in the fifth grade at a school in the Tsim Sha Tsui area, La Salle Primary School greatly expanded, and his father took him there to apply, where he was accepted.

Bashir was an extremely friendly and personable fellow and full of confidence. His dream was to get really rich and perhaps own the largest spice store in Hong Kong one day.

***

Richard Singh

Richard was tall and strong. He was over six feet tall with broad shoulders. Instead of giving him a Sikh first name, his father—a police inspector—gave him an English one instead, after his boss at the police station.

His grandfather came to Hong Kong with the British as a policeman. Before the Second World War nearly 60% of police forces were Sikhs, because they were big and strong and more reliable than the local Chinese. They were also less prone to corruption because of the cultural and language barriers.

I had no idea that Richard was a Sikh until he told me. I thought they always wore turbans, but he didn't keep his hair long or wear a turban like his father or grandfather.

When he was in primary school, he belonged to a field hockey team, but when he joined La Salle in Form 1, he stopped playing because there hadn't been a hockey team at the school for years.

I had played hockey for two years when I was in Malaya and I brought my stick with me to Hong Kong. During recess one day, I asked Richard if he'd be interested in playing again, and he said yes. "I think Bashir and Mody would be interested too," he commented. "And I know a few other South Asians in the other classes who might play too."

We had a meeting and the La Salle hockey team was re-activated. Richard wanted me to be the captain, but I told him I was already busy with track and Boy Scouts as well as working as a tutor, so I declined. Richard became the captain.

He knew some players at King George V School (KGV), so he contacted them and they agreed to a friendly match.

On a beautiful autumn Saturday morning in November, we had a game in King's Park on the grounds of the KGV. We lost 3 to 1, but we had a great time.

***

Danny Tong

In Form 4A, I noticed another very dark-complexioned fellow. He had a high forehead and short curly hair, large dark brown eyes and a big, toothy smile.

He definitely spoke English with a Caribbean accent. His Cantonese was also accented. I was very surprised to learn that he could understand and speak some Hakka. He told me that it was because his grandfather was a Hakka from the Bao'an district, not very far from Hong Kong.

He wasn't sure when his great-grandfather went to Jamaica, but he initially went to Panama to work on the sugar cane plantations as an indentured laborer. The conditions were exceedingly harsh, and many workers were dying from malaria and other tropical diseases. Through a relative in Jamaica, he learned that black slavery had been outlawed in that country and they were recruiting workers from China, just as his five-year contract was up.

In Jamaica, he signed up a five-year contract with a sugar cane planation, making $4 a day on a 12-hour work day, terms that were much better than in Panama. Under the British in Jamaica, the workers' rights were better protected than in Panama, where they had no rights. He saved as much as he could.

After fulfilling his contract, he, like many other Chinese workers, opened a small shop and married a local woman. Their son, Danny's grandfather, was thus half Chinese and half Jamaican. He also married a local woman who was half Chinese. When it was time for Danny's father to get married, he also chose a woman who was half Chinese.

The family prospered. From the store, his grandfather and father began making loans to the locals, charging interest as much as ten percent each month. Most of the locals lived from hand to mouth, and because many Chinese were living better than them, anti-Chinese sentiments arose.

Then Jamaica's economy took a downturn when the price of sugar plunged because of over-supply around the world. Between the weakened economy and the increasingly violent anti-Chinese movement, Danny's father could see that life in Jamaica wasn't going to get any easier. He decided to sell everything, and the family moved to Hong Kong in 1959.

They settled in the Hung Hom area, where Danny's father opened a store selling fruits and fruit juices. Life was difficult in a new place that was very different from Jamaica; and because of their darker complexions, they often faced subtle, and sometimes not-so-subtle, discrimination.

Initially, Danny found life in Hong Kong unbearable because he knew very little Chinese and he was often made fun of by his classmates. But he worked very hard and rose to the top of his class. After primary school, he was accepted into La Salle.

***

Soon it was Christmas. I didn't know Tommy Sung well, so I was surprised when he invited me to his Kadoorie Hill house for a Christmas party.

Kadoorie Hill was named after a Baghdad Jew who came to Hong Kong and became one of the richest men in the colony. It was the most exclusive residential area on the Kowloon side, a short distance from Prince Edward Road. On the hill were mansions and large condominiums. Tommy's residence was four or five times the size of our apartment. I was fairly certain that our entire apartment would have fit in Tommy's living room. His mother had organized the party and had the ABC bakery deliver the tastiest cakes and finger sandwiches. We did the Twist, the Limbo and the Cha-cha. Chubby Chucker was screaming his head off from the record player. When the slow dance came, with Cliff Richard singing my favorite, "When a girl in your arms…," there weren't many dancers; even at sixteen, few of us dated.

The Sung family was one of the few families that could afford to go overseas on vacation. They had been to Taiwan and Japan. On Tommy's return from Japan, he showed us the pictures of Mount Fuji, the famous Tokyo TV tower, the Ginza area, and a Japanese fishing village.

In Hong Kong, one could see the power of money: the luxurious flats, the limousines—Bentleys and Mercedes—Rolex watches, fancy jewelry, maids in uniform, clothes of the best quality. To me, these things gave wealthy people an air of invincibility, like they had no problems, or at least any problems they had could be solved with money. In Hong Kong, displaying what you had commanded "face," or a show of respect. This was partly due to the population being built on waves of successive immigration escaping from famines, wars and communism. These people had nothing when they arrived, and through hard work and shrewdness in business, they achieved financial success; after all the hardships, it was acceptable to show it off. They also probably realized that life is ephemeral, so when you had it, you should flaunt it.

After school one Friday, Tommy invited me to his house. His mother picked us up in her black Mercedes. Mrs. Sung had always been kind to me, and she told me that she liked me as a friend for Tommy, since Tommy had few friends.

She already had afternoon tea set up in their spacious living room when we arrived. She had picked up a five-layer cake from the famous Russian bakery, Cherikov Bakery. One of their servants brought out piping hot Lipton tea made fresh with real tea leaves.

Tommy was in a good mood. As I took a bite of the delicious cake, he asked, "James, you know the artist in our class, the fellow who drew all the posters?"

"You mean Ethan Pei," I responded.

"Yes. I was surprised when Phillip told me the other day that Ethan lives in the So Uk Government Housing. How could such a good-looking guy, so talented with his drawing and painting, who always wears nice clothes, be living in such a place?"

Tommy seemed puzzled that someone from La Salle had to live in housing meant for the blue-collar class, people with lower incomes. It was obvious that Tommy had never experienced poverty and just couldn't comprehend how people would not have money, or enough money to live in a decent place if they could study at La Salle like him.

"Tommy," I remarked, "you know your family is one of the wealthiest in school. Both of my parents work very hard just for us to afford a small apartment on Prince Edward Road, so my sister and I can be close to school. I don't know what Ethan's father does for a living, but perhaps that's the only accommodation they can afford."

When we finished our tea and cake, we went into Tommy's private, spacious bedroom to review trigonometry. Outside the window of his room were several *pak lan* trees loaded with flowers, and their fragrance was intoxicating.

Tommy's life was quite different from most of us in the class. He had a tutor for every subject: English, math, physics and Chinese. In contrast, some of us were trying to make a little money by tutoring others.

***

The school year flew by and before long it was June—final examination time. I had studied hard, and I thought I did all right.

When the finals marks for all the classes in Form 4 were posted, a number of students with poor marks were asked to leave. They weren't given a chance to repeat the grade. The school simply didn't want them to ruin its fantastic passing rate each year! Maintaining a pass rate over 95% distinguished La Salle and kept it among the most elite high schools in Hong Kong. These hapless students had to find themselves new schools. Those from wealthy families, such as Harry, whose parents owned a big hotel, simply found a foreign boarding school—Harry went to Sydney, Australia—and avoided the shame of having been kicked out of La Salle. Most of the students were good kids who really worked hard and abided by the rules;

they just fell short of the high standards required by La Salle. The practice wasn't limited to La Salle—it was done in other top schools as well. It was a merciless system.

One student in the C class whose name I never learned, a quiet, nervous boy with a bony face and dark-rimmed glasses, broke down in the hallway when he learned that he was one of those who had to leave. He was an older boy, perhaps nineteen, and I learned that he had already repeated the seventh grade. It was unusual for someone in the C class to be asked to leave, because there were many students below him in the D, E and F classes; but he had failed English language badly and in the school's opinion ran a high risk of failing the HKSC Exam. He had ranked in the C class because he had good marks in other subjects.

He just couldn't stop crying. He didn't dress like someone from a family that could afford to send him to Australia or England, so I assumed he had to find another school in Hong Kong. He was probably devastated to face his family. I felt very badly for him, imagining myself in his shoes. I wouldn't have known what to tell my parents.

At least two Portuguese boys were also not promoted. Rodrigo Gomez Alvarez was a skinny fellow with unruly, very wavy light brown hair. He wore a pair of gold wire-rimmed glasses and spoke in a high-pitched voice. The other Portuguese students gave him the nickname Professor Gomez, because with his glasses and unruly hair he looked like Albert Einstein. I learned that he had gotten a zero in math and did poorly in other subjects as well. I never knew Gomez, but I felt bad for him. However, like most Portuguese, he had more options than the poor Chinese fellow because most Portuguese in Hong Kong were wealthier and had more connections.

The other Portuguese student, Jerry Sousa Arruda, who was also not promoted, was a big fellow, weighing over two hundred pounds, with large buttocks like those of a woman. He had a big round face and thick, wavy dark brown hair below his ears. The other Portuguese students often teased him for being feminine, saying that he looked like a woman. *(Knowing about genetics now, he probably had some sort of chromosomal disorder that gave him a feminine appearance.)* He often chased after them for making fun of him. He had also done poorly and was felt to be a liability for the school. But like Gomez, he too probably had more options than me. I couldn't imagine what I would have done if I hadn't been promoted to Form 5—it would've been my worst nightmare.

The entire Form 4 (tenth grade) class of over two hundred students, sections A to F, with over 40 students in each class, would be reduced to only 5 sections, A to E, with less than 35 students in each. Doing the math, it makes sense that at least 50 students would be asked to leave the school!

It turned out that I didn't rank as high as I had the year before, although the rankings were amazingly consistent. In those days, all the students in the same grade took identical subjects, and the points from each class were added up at the end of the year to determine each student's rank.

***

Overall, I was pleased with my school year. I had done well in Form 4, and I had made a lot of new and interesting friends. I was looking forward to Form 5, and it was a fantastic summer for tutoring, especially in the extraordinary month of July. I took in almost $800 HK, the same amount my mother was making at her full time job. Working 10 hours a day, from eight in the morning until nine in the evening, and getting paid four Hong Kong dollars (about 50 US cents) an hour, I was making $40 a day. It was an incredible sum for a high school student, considering that a bus driver earned $300 HK a month at the time.

CHAPTER 5

Form 5 and the HKSC Exam

WHEN THE SCHOOL YEAR ENDED, our marks were posted as usual; but there were no rankings posted that year. We all knew that the teachers and principal knew the rankings. I assumed I would be in Form 5A, but to my surprise I was placed in Form 5B. Later I found out that during the summer after Form 3, the school held an examination to recruit top students from second- and third-tiered schools. They took in ten new students; all of them were top of their class and scored very high in math and the sciences.

Michael explained to me that the school didn't always follow the rule of ranking a student according to his total marks. As a rule they did, but they could place a student in any class they chose, no matter how they actually ranked. I had seen it with the French language students being kept together in the same class; although in Form 5, they were scattered in different sections. It seemed that this year the sections of the classes were ranked according to our marks.

***

Time was upon us to take the HKSC Exam, or the Hong Kong School Certificate Examination, which was the equivalent of the O-level in the British system. This critical exam determined one's academic future. If the student performed successfully at the O-level, then he would be promoted to the A-level, which would require two years of pre-university studies, Forms 6 and 7 (upper 6), i.e., grades 12 and 13. This exam was exceedingly competitive and only about five percent of high school graduates would go on to university.

The five classes (A to E) of Form 5 with 35 students each would be reduced to only two classes of Form 6 with 32 students each. Form 6A (Arts) was for the students going into non–science areas, and 6B was for those going into science, medicine included.

It was a cruel pyramid system. Your loss would be someone else's gain. We were competing with each other.

Fall 1963

I needed to study as much as I could for the exam, but I was still in need of money, so I couldn't give up my tutoring job with Chun Man. It might make the difference in whether I could afford to go to the University of Hawaii or not. I planned to make up for the time lost with Chun Man by studying extra hard over the weekends.

I'd done reasonably well at La Salle the last two years, so I knew that unless something unforeseen happened, I would pass the exam. It was just a matter of how well I would do. History had shown that performance at La Salle was a good indicator of how well we would do. It also proved that miracles never happened—mediocre students wouldn't pass with flying colors, and it was very unlikely for an above average student to fail.

My Private Study

Chun Man's parents and I decided that I didn't need to tutor him on Saturdays and I would only spend two hours on Sunday evenings helping him get ready school. That gave me more time to study; but it tended to get crowded at home. The living room was small and the bedroom was smaller, and it faced the living room of another apartment; sometimes I could even see what they were watching on TV! On many weekends, the neighbors played mahjong, and with their banging of the mahjong sticks and cries of joy or disappointment, it was simply too loud to allow me to concentrate on my studies. It was worse in the summer, because without air-conditioning we had to keep our windows open. To add to the confusion, Big Sister was giving private ballet and piano lessons to young girls in our apartment.

I needed a quieter place to study, but the library at La Salle was closed over the weekends.

The chapel at La Salle was on the fourth floor, with a stairway that led to an open area above the chapel: a covered deck with a wall on one side and the rest exposed. The stairs leading to the deck were never used, because an iron gate blocked entry to the deck area, and beyond was only for maintenance workers. I had started studying there during recess, and as far as I could tell no one else had discovered it. The steps were wide and long, and comfortable for sitting. It became my private study area on the weekends as well.

One Sunday morning after the nine o'clock mass, I had taken the 15-minute walk to La Salle and I was just settling into reading Charles Dickens' *Great Expectations*, a required reading for the HKSC Exam, when I was startled by a loud voice.

It was a young man I'd seen sweeping the floors before. He was yelling at me.

"What the hell do you think you're doing here?" he screamed.

"This is a private area. You can't be here."

I was taken by surprise and didn't know what to say, so I packed up my books and left. On the walk home I felt a little distraught. My plans had been ruined. Where could I study now? But by the time I got home I had calmed down, reminding myself that most problems have solutions.

The following day, I looked around for the young man and found him near the maintenance staff quarter's lavatory on the ground floor of the school.

I caught his eye and approached him, saying, "Mister, I'm sorry I caused a problem by sitting on those steps. Here's something for your trouble." I handed him an envelope with two 20 Hong Kong dollar bills (less than six US dollars total) in it. He looked perplexed initially but took and opened the envelope, raised his eyebrows and looked pleasantly surprised, then smiled. He knew what it was for.

"Oh, you really don't have to do that," he said. He actually sounded apologetic; but he pocketed the money. "You weren't really causing anybody a problem," he added.

From his facial expression and change of tone, I assumed that he meant it would be alright for me to study there.

The following Saturday, I was studying in the same area again when the man, whose name was Ah Lee, came up the steps; he had come with a key for me!

"The key is for the iron gate here," Ah Lee said. "Up on the deck, you'll find a desk and some chairs. It would be a lot more comfortable than the hard marble."

He opened the gate and handed me the key, smiling as if he was proud to have done me a favor.

"This is wonderful!" I exclaimed with joy. "No one will ever find me. It's so quiet." I dug into my pocket and gave him another 20 Hong Kong dollars.

There is a Cantonese saying, "Money can make the devil push the mill for you," meaning that as bad as the devil is, if given enough money, he would do the heavy lifting for you.

The following Sunday, Lee showed up with another key.

"This is the key to the bathroom in the workers' quarters. You must pee sometime during the day!" he grinned.

He was right. No bathrooms were open on the weekends and I tried to drink as little as possible to avoid having to urinate during the day. When I needed to, I had to walk all the way down to the Paris Café on Boundary Street. When I really couldn't wait, I had a bottle with me. For Lee's trouble, I handed him another $20.

After that, Ah Lee would show up every two weeks or so with different stories about his grandfather, aunt or cousins being ill and ask for help. Each time I would hand over twenty or thirty dollars, which I considered rent money. It intrigued me that he never used his parents as an excuse to get money from me, but I never asked if he had any parents.

Was offering a bribe to Ah Lee immoral? All I wanted was a quiet place to study and I wasn't hurting anybody. It was impossible to study at home on the weekends, sharing a tiny room with three other siblings of various temperaments, and there was nowhere else I could go. I felt guilty for a mere second.

In early fall, Hong Kong was cool and dry and it actually felt good to be out in the open. But the Hong Kong winter could get cold, with temperatures sometimes just above freezing. When the weather turned colder, I brought many layers of clothing and a blanket along.

Almost every Saturday and Sunday for the school year, I sat in the open air on the deck from morning until I could no longer read in the evening. I usually brought a large bottle of water and a loaf of bread, some fruit, and sometimes chocolate bars. It was the most exclusive and quiet private study I have ever had.

One especially cold day in late November after another cold front from Siberia, I was feeling preoccupied as I walked to the school. There were so many thoughts on my mind. I went back and forth in my head wondering if I'd made the right decision to tackle eleven subjects in the HKSC Exam, or if I should have concentrated on six or seven like most students. Most of my classmates had already decided to either be in the humanities or the sciences.

I was worried that if I spread myself too thin, I would only manage to get mediocre grades in all the subjects. My problem was that I was still hoping somehow to get into medicine, but I realized it was hopeless to do it in Hong Kong. If I didn't do well in the science subjects, I still wanted to go to university; but I would have to settle for being in the humanities—a thought that depressed me.

I walked up the stairs toward the deck, unlocked the iron gate and began to settle into my chair. The study plan for the day was to review English literature. We were assigned five books: Charles Dickens' *Great Expectations*, Thomas Hardy's *The Mayor of Casterbridge*, Homer's *The Iliad*, Fyodor Dostoevsky's *The Brothers Karamazov*, Shakespeare's *King Lear* and a number of his sonnets.

Even though *The Brothers Karamazov* was over seven hundred pages and the characters' names were often confusing, I enjoyed the book because I was curious about human nature, and I also wanted to understand my own weaknesses.

It was a sad morning. My mind was overloaded with worries that I couldn't pinpoint. I just couldn't concentrate, and I began to question myself again on the decision to sign up for English literature, which involved so much reading. It wasn't a subject I needed, and I thought I should probably concentrate more time on my weaker subjects, math and physics. This is also when I felt the frustrating nature of my personality: indecision. I got up, walked around the deck and looked down on Boundary Street, and then on the school field where there was a soccer practice in progress.

I sighed. It was getting close to five, which was when the sun went down in the winter. Since there were no lights on the deck, I would have to leave. Packing my books, the water bottle and blanket, unlocking the iron gate quietly and locking it again, I began to walk down the stairs. As I reached the chapel level at the bottom, a large group of Brothers and students were saying the Lord's Prayers in unison. They all looked very serious and sad. I entered the chapel, kneeling and saying a few prayers, then sat down on a bench at the back next to another student from a different grade. He told me that the mass was for President Kennedy who had been shot the day before, and they were praying for his soul. JFK was shot on November 22, 1963, a Friday in the US. Because Hong Kong is almost a day ahead, it was already November 23, Saturday.

I was stunned. President Kennedy had been one of my heroes. I had tried to read his book, *Profiles in Courage*, but I found it irrelevant to my life as it was about US senators. But I thought what he told the young American people, "Ask not what your country can do for you, but what you can do for your country," was meaningful even though I was a stateless person and really had no country of my own. Hong Kong was a colony, and neither China nor Britain was my country.

JFK was a Catholic, and Catholics all over the world were so proud that one of ours had become the President of America. I cried and felt numb. I'd heard that God worked in mysterious ways and I thought this must have been one of those mysteries. I kept asking myself why God allowed that to happen.

I was so troubled that I couldn't even concentrate on praying. I wondered about the purpose of life. What was the point of working so hard when one's life could be snuffed out like that? It saddened me for days. My mind felt numb, and I was unable to concentrate on my studies.

***

There was something about Vincent Ma that intrigued me, because even though he had a Chinese surname, he didn't look entirely Chinese and he spoke English with an Indian accent. He had thick black eyebrows, large dark brown eyes and a prominent nose.

It turned out that he was Hui Chinese, i.e., Chinese Muslim. Hui are Han Chinese whose ancestors converted to Islam hundreds of years ago, especially in northwestern China. Some of them were descendants of Arab men and Chinese women.

One day I was in the school cafeteria trying to get a curry bun and a bottle of soymilk, and I was in line next to him. We sat down and talked as we ate our lunches. I learned that his grandfather worked for a Hui Muslim warlord named Ma Hungkui in Qinghai province in northwestern China.

I learned from Vincent that most of the Hui people have the same surname of Ma, which means *horse*. The Hui people commonly adopted it as a translation of the first syllable of Muhammad.

"I was told that my Arab ancestor came along the Silk Road seven hundred years ago, and that one of my forebears had been general to the first Ming emperor," said Vincent proudly. "I'm certain that I have both Arab and Persian blood, which explains my looks. Many of our people are in the Xian area. Through intermarriage, the Hui people have become indistinguishable from the Han except for someone like me with my large nose and round eyes.

"We speak a regional version of the Chinese language and we follow most of the Han customs. It's true that the Chinese we speak contains a few Arabic words, but we're essentially Han Chinese," he explained.

In the spring of 1949, Mao was taking town after town. The escape route for Vincent's grandfather and his family was cut off. With the aid of the CIA, they traveled on horses and donkeys with a group of soldiers and their families through Tibet to India. From there they were helped by a group of Indian Muslim men with connections to the CIA to travel to Calcutta, where there was already an established Chinese community of over 20,000, almost all of whom were anti-communist.

I was surprised that there were so many Chinese in another very poor country, and I was curious to find out who these people were.

"The Chinese community consisted mainly of Hakka and Cantonese," Vincent responded when I questioned him. "The Hakka were mostly in the tanning, leather, lard and shoe businesses, while the Cantonese were mainly carpenters, barbers and dentists.

"Running tanneries and working with leather was traditionally not considered a respectable profession among upper-caste Hindus, and work was relegated to lower classes. But there was a high demand for quality leather goods in colonial India, and the Chinese with their know-how were able to make it into a lucrative business."

"But why were the Chinese there?" I asked.

"Immigration from China to India began in the 18th century and continued through the turn of the 20th century, and during World War I," said Vincent, "partly due to political upheavals in China—the two Opium Wars, the First Sino-Japanese War and the Boxer Rebellion. Millions of people died, especially during the Boxer Rebellion.

"We arrived in Calcutta when I was three," he continued, "so I don't remember any of the journey. But my parents often talk about it, so I've developed a vivid picture of it in my head. I was told that we're lucky it was early summer, because we never would've made it through Tibet in the winter.

"We lived in Calcutta until 1960, where I attended Catholic school and was given a Christian name instead of a Muslim one, in addition to my Chinese name."

I nodded. So that explained why he had an Indian accent.

"But we weren't devout Muslims and we still worshipped our ancestors, which was forbidden in the Muslim doctrine." He chuckled and added, "You know, I think the only Muslim thing about me is that I try not to eat pork. But even if I inadvertently ate some, I wouldn't lose any sleep over it."

I snickered.

"With the help of the CIA," Vincent continued, "our family managed to get to Hong Kong. They thought my grandfather would be more useful to America in rallying anti-communists and former Kuomintang people instead of being stuck in Calcutta with nothing to do. My grandfather and father were used to a good life with many servants, and being in Calcutta was not their idea of the good life. My grandfather especially disliked the smell from the tanneries that surrounded their house."

His grandfather's younger brother had fled to Hong Kong earlier in the year with enough money to buy a house in the Kowloon Tong area, not far from La Salle. So Vincent's family was taken care of when they arrived, which was a lot more fortunate than many other refugee families.

The family was still worried about what China might do to Hong Kong, and they were trying desperately to immigrate to America where his grandfather had some influential friends.

***

Louis Chu

The following Monday at lunch break, I decided to eat alone on the marble staircase behind the chapel to review my chemistry notes while my memory was still fresh. But when I arrived, Louis Chu was already sitting there eating his sandwich.

This was the first year Louis and I were in the same class. I hadn't talked to him much and only knew that he was the son of the French teacher at La Salle, Monsieur Pierre Chu, and that his family was originally from Shandong province in northeast China. I had heard that his father was half French and was born in France.

With his large round eyes and straight, delicate nose and slightly wavy black hair, Louis was an impressive-looking fellow, and one of the tallest in class at almost six feet tall.

When our family was in Malaya, my father had a friend, a fellow teacher from Shandong province, the same province that Louis's family had come from. Mr. Liu was over six feet tall and had very fair complexion. Father often said that the people from Shandong were the tallest and the strongest in China because many of them were part Manchurian. Louis, whose complexion was fairer than most in class, reminded me somewhat of Mr. Liu.

When he saw me, Louis waved for me to sit down. He was a friendly fellow with an easy, sincere smile, and he always seemed full of confidence.

"Please sit down, James," he said. "I've always wanted to talk to you. I heard that you come from Malaya."

As he spoke, I took my sandwich from my bag, sat down next to him and opened my bottle of soymilk.

"Yes," I responded. "Our family lived in Malaya for five years. I was from Hong Kong originally. Actually," I corrected, "I was born in China, but we came here in 1949 like most people, when I was three."

"I assumed you were part Malay because of your round eyes and slightly wavy hair," he commented.

"Yes, I've been mistaken for a Filipino, a Malay, and even one time, someone thought I was an Indian from Assam!" I exclaimed with a smile. "My older brother thinks we had some Arab blood in us from many generations ago, but I really don't know," I added. "How about you, Louis? I heard your father was from France."

Louis nodded. "My father certainly had a very unusual background."

"I'm always interested in our classmates' backgrounds," I commented, "because I think each of us has to story to tell. I'm curious to know how your ancestors ended up in France."

"It's a long story," Louis said, "but I'm happy to tell you. I don't know if you've ever heard of the Chinese Labor Corp during World War I?"

I shook my head and said that I hadn't.

"I think this is a part of the history of World War I many Europeans like to forget, because they treated so many Chinese men like work animals. At the beginning of the war, soldiers on both sides were dying because of the improved killing machines they'd developed.

"It's called a world war because so many countries were involved. It began in 1914 after the assassination of Archduke Franz Ferdinand and lasted until 1918. During the conflict, Germany, Austria-Hungary, Bulgaria and the Ottoman Empire—known as the Central Powers—fought against Great Britain, France, Russia, Italy, Romania, Japan and the United States—known as the Allied Powers.

"With their machine guns, cannons and all sorts of bombs, tens of thousands of soldiers were killed in just a few days. It was the era of trench warfare. Waves of young men were mowed down with machine guns in minutes. It didn't take long for there to be a shortage of soldiers.

"A French general came up with the idea that since China had such a huge population and many of the men were unemployed, perhaps they could be hired as laborers to help the war efforts. They could support the troops by building and repairing railways and roads, moving supplies, mail, troops and the injured, laying down and maintaining telephone lines, plus constructing all sorts of military facilities.

"As you may recall from history class, China had a revolution in 1911 and became a republic, and conditions were chaotic for years. Jobs were scarce and many men were happy to sign up for a military job. These people were called the Chinese Labor Corp.

"My grandfather grew up near Qingdao in Shandong province. It just happened that the French had a recruiting post there. My grandfather was nineteen years old and he signed up. He had a few years of education at a Catholic school run by French nuns, and he had learnt some French. He was exactly the kind of man the French were looking for to work as a foreman in charge of mostly uneducated, some totally illiterate, Chinese peasant workers.

"He signed up for a five-year contract. He would be paid twenty-five Chinese yuan a month and his family would be paid twenty yuan while he was away. He was told that he was making ten yuan more than the regular laborers, and his family was getting five yuan more. He thought it was a very good deal since he was unemployed at the time, and his family farm couldn't support them."

When Louis paused to take a few bites of his sandwich and a sip of water from his bottle, I remarked, "That's really incredible. I've never heard that Chinese men were used like that."

Louis nodded and continued. "I never met my grandpa. I wish I had. I'd have so many questions to ask him. But my father told me a lot about his father's adventures, hardships and close calls. He says it took Grandpa well over two months to get from China to Europe.

"In October 1916, he sailed from Shanghai to Vancouver. When the ship docked in Vancouver, the men weren't allowed to get off the ship until it was time to catch the train to Halifax. He and 1,000 other Chinese men were cooped up for days in horrible conditions, cramped together in tiny, filthy spaces.

"When they got on the train bound for Halifax, they were packed into cattle cars—apparently it was hell. It took them nine days of bone-jarring travel to get there. There was hardly enough space for the men to sleep, and they couldn't bathe during the entire trip."

I shuddered and shook my head, trying to imagine how awful it must have been.

"Then from Halifax they sailed to Liverpool, I think, and from there, they were taken to northern France.

"My father told me that Grandpa was lucky, because he missed the ship he was supposed to be on when he was delayed getting to the port in Tianjin. That steam ship sailed south through the Strait of Malacca, then on to the Indian Ocean and through the Suez Canal. When the ship was near Malta on its way to Marseille, a German submarine sank it. Half of the 1,000 Chinese laborers on board were lost. My grandfather could have been one of them—it was fate that he missed that ship," commented Louis.

"After that disaster, the French decided to use a safer route by going through Canada."

"I didn't know the Germans had submarines in World War I," I remarked.

"Yes, they did," said Louis, "but of course they weren't as sophisticated as those they had in World War II."

He continued after a couple more bites of his sandwich. "My grandpa was sent to help in the Battle of the Somme by River Somme in northern France. The battle went on from July 1 to November of 1916. He was sent there almost as soon as he arrived in France.

"The French and the British were on one side and the Germans were on the other side, each side trying to advance. One side would advance a few yards and then the next day, the other side would claim it back. It was this fierce back and forth fighting, with each side losing hundreds of soldiers in the matter of a few minutes.

"Grandpa's job was to help direct the other Chinese laborers to dig trenches and set up barbed wire barriers for the French soldiers, and also to remove the wounded and the dead. It was a very dangerous job. He was told when he signed the contract that he wouldn't be involved in any fighting, so he was surprised that he was pretty much on the front line.

"In the end, the battle was a stalemate. The total casualties on both sides topped one million, including the deaths of more than 300,000. My grandpa didn't suffer any serious injuries, but once a bullet grazed the right side of his neck and left a superficial scar. He was lucky. He could have been killed if the bullet had hit him a little deeper.

"Several hundred Chinese were killed, even though they weren't supposed to be on the front line.

"In the end, Germany surrendered in November 1918 because the domestic situation in Germany was also deteriorating, due largely to food shortages caused by the Allied blockade.

"Grandpa told my father a funny story about some of the Chinese who had signed up to work with the British on the same side as the French. They almost rioted because one of the sergeants called out "Let's go," and they thought he was calling them dogs."

We both laughed. "Gou" in Chinese means *dog*.

At the end of World War I," Louis continued, "Grandpa oversaw the Chinese laborers as they cleared the mines and filled the trenches they'd dug. When his contract was up, he was allowed to remain in France. He and another friend from Shandong pooled their savings and opened a Chinese restaurant in Strasbourg. He married a local French woman and they had my father."

"My grandpa told my father that he was glad he signed up with the French rather than the British because the French treated the Chinese laborers better, and when their contracts were up, Britain didn't allow their laborers to stay in the country. But the French actually allowed any of the laborers to stay if they chose to—in the end, about 3,000 remained in France.

"It was estimated that about 60,000 signed up with the French and about 90,000 with the British at the beginning of the war. In all, the authorities believed that about 10,000 Chinese workers died in the war effort, victims of shelling, landmines, poor treatment, or the worldwide flu epidemic. Some Chinese scholars contested these figures, saying the number of deaths was as high as 20,000.

"My father was fortunate that he grew up during a time of peace and was able to graduate from the University of Strasbourg. He initially studied law but later switched to economics."

It was interesting to hear that Monsieur Chu had studied something other than French. "How did he go from studying economics in Strasbourg to being the French teacher at La Salle?" I asked.

Louis chewed the last bite of his sandwich thoughtfully. "When World War II began, times were hard for everyone, but his family had it easier than most because the occupying Germans liked Chinese food, so they let my grandfather keep his restaurant open. But then when the war ended, Europe was in ruins and there weren't many jobs. In 1946, my father was hired to work at the French Consulate in Hong Kong. Shortly after arriving here, he met and married my mother, whose family was also from Shandong, and I was born in 1947.

"My father later quit his job when he learned that La Salle was looking for a French language teacher. He hated the job at the consulate because the other employees didn't regard him as a true French citizen."

At that point, the school bell sounded, and we gathered up our things to head back to class. As I stood up I exclaimed, "Wow, that's quite a story, Louis."

"I hope I didn't go on too long," he said sheepishly as we started walking.

"No," I protested, "I learned so much. I'd actually be interested in hearing more sometime."

When the afternoon session ended, I walked back out of class with Louis and down the steps of the school, asking him more questions about the Chinese Labor Corp.

"James, someday if you have a chance to go to Paris," he said, "you should visit the large public cemetery there. You'll find the graves of many Labor Corp workers there.

"A lot of the Chinese who chose to stay in France worked in factories. They started Chinatown in Paris, and if you meet a French citizen of Chinese origins today, there's a good chance they're descendants of a Labor Corp worker."

"Thanks Louis," I commented. "I feel like I know so much about these people already. I can't imagine the kind of hardships they endured."

"I think the Chinese people are very adaptable. It seems like they're all over the world," remarked Louis.

I agreed with him. When we reached his bus stop, we bid each other goodbye and Louis got on a bus, while I continued to walk home with a head full of thoughts.

***

The following Saturday was La Salle Sports Day. It was a beautiful, cool, sunny day in January. I was resting by the sports field railing, surrounded by crowds of people watching the races. I was getting ready for my last event—the long jump.

Ed King walked by with an agitated look on his face, and a Coca Cola bottle in his right hand. As he passed, he said to me, "I'm going to teach those hooligans a lesson. They should respect me when they're at my school."

I had no idea what he was referring to. I watched him break into a run after three fellows I'd never seen before, probably from another school. They weren't wearing track clothes, so I assumed they were just spectators. As Ed got closer, he splashed his drink toward them. A few drops of Coke hit the light brown jacket of the fellow in front. Then Ed ran away.

Later I learned that Ed thought they had been staring at him and challenging his authority.

Even though by then I'd run many races with Ed on the relay team, I never really got to know him. We were in the same year, but never in the same class. He was usually in the D or E class. He impressed me as a brash guy, a show-off.

I knew a bit about his background from Tony. He was the only child of a family from the Nanjing area. His father used to work for the notorious warlord, Wang Jingwei, who was a Japanese collaborator and traitor to the Chinese people.

Wang was a rival of Chiang Kai-shek of the Kuomintang, and he defected to the Japanese side in 1940 and formed a collaborationist government in occupied Nanjing, the traditional capital of China.

The new state claimed the entirety of China during its existence, portraying itself as the legitimate inheritors of Sun Yat-sen's legacy, opposed to Chiang Kai-shek's government, which was then in Chongqing after retreating further west from the Japanese. But in actuality, Wang's regime only had the Japanese-occupied territory under its control.

At the end of World War II and following the surrender of Japan in August 1945, Wang's regime was dissolved and many of its leading members were executed for treason.

Ed King's father was in Wang's inner circle and received an early warning to flee, so he took his family to Hong Kong with bags of gold bars and silver coins before the rest of the collaborators were arrested.

Once in Hong Kong, his father changed his name from Liu to King. It was rumored that he even had plastic surgery to avoid recognition by friends and relatives who had also fled to Hong Kong. They bought properties and became quite wealthy.

Moments after I'd watched Ed's strange behavior, Frankie Sing walked by and asked me what the matter was with Ed. I told him that I really didn't know but explained what I'd seen him do with the bottle of Coke.

Frankie shook his head and said, "That's Ed. He's always looking for trouble. He thinks he's so tough."

In spite of his outwardly flashy appearance, I found Frankie to be a very stable and considerate fellow. He stood out in school with the bluest cashmere blazer, the whitest pressed shirt, and the nicest pair of gray woolen pants; and of course, his James Dean hairdo. It was apparent that he knew he was cool, and he was very popular with the girls at Maryknoll Convent School two blocks away.

Tony had told me that Frankie also played the guitar, sang and was a good dancer.

As captain of the relay team, Frankie made sure that we practiced passing the baton several times before each race. Thanks to him, we had never dropped the baton.

Like so many Chinese men in southern China around 1900, Frankie's great-grandfather went to Fiji to work on a sugar cane plantation. And, like many other Chinese men who stayed to farm or open a business after fulfilling their contract, Frankie's great-grandfather opened a store and settled there. He married a local woman, who happened to be a Melanesian and Polynesian mixture.

By the time Frankie's grandfather took over the business, they had made some money, and he went back to China and married a Chinese woman. When his father grew up, he married an Indian woman he met in school. That explained why, in addition to English, Frankie spoke Fijian, Hindi and some Hakka. Also, after eight years in Hong Kong, he had learned to speak passable Cantonese. But he belonged to the French language group and the only Chinese he could write was his name. Once he remarked to me that learning the Chinese language was just too difficult for him as a non-native-speaker.

***

Rules of the HKSC Exam

With a certificate from the Hong Kong Education Department, a student could move on to the next step in a very competitive Hong Kong society. Without it, it would be almost impossible to leave Hong Kong for a higher education and extremely difficult to get a job. Even working in a hotel required the HKSC certificate. It was the minimum requirement for survival in Hong Kong.

To be awarded a certificate, the candidate needed to pass at least five subjects: English language, a second language (for the vast majority, Chinese), a science or math, and two electives. The requirements didn't seem so difficult. If the student had a good command of the English language, the rest would be easy. Subjects such as history, geography, biology, and biblical knowledge were taught and tested in English. I often wondered how students with weak English skills could answer the questions. That was why the fail rates in third- and fourth-tiered schools were so high—their students often didn't learn the English language well and, as a result, stumbled in all the other subjects.

The eleven subjects I'd signed up for were: English language, English literature, Chinese language, Chinese history and literature, Malay language, mathematics, physics, chemistry, biology, geography and biblical knowledge. I also signed up for oral Mandarin, which didn't count as a subject for passing but would be useful for jobs in Hong Kong that might require knowledge of Mandarin.

Eleven subjects were far more than required to pass, but I thought since I had studied them, I might as well take the exam.

A few in the class thought I was spreading myself too thin and that I might do better to concentrate on fewer subjects, which I'd been worrying about myself as the exam date neared.

The grades were as follows: 1 was distinction, 2 and 3 were credits, 4, 5 and 6 were passes and 7, 8 and 9, failing grades. Getting a distinction was very difficult. Each year, a handful would have as many as seven or more distinctions. These students would have their pictures splashed all over the papers. They would be interviewed and asked about their secrets of success. On the flip side, each summer after the exam results were posted in mid-July, a few young people would jump off tall buildings for having failed or not having done as well as they'd hoped.

Tremendous pressure was put on the students, their families, the teachers and the principals. The student's future depended on the results of the exam. The family's honor was at stake. The teacher's job often depended how well the students did.

***

My stuttering had improved but hadn't gone away completely. The English Language exam consisted of several sections: an essay, use of the language, grammar and the oral. In the oral section, each student would be tested by two examiners. A large picture would be shown to the candidate who then had to describe the picture and answer questions about it. Having spoken English regularly in Malaysia for many years, I didn't think it would be a problem; but I was worried about my stuttering. What if I became tongue-tied and couldn't get the words out? What if I had a mental block and couldn't think? With so much at stake, it would be easy for someone to lose their faculties and simply freeze. But I consoled myself with the fact that English had been consistently one of my best subjects at La Salle.

I didn't expect English literature to be a problem either. Chinese language and Chinese history and literature could be potential problems, but if I failed Chinese language, I was taking Malay language to make sure I fulfilled the second language requirement.

Mathematics could be a problem too. Through sheer hard work and sometimes by memorization, I had passed all my math subjects at La Salle; but it was a lot of work. I was confident with chemistry and biology, but less so with physics.

I was the belt-and-suspenders type; even if I only passed half of what I had signed up for, I would still be awarded the certificate!

***

In spite of an extremely busy schedule, I didn't give up on sports, trying to train at least once a week to maintain my 100m time of around 12 seconds. I continued to run the 4 x 100 meter relay for La Salle and we usually came in first or second at the invitational meets held at other English medium high schools.

With the little free time I had, I dreamt about studying at the University of Hawaii. By then, I knew my hopes for studying medicine at Hong Kong University were very unlikely to come true.

Chun Man's mother continued to be very generous, giving me one or two extra hundred-dollar bills each month for tutoring her son. I saved what I could, knowing I would need it if my dream of going to medical school became a reality.

The "rent" money I paid Ah Lee for my private study on the deck averaged $50 HK a month. After covering that and my other expenses, I was still able to save on average $200 HK a month.

Mrs. Wong was already worried about what Chun Man would do when I left Hong Kong for university, but I assured her that it would be a year and a half away if I did, and there was no guarantee that I was even going.

***

Every night, I was studying till one to two in the morning, and sometimes later. I began to notice that I was seeing flashing lights, which appeared like bright stars. I wasn't sure if they were real and something was happening to my eyes, but I was worried.

There was an eye specialist on Nathan Road named Dr. Chang who my father had seen once. I started to worry that I might be going blind, so I made an appointment with him. The doctor examined me, gave me some pills and charged me $100 for the five-minute visit, which I had to work twenty hours to earn! I went back for two more visits.

I then began to notice that the shiny stars only appeared when I stayed up past two in the morning. I decided that it must have been my eyes telling me not to overuse them. As long as I didn't stay up past two, my vision was fine. I also realized that the eye specialist's pills had absolutely no effect on my problem.

I continued to study hard, and I prayed regularly for good enough results to get into Form 6 (twelfth grade) in the Science section.

Exam week arrived in mid-May. The first week was for the important subjects, one in the morning and another in the afternoon. The second week was for the irregular subjects such as biblical knowledge, French, and in my case, Malay language and Mandarin.

The examination was held in the school auditorium. Desks and chairs were neatly arranged in rows and we were each assigned a desk, in alphabetical order. We had all been briefed on the rules beforehand: bring extra pens and pencils, get a good night's sleep and avoid having to go to the bathroom during the session. Each session lasted three hours.

After all my worrying, the oral section of the English language exam went surprisingly well. I was shown a picture of an American neighborhood with a boy riding a bicycle. I was able to describe the picture clearly and fluently and without any signs of stuttering. The two examiners congratulated me and were curious about where I was from, saying they didn't think I was from Hong Kong. It must have been my Malayan accent!

When I had finished the testing in all my subjects, I wasn't ecstatic, nor was I sad. I thought I did alright—there hadn't been any surprises. Math wasn't easy, but I thought I did well enough to pass. I was most pleased with chemistry.

It was a bit of an anti-climax after building up to it for so long. Now that we were done, all we could do was wait for the results. We went out and celebrated.

I started getting busy with tutoring again. The other students I'd had to stop tutoring during the school year wanted me to resume my service. Now that I was officially finished with Form 5 at La Salle, I was in greater demand. My reputation had spread! I was now making well over $800 HK a month.

CHAPTER 6:
Exam Results

F OR A WEEK BEFORE THE RESULTS CAME OUT, I prayed at St. Teresa's Church for hours every day—especially to the Virgin Mary. I was convinced that she'd answered most of my prayers. I prayed that I would do well enough to get into the Form 6 Science section at La Salle. I knew the competition was fierce, and many of my classmates had much stronger science aptitudes than me. I needed to score at least a 2 or 3 in three out of the four subjects of math, physics, chemistry and biology. That was usually the minimum requirement.

The exam results were posted on a hot, humid Friday afternoon in July. I joined the crowd gathered in front of the principal's office and waited anxiously until Mr. Hung, the office manager, came out and tacked the scores to the wall for everyone to see. There was no privacy.

I didn't get any distinctions. I had four credits: English language-2, chemistry-2, biology-3 and biblical knowledge-3. The other seven subjects were passes: physics-4, English literature-4, Chinese literature and history-4, geography-4, Malay-5, mathematics-5 and Chinese language—which I had opted for just a pass or fail in—pass. I also passed oral Mandarin. My shoulders slumped. It wasn't bad, but I knew it probably wasn't good enough to get into the 12th grade Science section.

A lot of students in the class would have been ecstatic with my results. Scores like that were good enough for entrance to the Teacher's College, or to be a bank trainee, a front office worker at one of Hong Kong's many hotels or a manager in a factory. There would also be openings in the civil service: post office employee, immigration officer, government housing inspector or police inspector.

Jackson, the perennial top student in our grade, was equally good in humanities and sciences and an excellent public speaker as well. He got more distinctions than anyone. To everyone's surprise, he indicated that he wanted to be in Form 6 Arts instead of Science. We all thought he was making a mistake. Why would anyone with distinctions in math, physics, chemistry and biology choose to be in the humanities? There was no doubt that he would get into medical school if he wanted to. That showed how narrow-minded I was! It was my idea of an ideal profession, and I couldn't imagine anyone wanting to do anything else. But to our amazement, Jackson indeed signed up for Form 6 Arts, without giving any reasons. Years later, he proved to be miles ahead of us all. He graduated from the University of Hong Kong with honors in economics and became one of the most influential leaders in the city.

Benny Cho was milling around the bulletin boards where the results were posted, checking and re-checking as if to see if there'd been a mistake. Benny was a transfer student from the American International School in Taiwan in Form 2. Only the very well-to-do Chinese could attend that school. His father had a dental office on Boundary Street.

I knew Benny from the sports team. At six feet two inches and well over two hundred pounds, he was the top discus thrower at the school. Several students in our class were half his weight.

Benny looked sad. He asked how I did and I told him my results.

"James, if you could only give me one of your eleven subjects, I would have passed," he said dejectedly. He had passed all the requirements: English, French as a second language, biology for science and biblical knowledge. All he needed was one more, any elective. But he wouldn't get the chance now, and without that piece of paper, it was almost impossible to move on.

One of my favorite Portuguese classmates was Alphonso Remedios. With his very fair complexion, almost blond hair and blue eyes, he didn't look Portuguese at all—more like someone from Northern Europe. He wore brown tortoiseshell-rimmed glasses and had a very scholarly look. He sat next to me in class and was always well behaved. When I saw him after the exam results came out, Alphonso looked dejected. He didn't pass math or any of the sciences, and he wouldn't be awarded a certificate. He had to look for another school to repeat Form 5 and to sit for the exam again.

I had always assumed that Brother Michael was English, but it turned out that he was Irish. He was a massive, bald, bespectacled man with a hearing aid. He must have been in his seventies. He was the school's Career Master, responsible for making the list of names to be in the two grade 12 classes.

In all fairness, I thought the system was transparent and favoritism was impossible, since we all knew each other's scores. Those of us who had passed with at least three credits could apply for promotion to the pre-university years in either science or the humanities. We would be ranked against each other. Out of a class of over two hundred, only sixty-four of us would go on to the next grade.

I was assured a place in the humanities, a consolation prize that meant I could at least remain at La Salle without having to look elsewhere to continue.

A student in the humanities section was automatically stigmatized as second-rate. In those days, a degree in humanities from the Hong Kong University provided limited opportunities: most graduates ended up as teachers or working for the government. There was little need for lawyers, as most people were still poor in Hong Kong and rarely sued each other. Since most of the housing was built by the government, there was also low demand for legal services to do property deeds. And there were no law schools in Hong Kong.

Those in science could go into medicine, engineering or another science that enabled them to go abroad and get advanced degrees. It would have been more difficult for a non-native English speaker to get an advanced degree in humanities, and even if one got a PhD, finding a job wasn't easy. But in science, the language is science. It was simply more practical.

It was the first time I had any dealings with Brother Michael, since none of us below Form 5 had any need to. He worked mainly with the upper classmen. I had made an appointment with him to find out if there was any way I could be in Form 6 Science at La Salle or even at another school, or if there were any other possible options. He showed me the list of rankings and I was number thirty-four; the cut off was thirty-two.

There was no way around it. If I wanted to stay in La Salle, I would have to be in the Arts section. I was disappointed, even though I knew that many students in Hong Kong would do almost anything to be in my situation. I checked out several second-tiered schools for Form 6 Science. They were very happy to accept me, but in the end I decided there was no way I would leave La Salle.

I had been so close to gaining entrance to Form 6 Science; perhaps my strategy to sign up for eleven subjects was indeed flawed. I could have used the time I spent on the extra courses to work on physics, which might have helped me get a 3 instead of a 4 and enabled me to make the Science section list. But that's the nature of life: we make decisions and have to live with them.

I did a lot of soul searching and went over my options by writing down the pros and cons of each. Trying to secure a place at the Hong Kong University Medical School was out of the question. I fell flat at the first hurdle. Even if I had made it into Form 6 Science, La Salle could only send three or four students to the medical school each year, and I certainly wouldn't be among them, being so far away from the top.

I learned that in the US, medical school was for people who had finished university, and it didn't matter whether the major had been in science or not, as long as the required subjects—called premed courses—were taken.

I went to some lectures given by US Consulate staff about the education system in America and was advised that Form 6 Arts would be a better choice for me, because it would be advantageous for a foreign student to take more English classes and be able to write better.

My options were:

Plan A: Go to the University of Hawaii after the Form 6 Arts year.

Plan B: If, for some reason, I couldn't go to the US, I would stay for Form 7 Arts and perhaps go to Hong Kong University for history or geography.

Plan C: My brother Paul had a classmate who was going to the Santo Tomas University Medical School in Manila, in the Philippines, and I could follow the same path and later try to go to America.

Plan D: As Hong Kong didn't have a dental school, the government was accepting the credentials of some dental schools in the Philippines. I talked to one dentist who had gone to the University of the East in Manila and was making a good living. Santa Tomas University also had a dental school. One advantage of going to university in the Philippines was that it wasn't expensive. I could work in Hong Kong for a few years to save enough money for it. Clement Tam and I had talked about this option at great length.

Plan E: When everything else failed, I still could join the Hong Kong Police Inspector Academy and become a police captain.

I had considered Australia and the UK, but there were few opportunities to work in those countries. I also looked into New Zealand, but at the time it had an anti-Asian immigration policy and essentially forbade Asian students. I read a great deal about New Zealand and thought it sounded like such a wonderful place. I fantasized about settling there and having a small farm.

***

A few others were also disappointed by the exam results. Tommy had scores almost identical to mine and he couldn't get into Form 6 Science either, even though he was planning to go into civil engineering and eventually take over his father's construction business.

Lester was a quiet boy with thick black hair cropped close to his scalp. He too was planning to go into medicine. He showed me his results with a sad face.

"James, I think we're in the same boat even though it looks like I did better than you. A distinction in Chinese language is useless," he lamented. "I got a 3 in chemistry and a 2 in biology, and 2 in English, biblical studies, Chinese literature and history, but a 4 in physics and math. If I did better in either of those two, I think I'd have a good chance. But now, I'm sure I won't get into 6 Science, because the other guys did so well in science and math."

I tried to sound positive, saying cheerfully, "We're going to the US anyway. This year doesn't really matter, because we can major in anything over there. We can certainly still try to get into medicine.

"There are just too many gifted people here. We're competing with the best students in one of the most competitive schools in Hong Kong. It's a little set-back. I'm sure ten years from now we'll look back and wonder why we were so sad."

He smiled and said, "I hope you're right."

As Lester and I commiserated, Xavier Keng came over to us. I often walked home with him because his house was half a block from mine. He had a pompadour hairdo and the greatest sense of Cantonese humor. With a smile on his face, he said, "This is the worst day of my life. I got a 2 in math, a 3 in Chinese language, and the rest of my seven subjects are all 4. There's no chance I'll be able to stay at La Salle, maybe not even in the Arts section." He continued smiling but also shaking his head.

Clement was walking slowly toward us. He too was smiling and shaking his head. "So close and yet so far away!" he said. "If I had scored a 3 in chemistry instead of a 4, I'd have a shot at 6 Science. The only consolation is that I think I can be in 6 Arts if I want to."

I laughed and said, "Yes, I know how you feel. If I scored a 3 in physics instead of a 4, I probably would still have a chance. But now, I think the die is cast."

Xavier added, "Que sera, sera."

We all laughed. But deep inside, some of us were crying.

I had always enjoyed Xavier's company because he had such a funny sense of humor. Not being Cantonese, I often had to get him to explain some of the colloquial terms he used.

Xavier was born in Hong Kong and his father was some sort of a draftsman, just below the rank of an architect. His father owned a three-story building not far from my apartment and he had hoped to go into engineering and perhaps develop his father's building into a high-rise residential condominium.

I never got to know Lester well. He was a very studious guy, even by La Salle standards. Whenever the teacher passed out our exam papers, he would close his eyes as if he was praying. I couldn't tell whether he was born in Hong Kong or China, but I thought his facial features—a square face, high cheek bones and light complexion—looked more like someone from the north.

***

As I was walking down the school steps to Boundary Street, Robert Remedios joined me. He was a distant cousin of Alphonso's, but he looked nothing like him. He had short black hair, deep-set brown eyes and a pointed chin. He wore dark-rimmed glasses. Robert was known as a bookworm, as he always had a book with him during recesses and lunch breaks.

He was all smiles, saying, "Hi James, I heard you'll be in Form 6A."

"Hi Robert," I replied. "I think so, because it looks like there's no way I could be in 6B. I didn't do well enough in science or math."

"Clement told me that you'd probably be in 6A just like him. I know for sure that I'll be in 6A, and I'm planning to major in English language and literature at Hong Kong University. You know me, I hate math and the sciences," he remarked with a grimace.

"I heard you got distinctions in English language, English literature and French," I responded. "That's really impressive. You'll have no problem getting into the university."

"Yes, I'm very pleased with the results," he said.

Robert had been in the same class with me for the full two and half years I'd been at La Salle. He was a taciturn fellow and I never really got to know him. I knew that his father, like many of the Portuguese and Macanese, worked for either the Hong Kong and Shanghai Bank or the Chartered Bank, and most of them lived in the housing provided by the banks in Kowloon Tong.

"Aren't you going to follow in your father's footsteps and work for the bank?" I asked.

"No, I like literature too much," he replied. "I'd like to be a teacher or a professor."

We reached the bottom of the steps and headed toward Boundary Street. "How long has your family been in Hong Kong?" I asked curiously, changing the subject.

"As far as I know, my family has been in Macau and Hong Kong for many generations, at least a hundred years," he responded. "This is the only home we know. Even though I look Portuguese, I've never been to Portugal, and I don't speak the language.

"You're lucky that you're Chinese, and you know you belong here. We know we don't belong here, but we don't belong anywhere else either. Maybe after I graduate from Hong Kong U, I'll go to Canada. I think I wouldn't mind living there. I've been reading about the vast country. I think I'd like to be in a place where it's not so crowded. Sometimes, I'm so tired of the crowds in Hong Kong. There are people everywhere here. I'd actually like to attend university in Canada and get a graduate degree, but my father says there's no way he can afford to pay for it. He's a mid-level manager and we just manage to get by."

"It's interesting to hear you say I'm lucky to be Chinese and that I belong here," I commented. "The truth is that I wasn't born in Hong Kong, but I'm not a citizen of China either. I can't even have a passport—only a document from the Hong Kong government stating that I'm a resident here. So really, I'm a stateless person. You know that the Portuguese and the Macanese have more opportunities in Hong Kong than the Chinese."

"I guess the grass is always greener on the other side," Robert chuckled. "I think the problem with Hong Kong is that it's a city that exists on borrowed time in a borrowed place. I'm not looking forward to 1997 when it gets returned to China. I can't imagine myself living in Portugal either—I have absolutely no connections there."

"That's interesting," I remarked. "I've always envied you guys and thought the Portuguese and Macanese in Hong Kong had it made. You all seem to have good jobs and be doing so well."

"No, James," said Robert with a shake of his head. "You know the British look down on us. But I think they trust us more than they trust the Chinese. I think the two banks have always preferred to hire Portuguese or Macanese because they think the Chinese customers will be more impressed with an assistant manager who's Caucasian-looking rather than Chinese. Also, for generations we've been perfect for the bank jobs because we can communicate with the Chinese customers in Cantonese, yet it doesn't matter that almost none of us write Chinese, because all the documents are in English. Of course, I would've liked to learn to read and write some Chinese," he remarked.

"I'm surprised to hear that you feel the British look down on you guys too," I said.

"Right. I don't like the British," he responded. "They think they're superior. But after World War II, we all realized that they aren't. They were simply slyer. Perhaps they were clever in how they exploited the locals in their empire. Imagine how they ruled India, several hundred million people, with only 50,000 soldiers. I think they're tricky in dealing with the local people, always working one group against another and causing division among them.

"My father told me that when the Japanese invaded Hong Kong, most of the British were scared and didn't want to fight. It was the Portuguese and Macanese who fought the hardest because they felt that Hong Kong was their only home. The British had Britain.

"Yes, my father told me many stories about how duplicitous, dishonest and underhanded they could be. And yes, my father used all those adjectives to describe the British," Robert commented with a smile.

"Wow," I exclaimed, "I'm really surprised to hear how you feel about the British. I always thought you were content because you all had jobs, while my parents, when they arrived in Hong Kong in 1949, couldn't find any work even though they had graduated from one of the best universities in China. My father was unemployed for five years."

Robert nodded sympathetically. "That was a difficult time for a lot of people, because so many refugees arrived in such a short time. Hong Kong really wasn't ready to handle them. We were lucky in that we've always been in Hong Kong and my father was educated in the British system. I think if your parents knew English, they might have been able to find jobs sooner," he remarked.

When we reached Boundary Street, we bid each other goodbye and Robert walked north on La Salle Road to Kowloon Tong while I continued west on Boundary Street to Prince Edward Road.

As I walked, I thought about what Robert had told me. It was quite a revelation, and it challenged some of the assumptions I'd made about his culture.

When I got closer to home, my thoughts returned to the exam results. I consoled myself that I could at least remain at La Salle without causing my parents to lose face. I also considered the possibility that our relatives and friends had no idea what Form 6A was. Perhaps they would even think that Form 6A was more desirable than Form 6B, not knowing that A stood for Arts!

CHAPTER 7

Form 6A

I WAS VERY GLAD THAT MY GOOD FRIEND MICHAEL was in my class. He was positive that he wanted to major in geography at the University of Hong Kong.

Out of the thirty-two in our class, four or five of us would've done anything to be in Form 6 Science. Tommy seemed to have accepted his fate and tried to be optimistic, saying that we'd worked so hard for so many years, and we deserved a year of taking it easy and preparing for university in the US the next year. Most fellows in the class were planning to major in humanities at Hong Kong U and stay in Hong Kong after they graduated. A degree from the university would almost guarantee them a decent job.

We were all taking the same subjects: English language, English literature, history, geography, Chinese language and Chinese history. We would study each subject in depth and take a university entrance exam after two years for the A-level. Those who wanted to continue their studies in the UK. could also take the A-level of the London University Overseas Examination, although it was quite rare.

For those of us who were planning to go to the US, it wasn't an important year. We just had to finish the 12th grade to begin as a freshman in an American university.

The students in Form 6 Science would usually study four or five college level subjects: pure math, applied math, physics, chemistry and biology, depending on whether they were going into physical or biological science. After five years, those who were accepted into medicine earned an MBBS degree: Bachelor of Medicine & Bachelor of Surgery, which is the equivalent to the MD in America.

Being in Form 6 and 7 was a big deal. We'd been through the meat grinder and survived. We even had a different color school tie to differentiate us from the rest of the students; and we had our own separate area each morning during the assembly. The rest of the school looked up to us, because the goal of every student was to be able to stay in La Salle after the HKSC Exam.

***

It was a good year for me to make money. After class at three, I tutored two boys who lived near the school for two hours. I then headed for the Wong's home, where a fantastic dinner would be waiting for me. Chun Man and I would work until after nine and then I would head home.

It wasn't a stressful year, except that I was worried about the three thousand US dollars I needed to show the consulate in order to apply for a visa. In those days, many families like mine just didn't have that kind of money. Most students would have enough money for the first few months and had to look for work right away in order to support themselves.

Tuition in the US in the sixties was low compared to today. Self-supporting in college was something many Hong Kong students were expected to do. We wanted a better life and we were willing to take the risks.

During my Form 6 year, I had more time to practice sports. I never made any progress and remained second or third in the 100 meters and long jump, but I maintained my 12.0 seconds for the 100 meters and the 18 feet distance of my long jump. I also remained on the 4 x 100m relay team.

I rejoined the Boy Scouts briefly but never completed the badges I needed to fulfill the Queen's Scout (Eagle Scout in the US) requirements.

I visited the US Information Office often and read about life in the US, poring over university catalogs. I spent a lot of time daydreaming about school in America.

La Salle didn't accept any new students from other schools in either Form 6A or B, so most of the students in my class were fellows I'd known in Forms 3, 4 or 5.

I noticed a quiet fellow who I'd seen in school but was never in the same class with until now. Henry Young spoke with an accent, but I had no idea what kind of accent it was. He was a stocky fellow with a swarthy complexion and thick black hair covering his ears.

During lunch break one day, we happened to find each other on a bench behind the main school building.

"Henry, I can't figure out what kind of an accent you have. Are you from England?" I asked.

Henry smiled and replied that he was from Australia.

I followed with another question. "How long has your family been in Australia?"

Asking more questions and making comments, I began to draw out the story of how Henry's great-grandfather got to Australia.

"My great-grandfather Ah Young was Hakka too," he said, after I told him some of my family background. "I believe his father died when he was nineteen and they had little land to support the family. An uncle suggested that he go to Australia.

"Some relatives contributed the money to buy his passage, and around 1880, he left his poverty-stricken village in Guangdong—a village not far from Hong Kong. He got on a boat in Hong Kong and arrived in Cooktown, the port in North Queensland in northeast Australia.

"He and a bunch of other Chinese men were hoping to find gold. In Cooktown he met other Chinese who'd been there since the 1850s for the first gold rush in Victoria. He realized that the rumors he heard in China about plentiful gold in Australia were untrue. Gold was elusive, the climate was oppressive and many of his countrymen were sick and starving in the alien land.

"Nevertheless, Ah Young and others made the arduous journey on foot to the goldfields many miles southwest of Cooktown. He worked very hard and did find some gold, but it wasn't enough for him to return to China a hero. When his gold ran low, he drifted south and ended up buying shares in a sugar cane farm near Cairns. While farming the cane fields, he had many skirmishes with the Aborigines. During one of the clashes he got hit on the head with a stone axe and lost his left eye.

"Ah Young was comatose in the hospital for over a week. The doctors were certain he wouldn't live. But he surprised everyone and woke up one day.

"In spite of the loss of his eye and a slight memory problem that resulted from his horrible injuries, he continued to work hard. He and his partners led in the development of the land around Cairns in North Queensland. As the climatic conditions in Southern China were similar to those in North Queensland, the Chinese farmers had experience in growing crops like mangoes, pineapples, bananas, corn, rice and sugar. They were experts in the art of hoe cultivation, which was necessary on the newly cleared ground, an activity the Europeans avoided because it was so tedious.

"Before long, Ah Young and other Chinese were the center of a vibrant community around Cairns. After years of hard work, he had become established, and he could seek a wife from China."

Henry went on to describe how Ah Young's future wife, White Lotus, arrived in Australia and almost fainted because no one had told her that Ah Young had only one eye and had been disfigured by the stone axe. However, his great-grandmother accepted it passively as her fate.

"Ah Young and his wife had one child, Charlie; sadly, White Lotus died when Charlie was three," Henry continued. "Charlie was brought up by men on the farm and sometimes he was boarded out to different families. When Charlie grew up, he married a woman who was a quarter Irish and three quarters Chinese. Charlie of course was my grandfather. He worked very hard and further diversified their farms, eventually opening a general store. Their mangoes and pineapples were distributed all over Australia."

"When my father William was born, Grandpa was considered quite well-to-do, and he was able to send my father to university.

"After he graduated, he married a Chinese woman he met at the university—my mother. I was born in Australia.

"When I finished primary school, my father decided to send me to Hong Kong to get some Chinese education, and that's how I ended up at La Salle," Henry finished.

We finished up our lunches, and then headed back to class. As we walked I asked, "What do you plan to do after this?"

"My plan is to finish Forms 6 and 7," Henry replied, "then return to Australia for university and major in journalism or writing in Sydney or Melbourne. I'm glad to be in Hong Kong and getting in touch with my Chinese roots. It's too bad that Australia isn't good for Asians, because they're still discriminated against. In fact, the country has the so-called 'White Australia Policy'—they welcome immigrants from Europe but forbid any from Asia. Even the Hong Kong students who go to Australia for university find it almost impossible to apply to stay and work or settle."

I was glad to have solved the mystery of Henry's accent, and I also felt I'd made a new and interesting friend.

Asmaraman Sukowati Tjong Kho Hoo

Tjong, as most of our classmates called him, was another fellow I'd run into but had never talked to. He was darker in complexion than most Chinese, and had large brown eyes and dense, jet-black hair that covered his forehead to about an inch or so above his eyebrows. He always had a soft smile on his face but said little in class.

During recess one day, we struck up a conversation.

"You certainly have a long name," I commented. "What sort of a name is it?"

"Well, it's Indonesian," he replied. "Tjong is my Chinese family name in the Hakka dialect. In Cantonese, it is Cheung, or Chang in Mandarin. It's one of the most common surnames. Asmaraman is my Indonesian name, Sukowati is my Indonesian middle name, and Kho Hoo is the Chinese name that my grandfather chose for me."

As he explained, he wrote the Chinese character 張 on a piece of paper and showed it to me. I nodded and said, "Of course! But I've never seen it spelled that way."

"Yes, I think this is the Dutch spelling," he answered. Sitting down over a small plate of rice noodle and a bottle of soymilk, Tjong explained further.

"Since you lived in Malaya for five years, you know the history of the Chinese people there. The history of the Chinese in Indonesia is somewhat similar, although Indonesia is a much larger country with many more people. Unlike Malaya, where the Chinese are almost as numerous as the Malays, the percentage of Chinese in Indonesia is small, something like 1.2% of the population. Even with such a minority, they controlled most of the economy, which really caused resentment among the locals.

"My parents told me that our family had been in Indonesia for at least a hundred years, but they didn't know when my ancestors first arrived because the family records were lost. As you can probably guess from my darker complexion and big eyes, I'm not pure Chinese. We're actually more Javanese than Chinese, but because of our family name we've always been identified as Chinese, which in Indonesia was and still is a disadvantage.

"By the time the Dutch arrived in the early 17th century, major Chinese settlements already existed along the north coast of Java. Most were traders and merchants, but some of them practiced agriculture in inland areas. The Dutch were impressed that the Chinese were skilled artisans and they hired many of them to help build Batavia, which is Jakarta now.

"The Chinese then branched out into farming spices that could be exported, such as cloves and nutmeg. Marriages between Chinese men and Javanese women were common and the Chinese didn't have to convert to Islam—at that point, Islam wasn't as powerful as it is today in Indonesia. The children of these unions took the Chinese names and became identified as Chinese."

"What did your family do there?" I asked.

"My father owned many acres of nutmeg and cloves in addition to a store. We lived in a town about a hundred miles southeast of Jakarta. I had a happy and worry-free childhood," Tjong said longingly.

I nodded sympathetically, remembering many carefree days in Malaya.

"Even though I have a Chinese name," he continued. "I don't think I'm very Chinese. I don't know the Chinese language, and we speak Indonesian at home. I never cared about China or what was happening there. It seemed that all the news I heard about China was negative. My parents always talked about how the Chinese people were always starving and that millions were killed after Mao took over and also during the Great Leap Forward. In my mind, nothing good was associated with China or being Chinese," he lamented.

"The Javanese are really kind and easygoing people. They're not as obsessed with money as the Chinese, and they didn't want to work as hard as the Chinese because they saw no reason to. You probably saw this in Malaya too—the Chinese regard the natives as lazy and stupid. It's just a cultural thing. I think the Dutch encouraged the attitude and really treated the locals badly, even as subhuman sometimes.

"The Dutch were crueler than the British as colonial masters, and they left the country a mess. Unlike the British, who left Malaya with a good system of roads, schools and hospitals, the Dutch left Indonesia nothing but chaos."

"How so?" I asked, as Tjong paused for a moment to take a bite of noodle.

"The Dutch took as much as they could," he explained. "They used the Chinese as middlemen in the exploitation of the natural resources such as timber, and crops such as cloves, nutmeg, sugar cane and coconut and palm oils. Often the natives who grew these crops weren't fairly compensated. Sadly, this earned the enmity of the local people against the Chinese, because it was the Chinese who they dealt with more directly than the Dutch.

"The Dutch also encouraged the Chinese to grow opium, then sent the opium to China. Many Chinese like my family got rich while the locals got poorer and became more resentful."

"When did you leave?" I asked.

"Things really began to change in 1959," Tjong replied. "The Indonesian government and military adopted an authoritarian rule and banned retail businesses by non-indigenous people, which meant the Chinese who owned almost all the retail businesses could no longer do so. My father decided that the future of Chinese people in Indonesia was going to get bleaker. So, three years ago, our family moved here. Sadly, because of my Chinese name, I had to leave a country that I truly love.

"Fortunately, my father was able to sell the land and businesses," he continued, "and with the money he was able to start a new business in Hong Kong. Many Chinese who left Indonesia with very little money weren't allowed to stay in Hong Kong and had to resettle in China. I've heard that their life in China has been terrible because most of them don't know the language and are very poor.

"I was educated in an Indonesian school all my life, but I was fortunate that my father realized how important the English language was and hired tutors for me. Otherwise, it would've been difficult for me to go to school in Hong Kong. In my town, many Chinese were attending Chinese schools. I never understood why they studied the Chinese language, Chinese history and even Chinese geography when they lived in Indonesia. Even as a kid, that made no sense to me," said Tjong, shaking his head.

It was clear to me that this was an emotionally charged issue for Tjong. Like him, I felt that my life was good where I was before we moved back to Hong Kong. It must have been difficult for him to be uprooted from an idyllic countryside in the tropics to a busy metropolis, packed tightly with very competitive people.

"You're right," I commented. "The Chinese in Indonesia and Malaya do have a lot in common. I can see why the locals resented the Chinese. The Malays and Indonesians share a common language and culture. They're a more happy-go-lucky kind of people and have a different outlook on life compared to the Chinese."

I could tell that Tjong was missing the town in Java where he grew up, just as I was missing Muar in Malaya. I again reminded myself that being at La Salle among so many classmates who had been born elsewhere was an education in itself.

We finished our food and went back to class.

Sondhi Tiamowong

At lunch break one day, Tony was sitting on a bench with a fellow I'd been somewhat curious about. About a year earlier, on several occasions when Xavier and I walked home together, I noticed a very fair complexioned fellow who always wore a hat walking up La Salle Road and disappearing into a mansion. I asked Xavier if he knew him, and he said he did.

Xavier had known Sondhi Tiamowong since they were both accepted into sixth grade at La Salle Primary School. Sondhi was Chinese and an albino from Thailand—the only albino I was aware of in school. As Sondhi and I had never been in the same class, I never got to know him. He had done well in the HKSC Exam and managed to qualify for Form 6 Science.

Sondhi's father was a very wealthy rice merchant in Bangkok. Like many wealthy Chinese men in Southeast Asia, he had more than one wife. Sondhi's mother was his father's second wife. When his father took in wife number six, his mother decided to move to Hong Kong where she had grown up, and brought her three children with her, including Sondhi.

I walked toward Tony and Sondhi with my luncheon meat sandwich in one hand and a bottle of Coke in the other.

"Do you mind if I join you guys?" I asked.

"Sit down, James," Tony answered, introducing me to Sondhi.

Sondhi, whose skin was fairer than that of even the whitest Englishman, squinted his eyes as he looked at me and remarked, "You know Joseph—he was in my class last year. He told me about you; and I saw you run on Sports Day."

I smiled. I was so notoriously curious about others that it struck me as funny to hear that others were also curious about me.

I told Sondhi that I had lived in Malaya for five years and had always been curious about the Chinese in Thailand, a country to the north of Malaya.

"I heard that all Chinese people in Thailand have Thai names and that they've been totally assimilated," I commented. "And even the king is part Chinese?"

"Yes," Sondhi replied. "The Chinese have been in Thailand for hundreds of years. In 1910, the wise King Rama VI realized that the Chinese in his country could become a problem, because they were getting rich and holding important positions in the royal court, and many Thai natives were jealous. He was worried that there would be a backlash against the Chinese, but he wanted the Chinese to help build his country. He decided that the Chinese should adopt Thai names so they could become Thai, and then there wouldn't be any resentment towards them when it became impossible to tell they were Chinese any longer. I think that was a very wise move.

"Now it's estimated that almost half the people in Thailand are part Chinese. It's difficult to tell who is pure Thai anymore, because for hundreds of years, even the royal family has been part Chinese.

"In actuality, we still can tell from a Thai-sounding name that has Chinese origins," Sondhi explained. "Take my name for example, Tiamowong: the last syllable 'wong' was my original family name. There's a famous Thai millionaire whose name is Limthongkul—his Chinese name is 'Lim', which is another common Chinese surname like my own."

"That's very interesting. Do you think it's better for the Chinese this way?" I asked.

"Yes," he answered, nodding emphatically. "It's much better for the Chinese to be assimilated. As you probably know from living there, it's a different story in Malaya. I think it's because of the Islam religion, which requires a non-Muslim to convert if he or she marries one. In Thailand, Buddhism is a much more tolerant religion and many Chinese married Thai people, and their children became Thai and nobody cared what religion they practiced.

"Sadly, Indonesia is like Malaya where the Chinese are discriminated against. I think the Chinese have it the worst in Indonesia. You know Tjong in your class? He's much more Indonesian than I am Thai, and yet his family suffered persecution and they sort of had to leave Indonesia.

"Most of the prime ministers in Thailand's history were more Chinese than Thai, and yet there's never been a problem," Sondhi continued. "It's really the religion. The Philippines have a lot of Chinese too, but you seldom hear about them being discriminated against there. As you probably know, most of the Filipinos are Catholic, and the Catholic Church doesn't usually require someone to convert in order to marry one. There are quite a few intermarriages too, and the Chinese simply blend into the Filipino people. Yes, they still keep their surnames, but they're so assimilated that people just don't care whether the person is Chinese or part Chinese or not."

"I think you're right, Sondhi," I commented. "If Chinese don't want to be discriminated against, they should take on the culture of the host country. That's what I would do. I think it's a matter of survival. Look at America. The second generation immigrants all become American, no matter whether they're from Italy or Ireland or China. Otherwise there could be divided loyalty."

Sondhi explained that he was Teochew (Chauchou), another dialect group in Guangdong province, and that they made up over half of the Chinese in Thailand. The other dialect groups were all from southern China such as the Hakka, Hainanese, Cantonese and Hokkienese.

***

Francois Tran Hoang
With a name like Francois Tran Hoang, I thought he probably had a Vietnamese connection. Francois was one of the two or

three fellows who rode a bicycle to school each day. I always admired him for having the courage to ride in Hong Kong traffic. He and I were in Forms 3 and 4 together.

Francois wore a pair of gray-rimmed glasses and always combed his Elvis hairstyle with a shiny cream. One day I complimented him on his bicycle skills after I'd seen him ride without his hands on the handle bar.

After school one Friday, I followed him and asked him if I could take a spin on his bike. I hadn't gotten on a bike since I left Shatin and I missed it. He was more than happy to let me do it, so I climbed on the dark blue 10-speed racing bicycle with upturned handlebars and took off. It was a great bike that rode easily uphill. After that we sat down on the grass and chatted.

"Francois, I heard that you're from Vietnam," I remarked.

"Yes," he replied. "I guess my family story isn't unlike others' in class. My father was a well-known physician in Guangzhou during the 1940s. Like most other Chinese families at the time, life was hard because of the warlord period, the civil war, the Japanese occupation and then World War II. When the war ended, my father thought there would be some good times ahead. But instead, the Chinese Civil War resumed with a vengeance.

"I guess my family lived more comfortably than many others, because my father was a respected physician, and he originally came from a wealthy family in Vietnam. As Mao was taking town after town, my father decided to leave China and return to Saigon where he grew up. His medical practice in Cho Lon, the Saigon Chinatown, soon became one of the busiest. We lived in a mansion surrounded by fruit trees and we even had servants."

Francois paused and adjusted his glasses, then took out a handkerchief and wiped his face.

"I didn't know there was a Saigon Chinatown," I chuckled, "but I think they must be everywhere! What language did you speak there?"

"I attended a Catholic school and learned French, Vietnamese and some English, but no Chinese. At home, we spoke Cantonese and Vietnamese," Francois replied.

"Your father was smart to get out of China. My family did the same; although I didn't end up in a mansion with servants!" I joked.

Francois smiled, but also looked a little sad. "Unfortunately," he said, "the good times didn't last. North Vietnam decided to absorb the other half of the country, the South. The Vietcong were and still are causing havoc everywhere in South Vietnam and Saigon, and now there are bombings almost daily. Assassinations of village leaders are frequent and innocent people are getting killed. The South Vietnamese and Americans are fighting an increasingly losing battle against the Vietcong and North Vietnamese army. My father was worried that I would be drafted into the South Vietnamese Army, so he sent me to live with relatives here in Hong Kong."

He sighed. "I miss my family. It's tough living with relatives. Sometimes my uncle isn't very kind. But there's nothing I can do about it. I've tried to encourage my father to move the entire family here, but he says he's too old for another big move. I haven't seen my family since I left Saigon five years ago, and I'm afraid to visit because I might be detained for evading the draft.

"James, you're lucky that you live with your family here. I don't know when I will see mine again. Perhaps I'll study in the US or Canada, and later I can try to have them immigrate there. I think that's the only way we'll ever be together again," he lamented.

I tried to console him. "Francois, I'm sorry to hear about your situation. I think your plan of going to America or Canada and then moving your family there is a sound one. I hope your dreams will come true."

He thanked me, and then said he had to head home. We got up and brushed the grass from our trousers, and then I waved goodbye as he got on his bicycle and rode away.

***

Hussein Bin Ahmad had been in class with me in all of my previous years, but he remained a mysterious figure to me. When I first arrived mid-year in Form 3, Michael told me that Hussein was from Malaya and his father was Malay, while his mother was Chinese—something I found very unusual, since Malays and Chinese rarely married each other because of the Islamic religion.

I don't think, in all the years of being in the same class, we even exchanged two words. He was somewhat taciturn and we never got the chance to know each other. Together again in 6A, he continued to remain a stranger to me.

He had a swarthy complexion and definitely looked more Malay than Chinese, with the large brown eyes of a Malay.

I thought since he knew that I'd come from Malaya, he'd be interested in talking to me. But he'd shown absolutely no interest in being my friend, and I already had more friends than I could handle. We would remain total strangers to each other, like two ships passing each other in the dark.

Felix Sapanov and I had become good friends, and we often talked about life and our future. His plan was to attend the London School of Economics and probably become a writer or journalist.

Max Mandel had actually qualified for Form 6 Science but chose to be in 6A, because he already knew that he was going to get a scholarship to Yeshiva University in New York where his father's younger brother was a professor. He wanted to take that year easy, and then take premed the following year.

He and I had also become good friends. We were having lunch on a Thursday and I was again asking him questions about the Jewish religion and people.

"If you're interested," he said, "I can show you the Jewish people's influence on Hong Kong."

I readily agreed, and the following Saturday at noon, a beautiful fall day with clear skies and a soothing breeze, we headed for the Jewish Cemetery on Hong Kong Island. We took a bus, the Star ferry and then another bus, and arrived at a peaceful green spot in a hidden corner of Happy Valley, tucked behind a Buddhist temple and surrounded by a cluster of apartment blocks. It was dotted with gravestones bearing a mix of English and Hebrew script.

The cemetery was quiet. With the exception of an old man with a crooked back and a head full of snow white hair and a woman who appeared to be his daughter, we were the only ones there. A few of my favorite fragrant *pak lan* trees dotted the cemetery here and there, giving off the most wonderful scent.

"The earliest recorded burial plot belonged to a Leon Bin Baruel, dated 1857," remarked Max as he pointed to a marble monument. "The first Jews to set up home in Hong Kong were Iraqi Jews who arrived in the 1840s. They were descendants of Jews expelled from Spain and Portugal during the Inquisition, which lasted from the late 15th to the early 19th century. They had worked their way east to Baghdad, where a sizeable community developed.

"During the 19th century, Baghdadi adventurers traveled to India and set up trading operations in the booming ports of Bombay and Calcutta. Later, as China gradually opened to international trade, they crossed the Indian Ocean and established outposts in Canton, Macau and Hong Kong.

"Although there were only a handful of Jewish families in Hong Kong in the mid-19th century, they enjoyed enormous success and several became fabulously wealthy. The Iraqi Jews are supposed to be the cleverest as far as business is concerned. They saw opportunities that other people either didn't see or weren't brave enough to pursue.

"This cemetery was created by the Sassoons, a family that was once dubbed the Rothschilds of the East. They bought the parcel of land from local farmers."

Max pointed out a plaque on the back wall that commemorated the opening of the burial ground in 1855 and then continued. "The family patriarch, David Sassoon, left Baghdad in 1832 and established himself in Bombay. He had seven sons whom he dispatched to outposts across the Orient, using his offspring to build a business empire. He had a son in practically every port," said Max. "In addition to Hong Kong, he had offices in Singapore, Burma, Canton, and even as far as Japan and Indonesia.

"The family started trading back and forth and invested in shipping, hotels and property, but its real fortune came from the trade in opium."

I nodded as I strolled along beside him and listened. As we continued the tour, we came across a small chapel and a tahara room, where bodies were ceremonially washed and prepared for burial.

"Few people realize that one of the most famous governors of Hong Kong was a Jew," Max continued. "Matthew Nathan served as governor from 1904 to 1907. Born in London, he was a soldier and an engineer with a reputation as a competent and decisive administrator.

"He wanted to develop Kowloon, which was a muddy backwater in those days. Nathan decided that for Kowloon to flourish it needed an access road to link it to the hinterland of the New Territories. Many thought he was making a mistake, but he was determined to push the project through.

"Now, Nathan Road is the Golden Mile, the shopping mega-strip that bears his name."

"I had no idea," I exclaimed.

Max nodded. "Like the Sassoons, the Kadoories were originally from Baghdad by way of Bombay. The first member of the dynasty to arrive in Hong Kong was Elly Kadoorie, who came in 1880 at the age of 15, to join the Sassoon family company. His brother Ellis joined him later. So, James, now you know who Kadoorie Avenue was named after."

I grinned and nodded. "It's fascinating," I commented.

Max smiled. I could tell he was pleased by my interest in his people's history. "The brothers amassed a fortune," he continued, "by investing in rubber plantations in Malaya, banking, docks and real estate. In 1914, Ellis made a major investment in Hong Kong and Shanghai Hotels. The Peninsula Hotel in Tsim Sha Tsui, an iconic Hong Kong landmark, was said to be 'the finest hotel east of the Suez' when it opened in 1928. Later, he bought into China Light and Power, the largest electricity-generation company in Hong Kong.

"Can you believe that in the lead-up to the Second World War, well over 20,000—perhaps as many as 30,000—European Jews like my father, fleeing Nazi persecution, took refuge in Shanghai? It was the only city in the world for which a visa wasn't required at the time," Max explained.

"They had no money, no nothing," Max continued passionately. "The Jewish community in Shanghai galvanized and looked after them. It was a huge undertaking, because there were an awful lot of them and only a relatively small established Jewish community. Not only that, but the established Jews were of a different origin, which I'll explain later."

I was impressed. Max really seemed to know the history of the Jewish people in Hong Kong.

He continued enthusiastically. "After the war, the refugees were repatriated to Europe or went on to start new lives in the US, Canada, Australia and Israel.

"Do you know who owns the Star Ferry and the Peak Tram?" he asked.

I shook my head.

"It's the Kadoorie family," he answered. "You've heard of Belilios School right?"

I nodded.

"It was founded by a Jew. Emanuel Belilios, a contemporary of the Sassoons and another opium millionaire, donated a large sum of money and made it possible to establish the school."

It was almost 4 o'clock, so we began walking back toward the entrance.

"For over a hundred years," said Max, "the British grew thousands of acres of opium along the Ganges River west of Calcutta and had massive factories to process opium. Tens of thousands of Indians were hired to cut the capsules of the opium plant to harvest the gum, which was then made into opium. The end product was shipped to Hong Kong and on to China.

"I'm not proud to admit that it was some of these Jewish merchants who helped the British distribute the opium to the Chinese. They justified it by saying that if they didn't do it, someone else would."

"I had no idea it was the British who grew the opium," I commented.

As we exited the cemetery and got onto the main road, all sorts of names were swimming in my head.

The iconic trolley traveled slower than the bus, and I thought there would be a better view of the city so I suggested that we take it instead of the bus. Hong Kong Island was still somewhat unfamiliar to me as I seldom ventured out there.

We sat in the front row on the upper deck, which gave us a perfect view of the street scenes. As usual, the streets were crowded, so crowded that it looked like people were just being pushed along from behind.

After a twenty-minute ride we got off the trolley and boarded the Star Ferry. We found seats by the window and felt the soothing sea breeze while enjoying the magnificent view of the harbor—rated as one of the most beautiful harbors in the world.

"What's the difference between your family origin—Ashkenazi, right?—and Baghdadi, to which the wealthy Jews in Shanghai and Hong Kong belonged?" I asked.

Max replied, "Ashkenaz was the great grandson of Noah. The term 'Ashkenazi' refers to Jewish settlers who established communities along the Rhine River in Western Germany and in Northern France dating to the Middle Ages.

"In the late Middle Ages, due to religious persecution, the majority of the Ashkenazi population shifted steadily eastward, moving out of the Holy Roman Empire into the areas of present-day Poland, Belarus, Estonia, Latvia, Lithuania, Moldova, Russia, Slovakia and Ukraine. This explains how my mother's family was from Poland, and why there were so many Jews in Lithuania at the time. Sadly, almost all of those who remained in Lithuania perished.

"The other main group is the Sephardic Jews. Unless you're a Hebrew scholar or a rabbi, it's very confusing to understand the history of the different groups. For the sake of simplicity, I would divide them just into Ashkenazi and Sephardic. There are other terms like Sephardim and Mizrahi, but I think it's just too complicated to explain.

"As I understand it," he went on, "the term Baghdadi Jew is not commonly used. Of course, it refers to their origin in Baghdad, like the Kadoories who had been in Baghdad for many generations and had adopted many of the local customs and language."

The short ferry ride was over quickly, and we boarded the number 1A bus home. I thought Max might be tired of talking, but he continued his explanation on the bus.

"Culturally, the Ashkenazi and the Sephardic Jews can be quite different. They dressed differently. They had different customs and spoke different languages, and even how they said their prayers was different."

I laughed and shook my head. "It's a lot to follow," I commented, looking down at the notepad I was carrying. I had been jotting down some of the names and places Max was talking about.

"Yes, it's quite confusing," Max acknowledged. "James, don't bother with all these terms. I guess you just need to remember the two basic origins—European Jews are Ashkenazi, and Sephardic usually means Middle-Eastern and the other groups!"

Max added, "As you can see, the Jews traveled all over the world to seek a better life. They were also known to have traveled along the Silk Road as traders throughout the ages. Some of them actually settled in China. It's been well documented that Jews were in China during the Tang Dynasty.

"There's a city called Kaifeng in Henan in Central China that they settled about 1400 years ago, and there's still a Jewish community there today. But these Jews are so totally assimilated that none of them speak or read Hebrew any longer. It's a mystery how they ended up there in Kaifeng. Some scholars think they were traders along the Silk Road. Some have even suggested that they belong to one of the lost tribes of Israel. I just learned a few weeks ago that some of them are immigrating to Israel and the Israeli government is welcoming them with open arms. It's interesting that many of them look more Chinese than anything else!"

I nodded and listened with amazement. "That's truly incredible," I remarked. "I had no idea. Max, before I met you, I only vaguely knew the history of the Jewish people. Now I have a much better idea of the whole picture. It's truly fascinating. I'm so glad you're such a good teacher! Maybe you can explain to me what the lost tribes of Israel are—another day!" I added quickly with a laugh.

Max chuckled and replied, "James, of course. I'd be happy to. This has been fun for me too. I'm so glad we went on this outing."

It had been a very educational day. I tucked my notepad away and promised myself that I would try to keep the details straight so I could understand the history of the Jews better.

Our conversation turned to other subjects, and we chatted easily until the bus got to our neighborhood. I bid Max goodbye and thanked him for a marvelous day.

***

Carlos Medina Leon Lee seemed happy to be in Form 6A, and was planning to study in Florida where he had some relatives who had emigrated there from Cuba when Castro took over the island. He was planning to study business administration.

Danny Tong was planning to attend Howard University in Washington, DC, where he had an uncle who had emigrated from Jamaica and was in the engineering department at the university.

Clement Tam was worried about his uncle's health. His aunt had been bedridden for years following a stroke, and his uncle was trying to take care of her and the store.

His father had died a year earlier in Madagascar, and Clement was worried about his two half-brothers and one half-sister there. He thought he would go to Manila to study dentistry and then return to Hong Kong to help his uncle.

***

After a few months, the disappointment of not getting into 6 Science had dissipated. It convinced me that I simply wasn't competitive enough to get in the University of Hong Kong medical school. I also reasoned that perhaps it was a good thing I didn't get into Form 6 Science, because even if I'd barely managed to get in, there was a good chance I'd be truly disappointed after Form 7 when I wasn't one of those picked for medical school. It would be an even bigger disappointment because I'd have to decide what to do next and I'd have missed my chance to go to the US. Yes, I was trying to rationalize my situation, but somehow it helped me move on.

There was no question that Form 6 Arts was much less stressful than 6 Science, because in Form 6 Science, once again, the smartest guys were competing against each other. I decided to use that year to take it somewhat easy so I would be charged up for university, hopefully in Hawaii. There, I would try hard to do well in premed, and hopefully get into medical school eventually.

Most students in 6A knew that if they applied to the University of Hong Kong in the humanities after La Salle, they would be accepted. The atmosphere in class was much more relaxed compared to Form 5.

For those of us still planning to go into science or medicine overseas, there really wasn't much we needed to do, as there wouldn't be a big exam at the end of the year. We were just waiting out the year.

I applied to several universities in the US, and to my surprise and delight, I was accepted to all of them. My first choice was the University of Hawaii. My second choice would be the University of Southern Illinois at Carbondale where Lester was planning to attend.

***

Tony, my friend from the 4 x 100m relay team for the last three years, always traveled with me to our track meets, as he lived just half a block from my apartment. As we were on our way to another meet one Saturday, he asked me why I was wasting my time tutoring these kids and trying to make a few dollars.

We were getting on the Star Ferry to Hong Kong Island on our way to St. Paul's College when he said, "James, you will have the rest of your life to work. You'll be able to make a lot more money than you can now. Just enjoy high school." He simply couldn't understand why I was wasting my time for so little money.

"I know," I murmured, because I didn't want to waste my time trying to explain why I needed to work. His father was part owner of a construction company, and Tony had probably never experienced poverty like I did, even though he often complained that his mother was his father's number two wife and he didn't have the same rights as the children of the first wife. Nevertheless, it looked like his father was providing well for Tony and his mother.

***

After overcoming several hurdles, I got my visa to study in the US. The day I got it was one of the happiest days of my life. But I also realized that it didn't mean my life would be easy from then on. Trying to attend a university in a foreign country without adequate money would be a challenge. But it was something I'd been dreaming about almost all my life, something that I had wanted very badly. I knew that if I wanted a better life, I had to do the work, and I was willing to make sacrifices.

In the meantime, one of the boys in the class, CC Woo, who was going to Dartmouth College, took the rest of us who were going to the US to his uncle's pawnshop. I bought a transistor radio and a Parker pen.

In June, I was still busy tutoring Chun Man, who still couldn't work on his own. His mother was worried that after I left, he would revert back to his bad habits. I talked to my brother Chung and he agreed to take over the job. Mrs. Wong gave me a bonus of five hundred Hong Kong dollars before I left. She probably knew that I would need the money.

CHAPTER 8:
Chasing Our Dreams

The President Cleveland

AFTER YEARS OF STUDYING DILIGENTLY, we were finally ready to chase our dreams. Some of us chose to leave Hong Kong, while others decided to stay. Each of us had our reasons for our decision.

The American President Lines used to be how most people traveled to America. In the early and mid-1960s, each summer, most Hong Kong students heading for the US and Canada would board one of the two ships—the President Cleveland or the President Wilson—which sailed between San Francisco and Manila, with stops in Hong Kong, Yokohama and Honolulu.

Those whose families could afford it flew, which cost three times as much as what I paid for my passage.

There must have been at least ten students from La Salle who boarded the President Cleveland on August 6, 1965. I didn't know all of them—some were from the class before us, and they had finished Form 7 and were heading mainly for Canada with advanced standing.

Sondhi was heading for Steven's Institute of Technology in New Jersey to study engineering and he was sharing a more expensive cabin with a friend.

Thomas Chang, a long-distance runner on the La Salle sports team who was in Form 4 with me, was heading for California, to Chico State University.

The largest contingent of La Salle graduates was going to the University of Manitoba in Winnipeg, Canada. Most of those students chose to fly. My old friend Xavier Keng was heading to Manitoba for electrical engineering, and John Chen, a good friend of his, was doing the same. Kwok Man Tai, a tall fellow who I barely knew, was also heading for Manitoba for engineering, as was Yeung Man Chi, who had been with me in the same class for two and half years.

James Yeung was a nice fellow who was also in the same class with me for two and a half years, until Form 6 when he did very well in the HKSC Exam and qualified for Form 6 Science. He was heading to Manitoba for premed and hoped to continue at the medical school.

Many of those heading for Manitoba had actually hoped to attend the University of British Columbia in Vancouver, Canada, because Vancouver had the largest number of Chinese immigrants, and it was the warmest province. UBC was also one of the most prestigious universities, especially in the eyes of people in Hong Kong. But for some reason, UBC accepted few if any students from Hong Kong that year, and certainly none from La Salle.

At least two La Salle graduates were heading for the world-famous California Institute of Technology (Cal Tech)—Hugo Ting and another fellow I didn't know very well. I heard that a third, someone I didn't know who joined La Salle in Form 4, was also heading there.

Raymond Hung and Edward Lau were heading for the UK to study accounting and business administration.

Ko See Man, who was originally from Penang, Malaya, and a few others were heading for Australia.

At least six from Form 6 Science were planning to study medicine at the University of Hong Kong, and quite a few others were planning to go into engineering there.

Michael Sze and at least half of the class from Form 6A were planning to study humanities at the University of Hong Kong, and Robert Remedios, who was with me for all three and a half years, was planning to study there as well, majoring in English Literature.

At least one student from Form 6A chose to attend the Chinese University of Hong Kong, which was a new university at the time.

A few fellows had left in Form 5 and were already studying at the Hong Kong Polytechnic College, which offered sub-degree programs such as drafting and other areas of engineering. In those days, the Hong Kong Polytechnic College wasn't yet granting degrees. I never could understand the difference between it and a university, because students essentially studied the same subjects. I was told that it was a holdover of the British class system designed to separate the working class (those in technical college) from the elites who were attending universities.

Max Mandel was heading for Yeshiva University in New York City and would be staying with his uncle who was a professor there.

Darius Mody and Felix Sapanov were heading for the London School of Economics.

Mark Moy, the nice fellow from New York, returned to the US after Form 3, and was accepted to Princeton University at age sixteen. He was going to go into medicine, following in his father's footsteps.

My fellow runner on the relay team, Frankie Sing, was headed for Auckland University in New Zealand to study law.

As I didn't know more than half of the class of 1964, I only had second-hand information about some of them. I knew that some began working in government positions such as immigration officers, government housing inspectors and some of the lower-level jobs that only required a Form 5 education. The others worked in various businesses in the private sector, especially in the tourism industry, since more Americans had begun visiting Hong Kong and service workers who spoke decent English were needed.

Our most famous old boy was Phillip Chan, who became a popular TV star as a detective and later a movie star. He appeared in a few Hollywood movies, usually playing the role of a Hong Kong police inspector.

***

August 6, 1965.

It was the most exciting day in my life. My dream of going to America was becoming a reality.

It was boarding time for the President Cleveland. At five in the afternoon, the summer air was still hot and humid. I had on my gray polyester suit, a white Dacron shirt and a narrow brown silk necktie and was sweating profusely. My parents, my sister Cathy, and my brother Chung were there. Chung helped me carry one of my suitcases as we found my cabin. Everyone was looking somber, but at the same time very proud that I was going to America. Cathy was especially sad. She and I were so close; now she would have no one to talk to, to tell her worries to. No one cried.

Sewn into a secret pocket in my undershirt were five $100 bills. I also had five $20 bills in another pocket. That money was all I had; and it was to last me until I found employment on campus.

The ship's horn sounded, indicating that it was time for the well-wishers to leave. As my family departed, I ran up to the uppermost deck and waved goodbye. There were hundreds of people on the dock—it was customary in those days for relatives and friends to come see someone off. Scanning the crowd, I located my family, but they were busy finding their way out and didn't look back. As I watched them leave, all sorts of feelings ran through my head.

The British Empire had created a unique culture with the Chinese in Hong Kong. It was truly where the East meets the West—a bi-cultural society. Many of us who had been educated in British schools were more comfortable using English as our written language; however, in communicating verbally with each other, Cantonese was by far the preferred language.

We had learned about Western values: human rights, democracy and freedom of speech. Many of us even adopted Western religion and had Western names. The Cantonese spoken in Hong Kong was unique in that even those who didn't speak English would intersperse their speech with isolated English words such as: "Ngo feel happi" for *I feel happy*, or "Ngo wui call nei" for *I will call you*.

Hong Kong had always been an exciting city. Not only could we get the pop music from America, but we were also getting it from Britain with music from artists like Cliff Richard and Helen Shapiro, who were little known in the US. Pop music had always been a big part of my life.

After dinner, too tired to stay to meet other passengers, I headed back to my cabin. In bed, my mind was still racing with so many thoughts.

The Catholic Church was a big part of my life; it provided me with security, stability and order in my life. Most important of all, I was provided a good education, thanks to people like Brothers Robert, Felix, Lawrence and Eugene, who left their own countries and devoted their lives to helping people like me. Without the Catholic Church, I wouldn't have had such a well-rounded education—academic as well as moral.

Growing up, I had always associated China with misery, cruelty and horror. One of my father's friends who escaped to Hong Kong in the early sixties recounted how he was tortured, had to watch his own brother being executed, and was made to kneel on pebbles for days until he became unconscious. He was subsequently sent to a hard labor prison for over a decade. His crime was being an official in the previous government—a chauffeur!

During the Great Leap Forward in the fifties, the situation was so bad that the people had to eat roots and tree bark for survival, because Mao was shipping much of the grain to the USSR for the re-payment of arms and other forms of assistance. There were horror stories about cannibalism—one story that specifically stuck in my mind was about an old lady in Guangdong whose grandchild had died, and as she had no one to care for her and nothing to eat, she cooked the child and ate it. Stories like that motivated me to work hard so that I could get as far away from China as possible. I couldn't understand why China, with such a long history of civilization, could have leaders that brought so much misery to its own people, and how the local Communist Party members could form committees, passing death sentences on their neighbors. The idea of one person killing another for no reason was incomprehensible to me. Often, it was how people settled their private grudges.

America was the hope and dream of millions all over the world. I had always heard that in America, as long as a person was willing to work hard, success was inevitable. I decided to have my own story of success, my American dream.

***

On the ship, the six of us shared one cabin at the less expensive lower level. There was a small round window that we could look out of. I got the top berth of one of the three double-decker bunk beds.

CC Chow, a witty fellow with a good, dry sense of humor who had been in my Form 4 class, was on his way to Dartmouth College. He would get off in San Francisco and then continue east on the train.

Ambrose Hung, a good-natured, fair complexioned fellow sharing the same last name 熊 as mine, which was not very common in Hong Kong, was heading for California. He had been with me in the same class for two and a half years and had attended the Hong Kong Polytechnic College after Form 5.

Danny Tong was heading for Howard University in Washington, D.C.

Lester Tung, who was planning to go into medicine, was heading for the University of Southern Illinois at Carbondale, which had also accepted me.

Pedro was heading for Auburn University in Alabama where he had a cousin who was studying microbiology. Pedro and I were in the same class in Form 3 only. After Form 5, he left and I hadn't seen him for over a year and had no idea where he went.

His full name was Pedro Hoy Chi Suen. Hoy in Cantonese means *sea*, and Chi Suen means *ambition pure*. He explained to me that the first two parts of his name, Pedro Hoy, could be mistaken for Spanish, as Hoy means *today* in Spanish. But Pedro was very Chinese and was actually born in Hong Kong. His father, Pablo Hoy, was born in Lima, Peru of Chinese parents from the Toi-shan area not far from Hong Kong in Guangdong province. At age sixteen, Pablo was sent to Canton (now Guangzhou) for a Chinese education and to be immersed in Chinese culture; and also perhaps to find a Chinese wife. Then World War II broke out and he stayed on in China and later moved to Hong Kong, like many other families.

Pedro's father was fortunate because he had graduated from the famous St. John's University in Shanghai, where English was used as the medium of instruction for many of the courses, and many on the teaching faculty were from America or England. At St. John's University, he met Pedro's mother, who was also a student there.

With both of them fluent in English, they had no problem finding jobs when they arrived in Hong Kong in 1949, about the same time as our family. His father worked in a large hotel as the front desk manager and his mother was a teacher in a Catholic high school.

I knew Pedro because we had talked about going to dental school in the Philippines if we couldn't go to the US. At the time, Hong Kong didn't have a dental school, but with a diploma from one of the better-known dental schools in the Philippines such as the University of the Philippines, Santa Tomas University or University of the East, all in Manila, we would be able to practice dentistry in Hong Kong. But going to dental school in the Philippines wasn't either of our top choices.

Like so many students in Hong Kong, Pedro had also been traumatized by the HKSC Exam. He had barely made it, only passing with the minimum requirement of five subjects, with scores in each subject of 5 or 6—6 was the minimum passing grade. He had to do Form 6 (12th grade) at a night school because no day school would take him.

He and I often spent time on the deck watching the waves, occasionally seeing flying fish jump out of the water and breathing the fresh sea air. As we talked about our dreams, I noticed that Pedro's minor speech impediment, which I'd observed before, had gotten better, even though he still seemed to have some trouble controlling his tongue. But he tried to talk slowly and even chose words he could pronounce more easily.

I also noticed that the left side of his face seemed a little larger than the right, and that his left ear was definitely longer than the right. Then I noticed that his right shoe was elevated about an inch with a thick sole, as his right leg seemed shorter than the left. I never asked any questions about my observations.

***

The air in the room smelled stale, probably from poor circulation and the diesel engines on board. The food looked beautiful and tasted good initially, but after a few days it all tasted the same. The air in the dining room also smelled stale; I lost my appetite quickly and craved my mother's cooking.

I tried to get out on deck as much as I could to breathe the fresh air, writing home and daydreaming. The flying fish jumping out of the water really seemed to be flying, and occasionally I saw some bigger fish that I couldn't identify.

Part of my daily activities was writing home each day, as I described the happenings on the ship and my feelings about leaving home. I waited to mail the letters when we stopped in Yokohama. I wrote about how surprised I was to find a balding, middle-aged American man in white overalls with a cigarette dangling from his mouth and a paint brush in his hand, touching up rust spots on the railing. I couldn't get over the idea that an impressive-looking American man like that could be a manual laborer! Growing up in Malaya and Hong Kong, I thought all white people must be wealthy and high class!

CC Chow was sick from the first day, unable to get up. We took turns bringing him food and drinks. After three days in bed, one of the personnel thought that he ought to be seen by the ship physician, who thought it was a case of the flu and prescribed some medicine. CC continued to stay in bed.

The rest of us tried to stay in the cabin as little as we could and be out and about on the ship, because the cabin was so small, and except for the three bunkbeds and a very tiny toilet and shower, there was nothing else. There wasn't even a chair, let alone a desk. But one of us always tried to be in the room when CC was awake so we could help him. If he was asleep, we would leave him alone and let him rest. It must have been horrible to be cooped up in a room and not able to get out to breathe the fresh air for so many days.

The sea was calm most of the time and I never got seasick. The only time I felt slightly unwell was after I'd stayed inside too long in the stale air.

There were many Filipino families on board, on their way back after visiting relatives in the Philippines. I learned that many of them were from the Watsonville and Salinas areas in northern California. Their parents or grandparents had been recruited to work in the lettuce and strawberry fields in the area. They were incredibly talented and consistently won the talent show contests with their singing and dancing.

The ship's band was a trio of American Japanese. They mostly sang and danced. One told jokes, but few of the students and new immigrants understood them, and only the returning Filipino families laughed.

One evening, an educational program was held to teach the students and new immigrants about life in America, such as what not to do and how to be polite.

After four days at sea, we were told that the ship would be arriving in Yokohama, Tokyo's main port, on August 10, at about ten in the morning. It would stop for two nights and would depart on August 12 at noon.

After the ship docked, Japanese immigration officials set up desks as we disembarked and checked our papers. Very few passengers were getting off in Japan. I mailed the thick letter I'd written to my family.

The five of us, without poor CC Chow who was still ill in bed, took a train and headed for Tokyo. The Japanese writing, Kanji, means *Han words*, i.e., Chinese words, so we had no problem reading signs. Having been told that the Tokyo Tower with the TV antenna was a must-see, we made it our first destination.

From the top of the Tower we could see Tokyo for miles. From there we went to the Imperial Palace. We were thoroughly impressed with how well the grounds were kept and how clean the water was in the artificial lake with the large koi fish, some as long as two feet, in various dazzling colors.

In the evening, we toured the Ginza district; the neon lights were much brighter and larger than those in Hong Kong! When we got hungry, we found a small noodle shop—a bowl of noodles was five hundred yen, which was about one US dollar at the time.

We got lost when we tried to return to the ship, but although we couldn't speak the language, we were able to write down what we wanted to say to ask for directions. A kind Japanese man with yellow, nicotine-stained teeth in his sixties showed us where the train station was. We discovered that he spoke a little English, and as we walked along the street, he remarked that he was in China during WWII. This was followed by an awkward silence from us, because we thought he was probably one of the Japanese occupiers who might have perpetrated some of the atrocities.

We thanked him and boarded the train, arriving back in Yokohama safely.

After another week at sea, the ship docked next to the Aloha Tower in Honolulu. I had arrived in America.

CHAPTER 9:
A Decade (1965 to 1974)

Today, IT WOULD BE INCONCEIVABLE for students to survive the way many Hong Kong students of my time did, leaving home with a few hundred dollars to attend university in a strange land. We did it because that was the only way we could get out of Hong Kong and as far away from the communists as possible. It was really more than just getting a college education. It was our escape route.

My first few months at the University of Hawaii were exceeding difficult. I got a D in my first zoology test, a course that was part of the premed requirements, and the job I'd found in the cafeteria dishwashing room was extremely unpleasant. We didn't really have to wash the dishes, but just fed them to the machine and picked them up when they were clean; but we were in a sweltering room with no windows. The air was filled with chlorine from the detergent and it irritated our eyes and nostrils.

The most traumatic event was that I met up with bullies. All my life, I had treated people kindly, and in turn I was treated with kindness. In Hong Kong, I was even respected because I was attending La Salle. But some of the boarders in the boarding house adjacent to the university just thought of me as an FOB—someone literally fresh off the boat. They thought they were better than me and that I wanted to be like them, like an American.

I shared a room with five other fellows that was no larger than 10 by 20 feet. It was noisy day and night. I'd never had any problems getting along with people, but for some unknown reason, perhaps because I was easy picking and couldn't defend myself, one of the boarders decided to make my life miserable. He and two other tough guys would order me to do chores when it wasn't my turn. The last straw was when they woke me up in the middle of the night and demanded that I clean the toilet.

The next morning, I packed my belongings on my old bicycle and left. For three nights, I was homeless and secretly slept at the Newman Center, a Catholic community center off campus, until I found a small room to rent in the basement of a house about a mile from the university.

Slowly I got my act together. I was able to drop the zoology course without penalty and I made a plan to take it another time.

By Christmas I was very glad that I had come to America.

My semester ended with a 3.00 (B) average. I even got a B for German 101, which was a difficult language because it was so different from Chinese and English, and I found the pronunciations challenging.

***

In the meantime, I was hearing from other La Salle classmates.

Tommy Sung wrote from New York University that civil engineering was difficult and that many students in his class had already taken advanced math, including calculus. He was very surprised, because he was told that students from Hong Kong usually had an edge in math over the American students. They were probably referring to those who had made it to the Form 6 Science section!

I wrote back to him that I was struggling and had gotten a D in my first zoology test.

***

Pedro wrote from Auburn University that he found himself in an unusual situation because Auburn turned out to be for whites only. The blacks had their own university, Tuskegee University, which wasn't that far away. For some reason, Auburn took in many students from Taiwan and considered East Asian students honorary whites.

He was pleased that there was actually a course worth 4 units that would help the premed and pre-dental students prepare for the Medical College Admissions Test (MCAT) and Dental School Admission Test. He was excited to take the class.

He wrote about his speech problem and said that because of it, he most likely wouldn't go into medicine. He reasoned that much less talking was required in dentistry.

***

Danny Tong sent a letter from Howard University saying that the culture of black Americans was so different from the Jamaican culture that he felt like a stranger there. Outwardly, he could easily pass for a black American, but that was where it ended.

His uncle from Jamaica had gotten a scholarship from Howard and was now teaching there. Danny said he was very kind and trying his best to help him. He was taking first-year chemistry, biology and calculus and did well on his first tests.

He thought he would like to stay at Howard for medical school as well. He wrote that he'd met a beautiful black woman from Oakland, California who was studying medical technology there. He sent me a photo of them together and I agreed with Danny that Evelyn looked very much like Sophia Loren with darker skin.

***

Juan wrote that things were going well in Upper 6 and he had decided not to apply to Hong Kong University. Instead, he planned to apply for a job at the Peninsula Hotel the following year as a concierge in training. A good friend of his father's had recommended him for the job.

Juan also wrote that Julia was now in Form 6 at Maryknoll Convent School and was thinking of working for Pan American Airlines as a flight attendant.

***

I received a letter from Lester at the University of Southern Illinois at Carbondale saying that being there was a culture shock, as the brand new university was in a small town in the middle of nowhere in the southern part of Illinois, amidst thousands of acres of corn and soya beans.

He complained that it was already very cold and snowing in October and that it was difficult trying to ride his bicycle to his dishwashing job at the dormitory cafeteria. He chose to live off campus and shared a house with five other foreign students, because the dormitory would be closed during the holidays and between semester breaks, and the foreign students would have nowhere to go.

***

I was hired as a temporary worker at the plush Kahala Hilton Hotel (now The Kahala Resort) and worked full time during the three-week Christmas break. At the end of the break, the assistant manager asked me if I would like to continue working there and I gratefully accepted the offer.

For the rest of my undergraduate years, I worked at that hotel almost full time.

When I finished my second semester, I was able to maintain a 3.00 B average. But I was told that to get into medical school I needed to have at least a 3.50 average.

When summer came, I continued my full time job at the hotel from 7 am to 3 pm. Each morning I would get up at 5:30, have a quick breakfast, then get on my bicycle and ride the 45 minutes to work.

From 4 pm to 9 pm, five or six days a week, I worked as a short order cook at the snack bar in the cafeteria of the East-West Center on campus at the university. It was mostly downhill from the Kahala, so it took just over half an hour on the bike. After taking a quick shower and putting on my uniform, I would be ready for work at 4 pm.

I truly thought I was on top of the world. My life was orderly, and I was responsible for myself. The people I came in contact with, whether they were co-workers or customers, all treated me nicely.

After saving up some money, I bought a used Honda 50 motorcycle for $150, which was much better than riding the bicycle, because Honolulu was such a hilly city and hot most of the time.

***

Summer of 1966: After the first year
Clement wrote from Manila that he finished his first year at Santo Tomas University and did well. He thought he had a good chance of getting into dental school after only two years. He was confident that he could finish all the pre-dental requirements in that time. He mentioned that for some reason not many Filipinos wanted to be dentists, and they all seemed to want to go into medicine. He also noted that most Filipinos didn't go to the dentist until they had rotting teeth or an abscess and were in severe pain.

Tommy Sung wrote from Hong Kong to say that he was home visiting his parents and that the first year at New York University went all right after all. He liked living in New York City, which he said was like Hong Kong.

Michael Sze sent a letter from Hong Kong saying that he'd been accepted by the University of Hong Kong to major in geography. He also wrote that he had visited my parents a few times and that he was helping my sister Cathy with her geography in preparation for her HKSC Exam.

He said that in Upper Form 6 Science, La Salle had a record number of students accepted to the faculty of medicine at the University of Hong Kong, a total of five. In the past, it was usually three or four. I would've loved to have been among them.

***

Fall of 1966: Second Year
The second year of university went well for me. I took 21 units during the fall semester and 19 during the winter semester and continued to maintain a GPA of 3.0 while still working at the hotel almost full time. By the end of my second year, I had fulfilled two thirds of the premed subjects including general chemistry, organic chemistry, physics, genetics and calculus, all of which were hard science subjects.

I was conflicted most of the time. The job at the hotel was too good to turn down and I needed the money; yet I knew I needed to raise my grade point average. I often thought of what Tony said to me about working in school and how I had the rest of my life to make money after I finished. Perhaps I was truly wasting my life trying to make a little money when I should be studying harder.

I went to a few Premed Club meetings and was discouraged that most of the other students had a much higher grade-point average than mine. One fellow even had a GPA. of 4.00!

I couldn't comprehend how some students could get A's in all their courses. How could someone be good in all subjects?

***

Summer of 1967

All was not well in Hong Kong. The anarchy of the Cultural Revolution in China had spilled over into Hong Kong. Pro-Mao elements in Hong Kong included rioting and planting bombs all over. Two young children were killed by a bomb disguised as a toy.

Michael wrote that he had been working on the tram as a conductor because many regular workers stayed home due to the threat of rioters.

My father wrote that he read about Michael's volunteering to work on the tram in the newspaper, and he was quoted as urging the people of Hong Kong not to give in to the pro-Mao rioters.

***

Fall, 1967: Third year

My third year was a disaster. I lost focus and simply didn't know what to do. I began taking history courses, thinking I would give up my dream of going into medicine and get a degree is history instead.

I also took a course in architecture and thought perhaps I should try that. At one point, I thought I would major in geography like Michael. Later, I took several courses in economics and thought I might get a graduate degree, but when I couldn't understand the course in mathematical economics, I concluded that it was out of the question.

Even though I was thinking about majoring in a non-science area, I could still try to get into medical school as long as I completed the pre-med requirements.

When I finished my third year, I had no idea which direction I was heading. I was still hoping to get into medicine, but I was discouraged that my grades weren't good enough. So, I made an irrational decision and decided to go to Indiana University.

***

Summer of 1968

I was happy to hear from Juan that he got the job at the Peninsula Hotel and enjoyed working there.

Michael had finished two years at the University of Hong Kong majoring in geography.

I was thrilled to hear from Julia, who wrote that she had been hired by Pan Am as a flight attendant.

Pedro wrote that he had flown to New Jersey with another boy from Hong Kong to work in the kitchen at the Preakness Country Club. He was quite certain that he would be able to save around fifteen hundred dollars, which should be enough for another year and might mean that he didn't have to work as many hours as a dishwasher.

Felix Sapanov was enjoying London, and was doing well at the London School of Economics. He explained that he would be getting a combined degree in economics and journalism.

***

Fall of 1968

At the end of summer, I flew to Bloomington, Indiana.

Even my application to the university was scattered. I had been accepted by the Indiana University Optometry School as well as the biology department to finish my bachelor's degree. I thought I would make the decision when I got there. When I arrived, it was getting cold and I had no winter clothes. I was missing Hawaii tremendously.

I attended the Optometry School orientation and also attended the first two biology classes, and then decided that I was really homesick for Hawaii and didn't want to stay in Bloomington.

So, I flew back to Hawaii and registered at the University of Hawaii again, but with no idea as to what I would do. There was no way I could graduate the following May.

I was totally lost. I had had too much freedom in Hawaii!

The fall semester of my fourth year was another fiasco. I signed up for four courses of 12 units, and I had to drop half of them because I didn't have the pre-requisite mycology course, which was an in-depth study of fungus. I also had to drop an advanced course in economics, which I simply couldn't understand.

Most of my old classmates from La Salle were planning to graduate the following May, which was less than six months away. I was nowhere near graduation, even though I would have more than the 124 required units, because I didn't have enough concentration in one area to declare a major.

I was back at work at the Kahala Hilton Hotel, but I wasn't feeling good about it. I couldn't stop wondering if Tony was right, if I should be concentrating on my studies instead of focusing on making money while I was a student.

***

In one of Michael's letters, he wrote that Jack Ng, a fellow we both knew, had graduated from the University of California at Berkeley in 1968, after only three years, and would be getting his MA in physics from Harvard in May of 1969.

There in Hawaii, I was nowhere close to a degree, paralyzed for some strange reason and unable to come up with a viable solution to the problem.

I was really ashamed to think that a fellow classmate would be getting an MA from Harvard when I couldn't even figure out how to get a bachelor's degree at a state university.

***

What Have I Become?
There were times when I thought about working at the hotel as my regular job and perhaps getting married. My coworkers at the hotel seemed happy, raising their families and owning their homes.

But I couldn't do that to my parents. They were already telling their friends and relatives in Hong Kong that I was on my way to becoming a doctor and that I was on scholarship. It was true that I was on a tuition scholarship, but only when my grade point average was 3.50 for one single, extraordinary semester!

It was as if I had been heading for disaster in slow motion during the past three and a half years, and yet I did nothing. But what could I have done?

Perhaps I should have been more focused, studied more, worked less and played less. I told myself that I had really tried, but in reality, I had become complacent and had gotten lost along the way without even realizing it.

For most of my life I had been exceptionally disciplined and always knew where I was going, with all sorts of plans and contingencies. But now I had no idea what my next step would be or what I really wanted to do with my life. I thought something must have happened to me and I was no longer ambitious. I didn't even want to think about my future. I had already spent far too much time thinking about it, and it was getting me nowhere. It seemed like the harder I tried, the worse things got.

Most of us had been told to shoot for the stars, but what about those of us who were never able to get off the ground? Some of us were probably aiming for something beyond our reach, outside of our abilities. Then there were the simple statistics of medical school admissions: four applicants for one spot. Every year, there were thousands of students who would never be able to achieve what they'd aimed for. Most of them were qualified to get into medical school but were simply outcompeted, losing out to even more intelligent students, higher achievers and better scores. Did these people who couldn't fulfill their dreams of becoming physicians have regrets, or did they just move on?

Feeling like a failure and getting angrier with myself by the minute, I dwelled on the fact that some of my classmates from La Salle were now thriving in places like Cal Tech, MIT, Dartmouth, Yale, Cornell and Harvard—and here I was floundering in a state university! How could this be happening to me?

Part of the problem of being Chinese was that you not only had to think about yourself, you also had to think about your parents, your family. It was a culture of shame. You wanted your parents to be proud of you and never to bring shame to the family.

My mind was going around in circles, and I was getting nowhere.

***

The Awakening
On December 6, 1968—I remember the date because it was a day before the anniversary of the 1941 bombing of Pearl Harbor by the Japanese—two weeks before the Christmas break, I had an awakening. I had no idea what I would be doing after the next

semester. I was supposed to be graduating in five short months, but I was nowhere close to completing the course requirements for anything at all. I had been busy working at the cafeteria and the hotel; school seemed secondary in importance. It was dusk. Tired from work at the cafeteria, I was walking my bicycle with my head lowered, feeling somewhat somber and deep in thought.

As I got near the water fountain on campus at the end of McCartney Mall by Varney Circle, I heard a voice from the other side of the fountain: "James, guess what? I've been accepted into medical school!"

It was Ka Seng, running toward me. He said he would be starting at the University of Hawaii Medical School the following September. He excitedly shared the details of how tough the competition was and said that the medical school had received hundreds of applications for just 40 first-year positions.

Ka Seng and I had met at the orientation for new students three and a half years earlier. He had been staying at the Baptist student dorm adjacent to campus. We knew each other but didn't spend much time together.

Ka Seng was also from Hong Kong, or more correctly from China. Unlike me, he left China much later. His family stayed when most people were leaving during Mao's takeover in 1949. His grandfather was the mayor of Guangzhou (Canton) at the time and was tortured and later killed in front of his family with a single bullet to the back of his head. To add insult to injury, the family was made to pay for the cost of the bullet. The scene of his grandfather's execution often returned to haunt Ka Seng.

When he was a teenager, he and his family escaped in a fishing boat in the middle of the night to Hong Kong, staying there for a few years before immigrating to Hawaii, where Ka Seng attended McKinley High School and then the University of Hawaii.

Ka Seng was not much fun to be with. He talked incessantly about himself and his problems, and he never listened. He told me that he had a privileged life growing up in Guangzhou and bragged that he had a Stradivarius violin. He had to explain to me what such a violin was, and that it was worth a great deal of money. I doubted many of his stories, but once at a concert given by the Baptist Church, Ka Seng played a violin solo and I was impressed.

We only met when he really needed someone to talk to, someone who would listen to him. One Sunday evening he showed up at the cafeteria when I was working at the snack bar and insisted on talking to me. He seemed a little agitated, his eyes widened as he talked.

Earlier in the day he'd been working in a country club as a bus boy at a private party for a banker's fortieth birthday. When the gigantic birthday cake was brought into the room, out jumped a beautiful girl in the briefest bikini, almost totally naked. Ka Seng was upset by the incident, disturbed that rich people could live such decadent lives, but at the same time aroused by this beautiful, shapely woman. His reason for wanting to talk to me was not so he could condemn such decadence; he was upset because it wasn't him who was living such a life. Talking about his future and medical school, he asked me what specialty I thought would be the most lucrative. When I told him that I thought a neurosurgeon made the most money, he said, "Then that's what I'll be."

That evening, after learning of Ka Seng's acceptance to medical school, I was very pensive. I was really disappointed in myself for having accomplished so little in my three and a half years at the university. I was ashamed of my meager success in life so far. One thing I knew for certain was that I was more capable than Ka Seng. His acceptance into medical school made me realize that I hadn't tried hard enough to reach for my dreams. I determined to redouble my efforts. I knew that if Ka

Seng could get into medical school, I must be able to as well. It was time to pick myself up and get to work.

***

MCAT

During the Christmas break of 1968 I decided to study for the MCAT and the Dental School Admissions Test. By then the deadline for medical school applications had passed. However, there were still a few dental schools I could apply to. I sent in three applications for the fall of 1969.

The results of both tests came back in early spring; surprisingly, I had done very well in both. In the Dental School Admissions Test, I did extremely well in science and my chemistry score was in the ninety-ninth percentile! It couldn't have been any higher. My overall score for the MCAT was in the seventieth percentile and over the eightieth percentile in science.

In May of 1969 I received letters of acceptance from all three dental schools I had applied to: the University of British Columbia in Vancouver, Canada, the University of Missouri in Kansas City and Meharry University in Nashville, Tennessee. The decision was easy: UBC was the most prestigious and the least expensive, as well as the nearest.

After four years at the University of Hawaii, I had no degree, but I was feeling much better than just a few months ago when I really had no idea what to do. Now that I'd been accepted into dental school, I would study hard to be a dentist. I was happy to learn that the life of a dentist would be stable and there would always be a demand for my services.

It was still a disappointment that I didn't graduate. It was so uncharacteristic of me not to finish a task or complete a project. Going to college was like running a race: rules must be obeyed, and if a runner stopped an inch short of the finish line, he or she hadn't finished the race. I had completed 128 units—more than I needed to graduate—but they weren't in the right groups. I didn't follow the rules. Technically I was a college dropout.

The news of my acceptance by the dental school at UBC had overshadowed my failure to graduate. In those days, the people of Hong Kong viewed UBC almost as highly as Harvard, because Canada was also in the Commonwealth, so a professional degree—medicine, dentistry or engineering—from UBC would be automatically accepted in Hong Kong, whereas a degree from Harvard may not. It was extremely difficult for a Hong Kong student to be accepted even as an undergraduate, let alone as a dental student. I simply told my parents that I was finished at the University of Hawaii and hoped they would assume I had graduated. After all, who wouldn't graduate from a university in four years? They didn't ask any questions and I didn't provide any more details.

I worked very hard that summer at the hotel and the cafeteria, requesting overtime shifts whenever I could. When it was time for me to leave for Vancouver, I had saved over five thousand dollars during the past four years, more than sufficient to see me through the first year of dental school.

Michael wrote that Jack Ng got his MA in physics from Harvard in May of 1969 as planned. Everyone I knew from La Salle had graduated, many from prestigious universities.

There in Hawaii, without a degree, I'd thankfully been saved from disgrace by my acceptance to UBC.

***

Julia
Summer of 1969
In mid-August, I began packing and getting ready to head for Vancouver.

I hadn't heard from Julia Anna Trujillo in over a year when she wrote to tell me that that she would have a two-day stop-over in Honolulu with her Pan Am flight crew.

I hadn't even had a chance to say goodbye to her when I left Hong Kong. In high school, we exchanged a few letters telling each other how much we liked each other and saying that school was busy. I visited her brother Juan at their home a few times, and on one occasion she joined us on a hike in the hills surrounding Shatin. We never really dated, as high school students rarely dated in those days.

Juan had filled me in with her news in his letters, and she had written to me a few times. I was thrilled to hear that she would be in Hawaii.

When the day arrived, my heart was racing as my motorcycle neared the Princess Kaiulani Hotel in Waikiki where she and her colleagues were staying.

A beautiful young woman with a short yellow sundress with red hibiscus flowers was sitting in the lobby when I walked in. When I left Julia had been a girl, and now she had become a woman. With a big smile, she jumped up from her chair and ran toward me, her hazel eyes as sparkly as ever. In my four years in America, I had learnt to hug (people in Hong Kong never did) and I gave her one. Then I put the single strand of tuberose lei I'd brought around her slender neck.

Her hair was cut short, displaying her beautiful neck. She was as stunning and vivacious as I remembered her. I thought she was even more beautiful than the Eurasian actress Nancy Kwan.

"What a wonderful fragrance!" she exclaimed, seeming very pleased with the lei.

We walked toward the beach to the Royal Hawaiian Hotel and sat down to have a drink and listen to a trio of Hawaiian musicians playing old-time favorites such as *To You Sweet Heart, Aloha.*

"How lucky you are to have studied here," she said.

"Yes, this is truly a magical place," I answered.

I asked her if she was hungry and she said, "Just a little."

I asked if she wanted to try seared tuna at a small restaurant in the hotel arcade, and she said she'd love to try something Hawaiian.

Julia had been working at Pam Am for two years, and so far she was enjoying it. Her parents didn't like the idea of her flying and suggested that she get a job with her brother at the Peninsula Hotel.

I asked about Juan, and she said he was doing really well at the hotel and enjoying meeting people from all over the world. He was often surprised how generous some Americans were.

"You know, just last week, an American couple gave him a $20 tip in American dollars," she commented. "That's so much money. He was just telling them the best place to dine or something like that. Most of them give him tips, usually a dollar or two, sometimes even in American dollars like that couple. Some months, his tips are more than his regular salary."

"I'm very happy for your brother," I said. "He's a nice guy. I really like him."

The seared tuna was something Julia had never tried before and she really enjoyed it. Afterward, we walked toward the beach and sat on a wooden bench. The sound of the waves was romantic and soothing. The fragrance of the tuberose around her neck put me in a dreamy mood. I extended my right hand and held her left hand. She looked into my eyes and smiled.

I asked her if she would like me to take her for a ride the next day on my motorcycle to show her the University of Hawaii campus as well as the hotel where I worked.

"I would love to!" she said excitedly, her beautiful eyes lighting up.

As I rode home, I felt intensely happy and content. It had been such a long time since I'd felt that way. I began humming the

Mario Lanza song that I liked so well, *The Loveliest Night of the Year*. I recalled an evening in Malaya when I was about thirteen, riding my bicycle home after track training in school. I heard that song on the radio and I felt exactly what the song described—it was the loveliest night and I was immensely happy.

I ought to be happy. My years of uncertainties were over and I was heading to a well-known university for dental school; and today, I had the company of a beautiful woman. Her hazel eyes still reminded me of one of my favorite Spanish songs, *Aquellos Ojos Verdes—Those Green Eyes*. It was truly the loveliest night of the year.

The next morning, I picked Julia up on my motorcycle. She smiled and declared, "My life is in your hands. I'm sure you're a good driver. This is so exciting! I will never tell my parents about this. But I think Juan will think it's all right."

We rode slowly along Waikiki, then up Diamond Head. Julia was surprised that Diamond Head was so barren and dry. We got off the bike and sat down on a bench to watch the surfers below riding the white waves.

We then rode toward the mountain to Tantalus Lookout a few miles north of Waikiki. Just ten minutes away from the bustling city, we came to a deep tropical jungle with huge trees on both sides of the road. As we climbed the steep mountain road, Julia clung to me tightly, which sent chills down my spine.

Riding the motorcycle with a girl at my back reminded me of a blind date I went on two years earlier when I still had my old Honda 50 motorcycle. My date turned out to be a plump girl from Pennsylvania who was in Hawaii for summer school. As we climbed further up the mountain, the bike's exhaust pipe was getting hotter and hotter, and then the engine noise stopped. The motor of the little Honda 50 had overheated and died. We had to turn around and coast down the mountain.

When Julia and I reached the top, we sat down on the grass and enjoyed the view of Waikiki, Diamond Head and the ocean. I related my experience of the blind date to Julia and she burst out laughing.

"It's a good thing you have a new and more powerful bike!" she teased.

"You are less than half that girl's size," I remarked.

We both laughed.

When we were ready to leave, we coasted slowly down the mountain road as I pointed out the different landmarks. I took her to the Kahala Hilton Hotel and introduced her to many of my coworkers.

"You seem to know everyone," she said.

"I've been working here for three and a half years," I responded. "I think this hotel is to Honolulu what the Peninsula is to Hong Kong. I've really been fortunate to work here."

"How could you attend university full time and work full time?" she asked.

"It wasn't that bad," I answered. "I guess I learned to use my time efficiently. I'm glad I was able to work here. Now I have enough money saved to attend UBC without having to work. I think it would be difficult to work in dental school."

"Yes, Juan told me that you'll be going to Canada for dental school. Do you think you'll come back to Hong Kong when you finish?" she asked.

"Probably not if I could stay in America or Canada because, as you know, my family left China because of the communists, and I just don't want to be too close to them," I said with a smile.

"I don't blame you," she said. "Especially with how bad things were in 1967 when there were the riots in Hong Kong. Everyone was trying to immigrate. People would be foolish to come back to Hong Kong if they could stay in America or Canada or

Australia." Her voice had become serious, and I suspected she was thinking about her own situation.

We sat down in the beach-front restaurant under a huge umbrella and had fish and chips for lunch. When I asked for the bill, the waiter, Eddie Flores, told me that the manager, Mrs. Benet, was paying for lunch as a going away present to me since I would be leaving in two weeks.

I thanked Eddie and Mrs. Benet.

As Julia and I walked back to the bike, I said, "If you fly to Vancouver, I would love to see you there."

"Of course, I would love to see you too," she smiled.

We left and drove slowly along the coast as I showed Julia the places I frequented, and then on to the University of Hawaii campus. She was really impressed with how lovely the campus was. She looked around and remarked, "This is like a botanical garden with all the beautiful trees. And many of them have signs showing the name of the tree and where it came from."

We sat down under the giant banyan tree next to the East-West Center where I had my first job as a dishwasher. She extended her hand and held mine.

"James, I think you are an amazing guy," she said. "You're so brave to do all these things on your own. I wish I had more courage."

"Well, you are flying all over the world," I defended. "I think you're courageous also."

Getting up, we continued our tour from the southeast of the campus to the northwest, while I pointed out the different trees along the way.

"This is called a cannonball tree because the fruits really look like cannonballs," I said, pointing to a tall tree loaded with almost perfectly spherical fruits.

She chuckled and exclaimed, "They really do look like cannonballs."

"This one is a sausage tree because as you can see, the fruits really look like huge sausages."

She chuckled again and remarked, "This is so strange. Are the fruits edible?"

"Not to humans," I answered. "I heard that wild pigs like them. But as you can see, they mostly just rot on the ground."

We arrived back at the motorcycle and climbed on, driving slowly back to Julia's hotel. She seemed to have really enjoyed the tour.

As I walked her up to the hotel, Julia was more somber.

"I wish we had known each other better back in school. We were both so busy," she lamented.

She raised her arms to give me a hug. It was difficult to let go of her.

"I hope to see you again," I said. "I hope you'll have stopovers in Vancouver."

As I started walking back to my bike, she ran to me and gave me a kiss on the cheek.

"Good luck in dental school!" she said.

I walked away slowly with a heavy heart, the song *Aquellos Ojos Verdes* playing in my head. I wondered when I would see her again.

***

1969, Fall

Dental school was a fiasco.

After failing my first biochemistry test, I went to see the professor and showed him my chemistry score in the 99.9th percentile on the Dental School Aptitude Test. He explained that general chemistry was quite different from biochemistry and told me to try harder and come see him again if I needed help.

By October, it was raining most of the time. The days were short and I was feeling depressed and anxious, and increasingly worried that I was going into the wrong field.

With the money I'd saved, I didn't have to work that year and could really concentrate on the studies. But my heart just wasn't into it. I was spending a lot of time studying, but the information wasn't sinking in.

By Canadian Thanksgiving, which was in late October, I knew that I just had to apply to medical school. I only applied to one— the University of Hawaii.

In late December, I received a letter of congratulations informing me that I'd been accepted to the School of Medicine of the University of Hawaii.

Finally, the dream of my life, I had another chance.

Again, I packed everything and flew back to Hawaii at the end of the school year.

***

1970, Fall: First Year of Medical School
Things went much better in medical school than they had in dental school. After the first mid-term exam, I passed every subject with mostly B's.

At the end of my first year I had 3.00 grade point average. Of course, a B average in medical school wasn't the same as in undergraduate studies, because I was competing with students who were highly motivated and had gotten into medical school.

I also met my future wife that year, Mary Louise Godfrey, a tall, slim, attractive young instructor in the University of Hawaii Dental Hygiene Department. She had just finished grad school at the University of Iowa. It was love at first sight, and we were married seven months later.

***

In the summer of 1971, I went back to Hong Kong for a visit. It had been six years since I'd seen my parents.

I stopped by the Peninsula Hotel and Juan showed me around. We sat down to have tea in the plushest hotel restaurant, simply called The Lobby. He told me that Julia had gotten married to a nice fellow, a navigator with Pan Am, and was now living near San Francisco.

I also caught up with Michael while I was there, who had been working for the Hong Kong Housing authority and was now the second to the chief.

***

1971, Fall: Second Year in Medical School
My second year went as well as the first, and I maintained my B average.

The medical school at the University of Hawaii was only five years old, and at that point it only offered the first two years, so we had to transfer to a medical school on the continental US for the last two clinical years.

Several medical schools accepted me for transfer. I picked the University of Nebraska.

In the summer of 1972, I passed part one of the National Board of Medical Examiners.

***

1972, Fall: Third Year in Medical School
Mary and I moved to Omaha, Nebraska. That year of medical school went very well, and I earned honors in almost every clinical rotation.

***

1973, Fall: Fourth Year in Medical School
My last year was also successful, with honors again in most of my clinical rotations. In May, I graduated and got my MD degree.

That summer, I did very well in part two of the National Board of Medical Examiners.

***

July 1, 1974: Internship in Fresno
The internship at VMC (Valley Medical Center), the large county hospital serving the indigent in the San Joaquin Valley, was a very difficult year. I was working thirty-six hours straight whenever I was on call, which was every third day. Sleep deprivation was a horrible experience. I barely survived.

I had originally planned to return to the University of Nebraska for my orthopedic residency, but decided to go into family practice because of the malpractice crisis at the time, during which malpractice insurance premiums for an orthopedic surgeon in California were over $200,000.00 a year.

At the last moment, I accepted an offer to be the chief resident of a new Family Practice program at the Natividad Medical Center in Salinas, California. It was a program run by the University of California San Francisco Medical Center.

CHAPTER 10:
Fifteen Years (1975 to 1989)

July 1975

THE FAMILY PRACTICE RESIDENCY PROGRAM started on July first. The bucolic country in the California Central Coast area is indeed idyllic: with its mild climate year-round, it's known as the salad bowl of the nation. It produces much of the nation's lettuce; other vegetables such as broccoli and artichoke are also widely grown. With Monterey Bay half an hour away, Mary and I felt like we were in paradise.

Later in July, I got the results of part three of the National Boards, and I had done very well. I was pleased with my score, which was in the sixty-fifth percentile—290 was passing and mine was 535. Shortly after that I got my California physician and surgeon license. With a diploma from the National Boards, I would be able to practice medicine in every state without further examination.

***

The very busy county hospital where I was to do my residency was Natividad Medical Center. It was a smaller version of Valley Medical Center, serving basically the same kinds of patients: all those who could not or would not go to the private sector hospitals. Much like Fresno, most of the agricultural workers were Mexicans, but the area also held a sizable population of Filipinos.

The Family Practice Program was brand new and had been established in response to the shortage of primary care physicians in California. I was given the official title of Chief Resident, since I was the sole second-year resident and also the only house staff with a medical license. None of the six interns could write orders or prescriptions without a signature from me.

There, I met Dr. George U. Thant Aw, the Mayo Clinic-trained urologist who was originally from Burma. He encouraged me to go into urology, as he was already busier than he liked to be and would be ready for an associate in a few years. I was flattered that he was already inviting me to join his practice.

***

Natividad was more than a hospital. It was the place that provided care for almost all of the Mexicans and indigent in the area. Next to the ER was the general clinic—the back of which had no wall, only a curtain—consisting of eight exam rooms. I literally ran from one room to another, seeing as many as six to eight patients an hour.

A few weeks into the program I realized that I had made a mistake. I was the workhorse and a source of cheap labor for the hospital, but I wasn't learning from anyone. Each morning, to psych myself up to face the general clinic, I had to drink two large cups of strong coffee and listen to marching music by John Philip Sousa before I could take the five-minute walk to meet the throngs of waiting patients. The red lights above all eight rooms would be lit up, indicating that a patient was waiting in each room. Once at the clinic, I worked nonstop, going from one patient to another without even sitting down. In addition to the general clinic, I also had to take care of whatever came in through the ER. I prided myself that I could suture up a child's cut in five minutes and still do an excellent job.

By noon my head would be pounding and spinning and I would escape to hide in the nearby bushes where a small creek flowed to calm my nerves. By then I was physically and emotionally drained and needed to recharge. In four hours, I would have seen over thirty patients and I needed some silence.

It was exceedingly stressful trying to manage so many patients with chronic diseases, many of whom had been patients at the clinic for years and never had a definitive management plan. How could anyone formulate a meaningful management plan when he had to see so many patients in an hour? There were many patients with chronic headaches who never had the proper workups. Each time, a patient's visit was much like the previous visit, usually ending with a prescription for more codeine pills. I lived in fear that some of them had more severe problems, but I didn't have the time to do the proper diagnostic workups. When I saw a patient with a headache, my own head began to ache from worrying that I was sitting on a time bomb such as a brain tumor growing inside the patient's head.

Many elderly people came in suffering from insomnia. When I didn't give them any medicine for sleep, their families often got angry. Grandma was keeping everybody up at night. When I did prescribe medicine for sleep, other members of the patients' families accused me of trying to turn Grandma into a drug addict. It was an impossible and often thankless job.

I was trying to manage the blood sugar level of one diabetic woman, but she wouldn't follow the instructions for her diet and would not lose weight. She told me that she'd been drinking diet Pepsi and was surprised that she still hadn't lost any weight— she thought the diet Pepsi itself had ingredients that would actually cause weight loss!

The patients with emphysema who continued to smoke were the most frustrating. A few times I almost lost my temper. How could I pretend to be taking care of these patients when I couldn't even make them value their own health? It was demoralizing.

Manuel Sanchez, a local union leader for the lettuce farm workers, had been a heavy smoker for over twenty years and was having problems breathing. During one of his visits, I couldn't contain myself any longer and told him that he really should quit.

"Doc, you think I wouldn't quit if I could?" he retorted, sounding annoyed. He could only speak in a whisper because of the shallow breaths and chronic fatigue of advanced emphysema. He was having trouble talking and walking as well, but continued to light up one cigarette after another.

Another group of patients that exasperated me was those with hypertension. They refused to exercise and stop eating high salt and fatty snacks, and instead expected some little pills to rid them of the problem that was shortening their lives.

Each day I had to face over sixty such patients! I truly believe that the process of taking care of a patient involves an exchange of energy: the positive energy flows from the physician to the patient, and the negative from the patient to the physician. I had nothing to prove it—it was only my own theory—but at the end of each day I would be totally drained and completely numb.

***

A Mexican worker showed up one day at the ER after slicing off the tip of his left thumb. It wasn't a deep cut, just the skin and a thin layer of flesh. The treatment as I had learned it was to take a small piece of skin from another area and graft it to the thumb to help it heal.

After anesthetizing an area on his forearm with Lidocaine, I scrubbed it with Betadine and then carefully dissected a dime-sized piece of skin and put it in a saline solution. Once the thumb was cleaned thoroughly, it too was anesthetized. I carefully placed the piece of skin over the injured thumb and stitched the edges with extremely fine sutures. Fluffy cotton balls were placed over the site, followed by layers of gauze, and the thumb was then wrapped. The patient's hand was placed in a sling to keep it elevated and prevent swelling. I prescribed antibiotics to prevent infection.

Ideally such a procedure should have been done by a surgeon, or even a plastic or hand surgeon, but this was a county hospital and sometimes the patient didn't have the luxury of choosing from the best physicians. I felt comfortable with the procedure and was satisfied that I did a good job—the graft took and it healed beautifully: a success!

I had felt for a long time that I should go into some sort of surgery, and with the success of the skin graft I was convinced that I needed to go into a surgical specialty. My unhappy experience at Natividad had proven that primary care was not for me.

***

Four months into the program I decided that I could no longer continue. I'd been thinking of going into ophthalmology or urology, because a physician in these areas could really help the patients, and the results would be almost immediate. It was October and many programs had already selected their residents for the following July. The Eye Residency Program at VMC was in the process of selecting their one resident for the following year, and I quickly sent in my application.

My brother Chung had now earned his PhD in microbiology and was in dental school at the Medical College of Georgia in Augusta. I decided to send an application in to the urology program there as well.

The director of the intern and residency programs at VMC called me a few weeks later and congratulated me on my acceptance into the Eye Program, telling me that there had been thirty applicants for that one position. I thanked him profusely and told him how honored I was, and gladly accepted the offer.

Shortly after that I heard from the urology department of the Medical College of Georgia that I had been accepted there as well. I thanked them and said that I had already made another decision.

Resigning my position as chief resident, I negotiated a contract to remain at Natividad as a staff physician, working as the main ER physician in the very busy department. I was doing the same work, but with fewer hassles and getting paid three times as much. Now we could finally save some money.

The work at Natividad was hard, but I was adequately compensated and I didn't mind it. At the same time, I was gaining more experience in general and emergency medicine and becoming a very competent general physician, obtaining knowledge that would be useful later on.

It was good that I had tried primary care and I left it with no regrets.

***

In the summer of 1976, I was at Stanford University taking a basic science course before I began my ophthalmology residency. Through Xavier Keng, I learned that Hugo Ting and Jack Ng were at the Linear Accelerator at the University doing post-doctoral fellowships. Both had gotten their PhDs in particle physics.

I invited them to our small apartment at the Escondido Village on campus. At that point, we only had one child; Melissa was two. I had cooked Malayan beef curry.

I hadn't seen either of them since I left Hong Kong in 1965. Hugo was as fit and trim as ever, with a smile on his face, and always appropriate. He had scored the highest in the A-level in Hong Kong and was awarded a scholarship to California

Technological Institute (Cal Tech), and got his PhD from MIT.

Jack Ng too had scored off the charts and had gotten a PhD from Harvard.

Physics and math were my weaker areas. I had always admired people who were good in those two subjects. I just never had the brain for higher math.

The beef curry cooked with coconut milk turned out to be quite good. Over dinner, I listened with fascination about the work they were doing, which was beyond my comprehension.

Hugo asked me about astigmatism, since I was going into ophthalmology. I hesitated and then declared that I really knew very little about the subject, which was the reason I was taking this course. As a physicist, he knew a great deal more about optics than I did, so he explained to me what he knew.

"Are you happy in medicine, James?" Hugo asked.

"I really am," I replied. "I'm especially happy that I'm going into ophthalmology. I truly enjoy doing surgery."

To my surprise, Hugo asked me about medical school and said that he was thinking about it. I told him that being a physician was a lot of hard work, unlike physics, which mostly used the brain.

"Why are you considering it?" I asked.

"There have been so many PhDs awarded in the physical sciences," he explained, "and jobs are scarce. Some of my fellow students in graduate school switched to medicine, and with their PhDs, a lot of them finished medical school in three years. Others who stayed in physics have had to do post-doc fellowships one after another, because there just aren't many permanent positions."

It was a surprising revelation. In my mind, I didn't even belong in the same league as Hugo and Jack. I couldn't even get into the science section of Form 6. Now Hugo was thinking of going into medicine, something I'd been able to get into.

He explained that he didn't think he would actually practice medicine, but an MD degree would open many more doors, such as research in new diagnostic equipment, which often came with huge grants. He thought he could invent some new machines, and a background in medicine would certainly help.

Like me, Hugo was born in China. His family was from Shanghai. They went to Hong Kong about the same time as mine, when the masses were fleeing China. His family was better off than mine, having arrived with more money, and life was more stable for them, unlike so many other refugee families in Hong Kong.

After getting his BS from Cal Tech, he continued at MIT where he got his PhD in theoretical physics, and he called himself a cosmologist.

"Sometimes people mistakenly call me a cosmetologist," he joked.

We all laughed.

I knew Hugo better than I knew Jack Ng because Hugo was also on the sport teams at La Salle. He had specialized in medium distance running, such as the 800m and longer. I remembered one day on the field very well as he talked about his dream of being in the Olympics, probably because the 1964 Olympics were held in Tokyo and many of us had been able to watch it on television.

He and Tony Hu were good friends. I asked him if he knew what Tony was doing, and he said Tony had graduated from the University of Sydney and was working somewhere in Eastern Australia.

***

With the money we had saved from my work at Natividad, Mary and I bought a house not far from VMC where I would be doing my three-year residency, a training program in Fresno affiliated with the University of California, San Francisco.

The three years went by quickly. I did well on the written and oral parts of the Board of Ophthalmology exam and became a board certified ophthalmologist.

MaryAnne, our second daughter, was born in March of 1977.

At the end of my residency I decided to do a fellowship in retinal surgery to increase my proficiency, considering the possibility of limiting my practice to retinal surgery.

I was accepted to the program at the University of California San Francisco, one of the top programs in the country at the time. During the interview, the director of the program pointed to a row of portraits on the wall of his office and said, "Your picture will be on the wall next." He went on to tell me that there were fifty applicants for that one position.

During my fellowship, our son James was born.

After the fellowship, I returned to Hong Kong to evaluate work opportunities there. The irony was that although American medical schools set high standards and the training was intense, in order to practice in Hong Kong I would have to sit for their basic medical licensure exam, because the Hong Kong Medical Council wouldn't recognize the credentials I had obtained in the US.

***

Summer of 1980

After a year in the San Francisco area, I had gotten used to the cool weather year-round. It was a surprise to me to feel the sweltering heat of Hong Kong in July. I felt sorry for the many businessmen who had to wear suits and ties.

I visited two ophthalmologists and enquired about practicing in Hong Kong. Both of them suggested that I work in a hospital first before setting up a private practice. The ophthalmologist I saw when I was in Form 5 who charged me so much and gave me useless medicine had retired.

Clement Tam and I decided to have lunch at the restaurant famous for Har Tu Si just as we had so many years ago.

Clement seemed pleased with how his life had panned out. In dental school, he met a local Chinese girl from Manila, Maria Elena Chua. They got married while still in school, and now she also worked out of the same office on Prince Edward Road, in the same building where they had a large apartment on the twentieth floor of Kirin Court, a huge luxury apartment complex three blocks from La Salle. They had three children, twin boys aged six and a girl of four.

His uncle who owned the store in Kowloon City, and who had been so kind to him, still hung around the store, but Clement had employed a manager who ran the day-to-day operations of the store. His aunt, who had been bedridden from a stroke and whom his uncle took such good care of, passed away soon after Clement went to Manila for university.

Clement had also helped his stepmother and three half siblings out of Madagascar, a wish that his father had before he died. They now lived with his family.

We compared notes on our dental school experiences. He laughed and commented that I was probably the first person in history who had failed dental school, then went to medical school and became a retinal surgeon.

I was surprised to hear that he had graduated from the University of the Philippines College of Dentistry instead of Santo Tomas as I remembered him planning. He said he changed his mind when he learned that the University of the Philippines dental college had a much better reputation and was less expensive, and also, he was guaranteed to get a license to practice in Hong Kong.

The next day, I met Michael and Juan at the Peninsula Hotel and had tea and scones in the famous restaurant in the lobby, The Lobby.

Michael had had many promotions and was now head of the housing authority. As always, he seemed to be beaming with confidence. He had married a Hong Kong girl he met at university who had also graduated with a degree in geography.

Juan revealed that Julia had moved to Honolulu with her husband and two children. "I really liked Hawaii," Juan reflected. "When Julia gets settled, perhaps at some point I'll consider moving there. Hong Kong is exciting but it's such a small place with so many people. It seems that everything is difficult here. In the back of my mind, I sometimes worry about what will happen when it's time for England to hand it over to the Chinese."

"Yes, Hawaii is wonderful. I just love the place," I agreed. "I thought about practicing there, but since my parents now live in San Francisco, I feel I should be around them," I added.

Juan seemed pleased with his job as head concierge at the Peninsular. They had treated him well at the hotel, and had bought him an apartment in Tsim Sha Tsui East, not far from the hotel. He said he was toying with the idea of going to the University of Hawaii to get a degree in hotel management so that he could move up into management rather than being a concierge all his life.

"Juan, you could look into getting a degree from the University of Hong Kong's College of Business Administration so that you don't have to uproot the family to Hawaii. You can study part-time and keep your job here," advised Michael.

Juan said it sounded like an excellent idea and that he would look into it.

As I sat in the fancy restaurant with my two old friends, I couldn't help but remember how the three of us would take the train to school together each morning. So far, our lives had turned out quite well.

In the end, I didn't sit for the Hong Kong medical licensure examination, deciding that my life was now in California and not Hong Kong. I had wanted to get away from Hong Kong for fear of the communists all my life. It would make no sense if I returned, especially now that my parents had moved to the US, and I had no close relatives left there.

I hadn't really planned where to practice because I was so busy with my training, but once I decided not to return to Hong Kong, I knew I would most likely stay in California.

Before we made the decision to stay in California, we did check out Hawaii just to convince ourselves that it was the right decision.

I interviewed at the famous Straub Clinic in Honolulu and was discouraged that the ophthalmologists were working very hard and not getting paid as much as those in California, and that living expenses in Hawaii were higher. Another reason that dissuaded us was that many families chose to send their children to private schools, which would be a great expense for us as we had three children then. Even though I loved Hawaii, to work and live there with children would be another thing.

On my return to the US I took an offer in Bakersfield, California, since they didn't yet have a fellowship-trained retina specialist.

***

A week into my job, I got a call from Pedro Hoy, who had seen the announcement my boss placed in the newspaper stating that I'd joined him in his practice. Pedro told me he'd been practicing dentistry in town for almost five years.

We met for lunch at the Bamboo Garden Chinese Restaurant and caught up on what we'd been up to since we last saw each other on the President Cleveland. He said his four years of undergrad at the whites-only Auburn University was interesting, but he didn't feel too out of place because there were over a hundred students from Taiwan and a handful from Hong Kong and India. While there, he met a girl from Taiwan and they got married during his last year of dental school.

From Auburn, Pedro went to Meharry University Dental School in Nashville, Tennessee, as it was the only dental school that accepted him. He was the only non-black student in the class. He joked that Auburn was an all-white school and Meharry was an all-black school, but being yellow, he managed to survive at both.

We chuckled.

After graduation, Pedro decided to move to Bakersfield where his wife had a cousin from Taiwan who had just opened his urology practice.

In the course of our lunch, he revealed that while at Meharry, he was diagnosed with Beckwith-Wiedemann Syndrome. For a long time, nobody knew why his left side grew more than his right side, or why his tongue was large and difficult to control, but now he knew it was because of this syndrome.

Fortunately, the Beckwith-Wiedemann Syndrome that afflicted Pedro wasn't severe. He didn't develop any kidney or liver tumors, which was a higher risk for people with the syndrome. The asymmetry of his face wasn't very obvious; but his large tongue interfered with his speech and he had difficulty pronouncing certain words. I remembered him telling me that the main reason he was pursuing dentistry rather than medicine was because he wouldn't have to do a lot of talking as a dentist. It seemed that he'd made a good choice.

Two months into my job, I realized that it was a mistake to have taken the position. My boss was an eccentric man and a horrible surgeon, but he refused to accept his incompetence and continued doing surgery.

Case after case, his patients' sight got worse after surgery. I decided that I couldn't be part of it and submitted my resignation.

My contract was for one year, so I had to finish the year. Since I had no training in setting up an office or billing, I decided to spend my free time with the billing department and learn how to bill for my services.

When my year was up, we returned to Fresno where I had done my residency and opened a practice.

A week after opening my office, I got a call from Danny Tong. He had been in practice in Fresno for over two years. He invited me to lunch and bragged that he knew all the owners of the best Chinese restaurants in town.

Over lunch, I learned that after medical school at Howard University, Danny did a residency in internal medicine at the Mayo Clinic in Minnesota. While at Howard, he met and married a woman who was studying medical technology there. She was from a prominent black family in Oakland, California.

"I heard there are two old boys from La Salle in the Chicago area," he commented. "Lester Tung, who went to the University of Southern Illinois and then graduated from the University of Illinois Medical School in Chicago. He did a family practice residency and now works for a large clinic there. The other is Mason Moon."

"I remember him," I said. "He was in Forms 4 and 5 with me. His English was so good he sounded like a native speaker. It turned out that his mother was from Vancouver, Canada."

Danny nodded. "Well he graduated from Northwestern University and is now an Ob-gyn in Chicago."

Danny also told me that James Yeung, who had gone to the University of Manitoba, had graduated from medical school there as well, and was now back in Hong Kong working as a GP.

James Yeung was born in Hong Kong and never had any intention of leaving Hong Kong, unlike many of us who were born elsewhere and always knew that Hong Kong was just a temporary place for us.

The five old boys who were accepted to the Faculty of Medicine of the University of Hong Kong (after the two years in pre-university) had graduated two years ahead of Danny and three years ahead of me, because of my year in dental school.

"You should join the Fresno Chinese Doctors Association," said Danny. "I helped found it last year."

"There are enough Chinese doctors in Fresno to have an association?" I asked incredulously.

"Yes," answered Danny. "We included dentists too. It's amazing that in a mid-size American town there are over twenty Chinese physicians and dentists. The majority are from Taiwan, and there are four local-born Chinese physicians."

"Speaking of dentists," I said, "Pedro Hoy is practicing dentistry in Bakersfield now."

"Great!" exclaimed Danny. "Next month is the association's bi-annual meeting. Why don't you get an extra ticket and invite Pedro? I haven't seen him since we left the President Cleveland."

The dinner and meeting was held at the Four Seasons Chinese Restaurant run by a Hong Kong family, who had the best Chinese food in town.

The occasion was to celebrate the jade exhibition at the Fresno Museum. One of the Taiwanese doctors who knew some important person in Taiwan managed to convince him to loan a number of famous jade carvings to exhibit at the local museum. Initially I wasn't happy about it, because two established, local-born doctors wouldn't take no for an answer when they asked me for a donation of a thousand dollars to fund the exhibition. As I had just begun my practice, money was scarce and it was a lot to ask for. At the same time, as a new doctor, I also thought it was important to have the good will of the established doctors, so I consented. In the end, I thought it was a good cause.

Sitting at our table were Pedro and Danny and the group of local-born Chinese doctors. One of them, Dr. Arthur Mar, was talking about how badly the local university football team had performed that year, with all losses and no wins, and the coach was fired.

His comments reminded me of a joke I'd heard, so I thought I'd try it out. "Art, did you hear that Fresno State University has hired a new football coach, and he happens to be a Chinese guy?" I asked.

Dr. Mar shook his head and looked surprised, saying, "No, I hadn't heard. What's his name?"

With a straight face, I declared, "Win Some Soon."

Dr. Mar smiled uncertainly, until I burst out laughing and he realized it was joke. Still chuckling, he went to the next table and announced, "Hey guys, did you hear what Jimmy said about the new Chinese football coach for Fresno State University?"

Everyone laughed. One doctor laughed so hard he almost fell of his chair.

When dinner was served, the most popular dish was the pork belly and taro cooked in sweet soya sauce. I remarked to Danny and Pedro, "These Chinese doctors certainly don't believe in a healthy diet!"

We chuckled. Everyone had a good time. Pedro had a two-hour drive south back to Bakersfield at the end of the night, but he was glad he came.

In August 1983, our youngest child Elizabeth was born.

1984

In the spring of 1984, I went to the Jules Stein Eye Institute of UCLA for an eye meeting, and after that I decided to pay Tommy

Sung a visit at his new Bel Air home on the west side of Los Angeles, in the foothills of the Santa Monica Mountains.

It was evening and the road was winding, making the drive a very difficult one. After struggling to find the address, I finally reached Tommy's house. It was a six-bedroom mansion with a swimming pool on the side of a hill. The driveway leading to his house was lined with royal palm trees.

He now had four children: three girls, and the youngest a son. His parents had insisted that he have a son to carry on the family's name. I noticed that he had two Mexican maids.

For a rich boy, Tommy had worked very hard. After La Salle, he got a degree in civil engineering from NYU, then an MS in civil engineering from UCLA, and then an MBA from Wharton's Business School of the University of Pennsylvania. Perhaps if I'd been in his shoes, I would have goofed off and lived off my father's riches.

Tommy seemed depressed. He was worried that the two hundred condo units he'd just completed weren't moving as fast as he hoped. He blamed it on the high interest rates, which were over twelve percent at the time.

"James, I can't believe that this is all there is to life," he said, looking distressed. "I seem to worry about everything. It's hopeless. I thought once I finished my education, I'd be a happier man, but it only got worse as the years went by. Now I worry about the children."

It was very sad to see someone who seemed to have everything in life so unhappy.

I was excited to share what news I had of the other old boys, but he didn't seem the least bit interested. He was consumed with worries, big and small. He complained angrily that his children didn't wipe the dirt off their shoes before getting into the car, and they had made a mess in his silver Rolls Royce.

Being with a friend who was so negative wasn't much fun. Certainly, I had a great deal more fun with Danny and Pedro than with Tommy, who I envied in school because he seemed to have it all. Now, it was clear to me that money indeed couldn't buy happiness.

With a young family and a busy practice, one year blended into another.

Fresno was an easy city to raise a family in. The children went to schools in the neighborhood and there was no pressure on them. It was quite different from being in Hong Kong, where parents would do anything to get their children into elite schools.

We encouraged them to participate in all sorts of sports so they would lead balanced lives. They all learned to swim when they were around three years old. They took piano lessons, tennis lessons, social dance lessons, or any extracurricular music or sports lessons they were interested in.

Each Sunday morning, after 9 am mass at St. Paul's Church next to Fresno State University, we would stop by a donut shop to take home our favorite donuts. Some Sundays, I had to see my patients at the hospital, and Mary and the kids would wait in the car.

The family grew and my practice prospered.

My parents were now living in Chinatown, San Francisco, where I would visit them once a month.

In 1987, Mary and I bought a building north of town next to the hospital. The building had about 7,000 square feet, which I rented half of to a plastic surgeon, and used the rest for my own office. It turned out to be an excellent investment.

Michael had written that he would be taking a leadership course at Stanford University in the summer of 1987. He also gave me Xavier Keng's phone number, who was working as a computer chip designer with Intel, and living not far from Stanford.

The three of us met at the Canton Chinese Seafood Restaurant in San Francisco's Chinatown. Michael was always full of news about everyone in our class. Xavier seemed distracted and a little sad. He finally revealed that while on an extended vacation in Hong Kong, he left his huge dog, a black Rottweiler, with his tenant at his mansion in Hillsborough, an exclusive neighborhood not far from Stanford University.

For some unknown reason, the dog bit the tenant's face, a Chinese woman who was an electrical engineer. She was hospitalized for over a month and needed extensive plastic surgery to reconstruct her face, which required a skin flap from her thigh. Xavier was in the midst of negotiations with her lawyers about compensation. "Fortunately," he said, "I have adequate insurance and it will involve very little, if any, out-of-pocket money." But he was obviously traumatized by the incident and truly felt very sorry for the woman, whose face would never be the same.

Later, Xavier drove Michael and me in his new silver Porsche to his mansion overlooking the San Francisco Bay. While at his house, I recounted my visit with Tommy in Los Angeles. Xavier and Tommy had been friends since the fifth grade. Xavier shook his head and commented, "Money really doesn't buy happiness, does it?"

"That's exactly what I thought," I agreed.

***

In the summer of 1989, China again seemed to be in chaos. Tiananmen Square was occupied by tens of thousands of students who demanded more democracy.

On June 4, the Communist Party sent in tanks and troops and slaughtered an unknown number (probably hundreds or even thousands) of students.

The people of Hong Kong were petrified. Their eyes were glued to the TV for several days as events unfolded. They worried about their own fates, as the handover date of 1997 wasn't far away.

In the back of my mind, and the minds of many others, it was exactly the scenario that we had feared. The communists could never be trusted. I was very glad that I had decided not to return to Hong Kong, and grateful for my life in California.

CHAPTER 11

25th Reunion

IN LATE NOVEMBER 1989, the class of 1964 had its first real reunion. In the past, old boys had gathered in Hong Kong, San Francisco, New York, Vancouver and Toronto whenever they could for a reunion, but usually in groups of less than ten. Under the leadership of my good friend Michael Sze and Vincent Lo, some of the old boys had organized the 25th reunion event.

Our class took the HKSC Exam in May of 1964. Who would believe that the year 1989, a year so futuristic in our minds, would ever become the present? We were seventeen or eighteen; our twenty-fifth class reunion was impossibly remote. Now it was here.

About a third of the over two hundred classmates from all over the world were expected to attend.

Most of us would now be around 43 years old—give or take a year or two—and would be at the peak of our careers. Of more than 200 in the class, probably a third had immigrated to places around the world. Most had gone to the US, Canada, Australia, and a few to New Zealand, England, Jamaica, Fiji and Singapore.

The class of 1964 was an impressive bunch. Among us, there were over ten PhDs, more than ten physicians, over twenty engineers, several lawyers and certified accountants, a movie star, several high government officials, many businessmen, and even one FBI agent.

Hong Kong in 1989 was very different from 1964 in many aspects, except that money and status were still the most important things. One only had to look at the Peninsula Hotel with its fleet of shiny green Rolls Royce limousines out front to know it.

I had brought along my son, James, and we left Hong Kong to visit my brother Paul in Guilin, China for a few days. Paul had graduated from the University of Hawaii in Hotel Management and was now the general manager of the Sheraton Hotel in Guilin. Tourist business was bad in China following the Tiananmen Square Massacre a few months earlier. The Sheraton Hotel in Guilin was devoid of foreign tourists and was almost empty.

After our visit, James and I flew back to Hong Kong for the reunion.

Sadly, the beautiful old Romanesque La Salle College had been replaced with a modern building, because the old building needed a great deal of upkeep and was costing more money than the school could afford. A deal was made with the billionaire, Mr. Li Ka Sheng, in which the school gave him a third of its campus, and in return Mr. Li built a new school for free. Following that, Mr. Li built luxury condos on the ceded land.

The first order of business was to meet in the new school's assembly hall. The president of the Old Boy's Association for the class of 1964 was Michael Sze, who gave a short speech welcoming those who had traveled from afar. Because of his contribution to Hong Kong's prosperity, he was awarded by the Queen and was now CBE (Commander of the Order of the British Empire), the highest title that could be awarded to a non-Brit.

He and I had remained in frequent contact throughout the years and had visited each other's homes. He was an excellent speaker and was full of humor at the reunion.

Next to speak was the current principal of the school. There used to be about ten or more Christian Brothers at the school, but now, with the fall in vocation, only the principal was a Brother.

The first event was a tour of the school building. Although new to me, it was already several years old, and not new to those who had remained in Hong Kong.

The new building was beautiful and was rated as one of the best-equipped high schools in Hong Kong. It still had a sports field and soccer field and, in addition, it now had an Olympic size swimming pool, perhaps the only high school in Hong Kong with one. It was truly impressive; but I missed the old building, especially the chapel where I had often asked God for favors.

Some of the old boys had brought their spouses and children along. James found a friend and was soon busy playing with another boy his age.

Following the tour of the school, we walked to nearby Kowloon City to a famous Cantonese seafood restaurant for a ten-course banquet. As we ate, one by one, the old boys stood up and spoke for a few minutes about what they had done since we left La Salle. Everyone was modest and many told interesting stories about life in a foreign country.

Sitting next to me was Henry Young, our Australian-born classmate. Henry was now a famous writer and photographer in Sydney. He recently had an exhibition in Hong Kong of photos he'd taken. I learned that he'd also had exhibitions in Tokyo, Taiwan, Sydney, Toronto, New York and San Francisco. He had also become a gay rights activist.

Henry had always been a quiet but outspoken fellow. He didn't talk much in class but when he did, it was always something meaningful. He seemed much more conversational than I remembered. He talked about his strict Hakka father and how he never had the courage to tell his father that he was gay. "I realized that he would never understand, and would be beside himself if he found out that his only son was gay," said Henry. "My father died without knowing. Which is just as well," he added.

"I only told my mother a while ago," he continued, "when I realized it was inevitable that she'd find out because I was becoming increasingly visible as an activist."

"How did she take it?" I asked.

"She cried for three days," he answered, "and then asked me never to talk about it again."

I shook my head sympathetically. I couldn't imagine being in his situation, but I knew I would never tell my parents if I were gay, because they simply wouldn't understand and it would only upset them. It was tough to be a Chinese son or daughter in that regard. Parents of a gay child would take it as a disgrace to the family, and believe that it was the result of bad karma. They would regard it as a reflection on them, that perhaps they did something wrong as parents.

Henry said that while in Sydney, he had become good friends with the three other La Salle fellows there, including Benjamin Cheung, whose house we were going to the following day.

The next day, Saturday, we met at Benjamin's mansion on the Peak. I barely remembered Benjamin, as we were never in the same class.

Michael briefed me about Benjamin's success story before we went. He was a true Hong Kong boy. He, his father and his grandfather were all born in Hong Kong. His grandfather started Cheung's Jewelry just before WWII. Their family had to flee Hong Kong when the Japanese occupied it, and when they returned to Hong Kong after the war, instead of selling jewelry, his grandfather opened a pawnshop. As over a million and half refugees poured into Hong Kong, many were poor like my family and had to sell their valuables. Business was brisk, and before long it was firmly established as the most honest pawnshop in the city.

Since most of the jewelry pawned was never reclaimed, Benjamin's grandfather, who had connections in Singapore,

Malaysia, Thailand and the Philippines, would sell the jewelry to his connections in those countries where there was a sizable Chinese population with money.

After Form 5, Benjamin went to Sydney and got a diploma from a business college. While in Australia, he was fascinated with the Australian opal, which had not yet become a popular gemstone in Hong Kong. After graduation, he spent some time studying the opal industry there, and visited opal mines such as Coober Pedy and also the famous mine that produced the spectacular black opals at Lightning Ridge.

On his return to Hong Kong, Benjamin convinced his father and grandfather to promote opals. He visited a small gem cutting shop in Aberdeen, Hong Kong and took a position as the chief cutter's apprentice. After two years, he had learned enough about the trade of cutting opal to move on.

In the meantime, the people of Hong Kong were getting richer. According to Michael, the real break for Benjamin came in the early 1980s when Hong Kong as a whole became rich, during the so-called "go-go years." Benjamin opened a large opal-cutting factory in Aberdeen and bought uncut opals directly from the miners he'd met in Australia. He also invested in the Argyle Diamond Mine in northwest Australia, and he opened a second factory in Aberdeen to cut the rough diamonds into gemstones.

Soon, Cheung's Jewelry became one of the largest importers of rough opals and Australian diamonds to Hong Kong, and Benjamin became a Hong Kong dollar billionaire.

Before long, Benjamin had cornered the market on naturally colored diamonds—champagne, cognac and rare blue diamonds. Recently, it was reported in the newspaper that Cheung's Jewelry sold the largest rare blue diamond in Hong Kong for ten million Hong Kong dollars.

Benjamin's mansion at the Peak—which he reportedly bought for $50 million US—was on almost half an acre of land, surrounded by all kinds of fruit trees: lychee, dragon-eye, mango, papaya, banana and so on. The property had a spectacular view of the Hong Kong Harbor.

As we strolled onto the grounds, Michael commented, "Remember that not so long ago, just before WWII, no Chinese were allowed to live at the Peak? Now, Benjamin's mansion is one of the largest."

It was a beautiful clear late autumn day, and a soothing breeze was blowing. The *pak lan* trees no longer had flowers on them. I imagined how fragrant the place would be in the summer when the trees were loaded with flowers.

Benjamin had arranged for stalls of street food to be set up in the immense garden. Most of us had grown up with this kind of food—*dai pai dong*, a type of open-air food stall in Hong Kong. The most popular were the soupy noodle stands, especially the wonton noodle. I had two bowls of fish ball noodle soup.

Every kind of childhood snack was also served: fried sticky rice balls, coconut and sticky rice, layered cake, all sorts of sweet buns and cakes, and even the Malay *jando*—a dessert made with coconut milk, palm sugar and red beans in shaved ice.

As the old boys and their families arrived, we strolled through the magnificent setting and sampled our childhood foods. It was the perfect setting for a reunion because we could mingle and talk to many different people instead of being in a restaurant, sitting next to someone we may or may not even know or like.

Large, outdoor speakers played the song *Below the Lion Rock* in the background. It was a popular Cantonese song composed by one of our schoolmates, James Wong Jim, who was a few years ahead of us, and sung by Roman Tam, the top male vocalist in Hong Kong at the time. Lion Rock was the name of a well-known mountain in Hong Kong that was visible from our school.

The song became immensely popular because it referred to the hardworking people of Hong Kong who overcame life's difficulties and became successful in spite of the fact that many of them had arrived as refugees with no more than the shirts on their backs. It was especially bittersweet because we felt that the song was referring to us. Many of us who left Hong Kong after high school also felt pride that we'd left with a few hundred dollars and managed to support ourselves through university and become successful.

At noon, Benjamin stood up in the gazebo and gathered us around, asking us to stand up to sing our school song.

Boys of courage, boys of daring, full of manliness and will; Spirits naught for danger caring, hearts to conquer every ill.... And they flourish high and mighty, but La Salle is something more.

Most of us remembered the lyrics by heart.

Benjamin then made a short speech and asked anyone who would like to share his life story to come up and say a few words. One by one, the old boys stepped up and talked for a few minutes. Everyone was humble and mainly talked about what they did after La Salle, and what they were doing now. No one bragged, except one who said something I thought was insensitive and probably upsetting to those who still called Hong Kong home.

Tim Long Sai Tong and I were in the same class for one year in the tenth grade. He was a slim man with a long, thin, bony face and a small nose.

He stood up, adjusted his dark-rimmed spectacles and began to speak. "After I left La Salle, I went to Sydney University and graduated with a degree in business. Now I am the regional manager for Garden Biscuit Company for all of Australia. We like living in Australia. I'm glad that I don't have to be in Hong Kong waiting for the 1997 handover back to China, because I don't want to have to kneel on pebbles." He chuckled.

There was total silence.

Kneeling on pebbles was a form of torture popular with the Chinese communists during the Cultural Revolution. A person would be forced to kneel on the ground covered with small pebbles for hours and sometimes days as punishment. This was one of the cruelest and also well-known tortures used by the communists.

It was a stupid thing for him to say, with memories of the June 4th Tiananmen Massacre still very fresh, and concerns about the 1997 return of Hong Kong to China running high. For the old boys who lived in Hong Kong, such talk was not comforting.

I lowered and shook my head with disbelief at his insensitivity. Tim seemed like a nice man, and he didn't strike me as someone who would be unkind or engage in schadenfreude. Perhaps the words just came out without thinking. We've all done something like that.

I heard my name and felt a pat on my shoulder, and turned to see Tony, my old running friend on the 4 x 100m relay team. He put his cigarette in his left hand and shook my hand; his hand felt bony. "Can you believe this guy?" he said. "He didn't have to remind us Hong Kong guys of this torture. But, I am glad that I hold an Australian passport too."

Later I learned that many of the old boys held dual nationalities, keeping their Hong Kong passports after moving away.

Tony told me that I looked good, smiling at me with nicotine-stained teeth. He coughed occasionally, the typical smoker's cough.

He introduced me to his wife—a beautiful well-dressed Hong Kong woman who had graduated from the Maryknoll Convent School. Their son Terrence was James's age. Terrence had grown up in Sydney and spoke English. The two boys decided to go do their own things. I was proud that James was very sociable and seemed comfortable in any setting.

When everyone was done speaking, Tony and I each grabbed a bottle of San Miguel beer, sat on a bench and talked. We hadn't seen each other for twenty-four years.

Tony was full of regrets. After La Salle, he went to the University of Sydney and graduated with a degree in engineering. From what I understood, it was the most difficult kind of engineering, which I'd never even heard of, mathematical engineering. He explained to me that in his field, their main job was to solve problems other engineers couldn't solve. I knew the three areas of engineering—civil, mechanical and electrical—but then I thought of another branch I'd heard of and asked Tony if it was the same as "structure engineering." He said no, it was even more difficult than that. I was impressed; but I still had no idea what his field was.

Tony wasn't the same person I remembered. I used to envy him—taller, faster, a better student in math, and he lived in a more expensive condo than I did. Now he was just a shadow of his former self. His face was gray, without any life or color. His cheeks were hollow and his hair was gray and thinning. His eyelids were so droopy that I could barely see his eyes. He said that his life hadn't been so lucky. He was laid off from his job in Sydney and retuned to Hong Kong two years ago. Now he was working for a major construction company. He said he picked up smoking out of boredom, and now he was smoking two or three packs a day. His voice was raspy.

"James, you know, I should have gone into medicine like you did," he said. "Mr. Leung, our biology teacher, encouraged me because I was his top student. But I chose engineering. I knew that I could've easily gotten into Hong Kong University or any Australian medical school if I wanted to. As an engineer, you're always working under someone. You're always an employee. But as a doctor, you are your own boss. Look at the GPs from our class who are now in Hong Kong—they're raking in at least a million or two Hong Kong dollars a year."

I felt sorry for Tony. I thought it must be terrible to live a life full of regrets. We got up to stretch our legs and walk around.

Perhaps Tony's disappointment with his own life caused him to look for it in others, because as we walked, he began pointing out the negative aspects of some of our classmates' lives.

"Look at the smartest guys in our class," he said. "Look at the three who went to Cal Tech, the most prestigious university of physical science in the world. They got their PhDs. Now they're just making enough money to get by.

"Look at Teddy Fong," he continued, shaking his head. "He got his PhD in biology from the University of California, Berkeley and now works as a professor at Montana State University, just getting by and freezing his ass off.

"And Allen Lau got his engineering degree from Manitoba University and now works in Saskatchewan. Do you know what life is like in a small town in Saskatchewan?"

Before I could comment, he went on. "Look at Lee Lok Ling. He got his PhD from MIT and works for the US government's Energy Department in Idaho. Who wants to live in Idaho?"

He seemed to know the story of everyone in our class. I wondered if he was trying to make me feel better because he knew how disappointed I was when I didn't make the cut for the science section. Perhaps what he was trying to say was that the guys who did well in the HKSC Exam didn't always become successful later in life. Or maybe he was simply venting his frustration with his own situation. I had always been wary of Tony, sensing that he was a fair-weather friend who often said things that didn't seem sincere. If he could bad-mouth other classmates, you never knew what he would say about you behind your back.

One ludicrous thing he said was that I should have gone to him when I didn't make the cut for Form 6 Science, because he had connections and would've gotten me in. This was of course ridiculous. It was so insincere and unbelievable that I wondered if he even knew what he was saying. I was reminded of the Cantonese saying: *Empty mouth talk white speech*, i.e., speaking with absolutely no sincerity.

I told Tony I'd see him later, and wandered off toward the food stalls. Tommy Sung and John Chun Man Lo were sitting down eating a plate of soft rice noodle wrapped with shrimp. Although Tommy had made Los Angeles his home, his parents were still in Hong Kong so he returned to the colony twice a year.

John Chun was one of my favorite classmates, ever so kind, modest and sincere. He had graduated from Hong Kong University and was now a senior official with the Hong Kong government. He smiled when I came over and said, "Hey, James, you look good. I saw your son there. He's a handsome boy— much better looking than his father." We laughed.

Tommy laughed too, but he quickly turned serious and began complaining, much as he had when I visited him in LA. "Is this all there is to life? After working so hard in primary school, high school, university, and now this?" He again talked about his worries over interest rates and real estate prices, and lamented the road rage and other hassles of living in LA.

I was surprised that he spoke like that in John Chun's presence, as I didn't think they knew each other well. But then I was surprised that he had confided such unhappiness with his life to me as well. In addition to the evening I drove out to Bel Air to see Tommy, I had also stayed with him for two nights on another occasion. He was always a good host. During that visit, he had complained to me about his Chinese Thai beauty queen wife. He had met her at NYU; now, her parents and two brothers were living with them in LA. He didn't mind supporting her parents, but the two brothers were in their thirties and didn't even try looking for jobs. Now they each had a BMW and spending money from his wife, which of course was his money.

I thought it interesting that he would marry someone from Thailand who spoke no Cantonese, and he spoke no Thai. The misunderstandings in communication must be frustrating.

At the pho stand, I recognized two men sitting on the little stools. It was Patrick Bon and Lau Tak Sing. The cook brought over a bowl of hot pho and placed it on the small table in front of Patrick. With a big smile on his face, Patrick dumped in the tiny red chili peppers and bean sprouts and inhaled the pungent steam of the broth. A second bowl of pho landed on the table for Lau.

Patrick looked very different from how I remembered him twenty-five years ago. He had been one of the most handsome boys in class, with a thick head of wavy black hair and an Elvis Presley nose. (Someone told me that his father was a Hong Kong Merchant Seaman who was half Irish.) I always thought that with the hairline on his forehead so much lower than mine, he would never go bald. Now, almost all the hair was gone, and his face was wrinkled and splattered with liver spots. Patrick had graduated from Hong Kong University with a degree in European literature. After graduation, he taught school for a few years, saved enough money and went to Sorbonne University in Paris where he earned a Master's degree in comparative literature.

"*Comment allez-vous*?" I asked, trying to impress Patrick and Lau with my French as I approached the table.

"Is there a Frenchman amongst us? *Qui parle en francais?*" quipped Patrick.

We all laughed, because in Cantonese, "Kam man tau lo fu," which sounded almost like "*comment allez-vous*," meant *tonight hunt the tiger*.

I was interested to hear about Patrick's two years' experience in Paris. I had always dreamt about doing something like that. He now owned one of the largest tutoring schools in Hong Kong, employing over twenty instructors.

In the 1960s, La Salle students from less wealthy families like mine were able to make our own pocket money by working as tutors. But now schools like one that Patrick owned dominated the tutoring business.

The economic situation for most families in Hong Kong had improved so much that most students didn't have to earn extra money. Their own school curriculum was so extensive as well as intensive that they simply had no free time for anything else. As a result, unlike in my days, it is rare for a student to work as a tutor for younger students.

The aim of schools like Patrick's was to help students do better in the HKSC Exam. To do this, the owners of tutoring schools would gather old exam papers, or cultivate relationships with teachers who were on the board that made up each year's questions. The students would then be taught how to answer these questions, which gave them an advantage over those who had never seen any old exam questions. Some tutoring school owners were making millions of Hong Kong dollars a year. Patrick didn't indicate how much he was making, but living in a large flat on Prince Edward Road suggested that he was doing quite well.

I later learned that Patrick had health problems—an autoimmune disease. The loss of hair, and the brown spots and wrinkles on his face were side effects of the long-term medication he was on.

On August 6, 1965, Lau Tak Sing and I had boarded the President Cleveland together. He and Sondhi had shared one of the higher-class rooms, paying a fare over $700 US, which was more than twice mine. Lau went on to McGill University in Montreal, Canada and got a degree with a double major in math and business, and now was a senior manager at AIG Insurance Company.

Mark Moy, Frankie Sing, Pierre Hoang, Clement Tam and Danny Tong were having coconut drinks at one of the stands, and I joined the group amidst handshakes, pats on the back and the cheerful noise of old friends greeting one another.

Mark looked pretty much the same as he had when I last saw him in May of 1964. He had always struck me as one of the smartest and most articulate boys in the class. I knew he had been accepted to Princeton at age sixteen, and I was impressed to learn that he went on to Harvard Medical School and got his MD degree at age twenty-three. He then went to the University of London for a few years, doing basic and clinical research in vascular surgery and obtaining his British medical license, where he was granted reciprocity by the Hong Kong Medical Council. He did his residency and fellowship in San Francisco and returned to Hong Kong to practice, where he was now one of the city's most prominent vascular surgeons.

As I had also trained at the University of California San Francisco Medical Center, we had some mutual friends. I told him that one of his fellow residents in general surgery, Dennis Flora, an Italian American with a fancy Elvis hairdo, had been practicing in Fresno also, but was recently diagnosed with Parkinson's disease and could no longer work. He said he was sorry to hear that.

Frankie Sing had gone to Auckland University after La Salle and became a lawyer. He had returned to his home country of Fiji to practice law and help manage his father's sugar cane plantation, but the country was getting restive as the native

Fijians tried to marginalize the Indians brought in by the British to work the plantations, so he had settled in Auckland.

When I first met Pierre Lung—the second Pierre in our class—I was impressed with how well he spoke French. It turned out that he had grown up in Papeete, Tahiti, and had been schooled in the French language. His father wanted him to be exposed to Chinese culture so he sent him to Hong Kong to live with a relative. After La Salle, he went to Sorbonne University and obtained a business degree, and now split his time between Hong Kong and Papeete, running the family business, which was one of the largest pearl farms in Tahiti. Their farm produced the best black Tahitian pearls and sold most of them to jewelers in Hong Kong, including Benjamin Cheung's Jewelry. I was surprised that he could speak my dialect, the Meixian Hakka dialect, which he explained was because most of the Chinese who had gone to Tahiti were from the Meixian area.

Danny still spoke English with a Jamaican accent. He was sitting down with Tjong and Sandhi next to a fish-ball stand and they were enjoying themselves. Sandhi teased Danny that he still talked like Bob Marley and we all laughed.

Tjong had graduated from San Francisco State University in business administration and now had an import-export business dealing mainly with importing hardwood from Indonesia.

Sandhi had graduated from MIT with a degree in mechanical engineering and was now managing one of his father's mega rice mills in Thailand.

James was happily kicking a soccer ball with Terrence. In the meantime, other boys and even a girl had joined in. I was happy that James was feeling so at home with a bunch of strangers. He always had the gift of talking to strangers no matter if they were young or old, man or woman.

Winston Ho Fan Cheung and Oliver Yue Kow Ling were at the curry noodle stall, wiping beads of sweat from their foreheads, commenting on how good the spicy noodle was. I joined them to have a small bowl of *lak-Sa*, a Malaysian dish made with prawns, coconut milk, curry and bean sprouts. Winston and Oliver had been two of the more serious students at La Salle, and in spite of being in the same class with them for three years, I never got to know them well. They had both been in Form 6 Arts with me.

Knowing they were both from Canada, I commented, "It must cold in Canada now."

Oliver nodded. "I heard there was heavy snow in Manitoba yesterday," he said.

"I lived in Vancouver for a while," I said, "and even that was too cold for me."

They both chuckled. To Canadians living in the interior provinces, Vancouver almost seemed tropical to them because it never got the kind of brutal cold found in the interior.

"What were you doing in Vancouver?" asked Winston.

I shook my head ruefully and told them the story of my failed year of dental school.

Winston had graduated from the Chinese University of Hong Kong in Chinese language and literature. After teaching school for a few years, he and his parents immigrated to Ottawa, Canada. But his teaching credentials weren't recognized in Canada, so he worked as used car salesman in the Chinese community for a few years, while at the same time attending classes to get a Master's degree in education. With that he was able to work as a teacher.

Oliver, after a year in Form 6, immigrated with his family to Alberta. He graduated from the University of Saskatchewan with a degree in Education, but he found it impossible to be a teacher in Saskatchewan because the students would make fun of his accent. So, he went back to school and got a law degree and was now a successful lawyer in private practice serving the province's Chinese community.

The other two lawyers in the class had spotted Oliver and were walking toward us.

Francis Mok had graduated from Hong Kong University with a degree in history. He returned to La Salle and taught for a few years before realizing that he didn't have the patience to be a good teacher. He found work in the office of an Australian lawyer for a few years before obtaining his own law license. In the 1970s, Hong Kong still didn't have a law school. Francis was now one of the busiest solicitors in the colony and dealt almost exclusively in real estate.

Vincent Ma Lun Ba, the Chinese Muslim who still spoke English with an Indian accent, left for London after finishing Upper Form 6 (grade 13) and got his law degree from London University. Each handed me a business card, and I noted that Francis called himself a solicitor while Vincent called himself a barrister.

"What's the difference between a solicitor and barrister?" I asked.

Francis answered, "In the British system, a solicitor is a lawyer who advises clients, represents them in the lower court, and prepares cases for barristers to try in higher court. A barrister's main role is to act as an advocate in legal hearings, which means that they stand in court and plead the case on behalf of their clients in front of a judge. And they wear a wig," he added.

"Who makes more money in Hong Kong?" Winston asked.

"In Hong Kong, solicitors make more money," Francis replied, "because business and real estate are where the money is now. When I first opened my office in the mid-1970s, sometimes I was making a thousand US dollars an hour. Then Hong Kong University opened a law school, and then more law schools opened. The Golden Days are gone. Those of us who made a name for ourselves still do well; but some young lawyers are hardly making a living."

Some years ago, I remembered reading in the *Economist* magazine about the unbelievable money that lawyers in Hong Kong were making. Soon lawyers from all over the British Commonwealth—UK, Australia, New Zealand, and even India and Malaysia—began setting up offices in Hong Kong.

Francis and Vincent were now partners and founders of one of the more prestigious law firms in Hong Kong. Michael told me later that Francis had donated a million Hong Kong dollars to La Salle a year earlier in the name of the Class of 1964.

The group widened its circle to make room as Mateo Ricci Fan Lee Bak joined us. He had told us that he was given the Italian name because his father really admired the Jesuit priest Mateo Ricci, who went to China during the Ming Dynasty and was one of the first Westerners to master the Chinese language. After Form 7 (grade 13) Science, Mateo went to Melbourne University and graduated with his MBBS (Bachelor of Medicine and Bachelor of Surgery, equivalent to the MD degree).

His father stopped by for a few minutes; he was on his way for a game of golf at the Hong Kong Golf Club with Benjamin's uncle. He remarked that Mateo had to pick the University of Melbourne, which was a six-year program, when he could have gone to Sydney University, which was only five years like most medical schools in the British Commonwealth, meaning that he had to support him for one extra year. Some of us chuckled, but others thought he was just trying to brag.

On one of my visits to Hong Kong a few years earlier, I read about Mateo's malpractice trial in the newspaper. A thirty-year-old woman had died during surgery when he was trying to remove a benign ovarian tumor in her abdomen.

During the surgery, he nicked an artery by accident and couldn't stop the bleeding. He called the vascular surgeon, who was performing surgery in the next room, for help. But when the vascular surgeon arrived, the patient had already lost too much blood and died. The case was settled for an undisclosed amount of money.

I left the group to look for James and found him drinking a bottle of Coke with another boy under a banyan tree. After checking on him, I noticed several old boys sitting at a table next to the gazebo sipping white wine. As I got closer, I realized that they were the lucky ones who got into the Hong Kong University Medical School. It looked as if they were having their own reunion.

I joined them and had a small glass of the white Zinfandel from California, which incidentally was from Madera, an area next to Fresno.

Gordon Chang had scored one of the highest marks in the Hong Kong University A-level exam. After internship, he began practicing in Hong Kong. He then decided to immigrate to New Zealand; but after a few years, he found New Zealand too quiet, and the payments from their National Health System too low. He returned to Hong Kong for a few years, but found Hong Kong too crowded. He finally settled in Sydney, Australia, where he now lived.

Richard Leung Hoi Tung also graduated from the Hong Kong University Medical School. After practicing for two years, he was disenchanted with primary care, and went to the US and got an MPH (Master of Public Health) from Johns Hopkins University and returned to Hong Kong to become a hospital administrator.

After graduating from the Hong Kong University Medical School, Paul Loon went to England for training in neurology and psychiatry. I'd always liked him, as he made a point of being kind to everyone in class, always addressing us by our names. He was the only doctor in Hong Kong certified in both neurology and psychiatry.

George Man Chi Lau, a tall and distinguished man with thick, wavy, jet-black hair, also became a doctor. After Hong Kong University, he went to New York and did a residency in pathology because, as he said, he didn't like talking to patients. After working in New York for a few years, he returned to Hong Kong and now owned one of the largest clinical laboratories in the city.

Thomas Hui was an articulate guy; he always spoke clearly in English and Cantonese. After Hong Kong University, he worked at Queen Mary Hospital for a few years, then decided to do a residency in anesthesiology in the US. He now lived in the San Francisco area.

Christopher Lu gave me a wave from the far end of the table. After Form 7 at La Salle, he was accepted to study medicine at the University of Manchester in England. After graduation, he went to London for his urology training and was now a well-known urologist.

I first met Chris in January 1962 when I joined La Salle mid-year in Form 3 (9th grade). My first impression of him was that he spoke English and Cantonese each with an accent. This mystery was solved when he told me that he had grown up in a town called East London, on the southeast coast of South Africa. Two and half years prior to that, at thirteen, his parents sent him to Hong Kong to live with an aunt so that he could learn Chinese and perhaps to get away from the apartheid South Africa.

Chris's great-grand father was recruited from the Canton area around 1900 to work in the Kimberley diamond mine. For political reasons that involved appeasing the much higher paid white workers as well as the unionized black workers, both of whom resented the Chinese, the Chinese were soon altogether banned from working in the diamond and gold mines. They found themselves unemployed in a very foreign land, unable to speak the local languages. Some of them set up small businesses or tried to find other forms of employment, but there were few opportunities. In addition, the Chinese were also caught up in the struggle of the blacks against the whites. Chris's great-grandfather managed to open a small grocery store in Durban, a town for the Coloreds (people of black and white mixture) and Asians (Chinese and Indians). Later, his father and grandfather moved to East London and extended their business to include making short-term loans to the locals and charging interest as high as 10% a month.

As Chinese, they were forbidden to live in towns reserved for the whites and had to ride public transportation with the blacks. Chris's father was concerned because Chris wouldn't be allowed to attend the better universities, which were for whites only. Life was getting more restrictive and confusing for the Chinese. The Japanese who were doing business in South Africa were regarded as honorary whites, thus enjoying all the privileges for whites, whereas the local Chinese were not. Later, when Taiwanese-Chinese businessmen began to do business in South Africa, they too were given honorary white status, while the local Chinese continued to be forbidden to use facilities for the whites.

In addition to having to know English, the Chinese also had to learn Afrikaans, a form of archaic Dutch brought by the Dutch settlers in the 17th century, who made it an official language of South Africa. Afrikaans was notoriously difficult to learn, and useless outside of South Africa. Seeing no future for Chris, his parents sent him to Hong Kong.

He still spoke English with a South African accent, and his Cantonese hadn't improved much either, still carrying the village accent he'd learnt as a child. We hadn't seen each other in twenty-four years. He had married a Chinese girl from South Africa, someone he knew when he was young, and they had two daughters. He seemed very pleased with his life. He was grateful that his parents sent him to Hong Kong and he didn't have to live in South Africa where he would always have been a second-class citizen.

Sitting next to Chris was James Yeung, who was in the Form 6 Science class. After La Salle, he went to the University of Manitoba and got his MD, then returned to Hong Kong and now had a busy practice in general medicine. Because of his Canadian license, he was able to practice in Hong Kong without having to take the licensure exam, which usually had a pass rate of less than 10% for non-Hong Kong University graduates. It was obvious that the local medical association used that barrier as an anti-competition ploy to keep the non-Hong Kong University physicians out. Physicians in Hong Kong have always been among the highest paid in the world.

Sitting further down were Lester Tung and Mason Moon, who both now practiced in the Chicago area. Lester talked little and seemed to be cautious with his words. Mason was funny and talked with animated hand gestures. He was now a well-known Ob-gyn and noted for his keyhole (laparoscopic) surgeries. Lester practiced internal medicine and also had a family practice.

Mason told funny stories about his work in a Chinese restaurant in Chicago when he was attending university. He recounted how some customers once complained that there wasn't enough meat and shrimp on their noodle dish. "So I pretended to go back to the kitchen, then rearranged the pieces of meat and shrimp on the top of the noodles, and told the customers that the cook had added more." We all laughed. "They were very pleased," he added. "One thing I learned quickly working in a Chinese restaurant is that the waiter should never ask the cook to redo or add anything to the dish. It would enrage them!"

Xavier Keng saw me from afar and called out to me. He still had his trademark thick, puffed up, permed wavy hair—now a little gray—and dark rimmed glasses. He had always been kind of a rascal who liked to make fun of people. He and I used to walk home together after school on many occasions as he lived close to my apartment.

After getting his EE (electrical engineering) degree from the University of Manitoba, he continued at UC Berkeley and got two Master's degrees. A few years ago, he quit his job as a chip designer in Silicon Valley, and was now devoting all his time to real estate investment, having bought over twenty houses in the San Jose, California area. He had finally gotten a divorce from his Hong Kong-born wife and was having fun playing the field.

"Xavier, can you believe this place?" I exclaimed. "Benjamin must have made so much money. I heard from Michael that he made his money in opals and colored diamonds."

With a smile, Xavier asked, "Have you met Benjamin's wife?" I said I hadn't.

"Do you know the billionaire Mr. Pui See Kong, the shipping magnate?"

I nodded.

"Have you seen his picture in the newspaper?"

I nodded again.

"Do you agree that he is a very ugly man?"

I smiled and nodded.

"Benjamin's wife is a female version of Mr. Pui," he finished with a laugh.

I laughed loudly. He was implying that Benjamin hadn't made his own fortune, and that his money had come from his wife, as she was an only child. I had always enjoyed his Cantonese humor and his funny descriptions of people.

We decided to walk toward a banana patch where the two physicists were sitting on a marble bench talking.

Both Hugo Ting and Jack Ng had gotten their PhD degrees in astronomy, in the area of the Big Bang theory. The last time I'd seen them was when they visited our Stanford University apartment in '76. As we approached them, I joked, "Are you guys talking about the universe?"

"As a matter of fact, yes," said Hugo. "We're talking about String Theory. I'm sure you know all about String Theory," he added, causing a round of laughter.

To me, Hugo was a genius. When the physics and math teachers at La Salle ran into trouble, he had always bailed them out. He had an aura of invincibility. When I was sweating it out in exams, he calmly sat down and looked over the questions, then answered them.

He never seemed to be worried about anything and wasn't afraid of any teacher, unlike some of us who cowered in fear whenever the very strict Mr. Tien announced a surprise test. He would say, "What is there to fear?" I had always admired him and thought perhaps when someone was that smart and knew that nobody was more intelligent, then there really was nothing to fear. He had probably never experienced any condescension in his life.

Jack Ng, after finishing his PhD at Harvard, had ended up at a university in South Carolina, where he was now the chairman of the physics department. Hugo reminded me how I had requested that they remove their shoes when they arrived at our small apartment, a habit I'd picked up in Malaysia.

"I remember you asked about medical school on that visit," I said. "Did you ever follow up on that?"

"No, I didn't." Hugo replied. "Sometimes I wish I'd gone into medicine, perhaps into research though—not the daily grind of seeing patients. I always thought I could've invented some new medical imaging machines or a new irradiation treatment for cancer."

Hugo had tried to explain his work to me in the past. Out of curiosity, I'd read some books in the field and really tried to understand it. I'd even taken an evening class on the subject; but

I just couldn't understand how they came up with their calculations about the universe.

I did remember that Hugo had told me years ago about protons and electrons being created shortly after the Big Bang, which happened over three billion years ago. Their research was about looking for particles that were smaller than the protons, and some had been discovered already.

I was curious and asked Hugo how big these new particles were.

He explained, "Let's say about 2,000 atoms put side by side is the width of a hair. You know that the electrons and protons orbit around each nucleus of the atom. The size of a proton in relation to the nucleus is equivalent to a golf ball orbiting around a golf course that is 400 meters in diameter, which as you can see, is very small. And these particles are smaller than the proton. For example, the gluon is one third the size of a proton."

"What do they do?" I asked.

"It's believed that they hold the matter in the universe together like glue, hence its name, gluon." Hugo replied.

Xavier had been listening intently and finally said, "It's amazing that you guys are studying things that may not even exist."

We all laughed again. Xavier had known Hugo and Jack since sixth grade, and he joked with them easily. He reminded them of the teacher who had a larger than normal bottom who they'd called *dai lor yau*, meaning "big bottom." He also brought up the teacher who had one leg shorter than the other and walked with a limp. His last name was Leung, and they named him Leung the Lame. He entertained us with many other funny stories about things they'd shared in primary school.

After chatting a bit longer, Xavier and I wandered toward where four men stood near a satay stand and dipping their skewers of meat into peanut sauce with one hand, and holding San Miguel beers in the other. They were Pedro Hoy, Clement Tam, Ronnie Ho and Juan Trujillo. As Pedro lived in Bakersfield, I would see him at least once a year, sometimes much more often. I had also become good friends with Clement and Juan, and we had regular contact. But I hadn't seen Ronnie Ho since I left Hong Kong.

Ronnie was now almost totally bald, so bald that his head appeared shiny with the reflection from the sun. He had gotten his PhD from Yale in linguistics and was teaching at a private university in the Midwest.

He had gotten into Form 6 Science without any difficulty and went to Yale for engineering. Xavier told me that when he went to visit him in New Haven, Connecticut after their first year in college, he noted that in his room was full of linguistics books rather than engineering books. Xavier asked Ronnie why. With tears in his eyes, Ronnie admitted that he simply found the engineering courses too difficult, but out of shame and fear of disappointing his parents, he didn't tell anyone that he'd switched to linguistics.

It was a sad testimony of the pressure we were under not to bring shame to our families that even just going to Yale wasn't good enough; it had to be in a more prestigious field like engineering.

Even though I didn't know Ronnie very well, I'd always thought he was a little eccentric. Even twenty-something years ago, he was trying to convert me to his church. He knew that I was happy with my Catholic religion, but decided that it wasn't right for me. He belonged to small sect of Christians who practiced speaking in tongues and taught that Jesus would come soon and we must repent. I never understood why people like that wanted to convert others into their religion.

Ronnie hadn't changed in that regard; the first thing he talked about was Jesus. He believed that AIDS was sent by God to punish the gay men in America. He often quoted the Bible.

Xavier mentioned that we had just talked to two of the smartest fellows in our class, the two physicists. He said Jack and Hugo had been explaining their research of the universe.

"Do you believe in their theories?" Ronnie asked.

Xavier shook his head and replied, "I really don't know enough to understand their research."

"So, they think the universe is three or four billion years old, and the earth too." Ronnie said with a smirk. "But the Bible says the earth is six thousand years old. So, they think the Bible is wrong?"

There was silence. Nobody spoke for a minute or more. Then Xavier said, "How do you explain dinosaur fossils? They've been tested to be millions of years old, and carbon dating is so accurate now."

The smirk on Ronnie's face turned to a sneer as he said, "We all know the fossils were planted by atheists. Nobody can prove that dinosaurs actually existed."

I remained silent. I wondered how someone with a PhD from Yale in linguistics could be so closed in his thinking. The very field of linguistics was about the study of mankind. It was absurd to hear Ronnie say that the world was only six thousand years old.

Pedro, who was also a Catholic, said, "I think we can believe what we want to believe. I don't think we should challenge someone else's belief. We do what's best for ourselves. As they say, never talk about religion or politics."

We smiled and nodded, but Ronnie shook his head as if to say that he disagreed.

A waiter came by pushing a small cart with all sorts of drinks. I picked a San Miguel beer. The others followed suit except Ronnie, who took a bottle of green sugar cane juice.

Clement excused himself, saying that he had to join his wife. I said I should look for my son, and Xavier and Juan joined me as I walked away, leaving Pedro and Ronnie by the satay stand.

The main topic of conversation throughout the day was the Tiananmen Massacre, which had occurred just five months ago. Many of the old boys who called Hong Kong home were edgy.

Those who had done well and had tons of money could always leave at their choosing and timing. But it wasn't that simple for many who worked as teachers, engineers or mid-level managers. Even if they could leave, what would they do once they got to a new country? They would have to start all over again.

A few were considering immigrating to Vancouver or Toronto.

At a distance, I could see James still playing ball with a few other children.

Xavier and I had lost Juan somewhere along the way, when we ran into Henry Hing, a civil engineer who was working for a large construction firm in Hong Kong. Henry was a tall, muscular guy, over six feet, and a soft-spoken man. His family, like mine, also escaped from China to Hong Kong in 1949. He felt that he needed to leave Hong Kong and explained that his application had essentially been approved. "I've more than met the Point System requirement to immigrate to Canada," he said. "I'm just waiting for the visa and tying up loose ends in Hong Kong."

He said proudly that he scored over 80, when only 67 were required. I was curious and asked him how the Point System worked.

"Countries like Canada, Australia and New Zealand use a Point System to determine if an applicant is a suitable candidate to immigrate to their country," he explained. "Canada requires at least 67 points. There are six areas in which they award or take away points. For education, up to 25 points can be awarded. I was given 20 points because of my degree in civil engineering. For language, a maximum of 24 points, and I was given 20 points. Work experience and approved occupations is given a maximum of 21 points, and I was given 15. Age between 21 and

49 receives 10 points. People older than 49 lose 2 points for each year. As I'm 44, I was given 10 points.

"If someone has already been offered a job," he continued, "it would be worth 10 points. My brother-in-law talked to his boss and he offered me a job, so I got 10 pts.

"Adaptability, spouse's education, previous work in Canada and family relations in Canada can be worth up to 10 additional points. As my sister and brother-in-law are already in Toronto, I was given another 5 points. So, I have 80 points.

"Actually, I would like to live in Vancouver," he went on, "but the housing is more expensive and there are fewer jobs. My sister lives in Toronto, so that's a good reason for me to be there. If I don't like it there, I can always move to Vancouver later."

Henry impressed me as a genuinely good person. He said he never thought he would be good enough to be accepted by the civil engineering department of Hong Kong University. "But," he said, "during the 1967 riots, so many people were leaving Hong Kong and there was a drop in the number of applicants. So, I was lucky that I got in."

"You might have been accepted anyway," I said. "Remember that you were good enough to get into Form 6 Science, while I was not."

We smiled and agreed that the HKSC Exam had affected us greatly, and some never recovered. We still had nightmares about failing or showing up at the wrong classroom for the exam. It was a brutal system. But this reunion proved that not everyone who did well on the HKSC Exam was successful in life. Book intelligence doesn't always correlate with financial success, and financial success was what was important in Hong Kong. Everyone was judged by how much money they had or could make.

Juan caught up with us again, and he, Xavier and I walked around enjoying the cool breeze in a beautiful setting in the most exquisite area of Hong Kong, moving from one group to the next, talking and reminiscing about our youth.

We found a round table to sit at, and a few others joined us. The waiter came by again with his cart and we each got a small sized ginger ale. A very fair complexioned fellow sat down across from me. He looked vaguely familiar. He still had a full head of hair, unlike many of us who had already lost much of our hair and a few who were completely bald. He was impeccably dressed in an Italian suit. He spoke to Xavier and asked how the computer chip business was. Xavier answered that he got tired of it and quit, and was now doing real estate full time in California. As I was trying to figure out who this fellow was, his voice gave away his identity. He was the Shanghainese boy, Dexter Pei, who used to listen to his transistor radio in class to follow horse racing.

I had heard that after Dexter failed the HKSC Exam, his family sent him to a boarding school in Melbourne. He later got into Melbourne University and graduated with a degree in business administration and was now the regional manager for East Asia and Oceania (Australia and New Zealand) of a large corporation.

Knowing that Dexter probably knew Benny Cho, the big discus thrower, as they were both from wealthy Shanghainese families, I asked if he knew what Benny was doing. He said Benny now owned a Chinese restaurant in Times Square in New York City and was doing very well. The restaurant was called Four Seasons, and it had been written up a lot in the newspapers and magazines.

Dexter and Benny were two examples of how money gave people options. They didn't study very hard, and despite failing the HKSC Exam, they both got second chances and went on to succeed in life.

As I was talking to Dexter, a portly fellow with gold-rimmed glasses came over to the table. The woman with him was equally portly and she spoke with what I thought was a German accent.

As I had taken a semester of German at the University of Hawaii, I was almost tempted to say a German few words to her; but I decided against it since I didn't know her, and I wasn't absolutely sure she was German.

This prosperous-looking man was Loh Kim Peng. He came over to me and shook my hand; his hand felt thick and meaty. A few days earlier, I had heard Michael remark to one of his millionaire friends after shaking his hand that he had *fat choi sau*, which meant "hands that would bring in wealth." I thought it was funny, so as I shook Loh's hand I said, "Wow, you have *fat choi sau*." Everybody laughed.

Michael had told me that after La Salle, Loh began working in a travel agency. In the 1970s, Europeans were beginning to visit Hong Kong, so the travel agency sent him to Frankfurt, Germany to run the branch office there. There, he met and married his wife, and returned to Hong Kong with her. He now owned the largest travel agency in Hong Kong with branch offices in Bangkok and Frankfurt, and lived in a mansion on Robinson Road.

Perhaps according to Hong Kong's criteria of success in life, Dexter and Loh were more successful than those with advanced degrees. Perhaps true success in life is in the eye of the beholder, the person experiencing it.

Loh began telling the group jokes. "The plane had been stuck on the tarmac for over two hours. The passengers were getting edgy. A British passenger was using the four-letter word. An American passenger heard two Chinese passengers who kept saying what sounded like 'Delay no more' and told his wife that the Chinese people were more civilized because they don't swear."

We all burst out laughing. In Cantonese, *Diu Lei Lo Mo* sounded like "Delay no more," but it actually meant *Go fxxx your mother*.

When the laughter died down, Loh said, "Last week, I had lunch with Phillip Chan and our agency made arrangements for him and his crew to film another movie in Thailand."

Phillip Chan was the fellow from our class and who became a singer and movie star. In the late 1960s and 1970s, he had his own television series, a show about a detective solving crimes in Hong Kong. He was also in several Hollywood movies, always playing a Hong Kong detective. I saw him in two of Peter Sellers' *Pink Panther* movies as well as Jean-Claude van Damme's movies.

Loh's wife, Erica, was very friendly. In spite of her German accent, she spoke fluent English with an excellent vocabulary.

"Erica, I have a question about the expats in Hong Kong," I said to her. "Do you think they have little to do with the locals by choice?" I had always been curious why these foreigners kept to themselves so much.

"James, I really don't have that much to do with the so-called expats anymore," she replied. "I have my family, children, so I have a busy life. I find that they're always complaining about their helpers, as if they've had helpers all their lives. Probably back in America, they had to do everything themselves. I got so tired of their small talk, about the best airline to get the best Business Class ticket, where to stay in Bali and Phuket.

"Some of them think if they speak slowly and loudly to the locals, they'll be able to decipher the foreign words, which I find hilarious," she continued. "Some expats really believe they're better than the locals. But the scene is changing as more American Chinese and Canadian Chinese come to work in Hong Kong. Many of the expats aren't white now. There are Japanese and Koreans too.

"Perhaps they've had so little to do with the locals because most of them live in Repulse Bay and Stanley, and they don't really need to mix with the locals. But also, I think Hong Kong people themselves are somewhat racist, so maybe they don't want to socialize with the expats. Perhaps language is a problem as well. Unless a Hong Kong person was educated in an English medium school like La Salle, it's just not easy for the locals to carry on any meaningful conversation in English."

Erica shrugged. "I guess if many of the foreigners know that they'll only be in Hong Kong for a few years, they simply don't want to invest their time in getting to know someone from here well. So, they do things they're familiar with, with people they already know," she finished.

It was something that had always puzzled me, and I was glad to hear about the experience from a true expat.

Far across the table, I could hear a woman speaking in the dead-giveaway singsong accent of Malaysia and Singapore, which was dubbed Singlish. Sitting next to her was Ko See Man, a classmate who had studied in Australia and got a degree in business or accounting. He had met his wife Sally in Sydney. Sally was lively and outspoken and I could hear her giggling and cackling every so often.

Tuning in to her conversation, I heard her say, "I really miss the food in Singapore and Malaysia. They try to make it here, but it's just not the same. After all these years, I'm still not used to living in Hong Kong. I think in the summer, it's even more muggy here than in Singapore.

"It was really difficult living with See Man's family when we first got married," she continued. "His mother did not like me and always tried to cause trouble between See Man and me. You know how the Chiu-Chau people are—they always treat their daughters-in-law badly. Just because the old lady was mistreated by her mother-in-law, she thought she had the right to abuse her son's wife. Fortunately, after six months, she had a massive stroke and died." She giggled.

We all laughed initially, but when we realized what she'd said, everyone at the table became quiet. We looked at Ko See Man and he was shaking his head. Xavier later remarked that he felt sorry for Ko See Man for having a wife like Sally. How could you rejoice at your husband's mother's death?

I thought about it later when I was alone, and shook my head again. It was so stupid that a wife would say something like that in front of her husband's friends. Showing "face," or respect, was so important in Chinese culture. At the same time, I did think it was a little funny that someone would say such a thing in front of a group of people.

Excusing ourselves from the table, Xavier and I meandered to the stand that served halal food. Felix Sapanov, Max Mandel, Carlos Medina Leon Lee, Darius Mody, Richard Singh and Bashir Ajmal were standing next to it eating bowls of lamb curry with roti.

Felix had immigrated to Australia and now worked a reporter for a newspaper in Sydney.

Max Mandel had graduated from the Albert Einstein Medical School and now worked as a radiologist in New York City. He later revealed that he was board certified in three areas: internal medicine, gastroenterology and radiology. He chose to work in radiology because he found dealing directly with patients stressful, but at the same time he couldn't find any way other than being a physician to make a living.

Carlos Medina was now living in Miami and worked as an accountant in a large hotel.

Darius Mody had graduated from the London School of Economics and was now helping run the family business in Hong Kong.

Richard Singh had become a lawyer and was now a prominent trial lawyer in Hong Kong, with many clients from the South Asian community.

Bashir Ajmal left La Salle after Form 6 and managed his family business in the spice wholesale and retail business. He was now known among the old boys as the King of Chung King

Mansions because he owned over ten stores in the building. He also owned several youth hostels in the same building, catering mainly to backpackers from the US and Europe. From what Michael told me, Bashir had done exceedingly well and was now a multi-millionaire, but not yet a billionaire like Benjamin.

Perhaps one of the reasons people who had grown up in Hong Kong loved the city was its fantastic food. The food carts Benjamin had hired reminded many of us how much we missed the wide variety of foods and flavors available there.

In Hong Kong, you could see the power of money. Most families had a maid. How many families in the US had maids? Even a successful surgeon like me still had to take the trash out!

It seemed that mostly the more successful classmates showed up for the reunion. Lo Tak Kan had graduated from Hong Kong University in chemistry and had taught school ever since. He was almost apologetic that he was only a schoolteacher. He described his job as *mo yun*, meaning "useless," implying that he'd been a failure in life. I was surprised that if he felt that way he would still show up for the reunion.

Talking to LoTak Kan made me wonder what Kam Tung Wo was doing now, as the two of them had been good friends. Kam was nicknamed *Lap Sap Lo*, meaning "garbage man," because he always looked untidy. He had been in my class for one year. It always saddened me when the other boys addressed him by his nickname as if it was his real name. I cringed every time I heard it. After the HKSC Exam, he left to attend the Polytechnic College, and got a diploma in drafting and design.

I asked Lo Tak Kan if he knew where Kam went. He said he had maintained contact with him and that he had immigrated to Australia and was working for the city of Perth in Western Australia in the maintenance department as a draftsman.

The crowd thinned out when it began to get dark at six pm. James and I left for the Hyatt Hotel shortly after we ate dinner. Michael was kind enough to give us a lift to the Kowloon ferry that would take us back to the hotel.

I thought it had been a truly wonderful day. I thoroughly enjoyed it even though I wasn't usually a party person. Visiting with our friends from high school was like visiting our own youth. It reminded us that we were young once.

Soon our two weeks were up and we returned to California.

CHAPTER 12:
Twenty-five Years (1990 to 2014)

In the Blink of an Eye

MICHAEL AND HIS FAMILY took a month-long vacation to the US in 1990. They toured the country's major national parks and their last leg was to visit us in Fresno.

They stayed with us. Their daughter Karen got to know our four children. I gave the entire Sze family the most thorough eye examinations they ever had.

Danny and Pedro drove up from Bakersfield one evening to see Michael and his family, and we met for dinner at the Imperial Garden Chinese Restaurant.

Another day, I drove the Sze family to Yosemite National Park. Michael commented on the remarkable translation of the park's phonetic name into Chinese—*Yau San Mei Tei* literally meant "Touring Mountain Beautiful Land," which we all agreed described the place perfectly.

We drove to the giant Redwood tree that had a hole in the trunk big enough for my Volvo to drive through, and we took some pictures.

We spent some time reminiscing about our youth, remembering how when we lived in Shatin our future seemed so uncertain and scary. We talked about how different our lives would've been if we had failed the HKSC Exam, and how many students who didn't pass now toiled in unrewarding, low-paying jobs.

We considered ourselves most fortunate.

***

1991

My work continued to be grueling. At the end of some days, having seen forty or fifty patients, my head would be spinning because I was moving so fast. In between seeing patients, I would do some laser treatments. When a patient with a detached retina came in, I needed to repair it as soon as I could, which was usually that evening, after a long day's work.

Our oldest daughter Melissa was accepted to Stanford University and the three younger children were busy with school and sports.

Each week blended into another.

Busy as we were, each Easter holiday we would spend a week to ten days in Hawaii at the Kahala Hilton (now called The Kahala Resort) where I had worked for almost four years during my undergraduate years.

1993

For over a year, I suffered greatly with neck and shoulder pain. I tried all different kinds of treatments, including traction to pull the discs apart to relieve the pressure, and cortisone injections into the spinal canal. Nothing was working, and I was angry that nobody was taking me seriously because they assumed, as a physician, that I knew what to do for myself. With the constant nagging pain, I was unable to sleep. In order to get some rest, I had to apply very cold compresses each night to distract from the pain, which burned my skin. When the cold compresses failed to provide relief, I would sometimes inject a local anesthetic into my neck.

Desperate, I sought the opinion of another neurosurgeon and pleaded with him to help find a solution to my pain. This surgeon was more sympathetic than previous ones I'd consulted. He said there was a procedure we could try, but the risks of the surgery included total paralysis and becoming a quadriplegic, and the potential loss of my voice, as the nerve that controlled the vocal cords ran very close to the operation site. At that point, I simply didn't care. I could no longer live with the pain. A friend, an ENT specialist, volunteered to be the assistant surgeon and promised to isolate the nerve and make sure nothing happened to my voice. *(Often a physician is reluctant to operate on another physician, as it's known or often appears that they have more complications than regular patients.)*

The surgery, which included taking a piece of bone from my right hip to prop up the spaces between the discs, went well. To my profound relief, as soon as I woke up from the anesthesia, the pain was no longer there.

During my recuperation, I hired an associate, a younger ophthalmologist of Japanese descent who was born and had grown up in the area.

With an associate, I was under less pressure.

***

Chinese New Year, 1995
Danny Tong invited me and my family, Pedro and his family and some other friends for a Chinese New Year's Eve party. He had hired the chef from his favorite Chinese restaurant to cook some of his favorite foods, which included deep-fried calamari rings, tiny deep-fried anchovies, salt and pepper prawns, fried noodle with seafood and other tasty foods. Qingdao beers were also served.

Danny's three children were charming. His daughter was petite like Danny and his black mother, who was actually a patient of mine being treated for glaucoma. He was very proud to announce that his daughter would be heading for Columbia University. His two sons were handsome, athletic and polite, and according to Danny they were doing exceptionally well in high school. Danny's wife was a beautiful and statuesque African American, tall and confident like a model.

At the party, our children got to know each other. Pedro's two daughters were beautiful and polite. I was told that they were in a magnate school for gifted children.

Danny seemed a little sad, and when we got a minute alone, he asked if I could meet him for lunch the following week to discuss a personal matter.

At lunch, Danny seemed a little distracted. We chatted about work a little, and then he said, "James, I think I'm going to get a divorce. Evelyn and I are just such different people. I think it was a big mistake to have her mother come live with us. For weeks now, she and her mother have done nothing but watch the OJ Simpson trial on TV. The house is in disarray. When I get home after a long day's work, there's no dinner and I have to eat a bowl or two of instant noodles, make a sandwich, fry some eggs or cook myself a hamburger. I'm getting angrier and angrier. I just can't understand why the trial is so important to them."

I sat there and listened. What could I say? After a few minutes, I commented that perhaps they should find a marriage counsellor. I felt very bad for Danny, but I had no advice for him other than that. I hoped it was enough that I was there to listen.

***

1997 Bird Flu

Two years earlier, I had taken my daughter Melissa to Hong Kong. She was studying city planning at Stanford at the time, and she remarked that Hong Kong was such as compact city that if there were any emergency, such as an epidemic, it would be difficult to deal with.

Her observation proved to be correct. In the early spring of 1997, chicken farmers in Hong Kong's New Territories noticed that thousands of chickens were dying. Their bodies were shaking and seemed to be suffocating. Their faces went dark green and black, and then they were dead. Some of the birds had blood clots in their windpipes. In the lab, scientists identified the virus that caused their death as the H5N1 strain, which was shown to be a thousand-fold more infectious than the typical human strains of flu virus.

In May 1997, a three-year-old boy in Hong Kong was admitted to Queen Elizabeth Hospital with a fever and died a week later in a horrible way, with internal bleeding and his lungs filled with blood, literally choking him to death. The cause of his death was the H5N1 virus, which previously had only caused disease in birds.

The Hong Kong government sought help from the CDC in the US as well as the WHO. The world authorities in virology felt that the spread must be halted, otherwise it would be the 1918 pandemic flu repeated, and millions of people around the world would die. With Hong Kong being such a small place packed with over seven million people, the spread of the virus would be catastrophic and unimaginable.

The Chinese people in Hong Kong believed in having their food as fresh as possible. They shopped at wet markets in which chickens would be slaughtered on site at the time of purchase. This created a condition for birds and humans to live in close proximity, and the potential for the bird virus could mutate and become deadly in humans. That was what happened in 1918 when the influenza pandemic infected one third of the world's population, i.e., 500 million, killing between 20 and 50 million of them. The cause was an H1N1 virus with genes linked to birds.

The second human to die was a 13-year-old girl who began with a headache, and also died a horrible death a week later with internal bleeding throughout her body. The experts still couldn't believe that a virus assumed to exist strictly in birds was directly attacking humans.

Then a 25-year-old woman died of the same cause.

All three had contact with chicken before their deaths. Realizing the disease was coming from the birds, world-leading scientists called for every chicken, duck and goose in the entire colony to be killed at once to stop any new human cases. For four days, hundreds of government workers engaged in the slaughter; when it was done, over a million birds had been killed. Scuffles broke out with chicken farmers and vendors who tried to stop the slaughter. Buddhist monks held a seven-day prayer chant for the birds' souls.

Overnight, new human infections stopped. In the end, a total of six people died. It could have been so much worse had the drastic measures not been taken.

A few years later, intensive research on the H5N1 virus revealed how close the world had truly come to facing a pandemic. There was evidence that during the Hong Kong crisis, the virus was rapidly adapting to its new human host, acquiring mutations that increased its ability to replicate in human tissue. If the birds hadn't been killed, it was likely that the 1918 flu pandemic would have been repeated, and millions of people would have died.

A year earlier, I had planned a trip to Urumqi, Xinjiang in northwest China and debated if I should cancel it or bypass Hong Kong. When I learned that the spread of the virus had indeed been halted, I felt there was no reason for me not to go ahead with the trip.

When I arrived in Hong Kong in late June, everyone including my taxi driver was complaining that they hadn't had fresh chicken for weeks, and that the frozen chickens from America were tasteless.

After the scary ordeal, life slowly returned to normal.

Many of my friends had been extremely worried during the outbreak. When I stopped by the Peninsula Hotel to pay Juan a visit, he indicated that he was thinking about immigrating to Canada or the US.

We met, as we usually did, in The Lobby. Juan had worked at the Peninsula for just about thirty years now. At fifty, he needed to make a decision soon, as after fifty-five, most countries wouldn't even consider him for immigration.

Juan revealed that he was tired of the hotel business, and that he felt he was getting too old for it. He was tired of pretending that he was overjoyed to welcome the arriving guests as if they were distant and extremely wealthy relatives, uttering phrases like, "How glad I am to see you. I hope your jet lag isn't too bad!"

"I'm too old to kiss up to people anymore," Juan sighed. "Now, each time I utter something like that, I think of Benny Hill's saying: *Be sincere even if you don't mean it.*

"I know it's everywhere in Hong Kong," he continued, "but I think at this hotel, you can really see the power of money. The hotel flies in its cheese and hams from France, its steaks from the United States, and frequently has gastronomic festivals when it flies in chefs from famous restaurants around the world.

"I think it's all a show. It's irrelevant to the people of Hong Kong, most of whom work very hard for a living.

"I think I'm just getting too old for this kind of nonsense. This hotel has been good to me. I can't really find any fault with it. It's just the system. They provided me with a good job, and after thirty years I have a secure nest egg. Our children all are university educated. I'm grateful, but I think it's time for me to move on and do something I like, and to live somewhere less stressful. Even after working here for so long, I dread that one day they'll tell me I'm no longer needed.

"You know how it is in Hong Kong. As long as you can make money for them, they'll keep you. But the moment the company decides you're no longer an asset, they kick you out. I've seen it happen to so many people. There's no recourse. It's a merciless and shameless business." Juan shook his head and looked

238

around the beautiful lobby of one of the most glamorous hotels in the world. "But," he added, "I'm in a good place. The most important thing is that my wife and I have saved enough so we can now do the things we like to do."

Since he was never among the top management of the hotel, Juan wouldn't get a pension when he retired. Through careful planning and investment, he and his wife would be able to retire, but he would still need to be engaged in some sort of work, since he was still in the prime of his life. Their spacious condo in Tsim Sha Tsui East was now worth four times what they paid for it, and could sell for at least $1.5 million US.

Juan felt that with about $2 million US, he could get a new start in the US or Canada. At the moment, it seemed that Canada would be the best bet because it seemed like a kinder society, and not violent like America, which I agreed with. Another reason was that even with Julia in the US, who could sponsor him and his family, the waiting time would be over seven years. Canada seemed to encourage more immigration and would only take a year or less.

Six months later, I heard from Juan in Vancouver—they had made the move.

***

July 1997

I hadn't planned the stopover to coincide with the handover of Hong Kong to China. This was the day that many people, including me, had worried about. Many of the city's residents had escaped from China to the safety of Hong Kong. Had it not been for British Hong Kong, we would have had no place to escape to.

Britain first took over Hong Kong Island in 1842 after defeating China in the First Opium War. In 1860, China was forced to cede

Kowloon, the area on the mainland across from the island. In 1898, Britain leased additional land, known as the New Territories, promising to return them to China in 99 years, which would be 1997.

Growing up, my greatest fear was the communists coming to Hong Kong. It was the main reason I went to America.

Michael had invited me to a party he had planned for the handover. He sounded optimistic that Hong Kong would remain as it was. As he said, "My bones will be hitting the drum when Hong Kong truly reverts to China rule." *("Bones hitting the drum" is a Cantonese saying, meaning "I will be long gone.")* He had arranged for a bunch of La Salle classmates to meet at the Golden Bauhinia Restaurant.

Juan had returned to Hong Kong to tie up some loose ends, so he joined us. Clement was there, now a well-known dentist. Richard Singh was still doing well in his law practice. In his early career, he was interested in defending the criminals, but then he got tired of it and was now practicing almost exclusively immigration law.

Bashir Ajmal's businesses in Chung King Mansions continued to prosper. Tjong's Indonesian teak wood import business had expanded to importing wood from Thailand (through the help of Sondhi), Malaysia, Cambodia and Burma. His company had become one of the largest importers of teak wood. Vincent Ma also had become a very prominent lawyer. Henry Young happened to be in Hong Kong for another one of his exhibitions of his photography. The theme of this exhibition was "The Street People of India."

We had a great time reminiscing about the "good" or perhaps the "bad" old days of our very competitive and stressful high school life.

1998

I was taking some equipment to the clinic in Urumqi, Xinjiang, and I stopped over in Hong Kong to stay at Michael's spacious condo in South Bay, near Repulse Bay. Growing up, we could only dream about living in such a place. Now, Michael had a condo with a view of the South China Sea.

He was on the board of directors of the largest condiment company in Asia—perhaps the world—the Lee Kum Kee Company. Anywhere we went, we saw bottles of Lee Kum Kee products in the grocery stores, whether it was in Australia or Zimbabwe.

The company was having a Christmas party at the Hong Kong Club and Michael invited me to go along.

It was an eye opener, as I'd never seen how the really rich people in Hong Kong lived. A beautiful Filipina singer was singing popular songs such as *Perfedia*, *Besame Mucho* and *Maria Elena* with an impressive band, which I was told were members of her family.

I understood why many really wealthy people chose to live in Hong Kong. Money was powerful and visible there. In the US, people were more or less equal, and their lifestyles weren't that different.

Truly, life in Hong Kong was a great deal more exciting than my life in Fresno. There had been moments when I wished I was living in Hong Kong, but then I would remind myself that the grass is always greener on the other side. I had thought the matter over carefully, and decided against it. I stood by my decision, no matter how exotic Hong Kong seemed sometimes.

****

In 2001, at fifty-five, I was taking more time off, working in the clinic in Guilin and another in Xinjiang. Hong Kong was the stopover for most of my trips, which was twice a year for two or three weeks in duration.

My father had been ill for a couple of years. His chief problem was his uncontrolled hypertension, which resulted in renal failure and necessitated him being on renal dialysis.

My brother Chung had flown from Newark on September 10 to help take care of him in Oakland. September 11 was the horrific day when the World Trade Center was demolished. If Chung had gone to Oakland a day later, he would have been on the flight that hit one of the towers.

My father passed away later that year at age 88.

***

SARS

In March of 2003, I heard the news that SARS (Severe Acute Respiratory Syndrome) had spread from the nearby Guangdong province, China to Hong Kong.

Hong Kong had become a ghost city. More health workers and patients had died. Restaurants were deserted. Everyone lived in fear and those who could leave, left for safer places.

At that point, the authorities didn't even know what was causing the dreadful disease. They had no idea how it was spreading.

Rumors were running rampant. When the Amoy Gardens apartment complex came down with 329 cases of infection and 42 died, people expected the worst.

More medical professionals at the Prince of Wales Hospital had been infected, and many of them died. People thought if doctors and nurses couldn't protect themselves, how could the general population protect itself?

The Hong Kong government took drastic measures, including quarantining the entire apartment complex that had the outbreak and also anyone suspected of being infected. Soon, the number of cases began to decrease. In the end, 1755 people had been infected and 302 of them died.

By June 2003, life had returned to normal in Hong Kong.

***

2005

I was once again in Hong Kong on my way to Xinjiang where I had set up another eye clinic, and Michael invited me for dim sum. His distant cousin, Flying Tiger Chen (Henry Chennault) was in town and joined us. I had only met Henry once, briefly, when I was walking to school with Michael decades ago. I remembered being curious about him then; I was interested to learn more about him.

Henry was in a conversational and expansive mood. Over lunch, he began explaining his mother's family background.

It turned out that Henry's mother's maiden name was Ho, and she was related to Robert Ho Tung, one of the most famous men in Hong Kong.

"My maternal grandfather was Ho Tung," explained Henry. "My mother's family name wasn't really Ho. I don't know if you're familiar with Robert Ho Tung's history. He was the son of a Dutch Jew named Charles Henry Maurice Bosman who came to Hong Kong via the Dutch East India Company. He went to Java first, and then came to Hong Kong. His name, Bosman, was pronounced Bo-se-man in Cantonese, which transliterated into Ho Sze Man. Bosman had a Chinese mistress whose name was Sze Tai, who was from what's now the Shenzhen area not far from Hong Kong. They had several children, and Robert Ho Tung was the oldest.

"Ho Tung went into the import-export business. As he spoke fluent English, the British gave him preferential treatment and he prospered." Henry paused to take a sip of Oolong tea from his small, almost-transparent, fine white porcelain teacup.

"I heard rumors that much of his business was importing opium from India and then selling it to Guangzhou," he continued. "I think some of the rumors were true, but I don't think they only dealt with opium. I think they also exported tea, silk and porcelain.

"I know it was very immoral for Ho Tung to engage in that sort of trade, and it made him the richest man in Hong Kong. I heard that he was probably the richest man in all of China at the time. I've tried to ask as many questions as I could about how my great-grandfather Bosman made his money, and I've to come to the sad conclusion that he used his connections with the Hong Kong government to import opium from India and then sell it to China; and, like his son, he too became immensely wealthy from it. In the process, he ruined many people's lives."

Henry paused to pick up a piece of *har kau* (shrimp dumpling) with his chopsticks and chewed thoughtfully for a minute. "But opium was legal in Hong Kong in those days," he said. "Many of my relatives have said that if they didn't do it, someone else would have; and indeed, many did.

"I heard that grandpa tried to move away from the opium business and branch into other areas."

I listened with fascination, thinking that life truly was happenstance. One man came from the Netherlands over a hundred years ago and left hundreds of descendants in Hong Kong, one of whom was Henry.

I was curious about Mr. Bosman asked Henry if he knew what happened to him.

"He prospered in Hong Kong and had his own company called Bosman and Company," answered Henry. "He was also part owner of the Hong Kong Hotel, which was the first luxury hotel in Hong Kong. Later, he left for England and never returned. He left enough funds so that his children were well taken care of. He was rumored to have immigrated to California later, but nobody knew for sure. There was also a rumor that he had a wife back in Holland."

"What did your mother do during the Japanese occupation of Hong Kong?" I asked.

Henry took another sip of tea and put another dumpling in his mouth before responding. "When the war broke out in Europe in 1939, Hong Kong wasn't affected much, even though Britain was suffering. China was in chaos, as the Japanese had occupied Manchuria and other parts of China years before, making people's lives miserable. The Nanjing Massacre occurred between the end of 1937 and the first part of 1938, in which Japanese soldiers killed as many as 300,000 Chinese, most of whom were civilians. Many refugees fled China to Hong Kong. From a population of 600,000, it went up to one and a half million. I was told that half of these people were sleeping on the street, since they had nowhere to go. They came to Hong Kong because they thought it was under British rule and they would be safe from the Japanese.

"After the Allied retreated from Dunkirk in May 1940, the government of Hong Kong was on its own, as Britain could barely take care of herself.

"My mother was eighteen when the Japanese attacked Hong Kong. The poor refugees who had arrived from China not long ago were fleeing back to China, again trying to get away from the Japanese.

"My mother's family initially fled to Kunming in southwest China, far away from the Japanese; but then they decided to go to Macau instead, where they had some relatives.

"My father was in Macau organizing his large fleet of airplanes to try and supply Chiang Kai-shek's army by flying over the Himalayas, because the army had been cut off by the Japanese blockade. That's when my father met up with my mother again, and I was born a year later."

Henry nodded his thanks as I topped up his cup with fresh tea, and then continued. "As Portugal was neutral during WWII, the Japanese didn't occupy Macau, which was considered one of the provinces of Portugal. But it was cut off from the world. Life wasn't easy—food was scarce—but the conditions weren't as dire as in Hong Kong.

"Many of my mother's relatives who were Eurasians suffered, especially those who had worked with the British. Many of them were interned at the Stanley Prison or the Shum Shui Po Police Station. Many men were sent to Japan to work as laborers. One of my uncles died there.

"Most of the wives and children of the British were sent to Australia. One of my aunts was married to a Scottish engineer who was the head of the Public Works Department in Hong Kong. He decided that he would stay in Hong Kong to fight the Japanese while the rest of the family would go to Australia. My aunt and the three children were put on board a ship to Sydney, but when they got there, she was refused entry because she looked more Chinese than Caucasian and she was sent back to Hong Kong. As you may know, in those days, Australia had the All White Policy and no Asians were allowed to settle there. That experience really shook her up, because she thought with her British passport, she could go anywhere in the Commonwealth.

"Before WWII, the British truly felt they were superior to the Chinese and Eurasians, and they also looked down on the Portuguese. But when the Japanese attacked Hong Kong, many of the British soldiers simply surrendered or went into hiding, whereas the Eurasians and Portuguese fought bravely. They knew it was their only home and they had nowhere else to go, while the Brits still had Britain.

"The fact that the Japanese were able to defeat the British so easily showed that the yellow people weren't inferior to the white race. I think that's why, after the war, the attitude of the

British changed and we weren't discriminated against as much. Now we're even allowed to live on the Peak."

I nodded my head as Henry finished a barbecue pork bun and Michael ordered a fresh pot of tea.

"This is a small world," said Henry. "You know, James, when I was at La Salle Primary School, Bruce Lee, the famous kung fu actor, was also there. Even though he was a year ahead of me, he was a little guy. I was much taller than him. We once got into a fight and he lost. This of course was long before he learned kung fu."

Henry chuckled and said, "Can you imagine that I beat up Bruce Lee?"

We all laughed, and Michael remarked that he'd never heard that story before.

We sat back and listened as Henry told one story after another. He went on to say that Bruce Lee had a good friend named Ricardo Chen who was part Mexican. He always saw the two of them together. Henry later kept in touch with Ricardo but lost contact with Bruce.

"In the 1930s and '40s, Mexico was anti-Chinese, and Ricardo's mother was Mexican, but his father was Chinese. They were kicked out of the country and settled in Hong Kong. Ricardo told me how his mother used to weep as she sang Mexican songs while she did the laundry because she missed her home so much.

"Ricardo was eight or nine when he arrived in Hong Kong and later got into La Salle. When he was in Form 4, the new Mexican president decided that the Chinese-Mexicans who were unfairly kicked out would be allowed to return. Ricardo was among the three hundred or so Chinese Mexicans from Hong Kong and Macau who returned to Mexico.

"For Ricardo, it was a bad move, because he hadn't learnt to write in Spanish, and when they arrived in Mexico, they were very poor. So Ricardo worked in a Chinese restaurant as a waiter and later owned a small pet shop selling tropical fish, barely scraping by.

"If he'd remained in Hong Kong and with a La Salle education, he could have done a lot better than he did by returning to a poor country that he barely remembered."

I thought about Juan and his family. It was fortunate that his family wasn't among the three hundred or so who chose to return. Most of them had to start all over again, and their lives were a great deal more difficult than they were in Hong Kong.

Henry got up and bid us goodbye, saying that he had to meet an old friend at the Hong Kong Jockey Club.

***

2006

Having worked hard all my life, I decided to greatly reduce my hours, as my associate had been with me for almost ten years and was extremely reliable and an excellent ophthalmologist.

I bought a house in Redwood City, about forty-five minutes south of San Francisco and close to Stanford University where I would take some classes. I also bought a condo in my beloved Hawaii, in the Kahala area near the hotel where I used to work.

Xavier and I reconnected in the San Francisco area. We met for dim sum at the ABC Seafood Restaurant in Foster City on numerous occasions. We would talk from eleven in the morning until after two. I laughed so hard at his Cantonese humor that it amused the waiters to see me almost crying with laughter. I hadn't laughed that hard or that much for a long time.

Our last meal together was before Christmas, and I asked Xavier if he had any plans or resolutions for the coming year. "My father died in his 50s," he responded. "I'm not optimistic that I'll live very long. I'm just living from day to day."

Sadly, a few months later, I learned that he had died of a massive heart attack, just like his father.

In 2006, all four of our children had graduated from university and were gainfully employed.

I began spending more time in Hawaii.

***

Back in Fresno...
I again had lunch with Danny. He had gotten a divorce and was very happy with his life and with his Mexican girlfriend. He was especially proud of his older son who had graduated from medical school and, like him, was doing a residency at the Mayo Clinic in internal medicine.

He had retired from his practice in Fresno and was living in Jamaica part of the year.

"James, you know, home is where you grew up," he said nostalgically.

I nodded my head and remarked, "I know exactly what you mean, Danny. Sometimes I really miss Malaysia and Hong Kong. I especially long for the food there. I may just do what you're doing and live in Hong Kong and Malaysia part time."

Many of the old boys I'd maintained contact with had succeeded beyond our wildest imaginations. Many of us now decided to relax more and to do things that we truly wanted to do.

I sold my practice to my associate and concentrated on my work in developing countries and my writing.

I tried to visit Hong Kong every year and Malaysia every two years or so.

One year blended into another, and soon, it was 2014—fifty years after we had graduated from La Salle.

CHAPTER 13:
Toronto 50ᵗʰ Reunion

H ALF A CENTURY HAD PASSED since we graduated from Form 5. A lot had changed in that time, including the advent of the personal computer, email, smart phone, and many other gadgets that made our lives more convenient.

As I did a great deal of traveling in the 1980s and 1990s, I hung on to the old technology for quite a while. Music has always been a part of my life, and I used to be proud of the mini CDs I'd carry with me on my trips. The tiny discs were less than a quarter the size of regular CDs and each could carry as many as thirty songs, which I thought was amazing, considering the huge records we used to have.

Then the Nano Ipod came along, which could carry over a thousand songs. This new invention did away completely with the CD. Both the player and the over 2000 songs were combined into one unit that was less than one third the size of each mini disc! I made the change and never looked back.

The first 50th reunion for the class of 1964 would be held in Toronto in May of 2014. Antonio Almeida, who was in the same class with me for two years, was one of the main organizers. I'd always been interested in Antonio's background since he had a Portuguese surname and had some Portuguese facial features, but he was taking Chinese language and Chinese history and literature.

It turned out that his father did come from Portugal. Unlike the other Macanese who had roots in Macau for a long time,

Antonio believed that his father hadn't come from Macau but from Portugal instead.

Since he left La Salle after Form 5, I lost contact with him and was surprised that he was now in Toronto. It turned out that quite a few old boys had immigrated to Toronto, including David Au, who was also helping with the organization of the reunion.

Another main organizer was Angelo Lee, who had become a dentist in the Toronto area. He was with me for one year at La Salle. His father was our biology teacher in Form 3. I was curious about his name, and when I asked about it he said his father was born in Peru and his first name was Javier, which I hadn't known. His father went to China to get an education when he was young and stayed, a familiar story of many overseas Chinese. Angelo left Hong Kong for the US the same year as I did and attended dental school at the State University of New York, and then settled in Toronto.

Robert Remedios, who was with me for all three and a half years at La Salle, had also immigrated to Toronto. After two years of pre-university at La Salle, he attended the University of Hong Kong and graduated with a degree in English Literature.

Henry Hing, who was with me in Form 5B, had also immigrated to the city. I vividly recalled him explaining the point system for immigration to Canada at the 25th reunion, and how the visas for him and his family had just been approved at that point.

Henry was extremely pleased with his decision to take the family to Toronto. After La Salle, he graduated from the University of Hong Kong in civil engineering. In June 1989, he was unnerved by the Tiananmen Square Massacre and made the tough decision to leave Hong Kong. I remembered him saying, "James, I could probably live in Hong Kong but for the children's sake. I simply cannot let them suffer as we did. The education system is inhumane, the housing is beyond the reach of most working-class people, and look at Hong Kong now—they're already letting the Beijing government chip away many of the rights that were supposed to last for fifty years. Now they're even telling the Hong Kong government what to teach in schools. They're trying to brainwash the young people as they've done to the young people in China."

Even though he'd been in Hong Kong most of his life and had a good job at a big construction company, Henry decided to start anew in a country where the lifestyle would be very different from what he was used to.

Pierre Wong, who was with me for a year and a half at La Salle, had also immigrated to Toronto and now ran a busy import-export business.

Peter Fan had graduated from the Chinese University of Hong Kong after La Salle, and then immigrated to Ottawa. He was now retired and was active in the Catholic Church as a deacon.

Paul Wong Kai Lun, who I didn't remember at all, had also immigrated. I was surprised that I simply had no memory of someone who was in the same year with me. I guess since we'd never been in the same class and didn't have any mutual friends, there was never an opportunity for us to meet.

Tony Yeung Man Chi had graduated from the University of Manitoba in engineering the same year as Xavier Keng. He had stayed in Canada and settled in Edmonton. I remembered him writing to me when I was at the University of Hawaii and kindly asking me to write more legibly because he could hardly read my handwriting. This was long before I became a physician, so I had no excuse!

Most of the reunion's activities took place in Markham, a sprawling suburb north of downtown Toronto. Most of the residents in Markham were Chinese, especially Chinese from Hong Kong. As I walked around the Markham Sheraton Hotel, I thought I could just as easily have been in Hong Kong, there were so many signs in Chinese.

Initially when I received the information that the reunion would be held in Toronto, I made a reservation at the Westin Hotel near the Toronto City Center. Then I received an email from Antonio saying that Markham was in the extreme north of the Toronto metropolis, and even in good traffic it would take at least half an hour, usually closer to an hour, to get to Markham, and the taxi fare would be almost a hundred dollars. I had no idea that Toronto was that big and I was glad he'd pointed it out to me. I changed to the Sheraton Hotel in Markham itself, right next to the Chinese restaurant where many of the activities would be held.

On a Friday afternoon at five, I walked toward the Ding Tai Fung Chinese Seafood Restaurant where we would be meeting. It was a huge restaurant with tanks of fresh fish swimming, crabs, prawns and clams of every variety. It was even grander than most restaurants in Hong Kong.

There was a welcome desk at the front of the dining room that had been booked for the event. We were each given a nametag and a T-shirt with the La Salle logo.

As I stood near the entrance catching up with David Au, he was just saying how pleased he was that he immigrated to Canada when a friendly face walked over to us. I had no recollection of ever seeing him, so David introduced us. Christopher Cheung had been David's good friend for over fifty years. He stretched out his right hand and said, "Congratulations on your book. I couldn't put it down; it reminded me so much of my own family background."

Christopher was referring to my first book, *Finding Fat Lady's Shoe,* a memoir of growing up in Hong Kong and Malaya. He asked several questions about my siblings, whose photos I had in the book.

"I guess your family had it tougher than most others," he said. "My family also fled to Hong Kong about the same time as yours, but my father found a job. He also worked with the Kuomintang regime, and if we hadn't left, he would've been killed by the communists."

He dug into the inside pocket of his jacket and took out a wallet, showing me a photo of his father. He was very handsome, and wearing some sort of uniform with a pistol on his side.

Christopher added, "When our family arrived in Hong Kong in 1949, my father was lucky to find a job as a newspaper reporter and our family managed. With this job, he dined out with clients often, and perhaps he ate too much rich food for too long, because he had a stroke. After that, our family fell into hard times as well."

I lowered my head and said I was sorry to hear that. "Life was truly precarious during those years," I commented. "There were no safety nets. If the breadwinner got sick, it was just too bad. I know of another classmate whose father died shortly after arriving in Hong Kong, and his family really had a difficult time. My father often remarked that we were lucky no one in the family got seriously ill, because that would have been a disaster in so many ways."

Christopher agreed, then went on to tell me what he did after graduating from Form 5 at La Salle. He left Hong Kong not long after I did and went to university in Idaho, where he too worked as a dishwasher to pay his own way. We both shook our heads and smiled, agreeing that it was a horrible job because the dish room was so humid, hot and full of chlorine from the strong chemicals used in the dishwashing machine, which burned our eyes and irritated our throats.

He then went to pharmacy school and now owned pharmacies in the Los Angeles area.

I noticed John Chan Ka Leung arriving with his Canadian-born wife Debra and I excused myself to go greet them. John had been very good friends with Xavier Keng and shared the same house with him in Winnipeg while they were attending the

University of Manitoba. We remarked that we really missed Xavier since his death a few years ago. I was imagining how much fun we would be having had Xavier been alive and there to entertain us with his Cantonese humor.

John had graduated from the University of Manitoba in electrical engineering like Xavier, and was now in the San Francisco area.

Lester Tung arrived with his Philippines-born Chinese wife Rosalia. They had met in Chicago when he was attending medical school. It had been fifty years since I saw Lester, when I got off the President Cleveland in Hawaii while he continued on to San Francisco. I hadn't seen him at the 25th reunion. Rosalia's eyes brightened and she seemed very pleased to see me, even though it was the first time I met her. She remarked, "I read your book about growing up in Hong Kong and Malaya. I grew up in the Philippines and your book reminded me so much of my childhood."

Rosalia was friendly and had many questions about the book. She too was interested in what each of my siblings was doing now. Being in Muar for five years, I had learned the Fujian dialect. Rosalia was surprised when I told her that I could get by in her dialect. She asked me about my surname, and I told her that in Chinese it meant "bear," and that it had a different syllable in different dialects. In Cantonese, it was Hung; in Hakka, it was Yung; and in Mandarin, it was Xiong, which bore no resemblance to the other two dialects. I asked her what the syllable for "bear" was in the Fujian dialect. She was embarrassed and confessed that she had forgotten; it was a word rarely used in conversations, as there were no bears in the Philippines.

After graduating from medical school in Chicago, Lester had remained in the Chicago area and was still working part time in internal medicine.

Mason Moon arrived with his Korean-born wife who he had met in college in San Francisco. He commented that he enjoyed my memoir and didn't realize that some families like mine had it so tough during those years in Hong Kong. His father was a well-known dentist in Hong Kong, one of the few practicing in the colony in the 1960s.

I remarked that I'd always admired how he spoke English like a native, and that I had only learned years after graduation from Danny Tong that his mother came from Vancouver, Canada. Mason nodded and said, "Yes, we spoke English at home."

We talked about the English language, which we agreed was a difficult language for non-native speakers, especially for the Chinese, because it was so different from the Chinese language. He laughed and said, "James, you know, the reverse is also true. Chinese is a very difficult language for non-native speakers, or even for native speakers, such as me. I failed Chinese language in the HKSC Exam. Mr. Yep was so upset and declared that I was the only person who failed, which made him look bad." I laughed.

Soon James Yeung arrived. He had lived in the same house with Xavier and John and a few other La Salle fellows while they attended university in Manitoba. At the 25th reunion, he had been a GP in Hong Kong. Now, after many years of practicing medicine, James had moved back to Canada and retired in Vancouver.

Seeing James and John reminded me of Xavier and some of the funny stories he used to tell. I remembered one of them and repeated it to James.

"A few years ago, at lunch one day, Xavier was telling me funny stories about your years in Winnipeg. Do you remember Alex Hui?"

"Yes," said James. "He was another La Salle boy."

"Right," I said. "He had arrived in Montreal to attend McGill University and was terribly homesick. So, he talked to Xavier and Xavier told him that Winnipeg was almost like Hong Kong. Alex flew to Winnipeg and was planning to attend the university there. On arrival at the house, he took a look around and decided that it was nothing like Hong Kong and flew back to Montreal to attend McGill."

We laughed and James said, "Yes, I remember Alex being terribly disappointed in Winnipeg when he came to our house. He flew back to Montreal two days later."

A few years earlier, I had met Alex for lunch in Hong Kong and he confirmed the story.

I chatted for a few minutes with Henry Pang, who I hadn't known very well because I'd arrived halfway through Form 3, and his family immigrated to the US a few months later when the school year ended. He had graduated from UCLA and had now retired from his job as a high school biology teacher. He lived in the Los Angeles area.

While we were catching up, the three fellows from the New York City area arrived. Victor Lee and I were in Form 5B together. He was the most fashionable fellow in class and I was told that he was a good dancer too. He still looked handsome and had a mustache.

Frank Lee and I were in the same class for two years. His father was a well-known Hong Kong police detective who had solved the most notorious kidnapping case in the city.

The other fellow from New York was John Chiu, whom I barely remembered.

After mingling for a while, we all found our seats. Angelo requested that we stand up to sing the La Salle school song. After we had sung it in English, we were handed the lyrics in Chinese. Most of us were surprised that there was a Chinese version of our school song. It turned out that one of the La Salle old boys named James Wong Jim, who was quite a few years ahead of us and who became a big name in the Hong Kong entertainment industry as a director, song composer and actor, had composed this Chinese version.

Angelo then made a few announcements about the following day's activities and we sat down for the ten-course dinner.

The first dish was a scrumptious soup made with chicken, Chinese Yunnan ham, dried scallops and black mushrooms.

The soup was followed by Peking duck with soft steamed buns and all sorts of sauces, steamed grouper, pork belly cooked with taro in sweet soy sauce, BBQ pork spare ribs, crabs with green onion, pepper and salt, a soft tofu clay pot with assorted seafood, and ended with fried noodle with seafood and fried rice with scallops. It was truly a delightful and delicious dinner, one of the best I've ever had. It was certainly up to Hong Kong standards.

Sitting next to me was Ryan Tui and his Chinese Muslim wife, Tabitha. I had no recollection of Ryan Tui as we were never in the same class, but Xavier had talked about him so I knew that he had graduated from Cal Tech, and that he'd scored very high at the end of his two years of pre-university in Form 7. After Cal Tech, he went on to UC, Berkeley for his PhD. He was a congenial and very low-key sort of fellow. When I told him that I'd gone into medicine, he remarked that his father was a physician and still practicing in Hong Kong in his eighties. His wife Tabitha was fascinating and very friendly. She said her family had been Muslim for generations. They now lived in Montana after Ryan had retired from his work as a physicist for the US Department of Energy.

Riley Kung was sitting across the table from me. He was with me in Form 5B, and after La Salle he went to McGill and got a PhD in chemistry. He had just retired as the senior scientist of a large pharmaceutical company and now lived in Vancouver.

Lau Ming Chee was with me for two years at La Salle. After graduating from the University of British Columbia in engineering, he was now working in Rhode Island.

With a smile on his face, he asked me if I knew that Rhode Island was not an island. I shook my head and said I had no idea.

I told him about my year of dental school at UBC, which was a fiasco, and he agreed that UBC did have very high standards.

Francis Nguyen and his wife, Yuemei, were also at the table. Francis had been in the same class with me for two and a half years, and was one of the classmates I knew quite well. After La Salle, he attended the University of Hong Kong and graduated with a degree in electrical engineering. He worked for an American company and was transferred to the US, eventually settling in the San Francisco area. I regarded Francis as one of the nicest human beings I'd ever met, always humble, sincere, helpful and kind, and he always spoke appropriately.

Andrew Chang commented on how good the soup was and I agreed. Andrew had graduated from the University of California, Berkeley in electrical engineering and had worked for a large chip company in Silicon Valley before retiring. I didn't know him well, but it turned out he had also been on the President Cleveland in 1965 when we left Hong Kong. When I told him that I had been on the same ship, his eyes widened and he exclaimed, "You couldn't have been! I never saw you."

I laughed and said, "I never saw you either. But I was definitely on that boat." I named the other fellows I'd shared a cabin with, and we shook our heads with amazement that we spent all that time on the same boat and had no recollection of seeing each other.

Christopher began telling me about another classmate, who also became a pharmacist. I had no recollection of Lou Dong. Christopher told me that Lou specialized in infusion type of medicine and had been exceedingly successful. He also lived in the Los Angeles area.

David Ho Tak Chuen was with me for one year, and I remembered him well. He worked for many years as an accountant in Hong Kong and also decided to immigrate to Toronto.

When the last dish was served, we were treated with sweet red bean soup, a typical Cantonese dessert.

We lingered a while and chatted with people we hadn't seen in fifty years, and other people we never got a chance to know even though we were in the same year in school.

***

The following day, a Saturday, we were to have a BBQ at the Thomson Memorial Park in Scarborough, a part of the greater Toronto area.

John Chan had rented a car and was kind enough to take me and two other old boys along.

This get-together also included La Salle alumni from all the other years, which numbered over a hundred. Most of those who showed up were younger than we were, some much younger, having graduated only a few years ago. We probably looked ancient to the younger old boys.

We all wore our T-shirts with the La Salle logo. As a big group, we sang the school song.

It was a beautiful spring day. Even though it was mid-May, it was still a little chilly. The trees had soft, new green leaves on their branches. Many blue jays were happily singing. Some of the birds seemed young and had probably hatched only recently.

Soon the BBQ was ready and each of us got a plate and loaded up with an ear of corn and a piece of our favorite meat or sausage.

I found a seat next to David Ho, who was already chewing on his corn. "James, you know," he remarked, "in Canada, at least you have a chance. In Hong Kong, unless you're a super student and your family is super rich, life isn't going to be easy. It's a disgrace how the young in Hong Kong have to study so hard and they don't have much of a childhood. It seems that their sole being is just to study. I'm glad I decided to immigrate here, where life is much more equal. I know it's true that no place is perfect, but Canada is definitely a more suitable place for children to grow up. The drawback here is that the winters are so cold and so long. Especially when you get older. It seems the cold bothers me more and more, and the cold gets into my bones."

I nodded in agreement.

Robert Remedios was sitting next to Antonio at our table, and I asked Robert if he knew what happened to Alphonso Remedios, another Portuguese boy in our class.

"Oh, you mean fei chai?" he responded. "Fei chai" was an endearing term in Cantonese meaning "chubby boy." Apparently, Alphonso had chubby cheeks when he was young, and his Chinese Amah gave him the nickname.

After Alphonso left La Salle, he eventually immigrated to the US, and sadly he had died a few years ago from heart attack. I was sorry to hear that.

As we ate, I saw a group of Muslim women wearing black burkas, their faces completely covered. Behind them were men with long beards and their heads wrapped in turbans.

Tabitha, who I had talked to at dinner the evening before, was sitting across the table and I asked her the significance of wearing turbans among Muslim men. "I remember that the Malay men in Malaysia, who were almost all Muslim, wore a type of a cap, the shape of a truncated cone, usually black," I added. "Do you know if it has a similar significance?"

She looked in the direction of the people I was referring to and answered, "I think these men are probably from Yemen. Their turbans are wrapped around a cap known in Arabic as a *kalansuwa* and they can be spherical or conical, colorful or solid white, and their styles vary widely from region to region. Likewise, the color of the turban wrapped around the *kalansuwa* also varies. White is thought by some Muslims to be the holiest turban color, based on legends that the prophet Mohammed wore a white turban. Green is held to be the color of paradise, and is also favored by some. But not all Muslims wear turbans."

I nodded as I listened, then asked, "What is the reason for wearing them?"

"Muslim men wear a turban or a cap because it reflects the spirit of Islam that seeks to remind people of God. When praying, Muslims are required to cover their heads as they are in the presence of their Lord. Covering the head is a sign of respect to God," Tabitha replied.

I still had questions about Islam and asked another. "Did the Koran have any instructions about the women wearing burkas?"

"I don't think so," she responded. "I think this was something passed down from Arabic customs. I don't believe the Koran mentions anything about women having to cover their faces. But I could be mistaken, as I haven't had much instruction on the Koran. I grew up in Hong Kong, and my family wasn't very religious. It was more or less as a tradition passed down the generations, rather than a real religion."

Following the Muslims was a group of Sikh men wearing large colorful turbans and women in traditional saris, also very colorful. They were laughing and talking loudly, obviously having a great time.

David Au enlightened us that Toronto was one of the most cosmopolitan cities in the world, with people speaking over a hundred languages.

We strolled in the park until after 4 pm, and then headed back to our hotels to get ready for another banquet.

That evening, we had dinner at another well-known Chinese seafood restaurant.

There were a few announcements about the bus tour we would be taking the next day. The old boys in Toronto had arranged a three-day, two-night bus tour to Quebec City.

***

Bus Tour

Sunday morning, I woke up at 6 and had a quick breakfast before dragging my suitcase across the street to the tour bus. The bus was already half full and everyone on it had big smiles on their faces, like children going on an outing.

Christopher Cheung waved at me to sit with him. He was very funny and told me joke after joke, making me laugh so hard. I was very glad I'd come to this reunion and met a new friend. We had good chemistry, and took turns talking. We were both very interested in what each other had to say.

The tour guide was a slim Chinese man who spoke passable English, and who was obviously from Hong Kong.

I overheard a woman in the back complaining that the tour company charged us ten percent for tips for the tour guide and bus driver before the tour began. Then I heard a man explaining that they had decided to do that because few Asian customers would pay the ten percent after the tour.

I smiled to myself as I listened.

At the back of the bus were about fifteen Indians who looked like they were from two or three families. As our group consisted of about forty people, the other seats had been sold to other customers.

I was truly excited about the tour, and happy to be among a group of fellows I'd spent time with in my youth.

As the bus passed major landmarks in the Toronto area, the tour guide would point them out and make comments. I was impressed with how expansive Canada was. Even though I spent a school year in Vancouver, I hadn't ventured outside the city, and really knew very little about the country.

It was very green along the freeway and most of the trees had sprung new leaves. Our first destination was Kingston.

Located midway between Toronto and Montreal, Kingston had been named the first capital of the Province of Canada. The guide commented that Kingston was a city rich in history, culture, critically acclaimed attractions and cuisine.

We made a short stop to tour the Kingston City Hall. I learned that it was built in 1844 and was once the main governmental building of the capital city of the Province of Canada. Today, it was the city hall of Kingston and a community hub.

We also made a short stop at Queen's University, a large public research institution in Kingston. One of the oldest universities in the country, it actually predated the establishment of Canada as an independent country.

Another short stop was made at the Royal Military College, which was the premier degree-granting military university in the country, where cadets were trained in academics, officership, bilingualism and athletics, considered by the Canadian military to be the four pillars of success.

The scenery was beautiful as we passed a river and some lakes. We soon arrived at Parliament Hill, located on the banks of the Ottawa River in Canada's capital city, home to the Canadian Parliament.

As we drove by the beautiful Ottawa River, the tour guide pointed out the border between Quebec and Ontario. Along the drive, we saw numerous Victorian mansions and expansive Canadian forests beyond the horizon.

After a two-hour drive, we arrived in Montreal. We visited the St. Joseph's Oratory and Notre Dame Basilica.

I was truly moved as I prayed at the Oratory, which reminded me of how I used to pray in the little church in Muar.

The basilica was dedicated to St. Joseph, to whom Brother André credited all his reported miracles. The miracles performed by Brother André mostly related to some kind of healing power, and many pilgrims—handicapped, blind and ill—poured into his basilica, including numerous non-Catholics. On display was a wall covered with hundreds of crutches from those who came to the basilica and were purportedly healed.

Pope John Paul II deemed those miracles to be authentic and beatified Brother André in 1982, and he was canonized a saint in October 2010. As I looked at the hundreds of crutches on the wall, a part of me really wanted to believe that miracles did happen, and indeed those people were healed. But another part of me was skeptical.

We made a stop at McGill University, which the tour guide touted as one of Canada's best universities. One old boy who had graduated from McGill stood up and took a bow, and we clapped amidst laughter.

On our way to the hotel, the tour guide enlightened us that Montreal was the second-largest city in Canada, and the center of French Canadian culture. He continued to praise McGill, saying that his son was a first-year medical student there. No wonder he went on and on about the university!

We then checked into our hotel, and later had dinner—rack of lamb, for which the hotel was famous.

The next morning, we got up for an early breakfast and headed for Quebec City.

We stopped at Olympic Park in Montreal where the 1976 Summer Olympics were held.

Christopher continued to entertain me with his jokes. We talked about getting old, and that his ninety-year-old father and his brother lived in Toronto, so he would come to this area at least once a year.

We arrived in Quebec City and checked into the Fairmont Le Chateau Frontenac, a famous grand hotel and a National Historic Site of Canada. The hotel was essentially a castle that sat on a hilltop in the city. I was told that it was one of the most photographed hotels in the world.

The rest of the day was free time. Christopher and I walked around the Old City and were impressed by the buildings that were hundreds of years old. He remarked that it would be difficult for him to live there because it got so cold in the winter.

We walked by a small Chinese restaurant and saw several workers busy serving. I commented that Chinese were truly everywhere. I wondered how they managed in the depth of winter when temperatures were minus 30° Celsius.

On a plaque, I read that the UNESCO World Heritage Site traced the history of Quebec City to 1620 and the establishment of the Saint-Louis Fort. I looked around and was impressed with the architecture of Old Quebec and how a bunch of brave men and women tried to find a new life in a new land, a land that was very different from their native France.

Christopher and I then went to the top floor of the Edifice Marie-Guyart, a 31-story building in Quebec City—the Observatoire de la Capitale. We read that the Observatoire measured a height of 725 feet, and we had a wonderful view of the city.

We had dinner in the hotel restaurant again. We were told that we wouldn't find better lamb anywhere else, so most of us had lamb again! It was certainly the best I'd ever had.

The next morning, we again got up early and had a quick breakfast, and were soon on the road again.

We were on our way to the Thousand Islands. Along the way, the tour guide gave us a history lesson on Quebec. He pointed out that not long ago, the English-speakers were considered the higher class, which was how a top English-speaking university, McGill, existed in a French-speaking province.

After several hours on the bus, we arrived at the Thousand Islands, which indeed consisted of over a thousand islands (1864 to be exact) straddling the Canada-US border in the Saint Lawrence River as it emerged from the northeast corner of Lake Ontario. We got on a boat and cruised among the many islands.

I laughed when the guide told us that to count as one of the Thousand Islands, an island must have at least one square foot of land above water level year-round, and support at least two living trees. In reality, many islands were nothing but a rock with a couple of trees.

Some of the islands were as big as 40 square miles and had many houses on them, some with impressive mansions; but most of the islands had no inhabitants.

We headed back to Toronto shortly after 4 pm. It was certainly a trip to remember and I was very pleased that I found a new friend in Christopher, who seemed like a genuinely sincere and kind person.

We said goodbye to each other as we exited the bus.

The following day, I flew back to California full of good memories. Not in my wildest imagination would I have thought in 1964 that we would be meeting in Toronto fifty years later. We were grateful for the lives we had lived so far.

In the class of 1964, there were well over 200 graduates. About a third were on the old boy email list, which meant that two thirds of the class wasn't in contact with the alumni group. I really had no idea where they were, or what they had done with their lives. I would've been very interested to find out.

CHAPTER 14

50th Reunion in Hong Kong

THE OFFICIAL 50TH REUNION had been planned to be held in Hong Kong in mid-November. The main organizers were the usual reliable, hard-working fellows—Michael Sze, Vincent Lo, Edwin Chan Yu Chow and Lambert Leung Ying Wah.

Michael had risen to a top position in the Hong Kong government and had been Chris Patten's right-hand man, especially in the negotiations with China for the 1997 handover. He was now retired and enjoying being on the boards of several major companies including Swire and condiment giant Lee Kum Kee.

Vincent was one of the top business lawyers in Hong Kong and both Edwin and Lambert were senior executives in major companies.

Michael stood at the front of the school building, which still seemed new to me even though it was now over thirty years old, helping to greet the returning old boys. A welcome desk was set up next to the entrance.

As I stood with Michael beside the statue of St. John Baptist De La Salle, the founder of the Christian Brothers School, a familiar figure came walking toward us. This man had a spring in his footstep, but his somewhat stooped posture and receding hairline betrayed his age. It was Max Mandel. His hair was still wavy and his eyes bright.

He walked over to us with a broad smile on his face and extended his right hand to shake ours.

"I can't believe that it's been twenty-five years since we saw each other. I'm glad that we're still alive," he chuckled.

We nodded in agreement.

"Wow, it's good to be back in Hong Kong," he continued. "I'm glad that I grew up here and my experiences here showed me another side of myself. I really miss Hong Kong sometimes. I'm lucky that I live not far from New York City's Chinatown. If I miss Hong Kong, I just walk around Chinatown and have some dim sum."

"Are you still working at St Vincent's Hospital?' I asked.

"Yes," he replied. "I do still show up four mornings a week and read the films. It's not really work. But I wouldn't know what to do with so much free time if I didn't do it. You've probably heard that most people kick the bucket five or six years after they retire. So, I'm afraid to really retire. There's only so much you can do with playing golf or other hobbies. I've done my share of traveling. As you know, traveling is getting to be more of a hassle. I do enjoy the part-time work, especially teaching the residents and medical students."

"Do you live around St. Vincent's?" I asked.

"Not too far. It's an area in Lower Manhattan called Gramercy Park. But the so-called 'park' is really misleading, because it's just a tiny place," Max added.

"I know where Gramercy Park is," I commented. "About forty years ago, just before I began my eye residency, I spent a month at the New York Eye and Ear Infirmary as an extern. I actually stayed at the Gramercy Hotel and walked to work each morning at the Infirmary on Fourteenth Street."

"It's turned into a premium neighborhood now," Max said, "and the house prices are ridiculous. When we bought the condo twenty years ago, it was still affordable."

"I guess it's the same all over. Hong Kong is even worse," I remarked.

I looked past Max's shoulder to see our Pakistani classmate, Bashir Ajmal, walking toward us. "How is the King of Chung King Mansions?" I teased as he got closer. We all laughed.

Bashir said hello to the three of us before responding, "Life is good. I have no complaints. The situation at Chung King Mansions is fine and getting better. Finally, we the owners got together and made some major decisions to improve the elevator situation as well as security. Now, we have three security guards around the clock."

Bashir was referring to the notorious building, where he still owned shops and youth hostels, on Nathan Road at the center of the tourist area. The sprawling building had been in the news recently because it had become quite run down and turned into an international ghetto, infested with petty crimes.

"You know, I remember that building when it was new," I commented. "It wasn't long after I arrived in Hong Kong from Malaysia. It was considered a sort of high-class residential area, and I remember that a two-bedroom unit cost only fifty thousand Hong Kong dollars. Now it probably costs five million."

"Probably well over five million," remarked Michael.

"That's a hundred times the price of forty years ago," I lamented, shaking my head. "I don't think you see that kind of appreciation anywhere else on earth."

I noticed Juan Trujillo arriving, and I waved him over. He hadn't changed much and still had a full head of hair and a spring in his step. I'd last seen him in Vancouver a year ago. A few years after our 25th reunion, Juan decided that Hong Kong would not be his permanent home, especially after the 1989 Tiananmen Square Massacre. He made the tough decision to immigrate to Canada at age fifty-two, and he hadn't looked back since.

With his extensive experience at the Peninsula Hotel, he was hired as an assistant manager at the historic Vancouver Hotel, which hosted many Hong Kong visitors. With his fluency in

Cantonese, he was perfect for the job. As more and more tourists were visiting British Columbia from Central and South America, his fluency in Spanish was definitely an added asset.

At age 67, he still worked part time at the hotel. All his children had also moved to Vancouver, and Julia had moved to the area with her family too.

Richard Singh and Darius Mody soon showed up and joined us.

Richard was now a well-known immigration lawyer in Hong Kong. He was happy that he had switched from defending criminals to helping people stay in Hong Kong. As more Nepalese were deciding to stay in Hong Kong, many of them had immigration issues. Richard was the one they usually turned to. Many of the retired Gurkha soldiers, who the British had hired to guard Hong Kong, were working on bringing their families to join them, and Richard was their man.

Darius had expanded his family businesses into money remittance outlets for the many Nepalese workers and maids from the Philippines and Indonesia. His family also owned many of the money exchange outlets.

Clement Tam arrived and came to say hello to us. While the others chatted, Clement and I went to the nearby table and each got a bottle of Coke.

"I can't believe that it's been fifty years since we graduated from here," Clement exclaimed. "Life has turned out much better than I ever dared to imagine. It's already been five years since I retired."

Clement's twin sons had also graduated from La Salle. After graduating from the University of Hong Kong Faculty of Dentistry, they took over Clement's practice.

I noticed Felix Sapanov looking around as he walked slowly towards us. He still looked fit, trim and relaxed.

"Hello old boys," he called out as he got closer. "This is an excellent idea for us to get together. Who knows how much longer we'll be around?" he chuckled.

"You're right," Juan chimed in. "Let's enjoy every day that we have."

"I recently read that we should all treat our lives as if we only have six months to live, because at some point, we really do only have six months to live," laughed Felix.

After working as a reporter for a number of years, Felix decided to get a PhD at the London School of Economics, and had been teaching at the University of Sydney specializing in the politics of Hong Kong and China. I had read some of his articles in the *Economist* magazine.

To my surprise, a large fellow was moving slowly towards us. His eyes were hidden behind heavy eyelids, and his heavy cheeks were drawn down by gravity, sagging. I had no idea who it was.

He walked up to the welcome desk and announced to Vincent Lo, who was checking the names, that he was Benny Cho. On hearing his name, I immediately went over and grabbed hold of his hand and shook it vigorously a few times, saying, "Benny, what a surprise that you showed up! I learned that you had gone to Kansas after Form 5, and then the next thing I heard was that you had opened a Shanghainese restaurant at Times Square in New York, then I had no news about you for the last twenty-five years. Nobody seemed to know where you were," I added.

"James," he said, returning my handshake warmly. "I still can recognize you even though we haven't seen each other for fifty years."

Benny and I sat down on a bench nearby and caught up on each other's lives for the last five decades. He was now retired in New York City and his son had taken over the restaurant, which had turned out to be very successful. He added that his sister

Cynthia had also moved to New York, the sister who had told me that Benny had left Hong Kong for Kansas fifty years ago.

"Those years at La Salle were such tough years," Benny lamented. "You did well and you passed the HKSC Exam. Do you remember me telling you that if you could only give me one of the eleven subjects you'd passed, then I would've gotten a certificate too?" I nodded. "I guess moving from Taiwan to Hong Kong didn't help. The school systems were so different," he added.

"Most of us were traumatized by that exam," I remarked. "But look at us now—we are alive and doing well."

It was truly a surprise to see Benny. I had always suspected that his father must have gotten his money somehow other than his dental practice. The fact that his father was able to send him to the American International School in Taipei meant that the family really had to have some money. The income of a dentist in Taipei or Hong Kong in the 1960s certainly wouldn't have paid for such a school.

Benny stood up and waved to a beefy fellow with a red face walking toward us.

"Hey, Ed King," he yelled.

I couldn't believe my eyes. It was the fellow who was on the relay team with me for three years. I had no idea where he went after Form 5. He too had gained weight, and like Benny, his eyes were barely visible behind his droopy lids. I could barely see his neck, which was covered by rolls of fat beneath his chin.

Ed came over and I shook hands with him. It turned out that he had also immigrated to the US, and had also settled in New York. He became a lawyer and had an office in Chinatown. He had gotten together with Benny in the city and they sometimes played mahjong together with two other friends.

Soon it was 5 pm, and we milled into the assembly hall, talking, laughing, gesturing and looking around for people we hadn't seen for a quarter or half a century or more.

Michael gave a short welcome speech. The principal of the college, Brother Steven, also spoke. He was now the only monk at the school. I learned that there were now female teachers at La Salle as well, which didn't exist in our time.

The assembly hall was set up with eight large round tables, so after the speeches we sat down. The organizers had arranged for a catered ten-course dinner from a famous Cantonese seafood restaurant.

Juan sat down next to me and asked how Danny Tong was. I told him that I last saw Danny a few years ago after I sold my practice to my associate. At that time, he had gotten a divorce from his wife, and his 90-year-old mother was living with him. He brought her into my office. She had dense cataracts and severe glaucoma in her right eye and needed surgery. Sadly, I wasn't able to save that eye, but fortunately her left eye turned out well.

"His mother was a petite black woman. She talked like a true Jamaican," I commented. "I haven't heard from him since I left Fresno. I really should have made more effort to stay in contact with him," I added.

A tall figure was ushered to our table, and Michael helped him sit down. It was Brother Lawrence, my Form 3 teacher. I had him for only a few months, and I didn't think he would remember me.

"Hi, Brother Lawrence, I'm James Hung," I said.

"What is your Chinese name?" asked Brother Lawrence. "It's difficult for me to remember the English names alone as there were so many similar ones."

"My Chinese name is Hung Yum Yin," I responded. "You probably don't remember me because I was your student for only a few months. I joined La Salle in February of 1962 after our family left Malaya. I'm sure you do remember Michael Sze, though," I added. "He sat next to me and really helped me in school."

"Yes, James," said Brother Lawrence. "I think I vaguely remember you, because you told me you had attended St. Andrew's School in Muar."

"That's right," I responded with surprise.

"After teaching at La Salle," he continued, "I was transferred to Sabah in East Malaysia. I knew all the Irish Brothers there. I met your old principal Brother Robert. I'm sure you remember that he was a very strict man and I heard he carried out a lot of canings," he remarked with a chuckle.

I smiled and nodded, replying, "Yes, Brother Robert was really strict. I was caned on several occasions in primary four, five and six. But after that, I learned my lesson and never got into trouble again."

Brother Lawrence smiled and added, "You know he was the principal of a reform school before he went to Muar."

I nodded again. "Yes, that was what we heard."

What a truly small world, that my Form 3 teacher would know the principal of a small school in a small town in Malaysia that I attended.

I was curious and asked, "What is Brother Robert's surname? None of the boys were even aware that he had one!"

"His surname was O'Sullivan," replied Brother Lawrence.

I told him that I had written a memoir about growing up in Malaya and Hong Kong and said I would happy to send him a copy.

"Please do," he responded. "I would love to read it. I don't think any of my former students in Hong Kong or Malaysia have written any memoirs."

Brother Lawrence turned his attention to Paul Lam, who had just sat down next to him, and shook his hand.

Paul also had an interest in writing and I had read of some his articles about the history of medicine. I asked if he was still practicing medicine, and he said yes. "I guess, not being a surgeon and just doing consultations in neurology and psychiatry, I don't have to retire like you," he commented. "I imagine doing eye surgery at sixty-seven or sixty-eight isn't the same as when you were forty or fifty."

"You're right," I responded. "Eye surgery is especially unforgiving. If something goes wrong, then the patient goes blind. I quit delicate surgery at the right time. But I still do laser treatments for diabetic retinopathy in developing countries such as Samoa and Cambodia. I think as long I still can move, and I don't have Alzheimer's, I will always be able to do lasers," I chuckled.

Vincent Ma soon showed up and joined our table. He still spoke English with an Indian accent. He was now a prominent lawyer in Hong Kong.

"Do your clients ever wonder about your Indian accent?" I asked.

"Yes," Vincent replied. "It's funny sometimes, especially with new clients I've only talk to over the telephone. When they show up at the office, or at a restaurant to meet for lunch, they're confused to see a Chinese fellow instead of an Indian man."

"I can see why," I responded with a snicker. "Do you know if there are still Chinese in Calcutta?"

Vincent nodded. "There are less than a thousand now, instead of around twenty thousand like when we were there. Many of the old tanneries have closed because of new zoning laws. Most people who could leave have left, especially after the 1967 Sino-Indian War, when many Chinese were rounded up and put in internment camps, just like what the Americans did to the Japanese," he remarked.

The dinner began with minced beef and egg white soup. It was full of flavor and very soothing. We decided not to have shark fin soup because of the cruelty inflicted on the animals. It would be unconscionable to still consume a soup that involved such an inhuman way to get one of the ingredients. A few old boys protested that it was our cultural right to still enjoy the soup, but they were just a handful of dissenters.

Henry Young walked briskly into the room and sat down across the table from me, just in time for the soup.

"I could not get a taxi," he declared. "Hong Kong has changed so much in just four years. It seems like there are so many more people now. I don't think I could survive here at all. I'm just not fast enough to compete."

I stood up and reached out to give Henry a firm handshake. His eyes widened and he uttered, "It's good to see you, James."

Brother Lawrence raised his massive hand and also gave Henry a firm shake, remarking with a smile, "I will always remember Henry Young because he was the only student I ever had with an Australian accent."

We laughed.

I noticed a very distinguished, good-looking fellow across the room, stylishly dressed with a colorful silk scarf around his neck. I asked Brother Lawrence if he knew who it was.

"Oh, he is Ethan Pei, the famous artist in Hong Kong," answered Brother Lawrence.

This was the fellow from our Form 4 class who Tommy had been so curious about, wondering why such a nice-looking fellow with such talent had to live in government housing. I later learned that Ethan had become one of Hong Kong's top impressionist artists, and any of his paintings would sell for at least a hundred thousand Hong Kong dollars. He had also made a name for himself in Japan, so many of his buyers were Japanese.

One by one, the old boys were invited to stand up to say a few words about themselves. Most of them had retired except the few who taught at the university.

The second course, which was abalone with large shitake mushrooms, arrived. As we dug into the shellfish and mushrooms, the conversation turned to the Umbrella Movement.

The movement consisted of individuals numbering in the tens of thousands who participated in a series of sit-in street protests, often called the Umbrella Revolution and sometimes used interchangeably with the Umbrella Movement, or the Occupy Movement. It occurred in Hong Kong from September 26 to December 15, 2014. The protests began after the Standing Committee of the National People's Congress issued a decision regarding proposed reforms to the Hong Kong electoral system, such as pre-screening of the candidates for the 2017 election of the chief executive of Hong Kong.

Its name arose from the use of umbrellas as a tool for passive resistance to the Hong Kong Police's use of pepper spray to disperse the crowd during a 79-day occupation of the city demanding more transparent elections.

At the table, opinions were split between the pro-Umbrella Movement and anti-Umbrella Movement. Some felt that to demand democracy in Hong Kong was totally unrealistic, and that under the British, Hong Kong people never had democracy either. I learned that in many Hong Kong families, the feelings were so strong on each side that many members of the same family didn't talk to each other if they disagreed. I thought it wise to stick to the policy of never talking about politics or religion in a setting like this one. In the end, no one was persuaded by the other side, and people just got angry.

I truly could see the argument of each side, and I didn't have a stand in that regard.

Felix felt very strongly that Hong Kong people should be given more freedom to pick their own leaders.

Clement felt that the Chinese people wouldn't know what to do with their freedom, and he was tired of the chaos caused by this group of people. He felt certain that they were supported by the CIA to be a thorn in the Chinese people's sides.

Vincent Ma also felt that sometimes, for the good of a country, the people should give up some freedom. "Look at India," he said. "They can never get anything done there because everyone wants to have their own interests protected. They couldn't even build a freeway because there were so many protests. Look at Singapore—it was sort of ruled by a benevolent dictator, Lee Kuan Yew, and he totally transformed a poor country into a modern one. If the people had been given true freedom, nothing would have been accomplished. There is no comparison between China and India now. China has one of the best infrastructures in the world, while in India, the sacred cows still walk on the roads and sometimes even freeways," he asserted.

I wished the subject hadn't been brought up because it only served to upset people. In a setting like that, we were all together to have a good time, not to argue about politics.

Since the start of the 2014 protests, movement activists have complained of harassment from political opponents alarmingly similar to the way mainland Chinese activists and their families have long been targeted and have been prosecuted and jailed for their participation in acts of protest.

Max chimed in, "I think too much freedom is not good. I agree with you, Vincent. For the good of a country, we all have to give up some freedom. I think part of America's problem is that there is too much freedom."

I was surprised by Max's stand. I thought it odd that someone whose father had to flee Nazi Germany would have such an opinion. Although I did think perhaps Max was correct about America.

Tjong spoke up and gave his opinion. "I think many of the young people participating in this movement never had to suffer hardships like our generation, such as being poor. I don't think freedom will solve their problems. I think it's important for Hong Kong to have the rule of law. This occupying major public places and disrupting public transportation is a crime. All I want is a peaceful Hong Kong. I don't want a return of the 1967 riots when it was close to anarchy. Hong Kong was brought to a standstill."

Henry couldn't hold his tongue any longer and announced that he was surprised to see so many old boys against the freedom movement. "I think we're all trying to protect our own interests. Many of you have done very well in life and have accumulated much wealth. Of course, you don't want to see real estate prices drop, or your businesses slow down. But these young people have nothing, and they have little to lose. Many of them are university graduates and the only jobs they can find pay far less than twenty thousand HK dollars a month. Even just to rent a room in a shared apartment costs ten thousand a month. They'll never be able to purchase their own homes. No wonder they're so angry. I think it goes beyond the issue of freedom. I think it has become a rich-poor income gap issue. The rich have too much here. I think we should listen to these young people, or Hong Kong will be destroyed and all of you will be losers," Henry warned.

The third dish arrived: lobster cooked in a black bean and egg sauce.

Mason, ever the diplomat, tried to change the subject. "Last year, we went on a seafood tour in the New England states," he said. "We were treated to fresh lobster almost daily, cooked in every which way. It was truly amazing. After a week of lobster, I finally said to the tour guide, 'Please give me a Chinese style steamed grouper!' I don't think I'll ever get tired of steamed fish like that. It's such a healthy food and so delicious."

Jack Ng, the physicist across the table, added, "I totally agree with Mason. Steamed grouper is my favorite dish."

"Yes, I agree too," I remarked. "I think the best Chinese food I ever had was the steamed grouper I ordered at the Man Wah Restaurant in the Mandarin Hotel. I had that meal over thirty years ago, and I still talk about it."

The next dish was roast pigeon. The dark meat loaded with iron almost tasted like liver. The flavor was exquisite and I could detect a hint of the five star spices with anise.

As we finished dinner, we stayed and lingered to catch up.

This was the twilight of our lives. Some of us looked back with satisfaction; some had regrets and wished they hadn't made certain decisions. But it was too late now.

Every year, a new class would graduate from La Salle, full of hope just like we were fifty years ago, and they too would seek their place under the sun.

***

Two days before I left Hong Kong I had a very long conversation with Frederick Ho, who had been a reserve runner on the relay team at La Salle. He was with me in Form 4A and Form 5B. In 1964, he did well on the HKSC Exam and got in Form 6 Science. Even though he still occasionally ran the 4 x 100m relay with me the following year, we drifted apart and hardly did anything together. After Form 6, he went to McGill University in Canada and became a civil engineer. After working in Canada and the US for two decades, he returned to Hong Kong and drifted from job to job. A few years earlier, he was laid off. Because he didn't work in one company for any length of time, he had no pension.

At his invitation one windy and cold afternoon in late December, 2014, we had lunch at the YMCA dining room in Tsim Sha Tsui. We talked—or more correctly, he talked and I mostly listened—from noon to five in the afternoon catching up. Frederick had so many regrets. He wished he had gone into medicine like I did. There was no doubt in my mind that he could have gotten into medical school, as he was a better student than I was. He regretted marrying the woman he did, saying that he should have married the younger sister he was initially dating, but he changed his mind because he thought the older sister was more beautiful. He now felt that his ex-wife was a gold digger.

"Rose, the younger sister, is a much more sincere and down-to-earth person. She seemed happy even though her husband was only a schoolteacher. Whereas my ex was always complaining that I wasn't making enough money," Frederick remarked with a sigh.

He regretted not spending enough time with his only son when he was young, a son he now hardly knew and who was barely talking to him. His ex-wife blamed him for their son being gay because he didn't spend quality time with him when he was young.

Frederick looked sad. With very little savings and no hope of a pension, he still had to work at whatever jobs he could find. He sometimes tutored high school students in math and science. He also made some money as a tennis teacher. He claimed that his ex-wife had really "cleaned him out" in the divorce. He couldn't even afford a flat in Hong Kong or Kowloon and was living in Sheung Shui close to the Chinese border.

"The worst thing is that I really disappointed my parents," he lamented. "They worked so hard to send me to Hong Kong and then to Canada. They wanted me to get rich so I could help my three younger sisters and make them proud. But in the end, my parents never got rich and my father still had to work as a Fafi man in Johannesburg until he passed away."

I interrupted him and asked, "What is a Fafi man?"

Frederick paused to take a sip of his water and then replied," Fafi, also written as fah-fee or known as umchina, the Zulu word for Chinese, is an illegal lottery game based on superstition and luck played throughout urban areas and townships in South Africa. Players bet on a number between 1 and 36, all of which correspond to a particular image."

I nodded and interrupted him again. "Yes, I think I know what you're talking about. I think the Chinese in Malaya also played a similar game. I remember a fellow in our Form 1 class was able to afford a motor scooter while everyone else rode bicycles. The rumor went that he was working as a runner or carrier for the boss of this game," I commented. "I'm sorry," I apologized, "I shouldn't interrupt you."

After another sip of water, Frederick continued his explanation. "Fafi participants choose the number they want to gamble on by interpreting their dreams. This dream interpretation or conversion is based on a variety of systems. When they've decided on their lucky number, participants then place a bet on it. A dream about robbers may indicate the number 7. A dream about a white person is the number 1, whereas a dream about the sea could either indicate the number 3 for a ship or 26, the number for water. The game requires a runner, usually a woman, to take a bag of bets, along with the names of the betters and their money, to someone, usually Chinese, who visits the station (house) of the runner holding the betting session. The Chinese person will take the bag from the runner and then whisper the winning number to her. The runner will then indicate with her hands to the betters which number has won, and that person will be paid out," he finished.

Frederick had arrived in Hong Kong in 1959 when his father realized that South Africa with its apartheid policy wasn't a good place for the Chinese, so he sent him to live with his uncle. The uncle had relocated to Hong Kong from Maputo in Mozambique, as the country was engaged in the war for independence from the Portuguese. Frederick's father had hopes that his son would get a good education, make some money and perhaps help the family get out of South Africa, either to Canada or the US, or just to a good life in Hong Kong.

I felt very bad for him. I thought how tragic it was for someone to look back at almost seventy years of age and have so many regrets, because there wasn't much he could do about it now.

I was searching for words to try to make Frederick feel better and was having difficulty deciding what I should say to him. Finally, I said, "Life is a mystery. We never know what's around the corner waiting for us. I guess at this stage of our lives, the most important thing is our health. You look very healthy and you still play tennis regularly. Some of the fellows in our class are no longer with us. You have had a life that is probably better than most people on this earth. As far as money, I think we all want more. Even though we know that money cannot buy happiness."

"James, thanks for listening," sighed Frederick. "I know you're trying to make me feel good. I know I should be grateful for what I have, and you're right that my life has been better than most people's. I guess in Hong Kong, we're always comparing ourselves to someone richer than us. I know sometimes I have an attitude problem and I should really work harder to be a happier person."

We bid each other goodbye, and I hurriedly caught a taxi back to my hotel to get ready for my dinner with Michael. I was meeting him at 7 pm at the Hong Kong Jockey Club, where he'd been the president for years in the past.

In the taxi, I thought about Frederick's life compared to Michael's, and there was no greater contrast. Life was indeed a mystery. So much in life was about luck, about being in the right place at the right time.

CHAPTER 15:
2015 and Beyond…

THE 50TH CLASS REUNION WAS A RESOUNDING SUCCESS. It was a time for reminiscing about how we were once seventeen or eighteen; now most of us were close to seventy. Some of us were visibly frail and had to walk with a cane. Most of those who remained in Hong Kong after La Salle had done exceedingly well. Some of them had gotten quite wealthy.

I pondered every now and then what my life would be like had I chosen to stay or return to settle in Hong Kong. As one of the old boys put it, "Those of you who have made your home overseas probably have a different perspective of life. Those of us who chose to live in Hong Kong only know Hong Kong, whereas you have another experience. Sometimes I wish I had gone away."

Just before I left, I visited William Win Hang Lam at Queen Mary Hospital, not far from the Meridien Hotel where I was staying. Liam had been in the hospital with advanced nasopharyngeal cancer, a malignant cancer in the tissues of the upper part of the throat behind the nose. This form of cancer was found most commonly in people of Chinese ancestry from the Canton (Guangzhou) area. Liam was the second classmate of mine to be diagnosed with the disease. It's one of the cancers believed to be associated with a virus.

Most scientists believed that this cancer was related to the salt-cured foods the people from the Canton area ate. The mechanism came from chemicals released in the steam when cooking (frying and steaming) salt-cured foods, such as fish and preserved vegetables entering the nasal cavity. Being exposed to these chemicals at an early age may increase the risk even more.

It was also believed that the cancer was related to the Epstein-Barr virus. Somehow the fumes from cooking the salted foods combined with the virus in the nasopharyngeal cells caused mutations of the cells behind the nose, leading to this cancer. Like many cancers, the cause was most likely multifactorial.

Liam was with me in Forms 3A and 4A. He was a quiet fellow. He was a whiz in math and helped me with algebra and trigonometry. After La Salle, he left for the University of Toronto, getting a degree in computer science when this branch of science was still in its infancy. He then went to the University of British Columbia where he got his PhD. After that he stayed and taught at UBC and became an authority on the subject. About fifteen years ago, he moved back to Hong Kong and was given the chair of the department of Computer Science at the Hong Kong University of Science and Technology.

Shortly after his second marriage about ten years ago, he noticed that he was having frequent nosebleeds as well as a sore throat that never went away. He was seen by his GP, who suspected he might have cancer and sent him to a specialist. The specialist, Dr. Kingston Wong, was the world authority on this kind of cancer. After extensive studies including multiple scans and biopsies, he confirmed the diagnosis. Liam had never smoked or drank.

Liam was advised that the cancer was localized to one area and that surgery followed by irradiation would be the best treatment.

He did well following the treatment and passed the five-year mark. He chose not to celebrate for fear of bringing bad luck. A year ago, he noticed ringing in his right ear and went back to see Dr. Wong.

He was told that the cancer had spread to his neck, including the right ear canal. He underwent more irradiation followed by chemotherapy. In spite of the chemotherapy, the cancer spread to his lungs and spine.

I was sorry to see Liam so gaunt. His cheeks were hollow and his eyes had no spark. Above his left chest he had an IV tube dripping into his subclavian vein. He was reading a book of Chinese poems by the Tang poet Li Bai when I entered the hospital room.

I went up to his bed and shook his right hand, which felt bony and seemed devoid of any meat. He smiled and said, "Hi James, thanks for coming. Yes, I remember you well as the boy from Malaya. Oh yes, you joined us in Brother Lawrence's class mid-year. I think it was January 1962. I felt bad for you that you lived in Shatin, which took you almost two hours to commute each way. I knew that you were kind of lost in the first few weeks and you were having problems with algebra."

"Liam, you really have a good memory," I remarked. "Yes, it was in late January 1962. I certainly appreciated your help. You and Michael Sze really helped me. I passed both algebra and Chinese language at the end of the school year."

Five years after we left La Salle, we had met up in Vancouver where Liam was getting his PhD, and I was in dental school. I didn't find out that he was at UBC until we were almost finished the school year.

I reminded him of the visit, and commented with a smile, "Yes, I really liked Vancouver and UBC, but I was just not smart enough to compete with the Canadians."

"I thought it was ironic that you had difficulty trying to become a dentist, only to become a successful retina surgeon," he remarked with a chuckle.

"I'm sorry I didn't see much of you at UBC because we were both so busy," I said apologetically. As I looked into Liam's eyes,

I noticed that they seemed a little yellow, which suggested that his liver might be involved.

"James, I have had a good life," said Liam. "I have made peace with my first wife. My two children are doing well in Vancouver. I feel bad that I didn't get to know my four grandkids. But at seventy, if I have to go, I am ready. I have faith in Jesus. I don't know why people have cancer. This is one of those things that just happens in life. Perhaps if we ate less fried salted fish when I was young, I might not have gotten this cancer. In reality nobody knows," he sighed.

I was relieved that Liam seemed to accept his situation. I supposed he had many years to come to terms with his fate. He didn't sound bitter or fearful.

"I know this cancer is very aggressive," Liam continued, "one of the worst kinds of cancer. In a way, I'm fortunate that it's been ten years since I was first diagnosed. I am luckier than many others who get this disease. At least I had a good ten more years. If the Lord wants me to be around this earth for a little longer, I would be very grateful. If the Lord feels that I should go, it would be all right with me too. I'm not afraid to die."

"Liam, you're getting the best treatment for this kind of cancer," I said, trying to sound positive. "I pray that you'll be around for our 55th reunion." As soon as I said it I felt perhaps I shouldn't have. I didn't want him to think I was being insincere, as he probably knew his prognosis and that he most likely would not make the reunion.

At that moment, the nurse showed up with a syringe of morphine and injected into Liam's IV.

"My back has been hurting so much," murmured Liam, becoming groggy.

I held his right hand firmly and said goodbye as he drifted off to sleep.

Two months after I returned to Hawaii, I learned that Liam had passed away. His children and grandchildren were at his side.

***

In 2015, I was busy working on my third book, *Silk Road on My Mind.* It was about my travel and work in Xinjiang and part of the Silk Road.

Early in 2016 I heard from Michael Sze that our classmate George Man Chi Lai had passed away in Hong Kong. George had a very fast-growing brain tumor, a glioblastoma multiforme (GBM)—the worst kind of brain tumor. The time between his first symptoms of headaches and the end was less than three months.

Initially the doctors didn't know what was happening to him after he developed the "locked-in syndrome." He was completely paralyzed, except for the muscles that controlled his eyes. He was conscious and could communicate by blinking his eyes.

Unlike a persistent vegetative state, in which the upper portions of the brain are damaged and the lower portions are spared, locked-in syndrome is caused by damage to specific portions of the lower brain and brainstem, with no damage to the upper brain.

Eventually scans showed the tumor in his brainstem.

George's family background was somewhat similar to mine. In late 1949, weeks before the British closed the border from China, George arrived in Hong Kong with his extended family. They had taken the same train as our family. It was more difficult for them to get out of China because they lived in Wuhan in central China. They traveled in a boat, then a car, and then another boat to get to Shanghai, where they boarded a train to Guangzhou and transferred to a train bound for Hong Kong.

George's father had graduated from Columbia University in New York City about the same time as my father graduated from

Sun Yat San University in Guangzhou. His father also worked for the Kuomintang regime like my father. His mother had graduated from St. John's University in Shanghai about the time my mother too graduated from Sun Yat San University.

His father's father chose to remain in Wuhan, as he felt he was too old to start a new life somewhere else. His mother's father was one of the wealthiest jade and gemstone merchants in Wuhan and had brought with him a large amount of gold, jade and gemstones—according to George, the equivalent of over half a million Hong Kong dollars. In 1949, that was a fortune.

His maternal grandpa bought a large house for twenty-five thousand dollars on Robinson Road, the choicest residential neighborhood on Hong Kong Island at the time. Nobody in the family had to work early on.

Sometime in 1956, his family's fortunes changed drastically. His maternal grandpa lost big in a card game. Not only did he lose all the gold, jade and gemstones, but he also owed a large debt. They had to sell the house on Robinson Road and move to a very modest house.

Around the same time my family was leaving for Malaya, in December of 1956, George's family was moving to a small house in the Kau Wah Keng New Village. As more and more refugees from China arrived, the hills east of the original Kau Wah Keng Village were developed to build small houses, which became known as the New Village. His family bought a house on top of the hill for five hundred dollars. It was more of a cottage than a house.

George was in the same class with me for only one year in Form 5B. We never got to know each other well. He was a fellow of few words. I had no idea that he had lived in the village until decades later.

Sadly, shortly after they moved to the village, both his mother and maternal grandpa died of meningitis. His father found a job teaching science in a private high school just like my father did.

His father's salary was around three hundred Hong Kong dollars, similar to what my father was making before he got his job in Malaya. Years later, his father was remarried to a family friend, a widow from Wuhan who was a nurse.

George did well in the HKSC Exam and got into Form 6 Science, continuing on to the Hong Kong University Medical School. After graduation, he went to New York for a pathology residency. After starting a family and working in New York for a decade, he returned to Hong Kong and started one of the biggest clinical laboratories in the city, becoming immensely successful. About the same time that I published my first book, *Finding Fat Lady's Shoe*, he published his memoir, *From Robinson Road to Kau Wah Keng Village*. It was from his book that I learned about his family history.

Over the following five decades I would see him every year or two at the luncheons given by the old boys whenever I visited Hong Kong. He remained a man of few words and I rarely had a chance to talk to him, except after he published his book when he gave me a copy. I in turn gave him a copy of my book.

***

In the latter part of 2016, I got a letter from Helen Tong, Danny's second wife, saying that he had passed away. Six months earlier I had met with Danny and Helen in San Francisco. They were on their way to Miami where they had bought a condo and were now spending most of their time. They chose Miami because of its proximity to Jamaica.

During the last few years of his life, Danny was having a host of health problems. His chronic back pain had gotten worse. He had surgery for it about ten years earlier, which had provided some relief, but the pain had returned. He was walking with a cane. He was also diagnosed with diabetes and high blood pressure and was on several medications.

We had dinner in Chinatown at the Golden Dragon Restaurant. Years ago, it was one of the best restaurants in San Francisco, but I was sad to see that it had deteriorated so much and the food wasn't at all good. Every dish was too salty.

"James, how can this restaurant serve this kind of food?" Danny asked.

"I'm sorry," I apologized. "I didn't know that it had gone downhill so much. I think it mostly caters to the tourists now, as most San Franciscans don't like to come to Chinatown anymore because the parking is so bad. It's just very inconvenient to come here."

Even as we ate, I could see the agony on his face as he tried to find a comfortable sitting position.

"This pain is really getting me down," Danny confessed. "I think I'll have another surgery soon, because I can't live like this. I found a good neurosurgeon in Miami. He seemed like a nice guy and also trained at the Mayo Clinic. I'm sure he'll take good care of me."

In her letter, Helen wrote that after his surgery, he had one complication after another. He had pulmonary embolism in the recovery room, and then he developed pneumonia and renal failure. Finally, his body simply gave up. Helen was especially distressed that his ex-wife and the children were challenging the will, as Danny had left the condo as well as a rental house in Miami to her.

I was sad to hear about Danny's passing. Not only had I lost an old friend, but it also reminded me of my own mortality.

***

At least ten from the class of 1964 that we knew of were no longer with us. The Old Boys Association still only had contact with about a third of the class and we had no idea what the other two thirds were doing.

One of the old boys joked that at our age each year would be a bonus, and as another one put it, "From now on, every year is gravy."

***

For some of us, how we spend our time depends on how much time we perceive ourselves to have left on this earth. When we were young and healthy, we believed we would live forever. We didn't worry about losing any of our capabilities. We heard sayings such as "the sky's the limit" and "the world is your oyster." We were willing to delay gratification to invest years in school and resources for a more promising future. But as we got older and our horizons contracted, we began to see our lives as uncertain and finite and we focused our goals on the here and now.

I too felt a sense of urgency. After my retirement from my practice, I set more goals, one of which was to write more books, and to continue my volunteer work in Cambodia and islands of the South Pacific.

As both my parents died at age 88 and they showed no signs of dementia, I was optimistic that I would be as fortunate.

The topic of conversation now among the old boys was about getting old. We all feared dementia, poor health and being burdens to our children.

One old boy again remarked that we should live as if we only had six months left, because at some point it would be true.

Indeed, every few months or so I would reassess my situation as if I only had six months. I really wouldn't have done things any differently. I felt this was the best time of my life, as I didn't have to prove anything anymore. I simply needed to make each day as wonderful as I could and avoid the hassles of life as much as possible, knowing that sometimes hassles do come up no matter how hard we try.

I often reminded myself of a saying by Anton Chekov, "Any idiot can face a crisis—it's day-to-day living that wears you out." I thought perhaps he wasn't being fair to day-to-day living.

A few months ago, when I was in Hong Kong having lunch with a group of old boys, David Lau, who was with me for at least two years at La Salle, conveyed his thoughts about getting old to me. He had just been diagnosed with an autoimmune disease and was put on cortisone and now walked with a cane. With a smile on his face and shaking his head, he said, "James, you know, looking at my parents, I don't think I want to live as long as they have. They're both ninety-six now, but they have dementia. Even though they still know me, I don't think they know much else. My consolation is that they're docile and easygoing, unlike some of my friends' parents who have the disease—they scream bloody murder day and night, and sometimes even become violent. Henry Lee told me that his mother was so bad she would bite people. I think another ten years or so will be enough for me. When I look at my parents, I certainly don't want to be alive like them. What sort of life would that be? I'd be happy with another ten years if I can stay healthy and mobile."

"I know what you mean, David," I remarked. "It's the quality of life, not the length that counts."

As our time on this earth gets shorter, we all seek comfort in simple pleasures—our family, everyday routines, the taste of good food, music and naps. I no longer longed for adventures such as my travels to Xinjiang and the Silk Road or riding my motorcycle all over Cambodia.

We become more concerned for our legacy as we age. One of the reasons I write is because I think it might help my children, their children and so on to find out where they come from. I wish I had asked my parents more questions about their lives. I would be delighted if they had written books.

Another reason I write is because it's is a good way to recall my own life. There are days when I read my books to relive certain events. I think one's memoirs would be especially helpful if he or she developed dementia, which is estimated to occur in over half of people over eighty. If a person has dementia, his or her life story disappears forever.

Even though I was enjoying distant travel less, I was still making a trip once a year to a developing country to help train eye doctors and to donate equipment—something I had promised myself to do when I retired from private practice. Being a doctor is part of my *raison d'etre*, part of my identity.

Looking back at my life, I'm pleased to think that I have achieved all the goals I set for myself. In fact, I achieved more than I set out to, more than I thought possible. Each day I remind myself of what an interesting life I've had and how grateful I am for everything.

I think what happens in life is about luck as well as our effort. Without luck, I think sometimes no matter how hard we try, things just don't work out. I view myself as extraordinarily fortunate. Life hasn't always been easy. I had many frustrations, failures and disappointments. I used to envy my classmates at La Salle who did so well in math and physics—two of my weakest subjects. I thought those fellows really had it made.

With the benefit of hindsight now, almost sixty years later, it didn't turn out that how happy or successful one would be depended on one's intelligence. I'm convinced that I have fulfilled my potential. I was never the very top student in class, but all my life I worked hard and gave my best.

Another old boy once told me that if someone had to work very hard to get something, he would appreciate it more than someone who didn't. I agreed with him.

I sometimes look back the first time I thought I wanted to be a doctor. I was about twelve years old and was raising a few pigeons at our house in Muar. After school one day, I discovered that the neighbor's cat had ambushed one of them and left its right leg broken. I applied antiseptic to the wound, then re-approximated the two ends and immobilized the broken leg with a splint made from a popsicle stick. A week later, the pigeon was walking with its two legs again. As I had always wanted to help people, I thought being a doctor would be a perfect profession, even though my patient at the time was a pigeon.

The four doctors in Muar had the biggest houses on the nicest tree-lined street called Jalan Junid. I often bicycled past them after school and thought how great it would be if I could be one of them. I thought it would be wonderful to help others while providing myself with a good lifestyle.

***

In 2017, I went to New Zealand to visit my old friend from grade school in Muar, Chua Huck Cheng, who was now retired and living in Auckland.

Over fifteen years earlier I had purchased a house in Auckland, as I was considering moving there. It was my mid-life crisis. When I realized how inconvenient it was to travel there frequently, I sold the house. I still think of New Zealand fondly, especially since my good friend lives there.

I had a wonderful time with Huck Cheng and his wife Doris.

I traveled from town to town on a bus, from the North Island to the South Island.

Following my trip to New Zealand, I flew to Western Samoa (now known simply as Samoa). After working for a week at the Apia General Hospital doing laser treatments on patients with diabetic retinopathy, I spent some time touring the country.

On the recommendation of one of the doctors, I went to the Samoan Circus Show. It was a circus without animals, mostly acrobatics. The star attraction was the tallest man in the world, a Turkish man named Sultan Kosen who was 8 feet 3 inches tall.

Two days earlier, I had given a lecture on diabetes and endocrine problems, using acromegaly as an example of when a tumor in the pituitary gland secreted excess growth hormones and led to growth such Sultan's. I was interested to see him and take a picture with him so I could add the photo to my future lectures. He looked very uncomfortable standing up because he was so tall, and he had to sit down after a few minutes. It was an interesting show.

I hired a small boat to Manono Island, a small island situated in the Apolima Strait between the main islands of Savai'i and Upolu.

It was one of the scariest boat rides I'd ever taken, as there were no life vests, we were out in the open ocean, and the small boat was continually splashed with water. I had never really learnt to swim for any distance. I thought I could probably save my own life if the boat capsized within twenty feet from shore! The entire time I was on the boat, I worried that my wallet would get wet. I don't know why I had such a silly obsession, never mind that I could have lost my life if the boat tipped over!

I walked around the island. I had a chance to experience truly authentic Samoa, where many trappings of modern life, including traffic, were left far behind.

Home to just four small villages, Manono is only 3 square kilometers (1.1 square miles) in size, and Samoa's third most populated island. Although it's just 4 km off the coast from Samoa's main island, Upolu, Manono Island seemed a world away. People lived and cooked according to thousands of years of tradition. Life was more traditional, and no cars or dogs were allowed there. It was so much more peaceful than the main islands.

It took me less than three hours to stroll around the entire island. I hiked up to its highest point, Mt. Tulimanuiva, an archeological site at 110 meters (360 feet) overlooking the marine-protected lagoon. I checked out the few archaeological sites, including the star mound on top of the mountain.

At Lepuiai Village in the southwest of the island, I visited another archeological site, the Grave of 99 Stones. Each stone represents one of the wives of the high chief Vaovasa!

While in Apia, I stayed at the historic Aggie Greys Hotel, now the Sheraton Hotel. I visited the Robert Louis Stevenson Museum, which was the house that he and his family stayed in for many years until his death. He moved to Samoa because he was a sickly young man and the family thought the warm weather would be healthier for him than the damp cold air in Scotland.

Samoa is probably what Hawaii looked like a hundred years ago. I left the islands with fantastic memories.

***

In 2018 I went to Spain on the "Pilgrimage of Compostela," i.e., *O Camiño de Santiago*, which is known in English as the Way of St. James.

The Way of St. James is a network of pilgrims' ways or pilgrimages in northwestern Spain that lead to the shrine of the apostle Saint James the Great in the Santiago de Compostela Cathedral in Galicia, where tradition has it the remains of the saint are buried. I wasn't doing it as a form of spiritual path or retreat for spiritual growth but rather just to experience the travel.

The Way of St. James was one of the most important Christian pilgrimages during the later Middle Ages. Legend holds that St. James's remains were carried by boat from Jerusalem to northern Spain, where he was buried in what is now the city of Santiago de Compostela.

During the Middle Ages the route was highly traveled. However, the Black Death, the Protestant Reformation and political unrest in 16th century Europe led to its decline. By the 1980s, only a few hundred pilgrims per year registered in the pilgrim's office in Santiago. In October 1987, the route was declared the first European Cultural Route by the Council of Europe. It was also named one of UNESCO's World Heritage Sites. Following that, the route has attracted a growing number of modern-day international pilgrims.

I flew first to Madrid and spent a few days there, then took a train to Pamplona. Each day I walked about five to ten miles along the route near the town where I was staying. It was an easy 'pilgrimage', as instead of walking for several weeks and staying at hostels, I stayed in decent hotels and didn't walk as much.

From Pamplona, I took trains to Puenta la Reina, Logrono, Burgos and León, staying in each town for one or two nights. I then went north to Oviedo, then finally to Santiago.

The pilgrimage route in general was lined with the ruins of the past, especially along the stretch from Burgos to León.

I immensely enjoyed the stunning cathedrals, great urban architecture, fine museums, and marvelous food in both Burgos and León.

I took a train from Santiago de Compostela to Salamanca, staying two nights, and visited one of the oldest universities in the world. I sat in a classroom on a bench that was used by students at the university over four hundred years ago.

***

In 2019, I went to Hong Kong and Cambodia. I had brought a laser to donate to the Medical School in Phnom Penh. I stayed to set it up and teach the ophthalmology residents how use it.

In 2016, I had published my book, *Practical Ophthalmology: A Concise Manual for the Non-Ophthalmologist.* It had great reviews and I made it available for download free of charge on my website. I learned that it was now widely used in Sri Lanka, Bangladesh, the Philippines and Nepal. The head of the eye program at the university in Phnom Penh was very interested and indicated that he would like to give a copy of the book to every senior student at the medical school. He checked with a local printer and was able to get a copy printed for less than two dollars. There were 300 medical students each year at the only medical school in the country. With my donation of $2,000, a thousand copies could be printed and there would be enough copies to last for three years. I agreed to reassess the project at the end of three years. If it turned out to be an effective way to educate the medical students, I would certainly renew the grant.

Then I spent a few days in Siem Reap visiting the Angkor Watt.

From Cambodia, I flew to Hong Kong to attend the 55th reunion.

Five years ago, during our 50th reunion, we had been in Hong Kong during the Umbrella Movement. The protests in 2019 turned out to be a much more violent movement than the last one. Getting to restaurants for the reunion events was made difficult by the widespread and often violent protests. Protesters threw Molotov cocktails. Fires broke out in different parts of Hong Kong. Some of the MTR stations were closed because they were damaged. People were very angry with the government.

The protests started in June against plans to allow extradition to Mainland China. The majority of the people of Hong Kong feared this could undermine judicial independence in the city and the Chinese authority could use the extradition law to silence the dissidents.

Under the "one country, two systems" arrangement agreed upon by Britain and China in 1997, Hong Kong would have some autonomy and its people more rights than those on the Mainland.

The extradition bill, which triggered the first protest, was introduced in April. It would have allowed for criminal suspects to be extradited to Mainland China under certain circumstances. Opponents said this risked exposing Hongkongers to unfair trials and violent treatment. They also argued that the bill would give China greater influence over Hong Kong and could be used to target activists and journalists. Hundreds of thousands of people took to the streets.

After weeks of protests, leader Carrie Lam eventually said the bill would be suspended indefinitely. But protesters feared the bill could be revived, so demonstrations continued, calling for it to be withdrawn completely. By then clashes between police and protesters had become more frequent and violent, with police firing live bullets and protesters attacking officers and throwing petrol bombs.

In September, the bill was finally withdrawn, but protesters said it was too little, too late. Demonstrations continued, demanding full democracy and an inquiry into police violence against the protesters.

On October 1, while China was celebrating 70 years of Communist Party rule, Hong Kong experienced one of its most violent and chaotic days.

An 18-year-old was shot in the chest with a live bullet as protesters fought officers with poles, petrol bombs and other projectiles.

In November, there was a standoff between police and students barricaded on the campus of Hong Kong's Polytechnic University. The police shot at the protesters while they lobbed Molotov cocktails at them.

All the talk at the reunion was about the situation in Hong Kong. Most of the old boys felt that they could live out their years in the city, but some of them were worried about their children and grandchildren. As many of them were well off, they were encouraging their children to immigrate, and their grandchildren to study in the US or Canada.

In 1965, when I left Hong Kong for Hawaii, my main reason for wanting to leave was the very same reason my family escaped to Hong Kong in 1949—to be as far away from the Chinese communists as possible. Watching the near anarchy in Hong Kong, I was very glad that I had made my home in the US.

***

The Meridien Hotel at Cyberport, not far from Hong Kong University, was a small hotel in an exquisite residential area by the South China Sea. During the last fifteen years or so, it was my hotel of choice whenever I was in Hong Kong. I liked it because it was quiet and not in a tourist area, located next to a park by the water where I could take walks. This was also the hotel where I got my thoughts together and began writing.

I had always enjoyed writing and decided that after I retired, I would begin to write my first book. For several years, I had many thoughts floating in my head, but it was difficult to organize them and to put those thoughts into a book. Without distraction in my quiet hotel room, I began putting my thoughts on paper and it resulted in my first book, *Finding Fat Lady's Shoe*.

***

If our family hadn't left communist China when we did, without a doubt my father would have been executed right away, as they did with millions of people they considered enemies. Anyone who worked for the previous government was labelled an enemy—even someone who only worked as a driver for my father's boss was executed.

From 1949 to 1956, our family stayed in the Kau Wah Keng Village, a Hakka village at the northern tip of the Kowloon Peninsula. Life was exceedingly difficult during the five years my father was unemployed, and we survived through the largess of relatives and friends, and also through the kindness of the Hakka natives in the village.

The seven years we spent in the village were some of my most trying ones. It was there that I met my first good friend, Tsang Shui Tseung, who was in my class from first to fourth grades. His family was one of the original settlers of the village a couple hundred years ago.

We had to seek education elsewhere after fourth grade. Shortly after the school year ended, our family moved to Malaya and Shui Tseung continued in a Chinese medium school outside the village.

I took bus number 6 to Kau Wah Keng Village. It was the same route that I used to take over sixty years ago. Much had changed along the route, with most of the factories now gone and replaced by high-rise residential buildings.

After I got off the bus, I traced the familiar path leading to the village. Even though so much of Hong Kong had changed, the old village remained much the same, except that most of the original Hakka residents had moved out. Shui Tseung and a few families had stayed.

After high school, Shui Tseung worked for the government as a meter reader for the electric company. He got married and raised two sons, who were now successful engineers with families, living outside the village.

Shui Tseung was smoking a cigarette outside his house as I got near. The house was at the northern end of the village on a small hill. He invited me inside and his wife served us tea. This was the same house I used to visit, except now it had plumbing. A large 4K Samsung television was playing the National Geographic channel showing the Egyptian pyramids.

After tea, I suggested that we take a walk around the village. The house that our family rented a room from was now boarded up. The entrance to the well next to it was locked. But the houses around it still looked the same, although many of them were empty. The giant mango tree was still there, but Shui Tseung remarked that it must be over a hundred years old now and it only produced a few mangoes that weren't very tasty. I remembered how sweet and full of flavor they were sixty odd years ago.

We talked about old times. We walked by his distant cousin Ah Bai, meaning 'the lame' in Hakka. He owned a small store in the village. Poor Ah Bai had polio when he was young and both his legs were severely deformed. He hobbled around with great difficulty. I recalled him as a quiet boy, and now he was an old man, still quiet. I really felt for him as I shook his hand. Because of his disability, Ah Bai never attended school even though the schoolhouse was only a few buildings from his house. All his life, he eked out a living in the village by selling soft drinks and snacks. He had remained single.

For Shui Tseung and Ah Bai, the village was the only home they knew. It was their world. It seemed unfair that I had moved on and was able to study in America and travel around the world. Life was certainly unfair to Ah Bai.

Being in the village was like being in a time machine for me as I was transported back to my childhood. Many memories flashed in front of me. My favorite teacher was Mrs. Chai who used to tell us Sherlock Holmes stories. As I walked past the old schoolhouse, I was reminded of when I stole a few foreign coins from another student whose father was a merchant seaman. This boy's desk contained over a hundred coins from different countries. He seemed not to care about them and each day left them in his desk after school. My parents hadn't been home for a few days and I was hungry. I took five coins that looked like the fifty-cent silver colored Hong Kong coins and used them to buy food. I took a loaf of bread and gave the shop owner, Mr. Lai, two coins. He looked at them closely and to my surprise then put them in his pocket and smiled, saying nothing. He must have known that they weren't Hong Kong coins but accepted them anyway. I speculated that either he felt sorry for me or he was a coin collector. My guardian angel was looking out for me that day!

We walked east and up the hill to the cemetery where Shui Tseung's parents and his younger brother were buried. That day when his younger brother, then aged seven, fell off a large rock and died still haunted me sometimes. That was my first experience with death.

The steps up the hill were the same ones that my older brother Chung and I took on a hot summer day when we tried to make a little money by selling soft drinks to tourists from the city on top of the hill. I was eight and Chung was twelve. We carried twenty bottles of soft drinks up the hill, but didn't sell even one. Nobody bought from us because the other vendors had ice, and we didn't. So, we carried the heavy load back down the steps at the end of the day. Thirsty as we were, we couldn't afford to drink any. To add insult to injury, I lost my grip on the crate containing the bottles and dropped it, breaking a bottle. Fortunately, the storeowner was sympathetic and didn't make us pay for it, and even gave us some day-old bread. He knew we were hungry. I have always remembered Uncle Ah Dui Pak's kindness.

As we walked around the old village, more memories returned. Some of them were very vivid.

Every couple of years Shui Tseung and I would meet, and we would pick up where we left off. We renewed our friendship without missing a beat.

After our visit, he walked me to the bus stop in front of the village, the same location where it was over sixty years ago. He insisted that we have a bowl of wonton noodles before I left. The meal didn't disappoint—typical Hong Kong style with fresh shrimp and pork filling for the wontons, and al dente yellow egg noodles.

We said goodbye until the next time.

***

On my last day in Hong Kong before flying back to Hawaii on December 31, I read in the South China Morning Post that in Wuhan in Central China, people were getting sick with an illness that reminded some doctors of SARS in 2003. Nobody seemed to be worried in Hong Kong.

I returned to Hawaii on January 1, 2020. Soon, stories were coming out of China that more people were getting sick in Wuhan, but still no one sounded any alarms outside of China. Then it became clear in February that the illness was a very serious one.

In early February things in the US were still very normal. We were dining out. But the situation in Wuhan was so serious that the US stopped allowing travel from China to prevent spread of the virus.

In March, much of America was asked to stay home. I learned that one of the old boys, John Chan and his wife Deborah, were stranded on a cruise ship, the Diamond Princess, because there were a few passengers with the Wuhan virus—which wasn't yet named COVID-19. The ship was anchored off Yokohama and the Japanese government would not let the passengers disembark. The ordeal went on for three more weeks before John and his wife were allowed to fly to California to be quarantined for fourteen days at an army facility. Later, John learned that almost a fourth of the passengers had contracted the illness and four or five of them died.

With dreadful news coming out of Italy and Spain that hundreds of people were dying each day, I was reminded of my own mortality. I was especially sad to learn that almost a hundred medical doctors died from the illness in Italy while taking care of the patients.

With so much time confined to my condo in Hawaii, I passed the time reading, writing and thinking.

When I was fourteen years old, I read a book that greatly affected me. During the time of voluntary confinement, I reread it. The book was about Thomas Anthony Dooley, MD. He was an American physician who worked in Southeast Asia at the outset of American involvement in the Vietnam War. While serving as a physician in the United States Navy and later as a civilian, he risked his own life to save the lives of countless refugees in the jungles of Laos. Sadly, he died in 1961 at age 34 of malignant melanoma.

I was immensely touched by his life story, but it had raised many questions in my young mind. I couldn't understand how a merciful God would allow such a good person to die so young.

I also reread another book that had affected me greatly, entitled *Life in the Balance*. It was the memoir of Dr. Thomas Graboys, a cardiologist in Boston who wrote about his battle with Parkinson's disease and dementia in the prime of his life. It was a moving account of how he first lost his mobility, his dignity, then his mind to the point where he no longer could tell what was real and what was not. It was a slow death of the worst kind. I tried to put myself in his shoes and imagine how I would cope with such disability.

Another book that truly moved me was *When Breath Becomes Air* by Paul Kalanithi, a young surgeon who had never smoked in his entire life, and died of lung cancer at age 37. I also reread this book.

Kalanithi discovered he had inoperable lung cancer at the age of 36. The cliché about someone having everything to live for could have been formulated for him: he was on the verge of qualifying as a neurosurgeon at Stanford University after a decade of training, and he was planning to start a family with his wife. Instead, he found himself confronting not only a terminal illness, but also a profound identity crisis.

Prior to his illness, Kalanithi's life had been one of relentless striving and exceptional achievement.

The book reminded me of my own life, as I had nearly suffered the same fate as he. In 1981 at age 35, I had just finished all my training, including a prestigious fellowship in retinal surgery at the University of California San Francisco Medical Center. Three months into my new practice, a day before Thanksgiving in 1981, I was admitted to the hospital for paralysis. I was no longer able to use my hands and legs, and I was gasping for air, barely able to speak. I was quickly put on a ventilator.

The diagnosis was Guillain-Barre Syndrome (GBS)—an autoimmune disease probably brought on by stress. I got sicker and developed severe bilateral-lobed pneumonia. The doctors didn't know if I was going to make it. After a couple of weeks in the ICU on a ventilator, my condition improved. I had to learn to walk, to write and to talk again. After three months of rehabilitation, I resumed my practice. I made a full recovery with the exception that I could no longer whistle like I used to— I used to be an excellent whistler! Somehow the only nerves that didn't regenerate were the ones that enable a person to whistle. That was truly a close call.

One week blended into another, and soon we were in April during my confinement in the condo because of the COVID-19 crisis. With so much time on my hands, I decided to reread the book on Socrates.

When I was in high school, I read about Socrates, his teaching and his life. He was accused of impiety and corrupting youth, and at his trial the jury sentenced him to death. He was taken to the nearby jail where his sentence was carried out—death by drinking a cup of poison hemlock, as Athenian law had prescribed.

As described in Plato's *Apology*, Socrates reportedly uttered before he died, "The unexamined life is not worth living." Since reading that, I have often examined my own life to determine if it's a meaningful one.

***

Day after day we were bombarded with the number of deaths caused by the COVID-19 or Wuhan virus. I thought it was ironic that we humans, who invented the atomic bomb, landed on the moon and sent crafts to Mars, were almost powerless against the virus—a mindless bit of protein coated with nucleic acid containing some genetic information.

So, what is a virus?
Humans got interested in viruses because of their association with diseases—the word "virus" has its roots in the Latin term for "poison."

In the late 19th century, researchers realized that certain diseases, including rabies and foot-and-mouth, were caused by particles that seemed to behave like bacteria but were much smaller. Because they could be spread from one victim to another with obvious biological effects, viruses were thought to be the simplest of all living, gene-bearing life forms.

Later, scientists were able to crystallize a virus—tobacco mosaic virus—for the first time. They were then thought of as inert chemicals. They were regarded as a package of complex biochemicals, which lacked the essential systems necessary for metabolic functions, the biochemical activity of life. Therefore, they must not be alive.

Further research established that a virus consists of nucleic acids (DNA or RNA) enclosed in a protein coat that may also shelter viral proteins involved in infection.

A virus seems more like a bunch of chemicals than an organism. But when a virus enters a cell, it seems to come alive. It sheds its coat, bares its genes and induces the cell's own replication machinery to reproduce the intruder's DNA or RNA and manufacture more viral protein based on the instructions in the viral nucleic acid. The newly created viral bits assemble and give rise to more viruses, which also may infect other cells.

These behaviors are what led many to think of viruses as existing at the border between chemistry and life. With their dependence on host cells, viruses are thought to lead a kind of "borrowed life."

Viruses depend on the host cell for the raw materials and energy necessary to duplicate themselves, allowing them to multiply and spread. They cannot sustain themselves without a host.

In 1992, scientists sequenced the genome of the largest known virus, Mimivirus. This virus is about the same size as a small bacterium and it infects amoebae. Sequence analysis of this virus revealed numerous genes previously thought to exist only in cellular organisms.

It seems that viruses have their own, ancient evolutionary history, dating to the very origin of cellular life. For example, some viral-repair enzymes—which excise and resynthesize damaged DNA, and so on—are unique to certain viruses and have existed almost unchanged probably for billions of years.

So where do viruses come from?

Some scientists believe that viruses came from host genes that somehow escaped the host and acquired a protein coat. In this view, viruses are fugitive host genes that have degenerated into parasites.

Most evolutionary biologists are of the opinion that viruses have had some role in evolution, including human evolution. Most known viruses are not pathogenic. They take up residence in cells, where they may remain dormant for a long time. They may take advantage of the cells' replication apparatus to reproduce at a slow and steady rate so as not to kill the host. These viruses have developed many clever ways to avoid detection by the host immune system.

Viruses affect all life on earth, from single-celled organisms to human populations. They often determine what will survive.

Viruses do evolve. New viruses, such as the COVID-19, SARS and AIDS-causing HIV-1, may be the only biological entities that scientists can actually witness come into being, providing a real-time example of evolution in action.

After reading up on viruses and pondering their purpose, the mystery of life only deepened.

If there is a creator of the universe, why was the virus created?

Why are we having this pandemic?

The truth of the matter is that the people who are most adversely affected by it are the poor and innocent.

***

The COVID-19 crisis led me to re-examine my own faith, my view of the natural world, my life and my mortality.

Even when I was young and my faith was very strong, when I prayed and thought about God, I wondered how He could even listen to the prayers of several billion people.

Many years ago, at the University of Hawaii, I met a very intelligent and intellectual Jesuit priest at the Newman Center named Father Evers, who seemed to think that our God may not be the supernatural God, someone who micromanages our lives, but rather a creator who created the world but did not continue to interact with it, letting the creatures make their own decisions, good or bad. Perhaps that was what the teaching of 'free will' was all about. This priest even suggested that when bad things happen on earth, God suffers with us. I like this concept, as it makes the most sense to me.

Such explanations about the universe aren't new. This movement is called Deism. Deism is a belief in the existence of a supreme being, specifically a creator, who does not intervene in the universe. The term is used chiefly to describe an intellectual movement of the 17th and 18th centuries that accepted the existence of a creator on the basis of reason, but rejected belief in a supernatural deity who interacts with humankind.

Even if we accept that the world was designed, it cannot be assumed that its designer is God. And if God designed it, then the existence of evil and suffering in the world would suggest that the belief that God is all-good cannot be true.

But when I think about my own consciousness, that I am a unique person with my own unique story, it makes me believe that there has to be a God or a creator of the human mind. I can understand and accept how animals evolved. But how is it possible that our intelligent minds are the product of a series of blind mutations through evolution?

As an eye doctor, I often marveled at the beauty of the human eye, how delicate, complex and wonderful it is. It's hard to be convinced that this marvelous and super sophisticated organ could be the result of a series of accidental mutations.

I suppose throughout the ages, many people who were much more intelligent than me have asked the same questions. Why are we on earth? Where do we come from? Is there a God?

Life is truly a mystery.

***

As I pondered life, I wondered what would happen for our 60th anniversary in 2024. How many of us will be there? What will the world be like?

We never know what is waiting for us around the corner. We are on this earth for a short time and then leave, but to where?

www.ingramcontent.com/pod-product-compliance
Lightning Source LLC
Chambersburg PA
CBHW071059250626

47159CB00002B/524